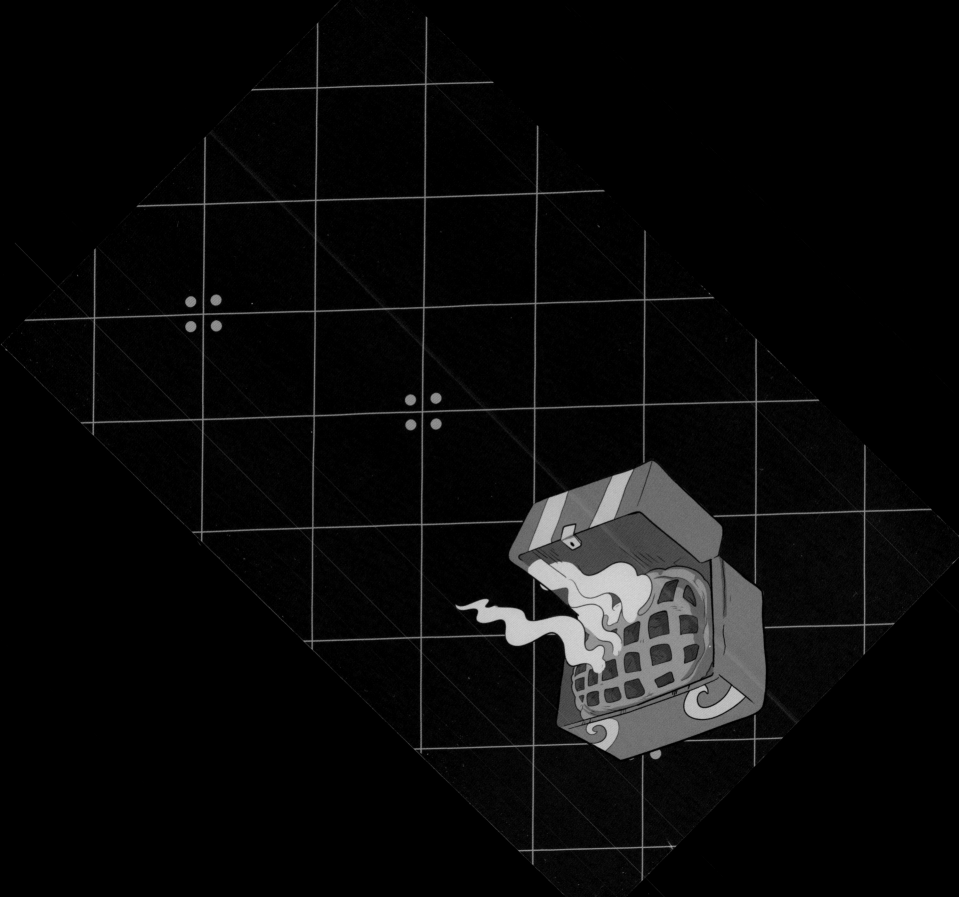

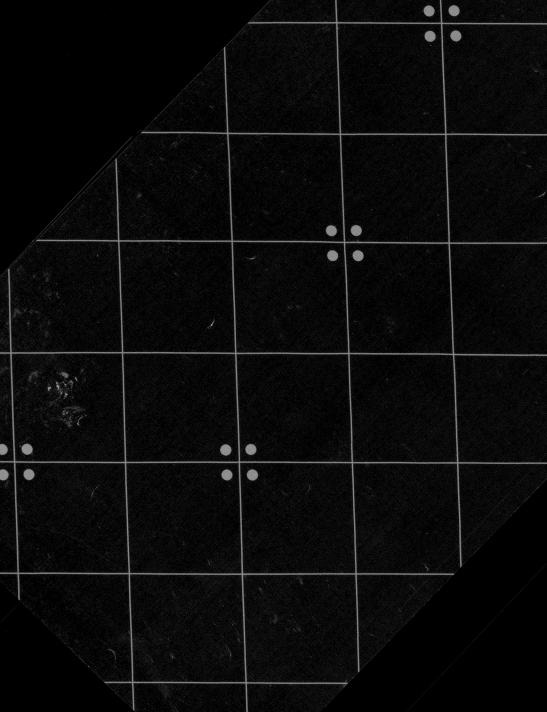

DRAGON KINGDOM
of Wrenly

INFERNO NEW YEAR

By Jordan Quinn

Illustrated by Ornella Greco at Glass House Graphics

LITTLE SIMON

New York   London   Toronto   Sydney   New Delhi

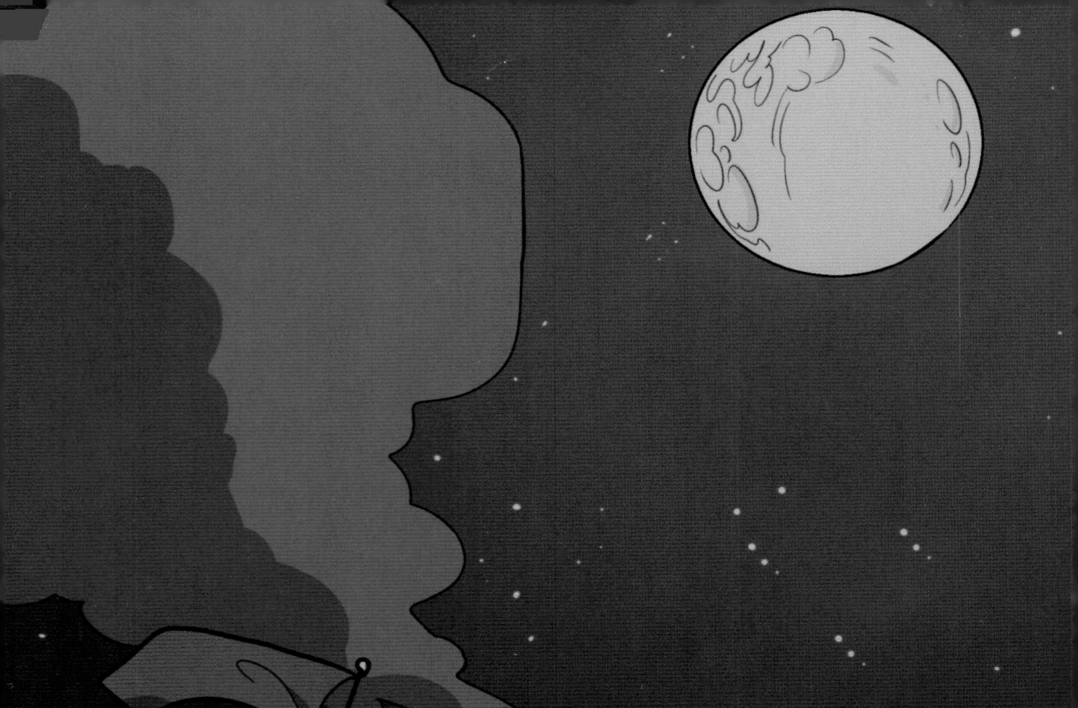

LITTLE SIMON
An imprint of Simon & Schuster Children's Publishing Division
1230 Avenue of the Americas, New York, New York 10020
First Little Simon edition September 2021

Designed by Kayla Wasil
Text by Matthew J. Gilbert
GLASS HOUSE GRAPHICS Creative Services
Art and cover by ORNELLA GRECO
Colors by ORNELLA GRECO and GABRIELE CRACOLICI
Lettering by GIOVANNI SPATARO/Grafimated Cartoon
Supervision by SALVATORE DI MARCO/Grafimated Cartoon
Manufactured in China 0721 SCP
2 4 6 8 10 9 7 5 3 1
Library of Congress Cataloging-in-Publication Data
Names: Quinn, Jordan, author. | Glass House Graphics, illustrator. Title: Inferno New Year / by Jordan Quinn ; illustrated by Glass House Graphics. Description: First Little Simon edition. | New York : Little Simon, 2021. | Series: Dragon kingdom of Wrenly ; 5 | Audience: Ages 5-9 | Audience: Grades K-1 | Summary: The island of Crestwood's largest volcano erupts and sends Cinder, Groth, and Roke to the palace to stay with Ruskin until it is safe to return, but after the spectacular explosions are finished danger continues to follow the dragons.
Identifiers: LCCN 2020048831 (print) | LCCN 2020048832 (ebook) | ISBN 9781534484771 (paperback) | ISBN 9781534484788 (hardback) | ISBN 9781534484795 (ebook) Subjects: LCSH: Graphic novels. | CYAC: Graphic novels. | Dragons—Fiction. | Fantasy Classification: LCC PZ7.7.Q55 In 2021 (print) | LCC PZ7.7.Q55 (ebook) | DDC 741.5/973—dc23
LC record available at https://lccn.loc.gov/2020048831
LC ebook record available at https://lccn.loc.gov/2020048832

Contents

Chapter 1
Normally Visitors Entered through the Front 6

Chapter 2
Ruskin Led His Friends 20

Chapter 3
Welcome to the Royal Library 33

Chapter 4
This Is Bad 48

Chapter 5
Later 62

Chapter 6
Interesting! 75

Chapter 7
Moments Later 91

Chapter 8
The Dragons Launched 105

Chapter 9
Ruskin Flew to the Far Side 117

Chapter 10
A Few Days Later 134

Chapter 1

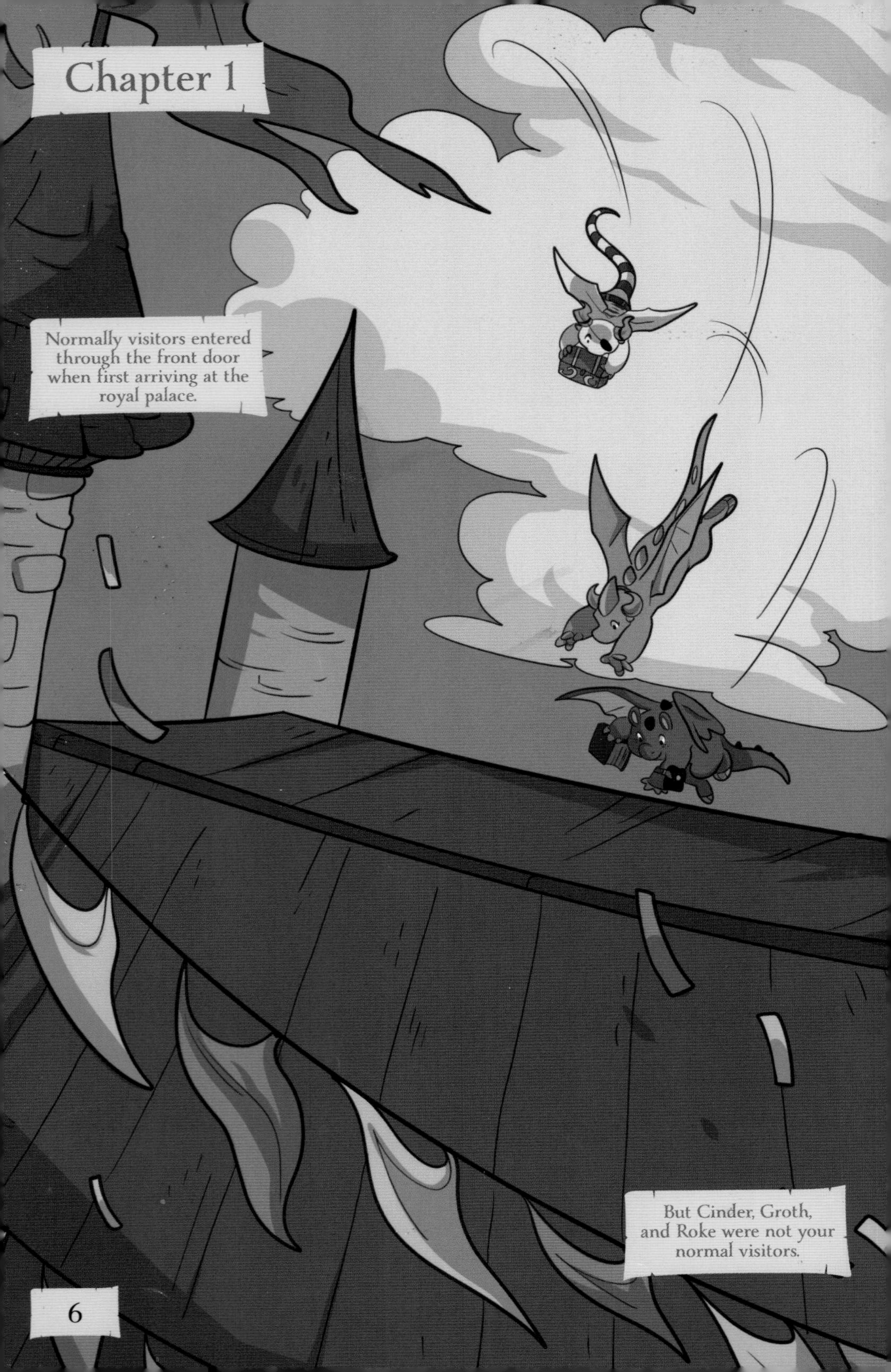
Normally visitors entered through the front door when first arriving at the royal palace.
But Cinder, Groth, and Roke were not your normal visitors.

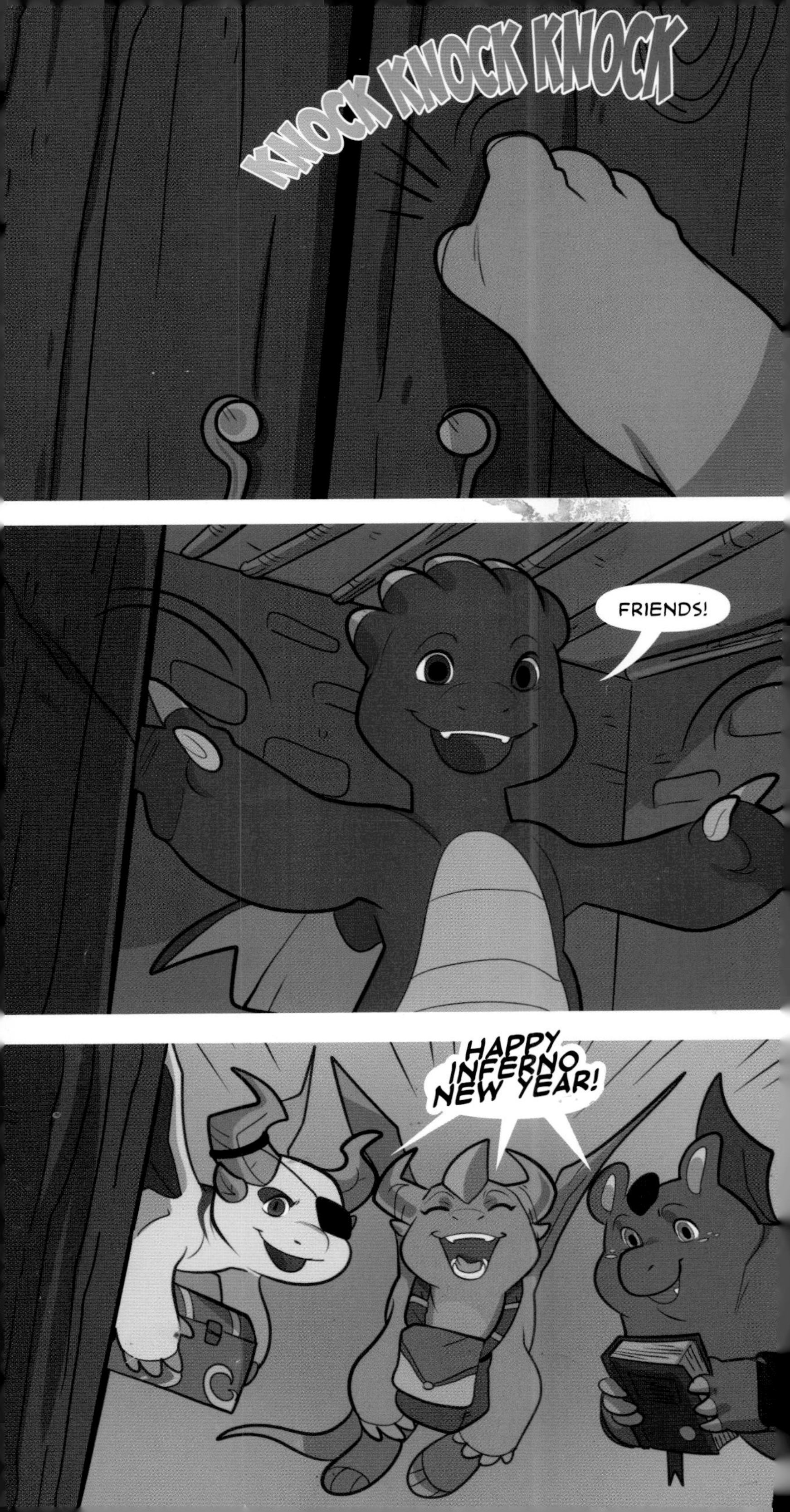
KNOCK KNOCK KNOCK
FRIENDS!
HAPPY INFERNO NEW YEAR!

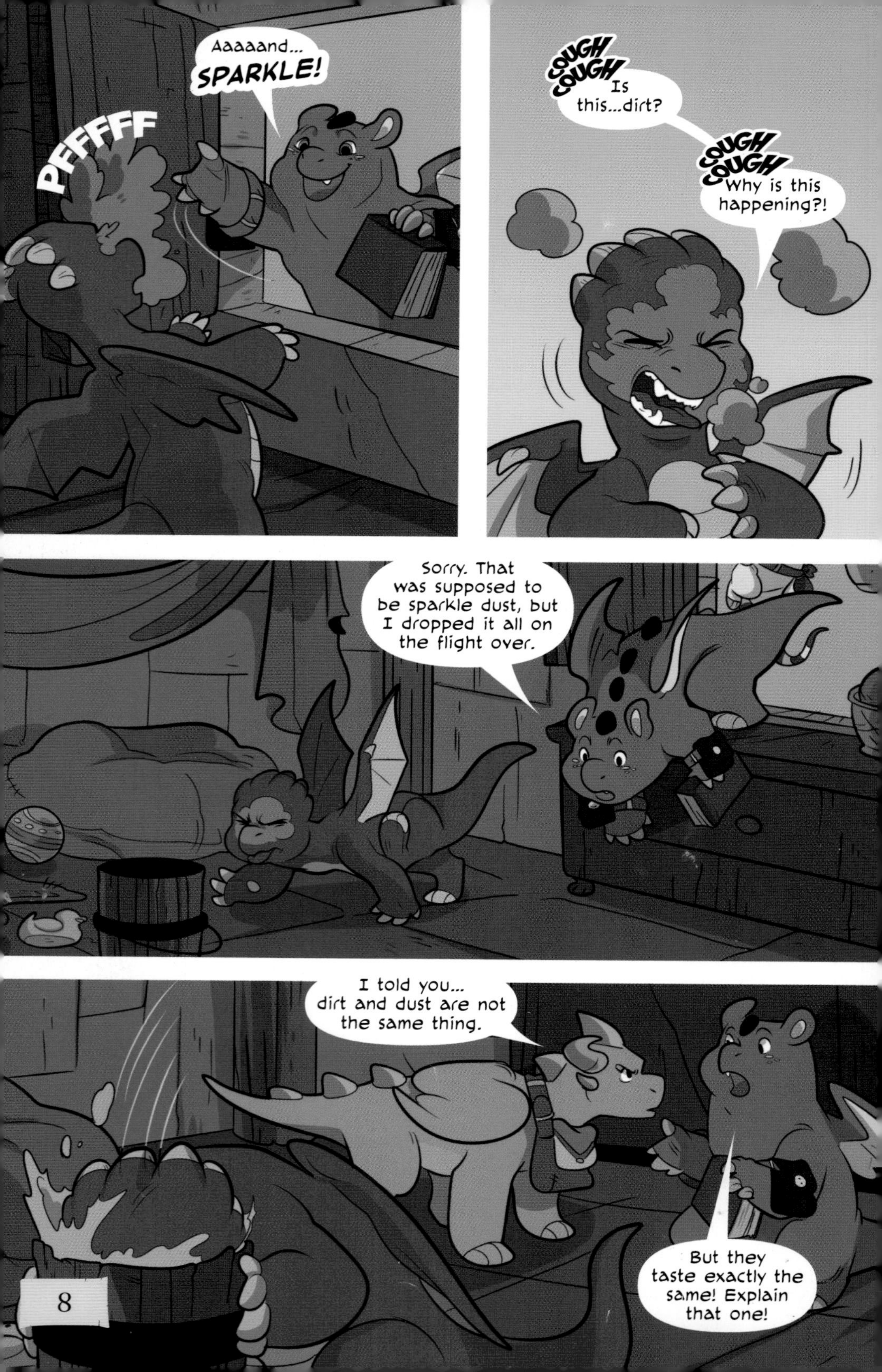
Aaaaand...
SPARKLE!
PFFFFFF
COUGH COUGH
Is this...dirt?
COUGH COUGH
Why is this happening?!
Sorry. That was supposed to be sparkle dust, but I dropped it all on the flight over.
I told you... dirt and dust are not the same thing.
But they taste exactly the same! Explain that one!

SHAKE SHAKE
That's better—now what's all this about New Year's being... *invisible?*
We didn't say "invisible." We said "inferno," as in...HAPPY INFERNO NEW YEAR!
SHAKE SHAKE
Inferno New Year is a Crestwood holiday... *and* a world-changing marvel of nature...AND a dragon celebration, all rolled into one!
How do you celebrate it? With a feast? A surprise party?
Even better. We celebrate with a huge volcano that covers our whole island in fiery lava and burns everything until it rains ash.

That sounds *terrifying!*

It really isn't.

From a geological perspective...it is safe, and it—

Do *NOT* say "rocks."

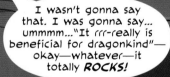

I wasn't gonna say that. I was gonna say... ummmm..."It rrr-really is beneficial for dragonkind"— okay—whatever—it totally *ROCKS!*

Inferno New Year does indeed *ROCK,* and I'll tell you why, Ruskin...

You know the volcano where my ad and I live? Well, every two hundred years it decides to wake up...
The ground shakes, and then a big BOOM happens like...
KA-BOOOOM
The lava fall brings an *inferno* that melts the island, transforming the Crestwood of old...
This is my third Inferno New Year. I liked it before it was cool...
...into an incredible *new* world.
A ***NEW CAVE!*** I call dibs!

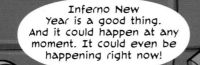

Inferno New Year is a good thing. And it could happen at any moment. It could even be happening right now!

Which is her long-winded way of asking...can we crash here for a sleepover while our homes are being *melted*?

HAPPY INFERNO NEW YEAR!

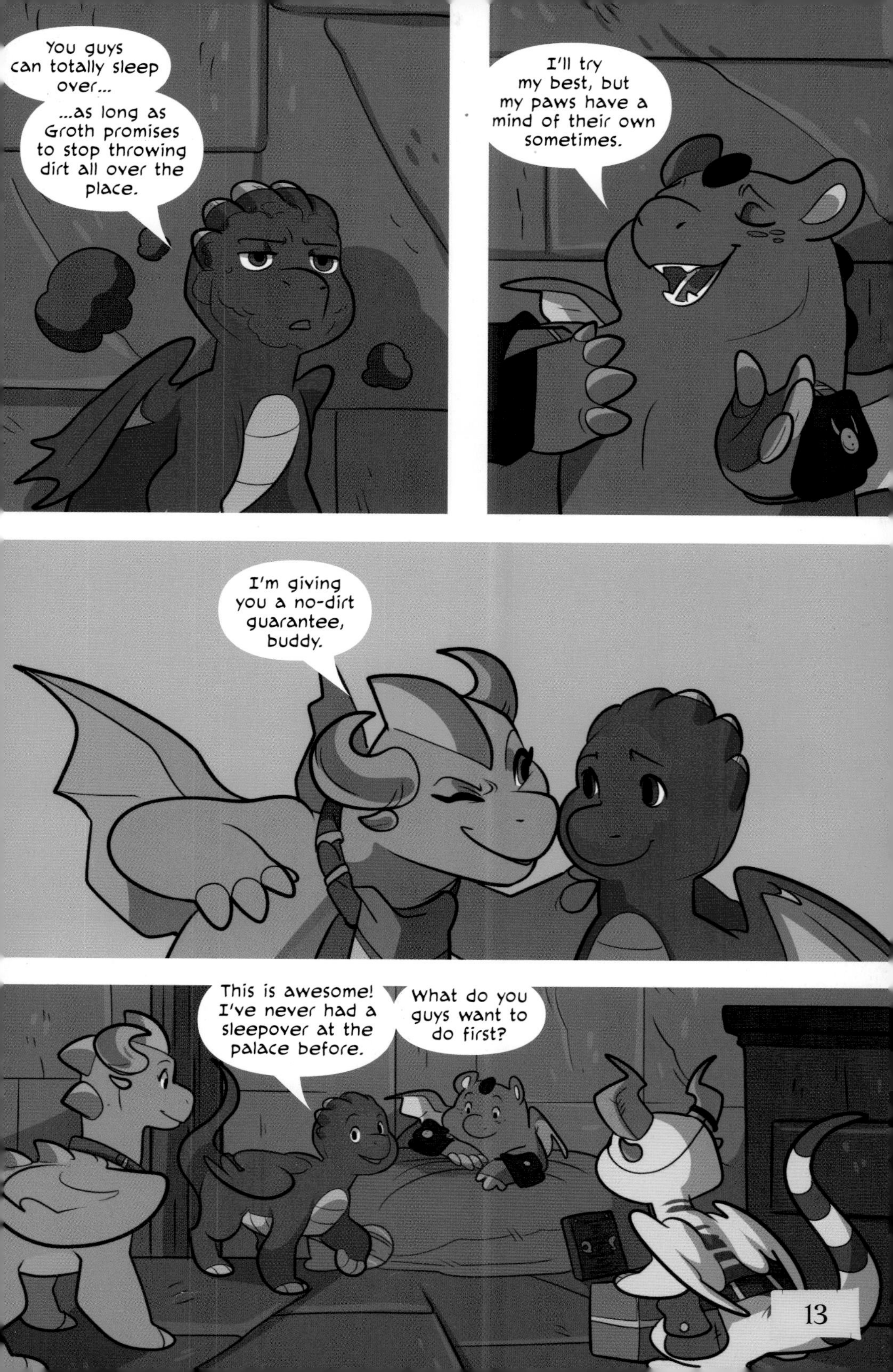
You guys can totally sleep over...
...as long as Groth promises to stop throwing dirt all over the place.
I'll try my best, but my paws have a mind of their own sometimes.
I'm giving you a no-dirt guarantee, buddy.
This is awesome! I've never had a sleepover at the palace before.
What do you guys want to do first?

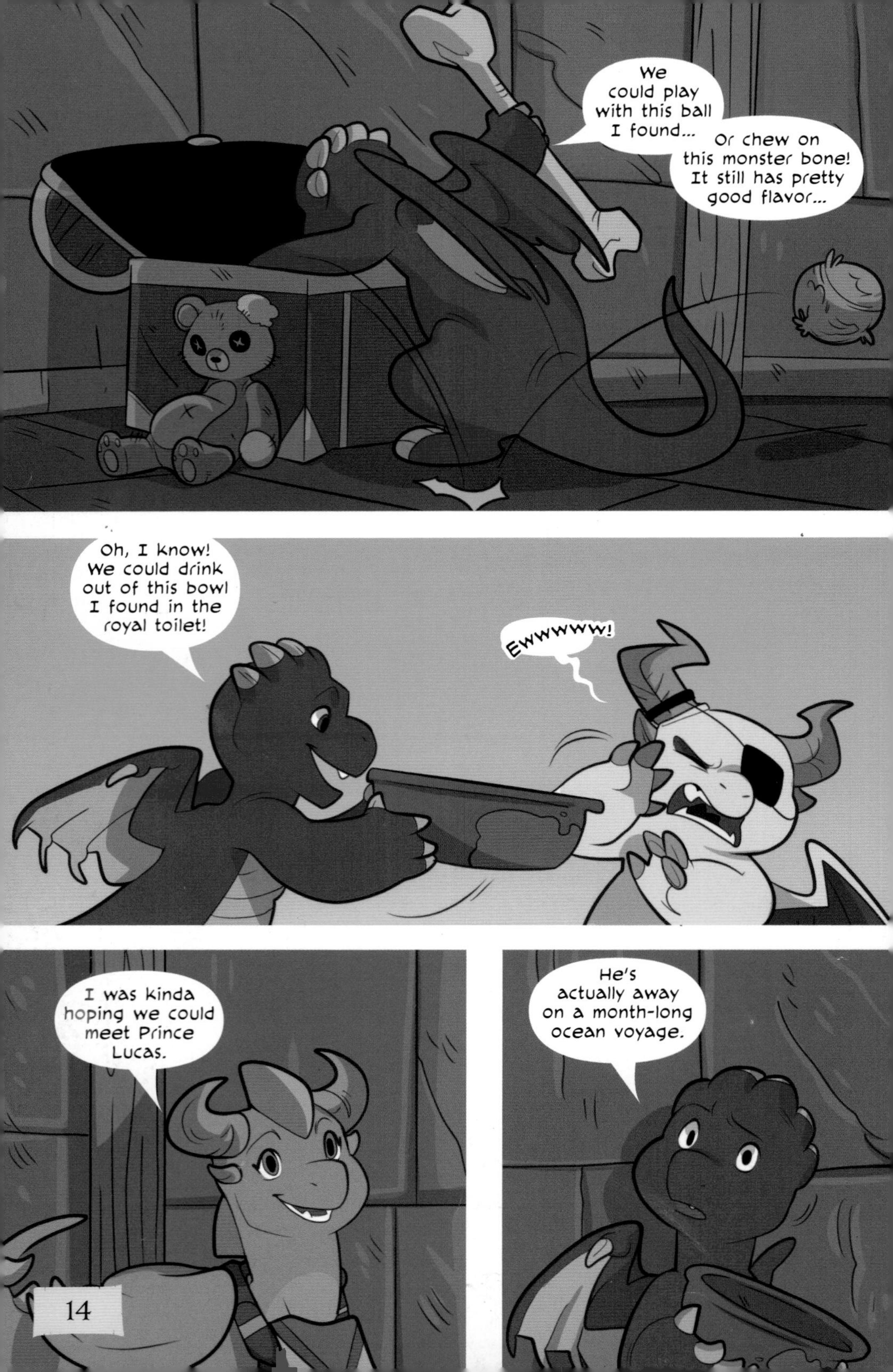
We could play with this ball I found...
Or chew on this monster bone! It still has pretty good flavor...
Oh, I know! We could drink out of this bowl I found in the royal toilet!
Ewwwww!
I was kinda hoping we could meet Prince Lucas.
He's actually away on a month-long ocean voyage.

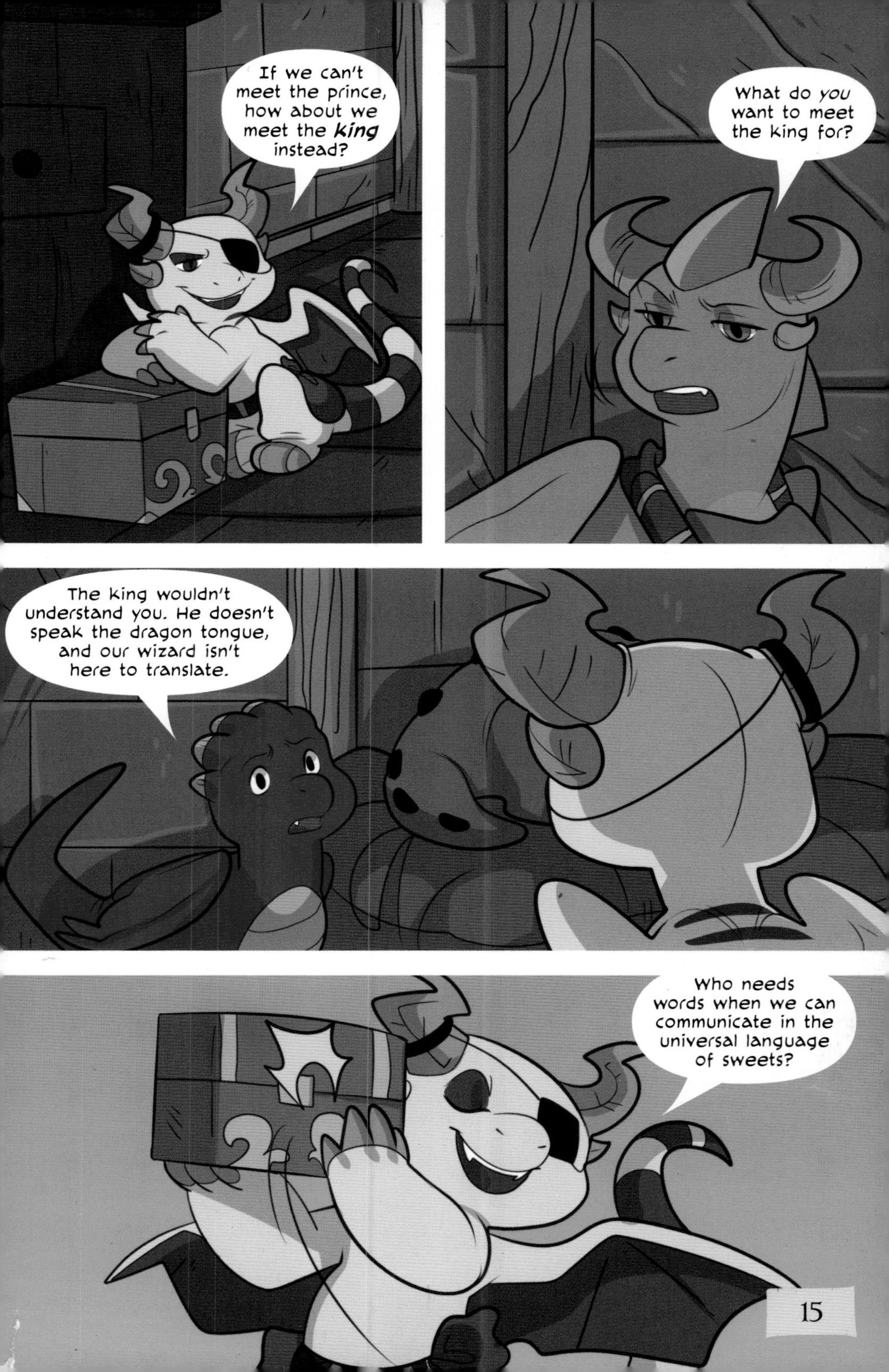
If we can't meet the prince, how about we meet the ***king*** instead?
What do *you* want to meet the king for?
The king wouldn't understand you. He doesn't speak the dragon tongue, and our wizard isn't here to translate.
Who needs words when we can communicate in the universal language of sweets?

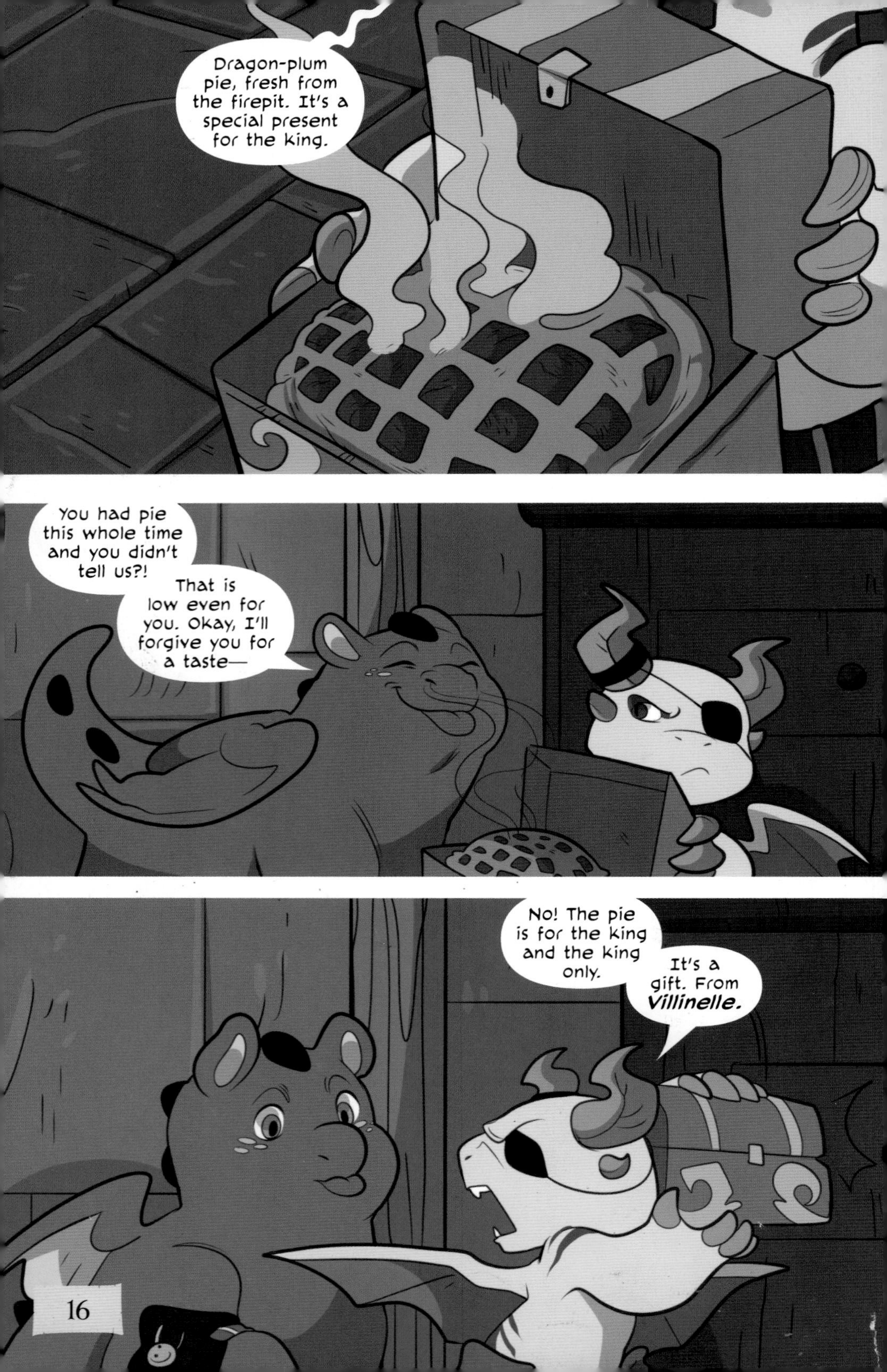
Dragon-plum pie, fresh from the firepit. It's a special present for the king.
You had pie this whole time and you didn't tell us?!
That is low even for you. Okay, I'll forgive you for a taste—
No! The pie is for the king and the king only.
It's a gift. From *Villinelle.*

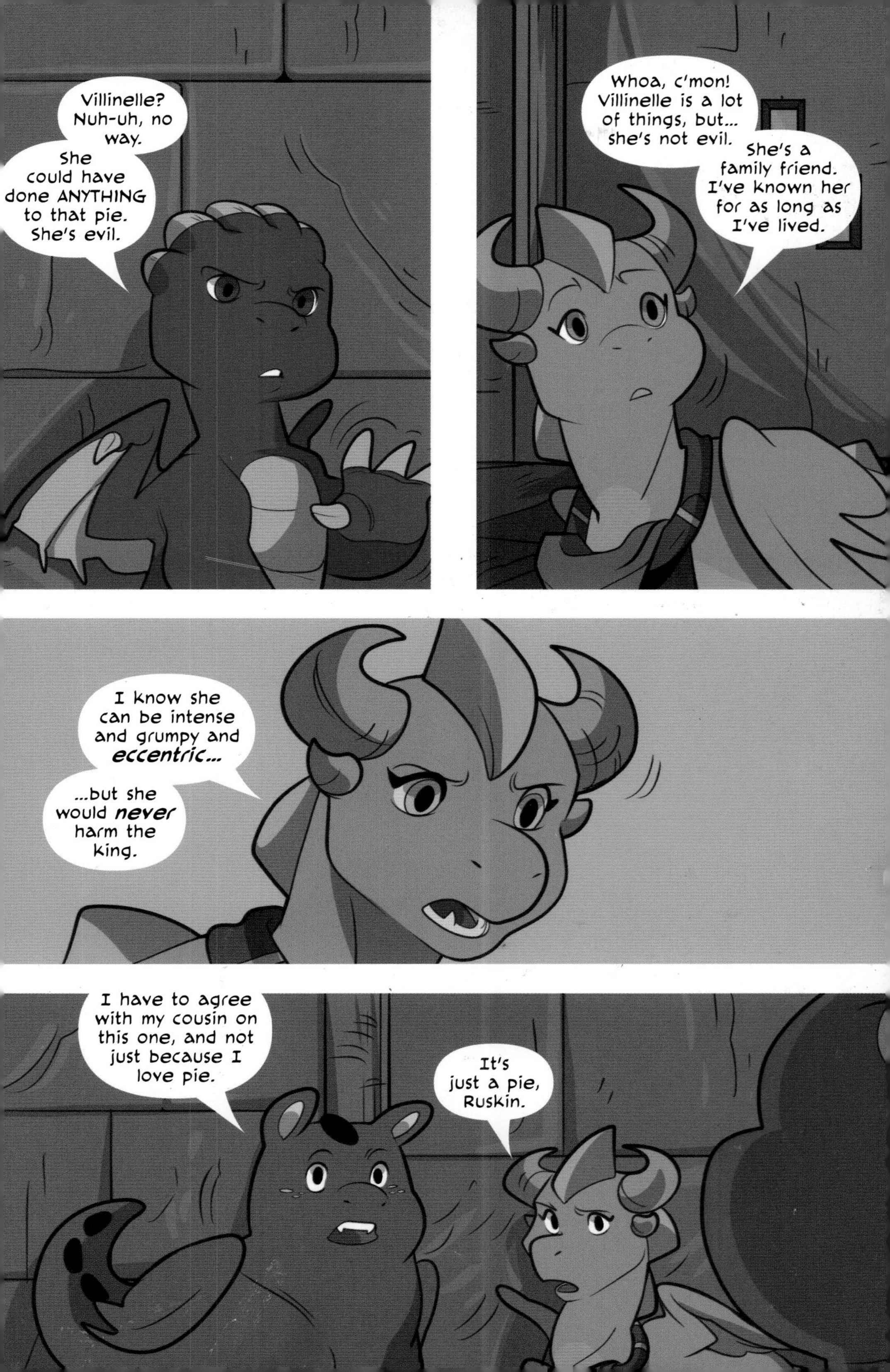
Villinelle? Nuh-uh, no way.
She could have done ANYTHING to that pie. She's evil.
Whoa, c'mon! Villinelle is a lot of things, but... she's not evil.
She's a family friend. I've known her for as long as I've lived.
I know she can be intense and grumpy and *eccentric*...
...but she would *never* harm the king.
I have to agree with my cousin on this one, and not just because I love pie.
It's just a pie, Ruskin.

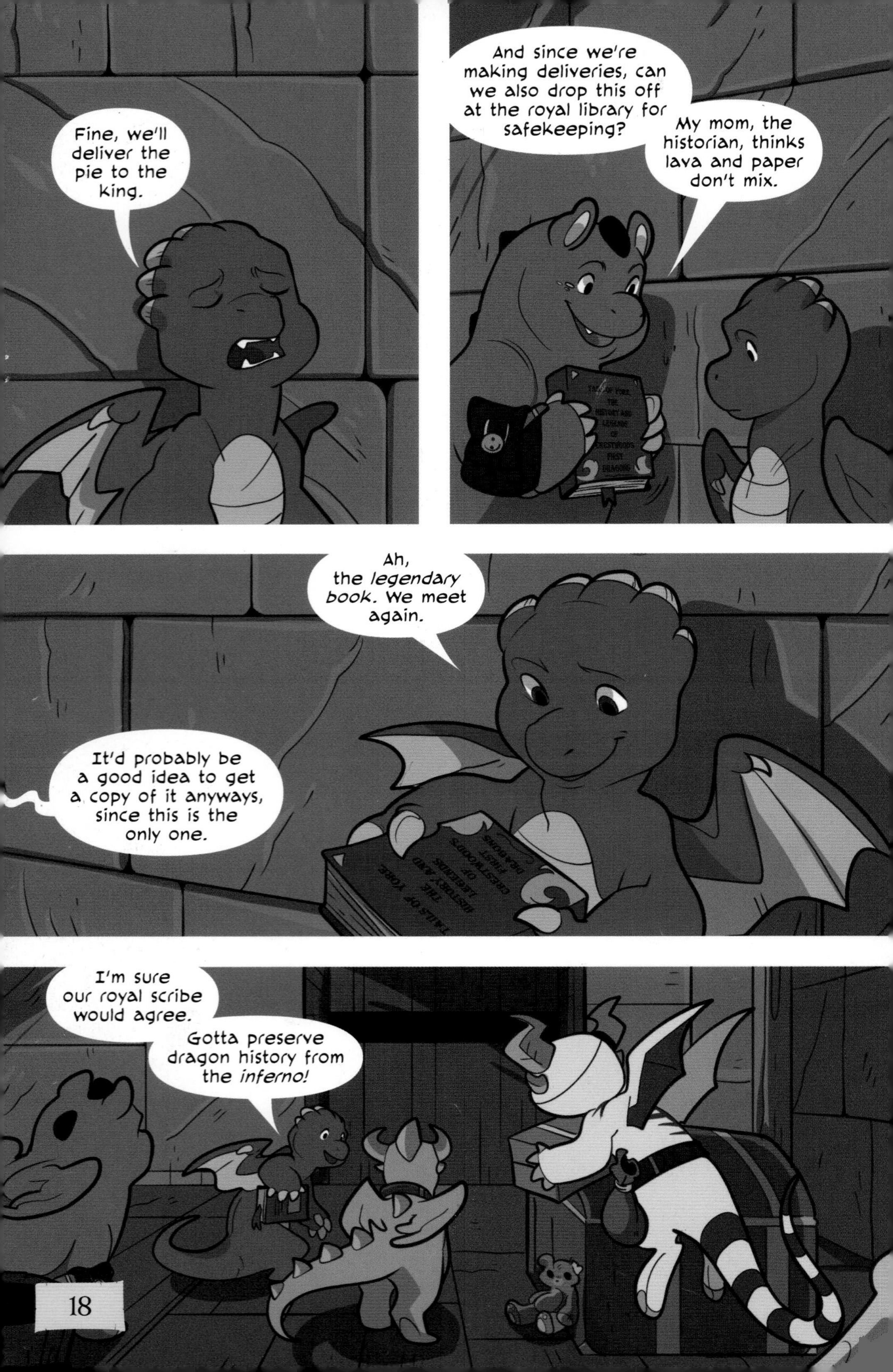
Fine, we'll deliver the pie to the king.
And since we're making deliveries, can we also drop this off at the royal library for safekeeping?
My mom, the historian, thinks lava and paper don't mix.
Ah, the *legendary book*. We meet again.
It'd probably be a good idea to get a copy of it anyways, since this is the only one.
I'm sure our royal scribe would agree.
Gotta preserve dragon history from the *inferno!*

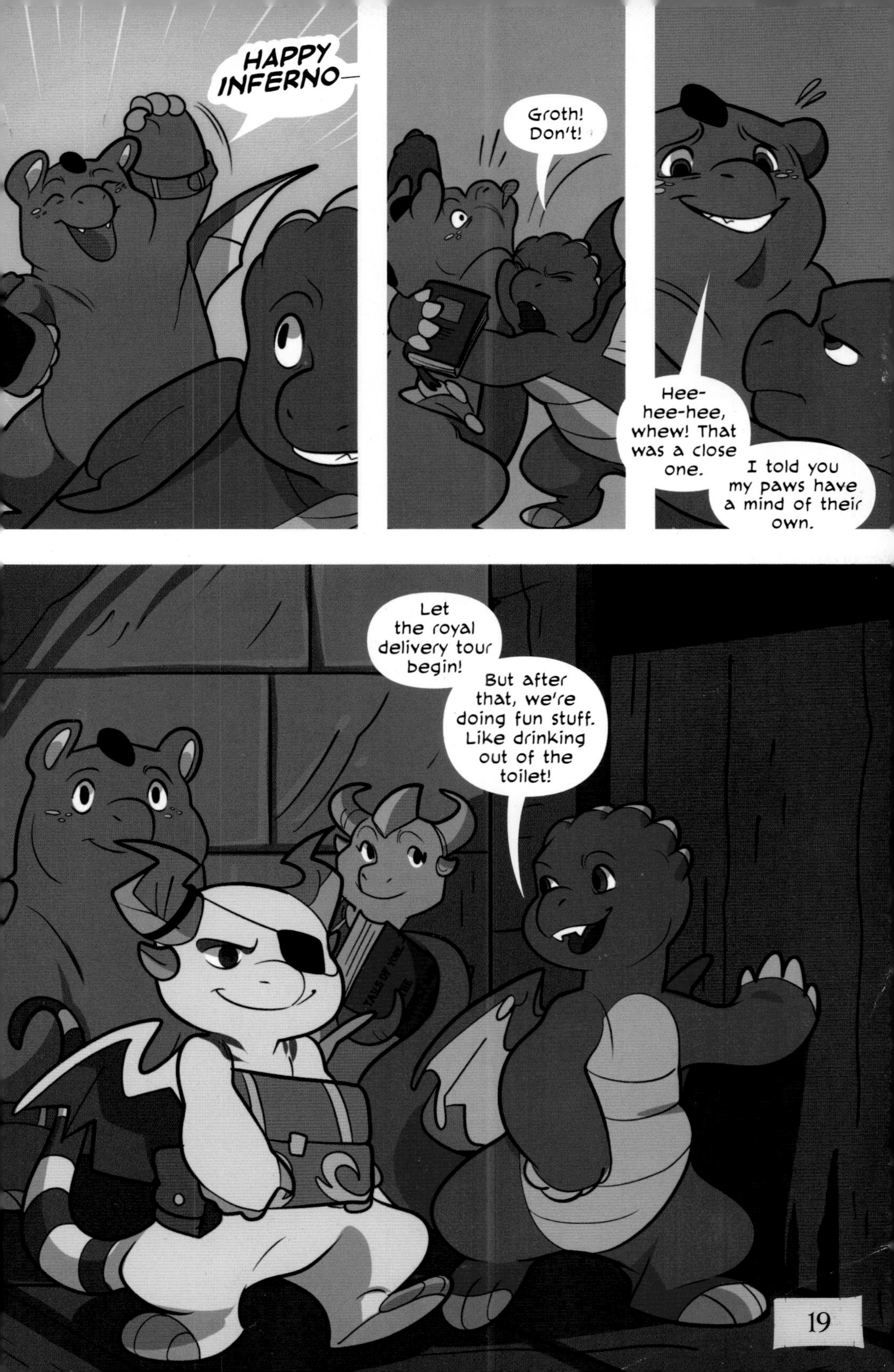
HAPPY INFERNO—
Groth! Don't!
Hee-hee-hee, whew! That was a close one.
I told you my paws have a mind of their own.
Let the royal delivery tour begin!
But after that, we're doing fun stuff. Like drinking out of the toilet!
TAILS OF YORE

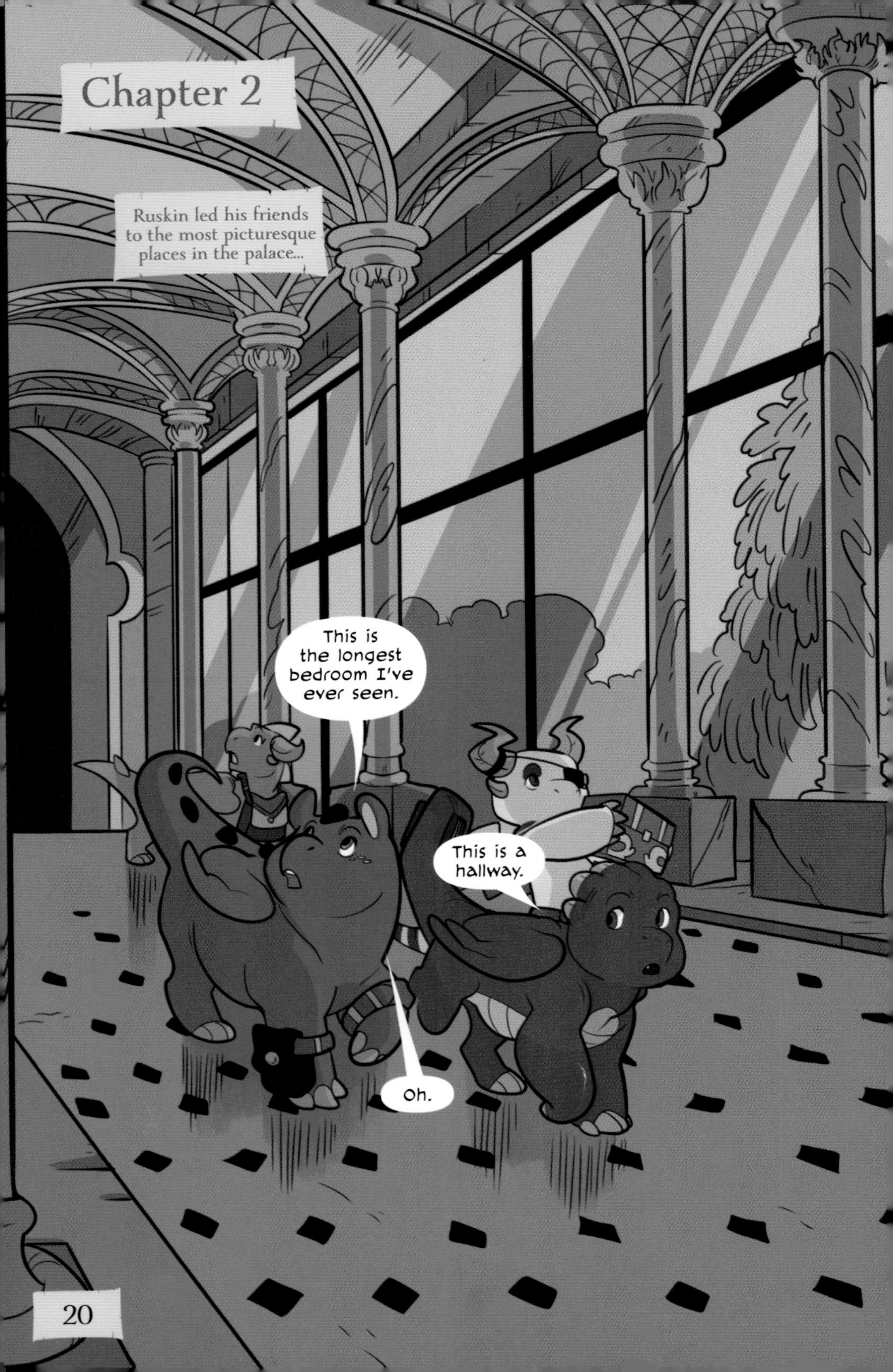
Chapter 2
Ruskin led his friends to the most picturesque places in the palace...
This is the longest bedroom I've ever seen.
This is a hallway.
Oh.

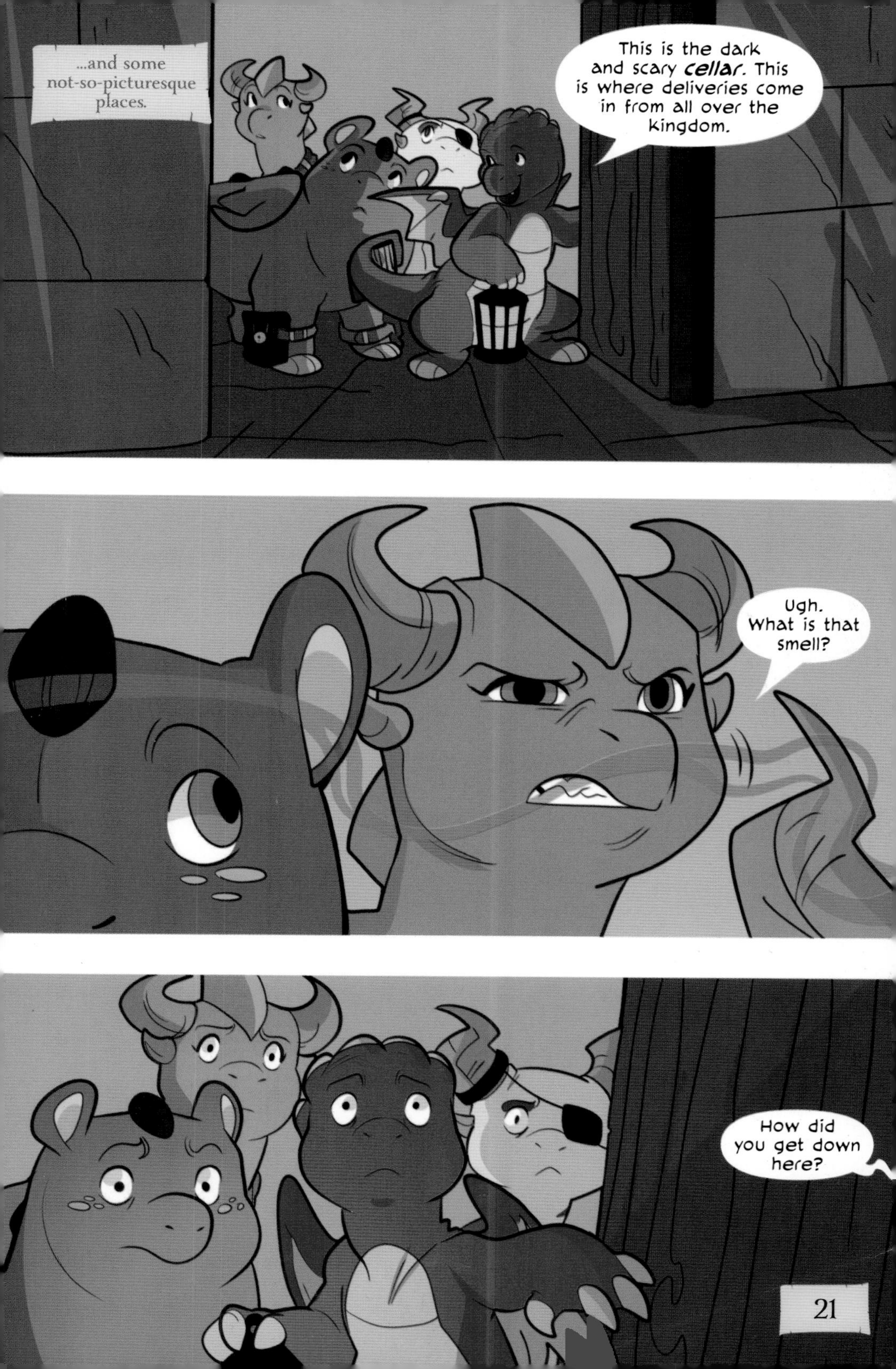
...and some not-so-picturesque places.
This is the dark and scary *cellar.* This is where deliveries come in from all over the kingdom.
Ugh. What is that smell?
How did you get down here?

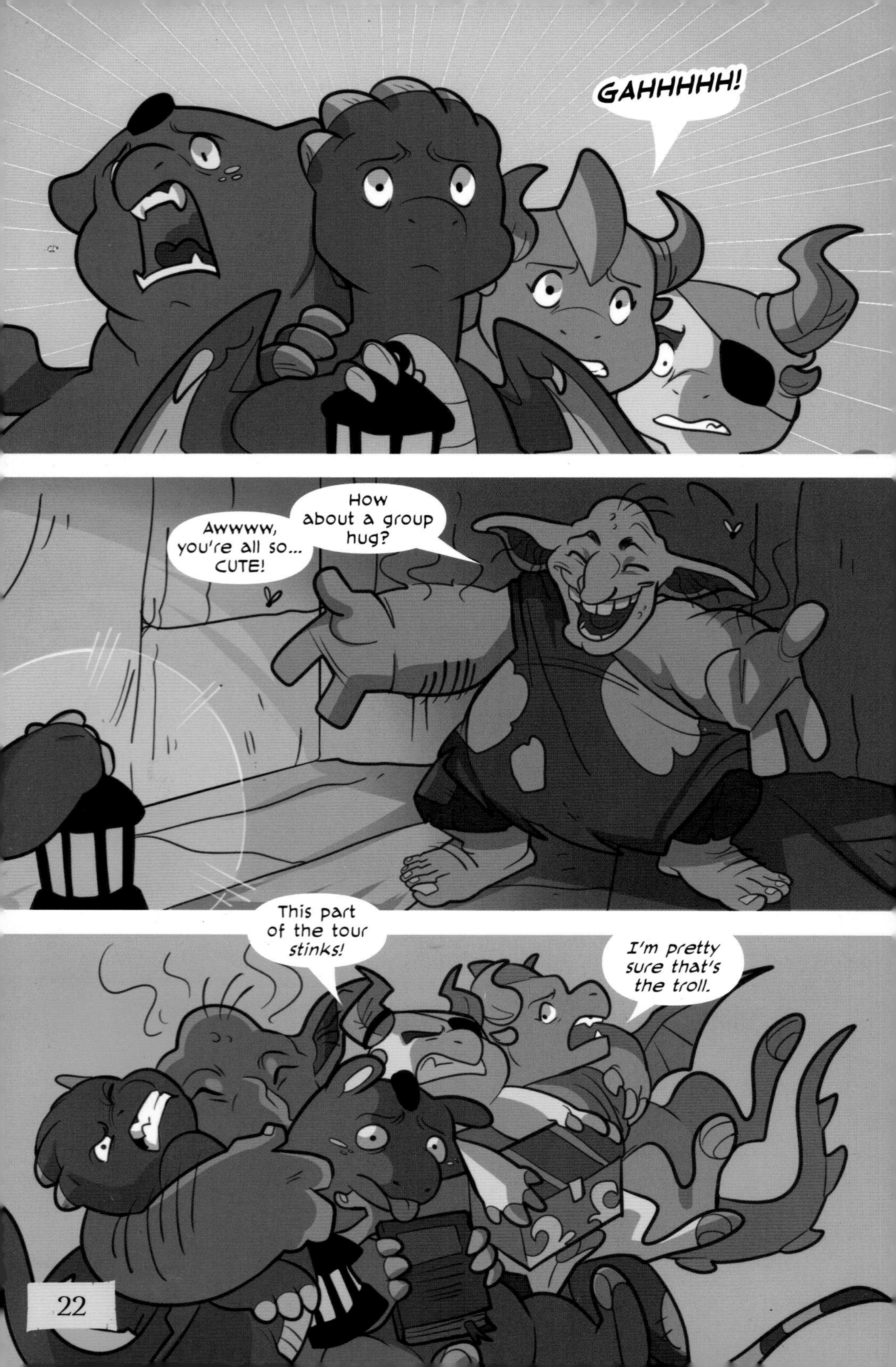
GAHHHHH!
Awwww, you're all so... CUTE!
How about a group hug?
This part of the tour *stinks!*
I'm pretty sure that's the troll.

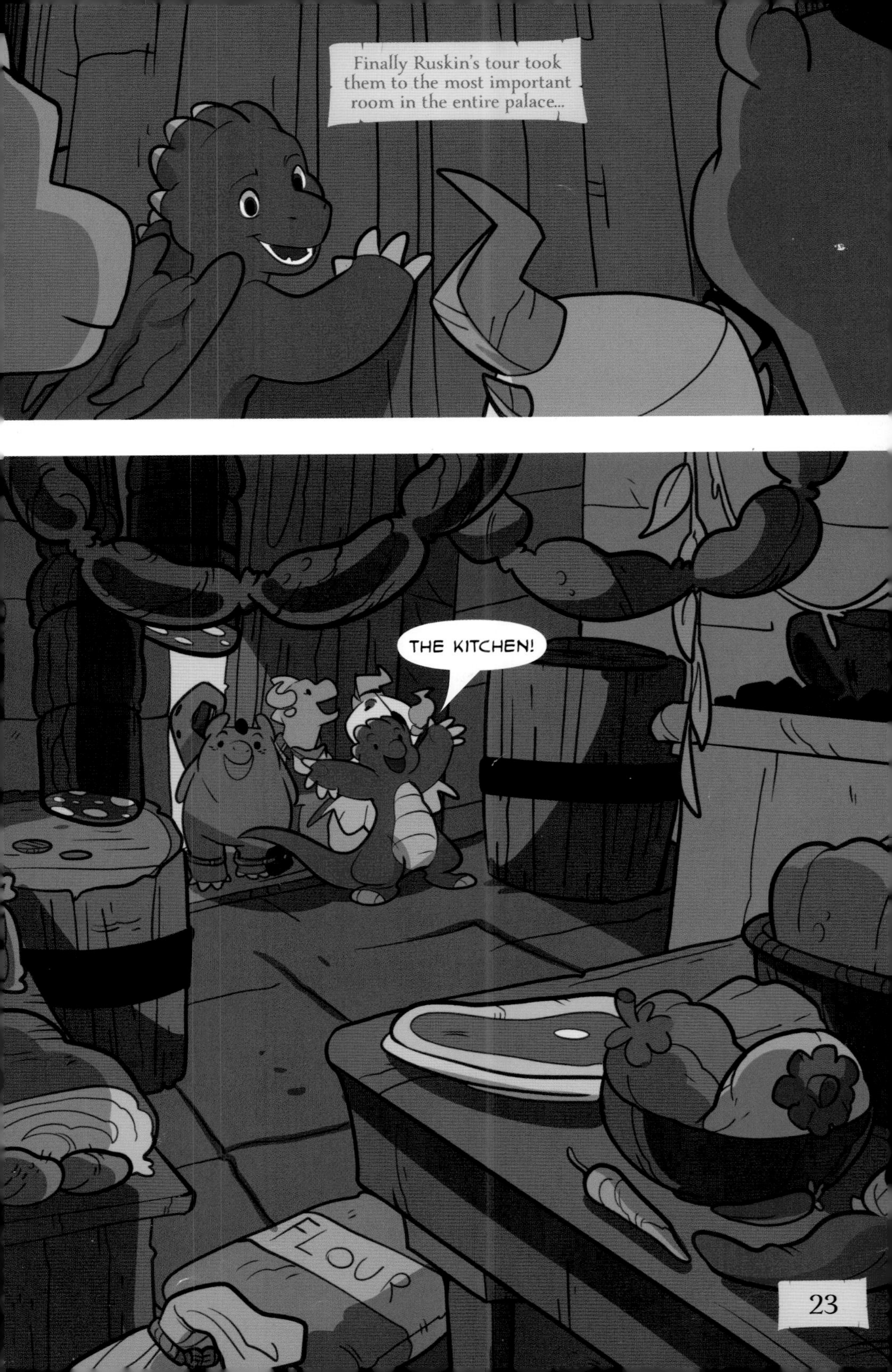
Finally Ruskin's tour took them to the most important room in the entire palace...
THE KITCHEN!
FLOUR

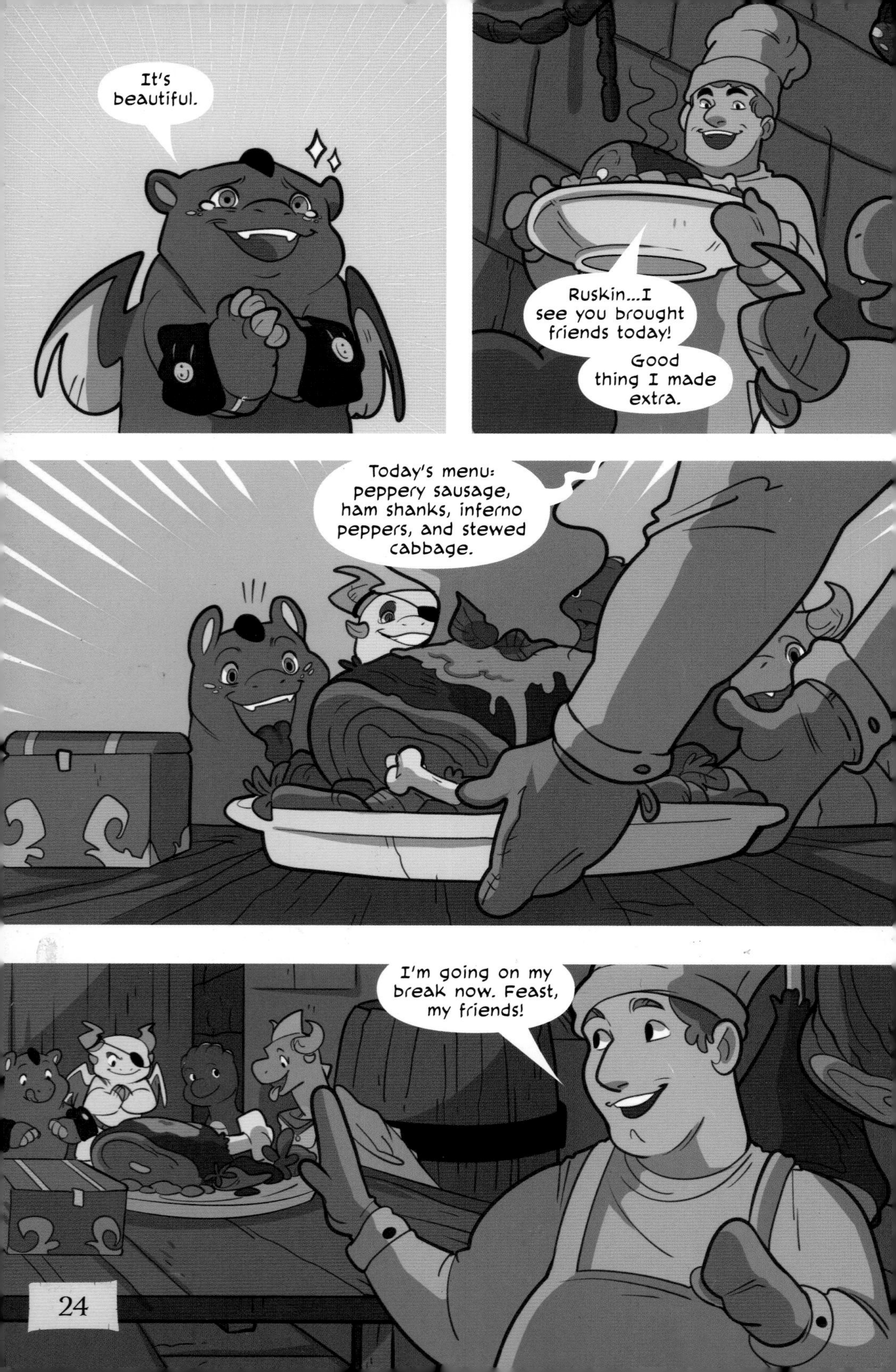
It's beautiful.
Ruskin...I see you brought friends today!
Good thing I made extra.
Today's menu: peppery sausage, ham shanks, inferno peppers, and stewed cabbage.
I'm going on my break now. Feast, my friends!

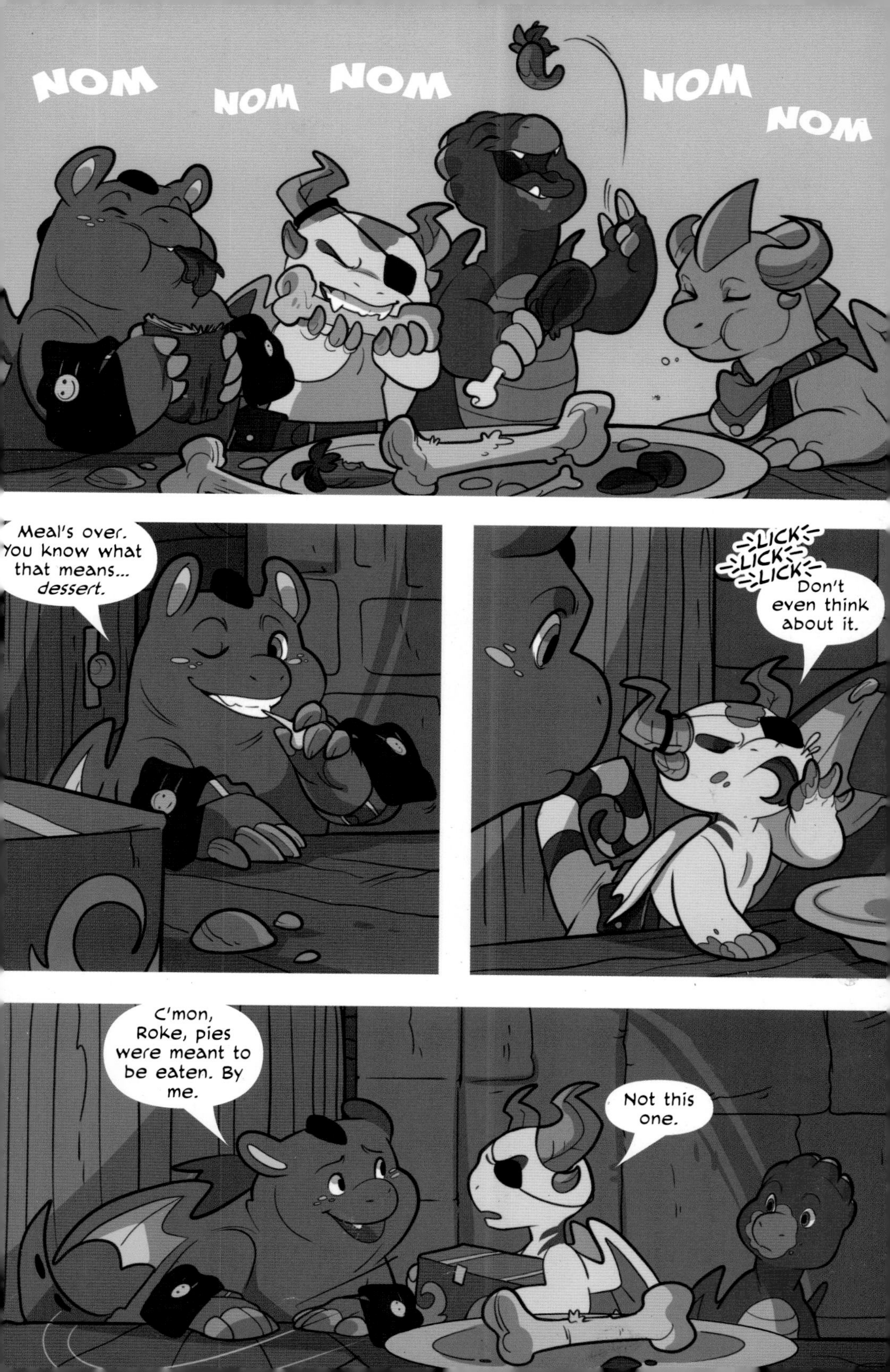
NOM
NOM
NOM
NOM
NOM
Meal's over. You know what that means... *dessert.*
LICK LICK LICK
Don't even think about it.
C'mon, Roke, pies were meant to be eaten. By me.
Not this one.

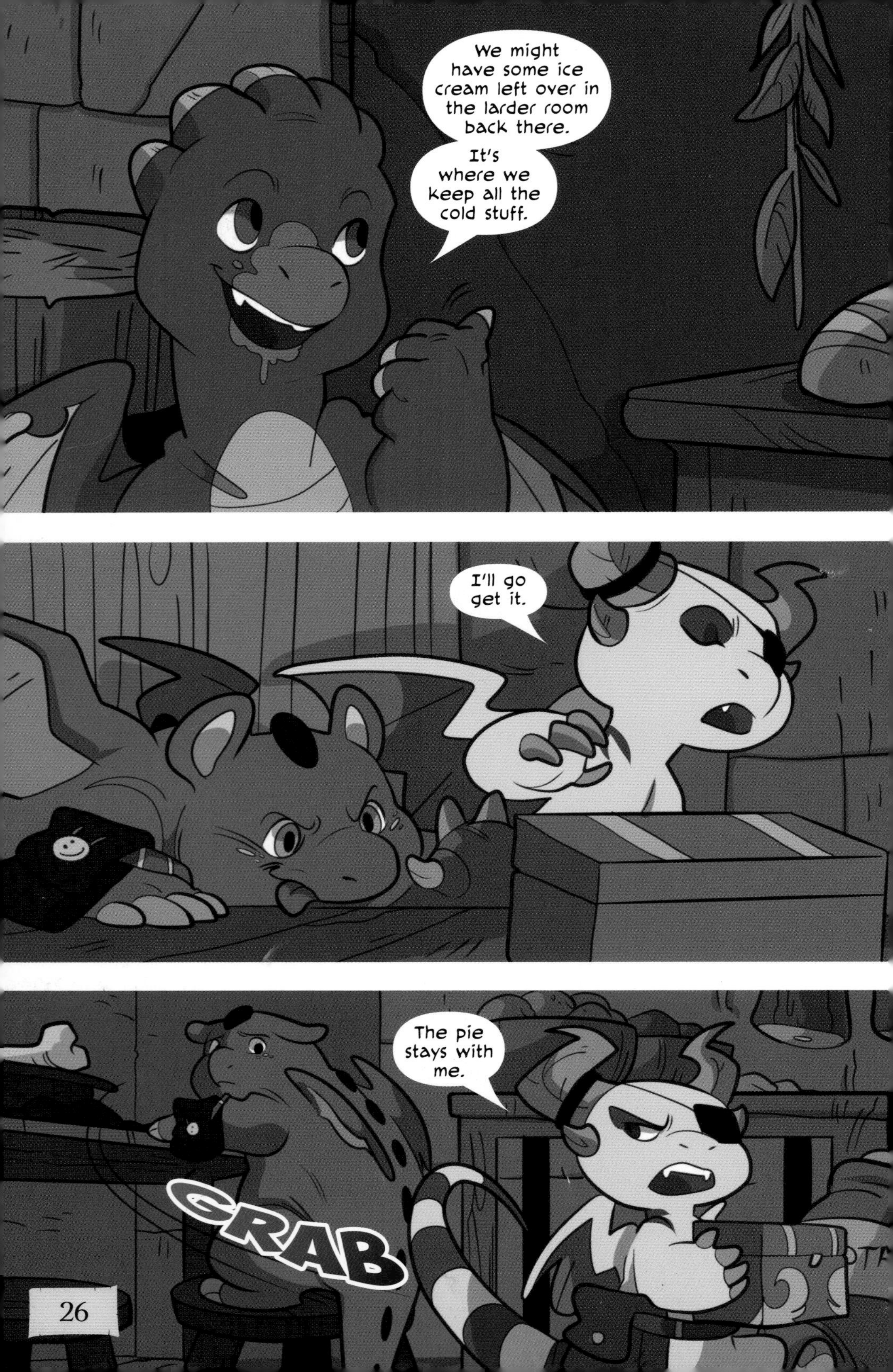
We might have some ice cream left over in the larder room back there.
It's where we keep all the cold stuff.
I'll go get it.
The pie stays with me.
GRAB

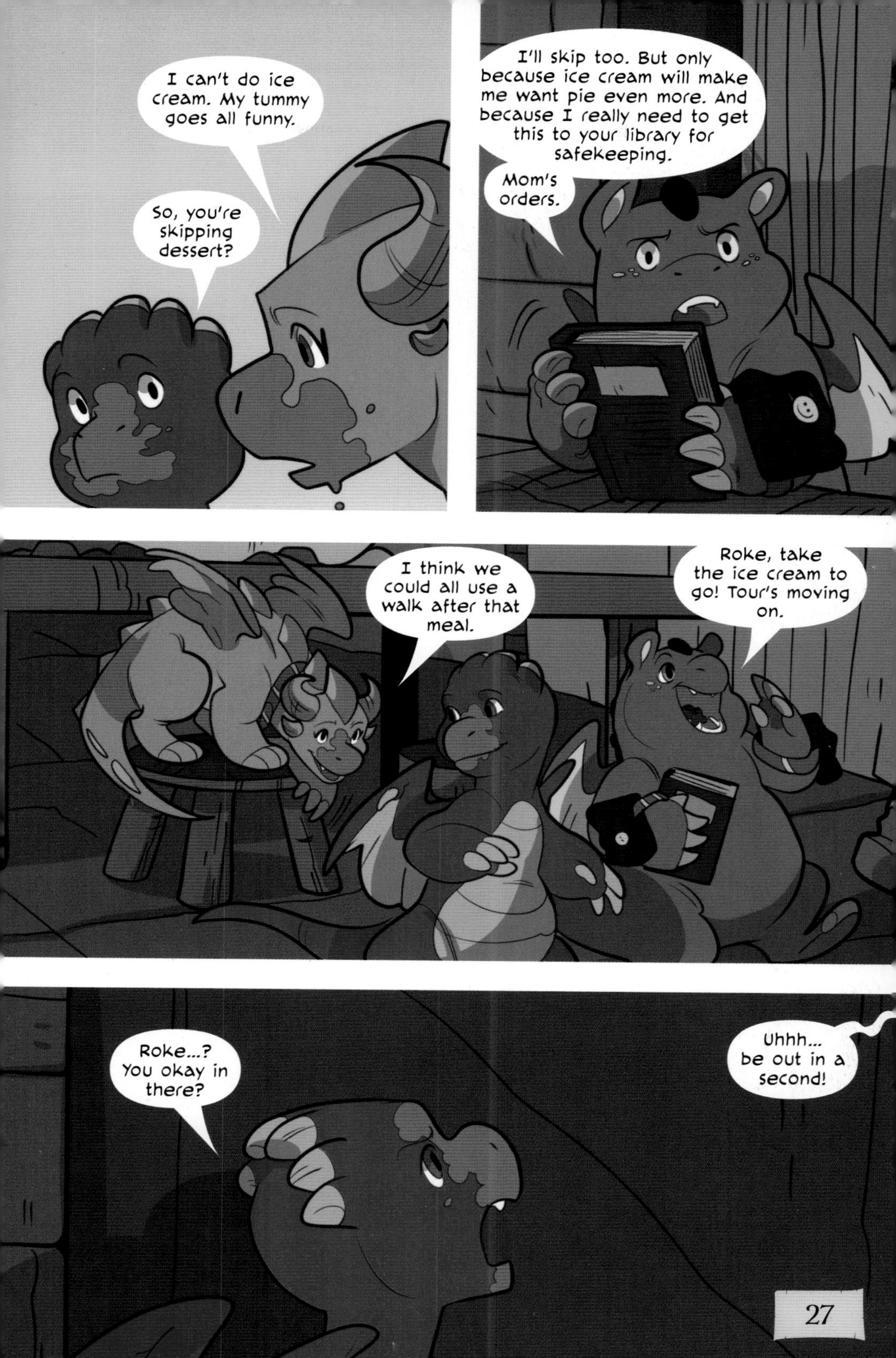
I can't do ice cream. My tummy goes all funny.
So, you're skipping dessert?
I'll skip too. But only because ice cream will make me want pie even more. And because I really need to get this to your library for safekeeping.
Mom's orders.
I think we could all use a walk after that meal.
Roke, take the ice cream to go! Tour's moving on.
Roke...? You okay in there?
Uhhh... be out in a second!

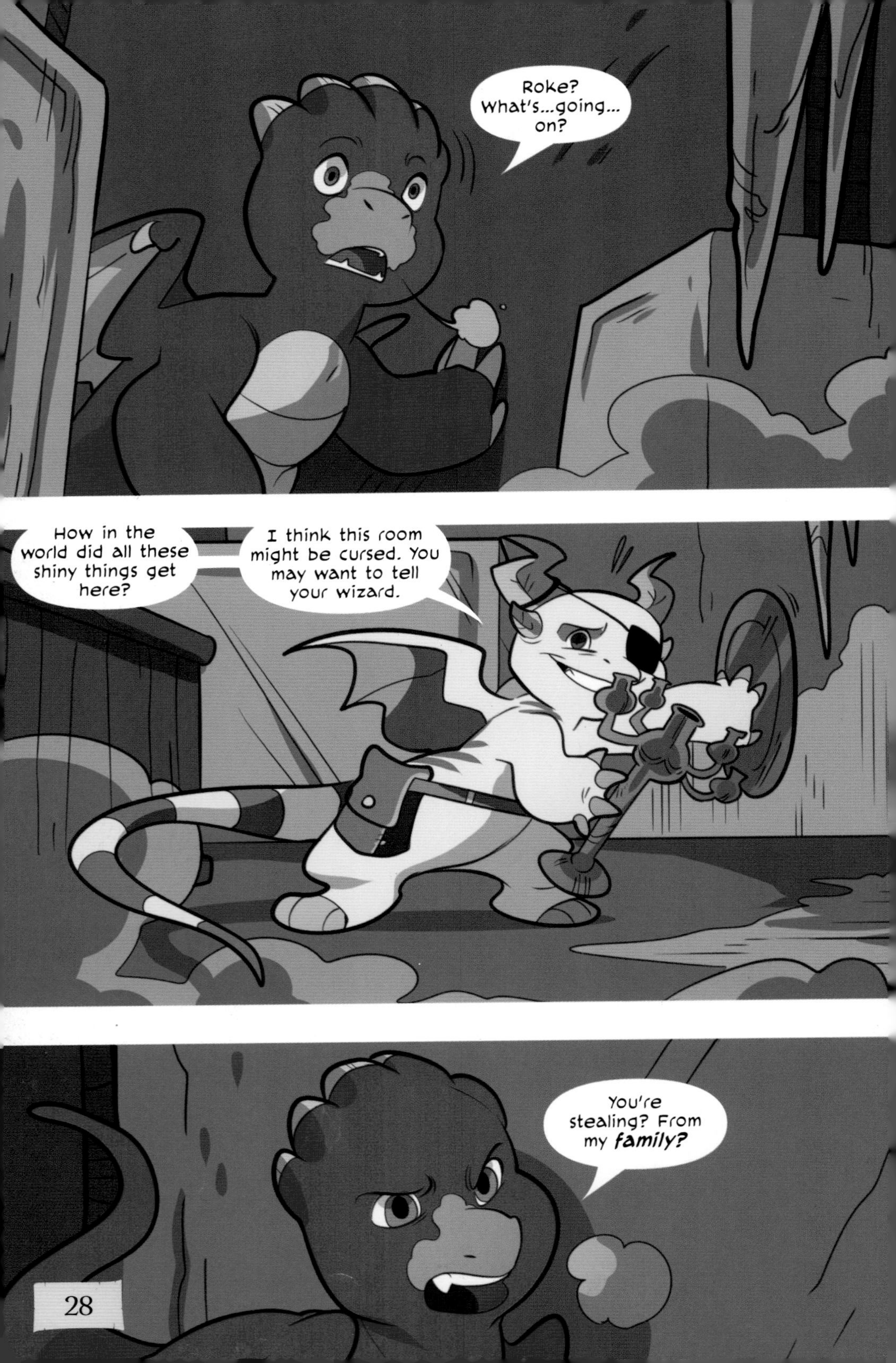
Roke? What's...going... on?
How in the world did all these shiny things get here?
I think this room might be cursed. You may want to tell your wizard.
You're stealing? From my *family?*

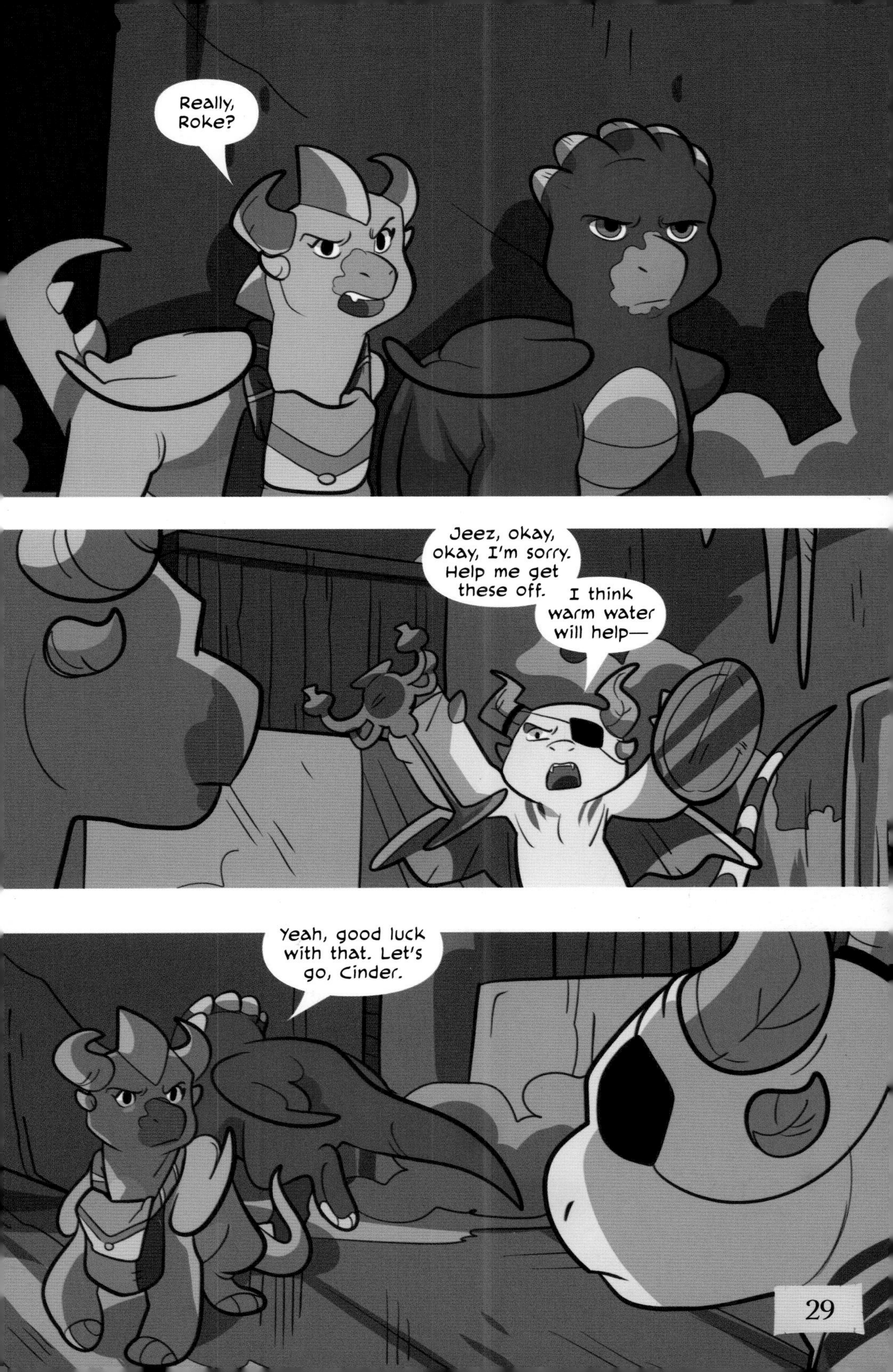
Really, Roke?
Jeez, okay, okay, I'm sorry. Help me get these off.
I think warm water will help—
Yeah, good luck with that. Let's go, Cinder.

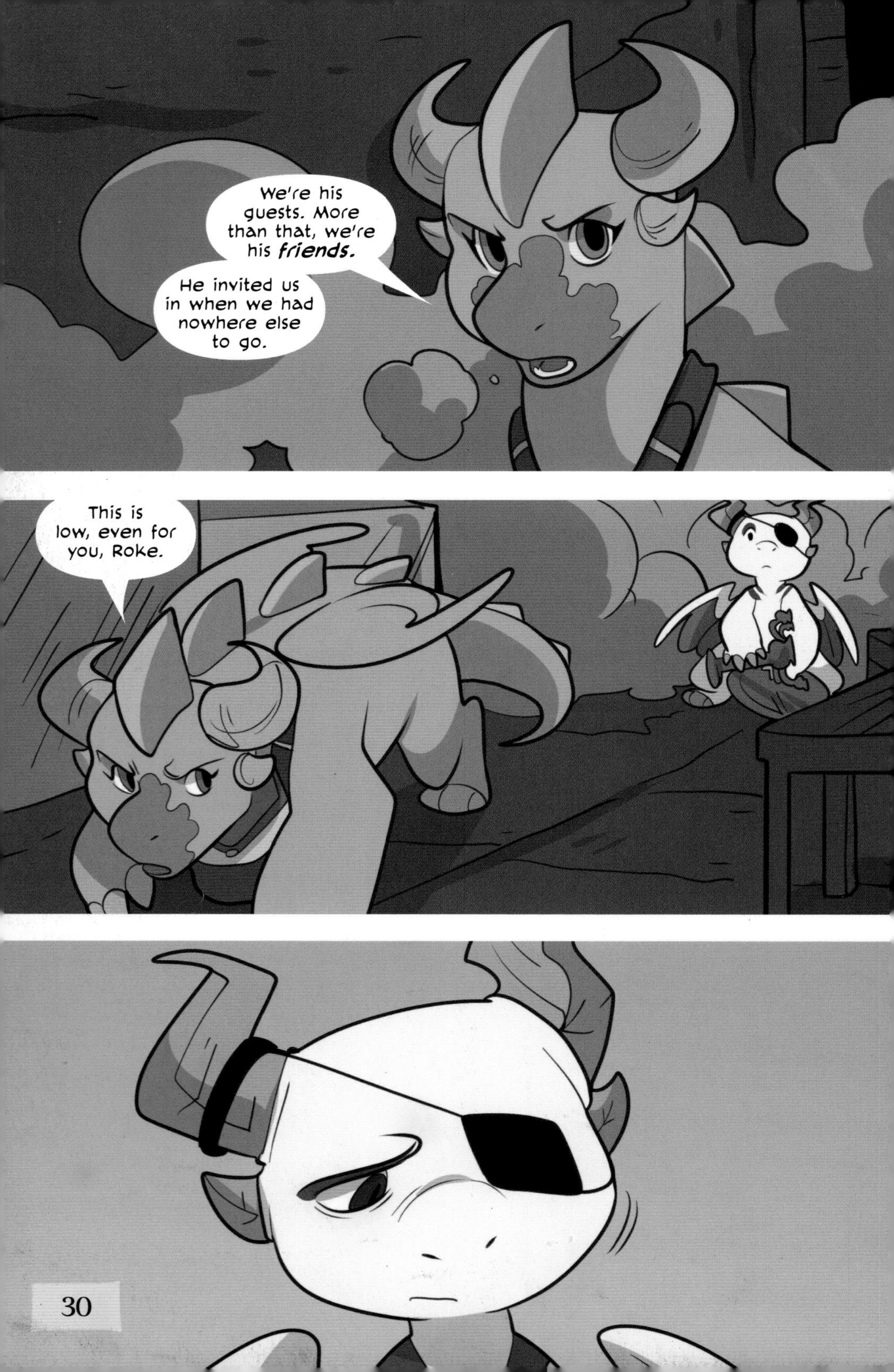
We're his guests. More than that, we're his *friends.*
He invited us in when we had nowhere else to go.
This is low, even for you, Roke.

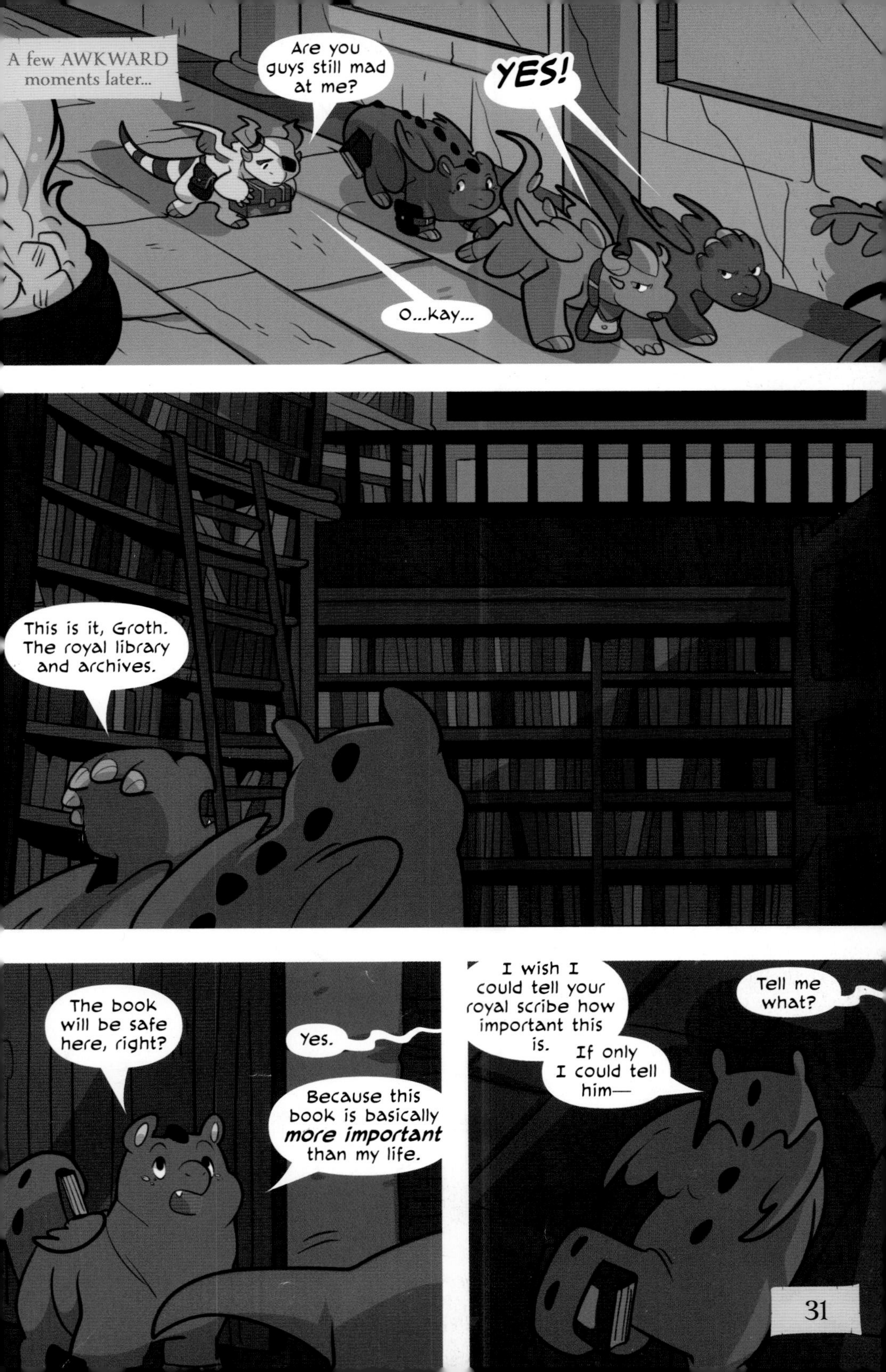
A few AWKWARD moments later...
Are you guys still mad at me?
YES!
O...kay...
This is it, Groth. The royal library and archives.
The book will be safe here, right?
Yes.
Because this book is basically *more important* than my life.
I wish I could tell your royal scribe how important this is.
If only I could tell him—
Tell me what?

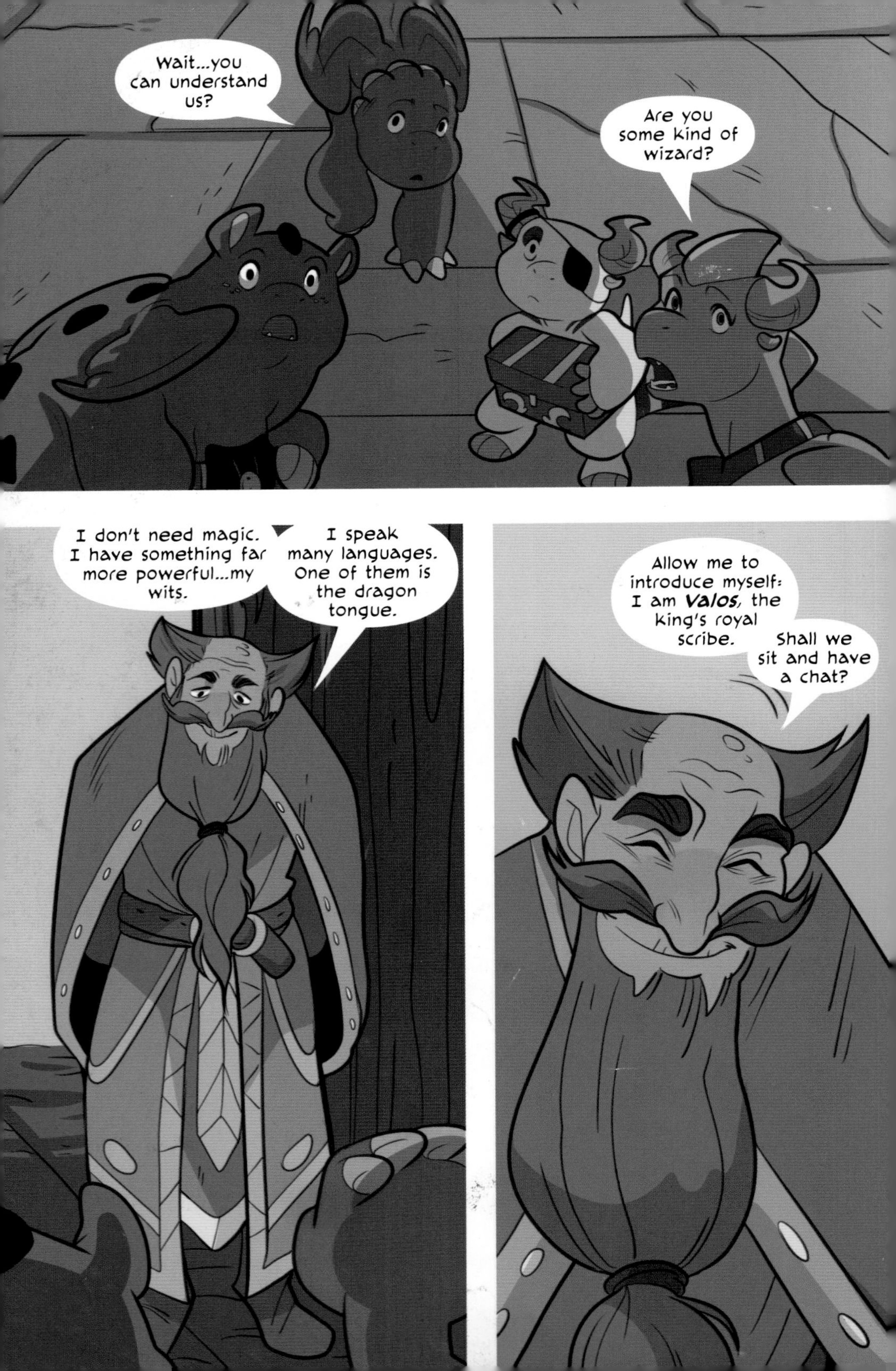
Wait...you can understand us?
Are you some kind of wizard?
I don't need magic. I have something far more powerful...my wits.
I speak many languages. One of them is the dragon tongue.
Allow me to introduce myself: I am *Valos*, the king's royal scribe.
Shall we sit and have a chat?

Chapter 3

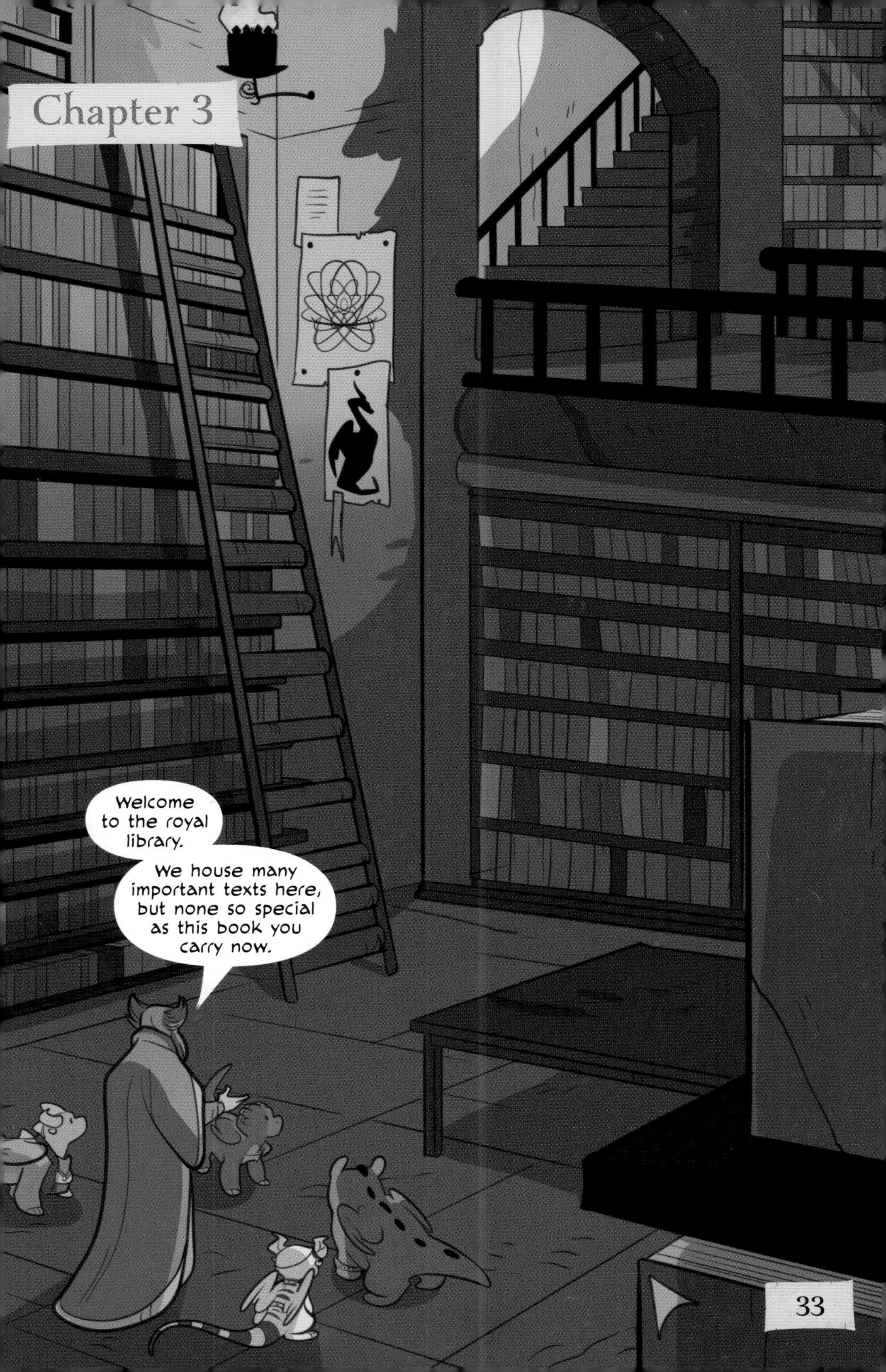
Welcome to the royal library.
We house many important texts here, but none so special as this book you carry now.

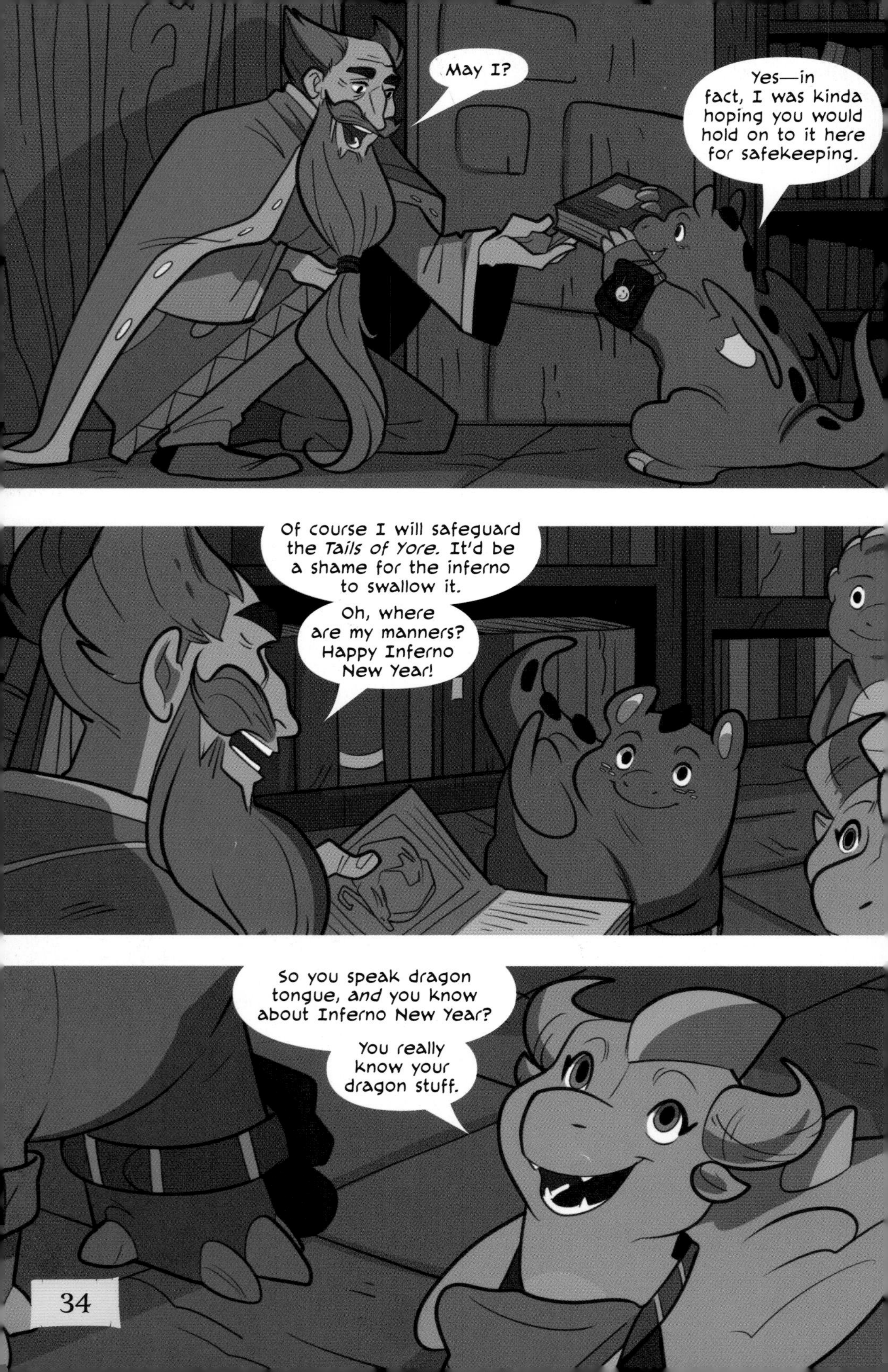
May I?
Yes—in fact, I was kinda hoping you would hold on to it here for safekeeping.
Of course I will safeguard the *Tails of Yore.* It'd be a shame for the inferno to swallow it.
Oh, where are my manners? Happy Inferno New Year!
So you speak dragon tongue, *and* you know about Inferno New Year?
You really know your dragon stuff.

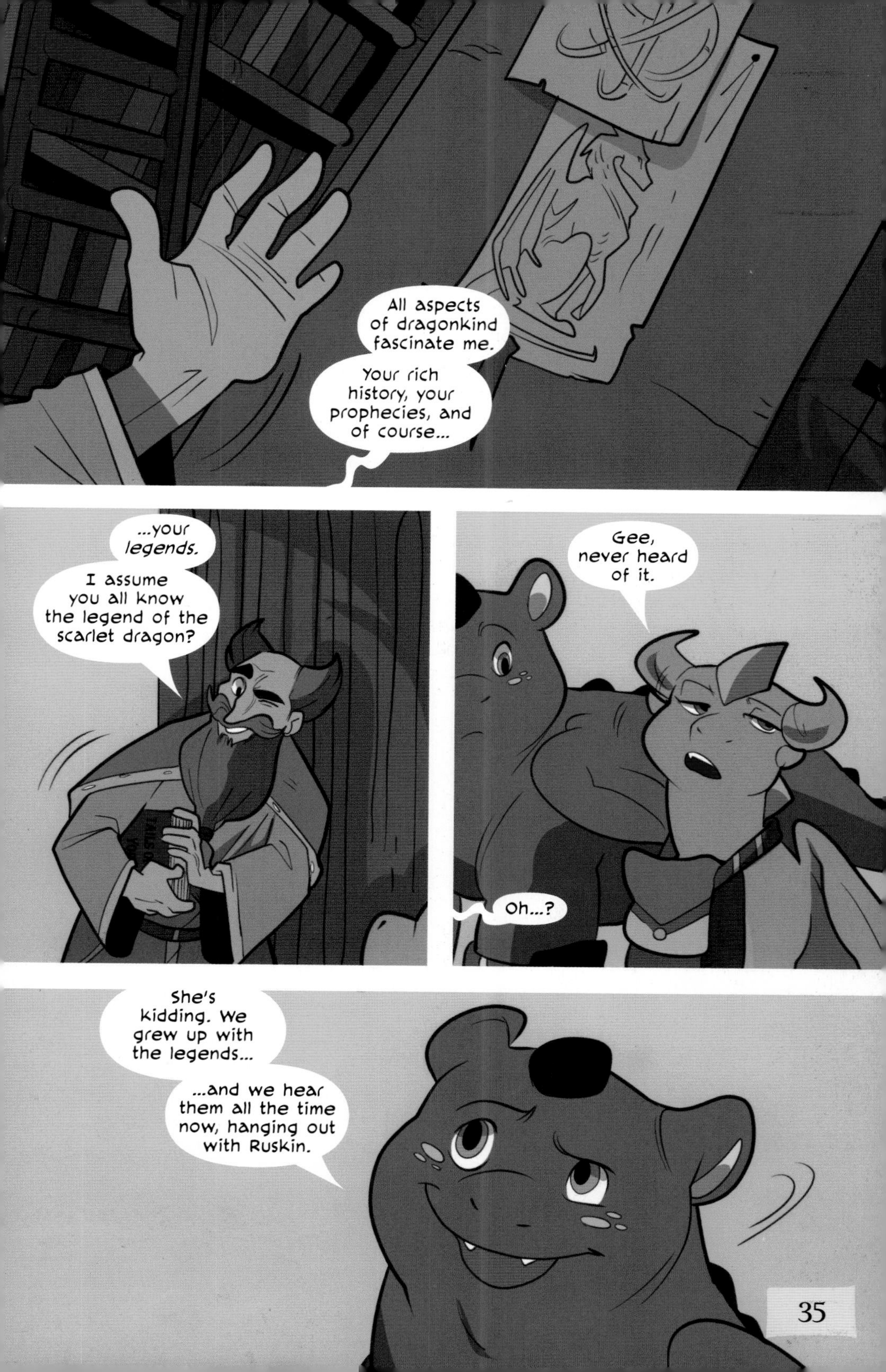

All aspects of dragonkind fascinate me.
Your rich history, your prophecies, and of course...
...your *legends.*
I assume you all know the legend of the scarlet dragon?
Gee, never heard of it.
Oh...?
She's kidding. We grew up with the legends...
...and we hear them all the time now, hanging out with Ruskin.

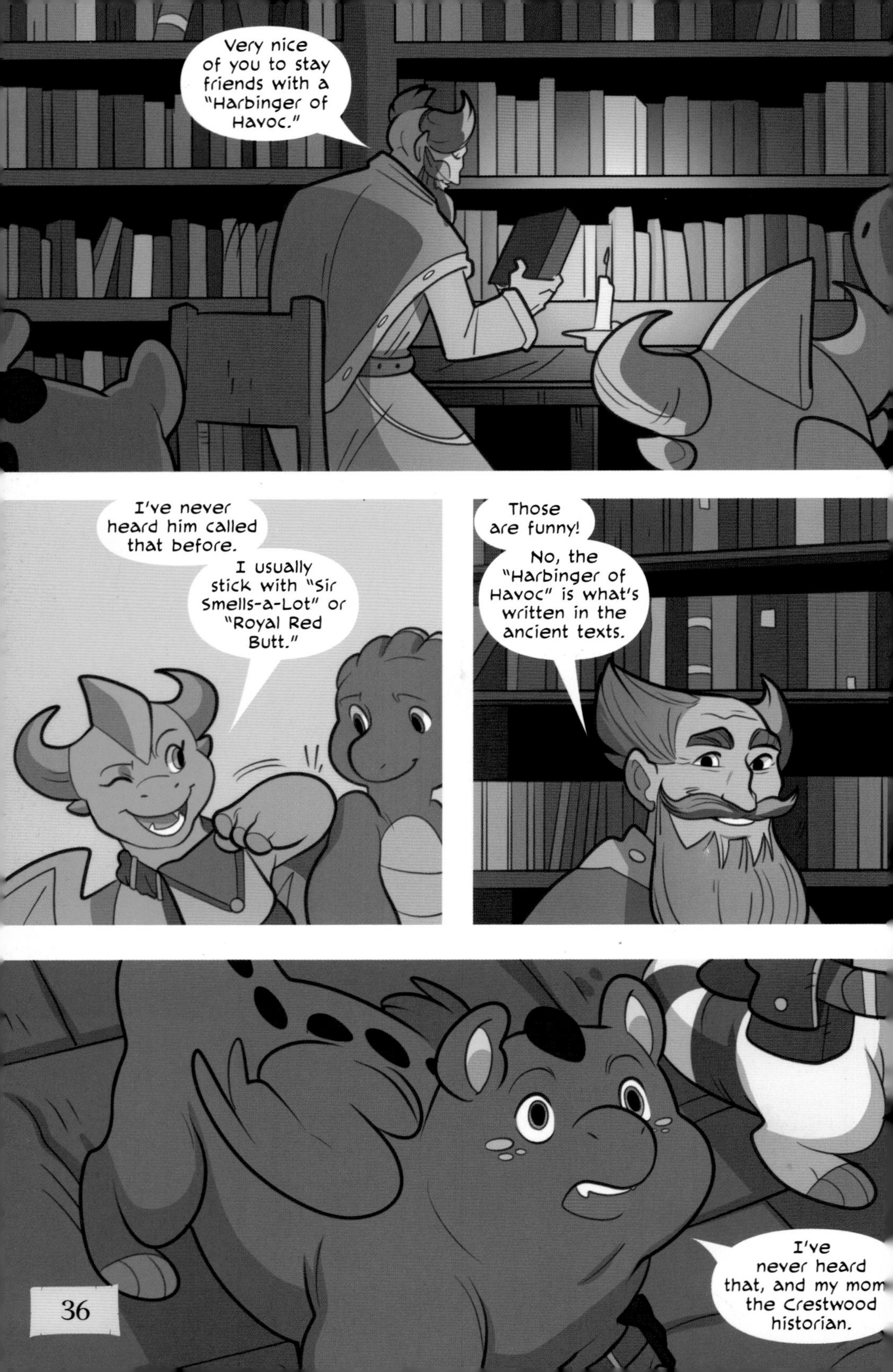
Very nice of you to stay friends with a "Harbinger of Havoc."
I've never heard him called that before.
I usually stick with "Sir Smells-a-Lot" or "Royal Red Butt."
Those are funny!
No, the "Harbinger of Havoc" is what's written in the ancient texts.
I've never heard that, and my mom the Crestwood historian.

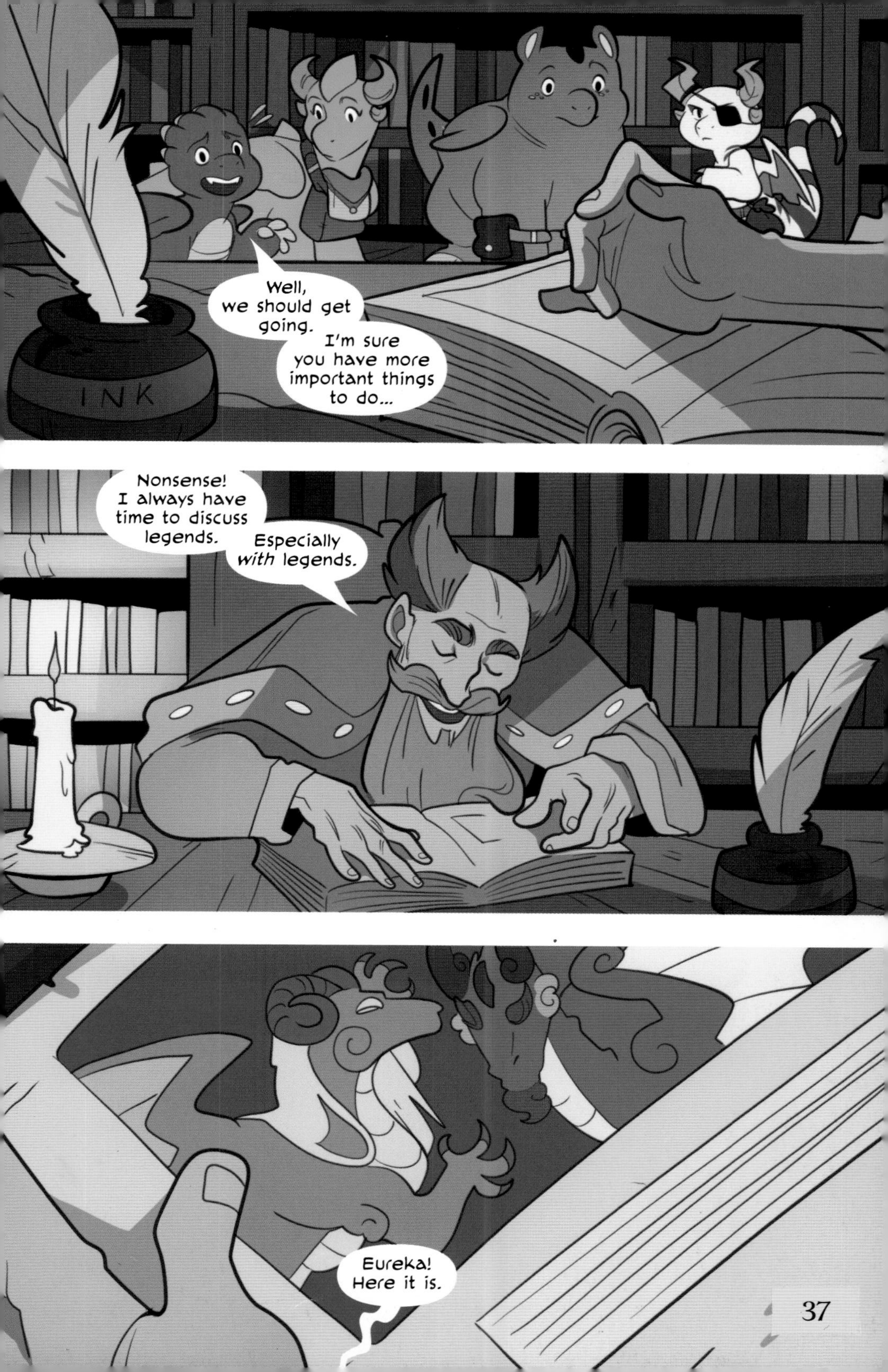
Well, we should get going.
I'm sure you have more important things to do...
Nonsense! I always have time to discuss legends.
Especially *with* legends.
INK
Eureka! Here it is.

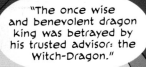

"The once wise and benevolent dragon king was betrayed by his trusted advisor: the Witch-Dragon."

"She weaved a story about an uprising of all of Wrenly's subjects.

She warned him they would invade Crestwood, hungry for a war with the dragons."

"Of course, this was trickery. A way to get the dragon king desperate enough to turn to dark magic to help his kingdom..."

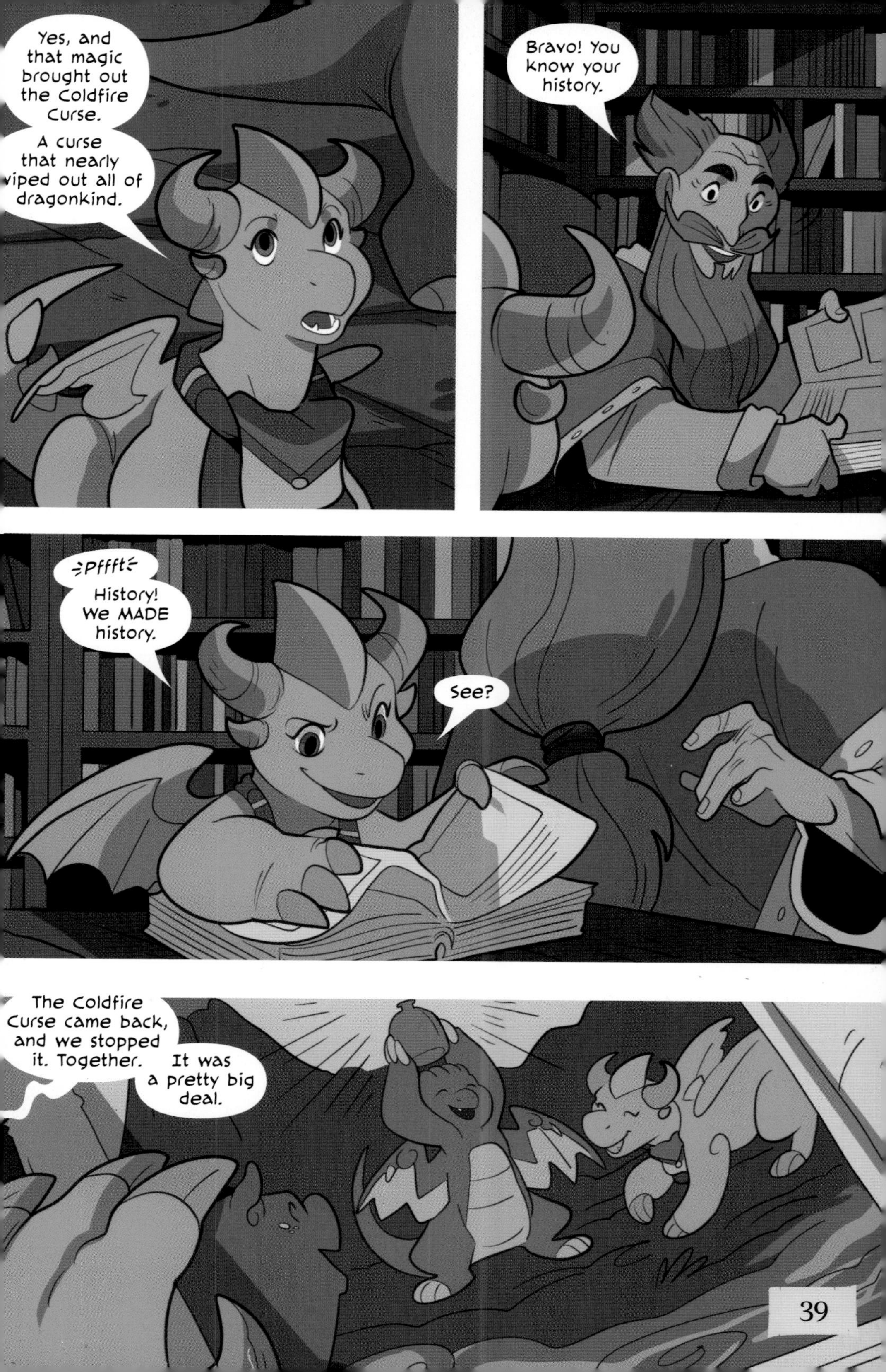
Yes, and that magic brought out the Coldfire Curse.
A curse that nearly wiped out all of dragonkind.
Bravo! You know your history.
Pffft
History! We MADE history.
See?
The Coldfire Curse came back, and we stopped it. Together.
It was a pretty big deal.

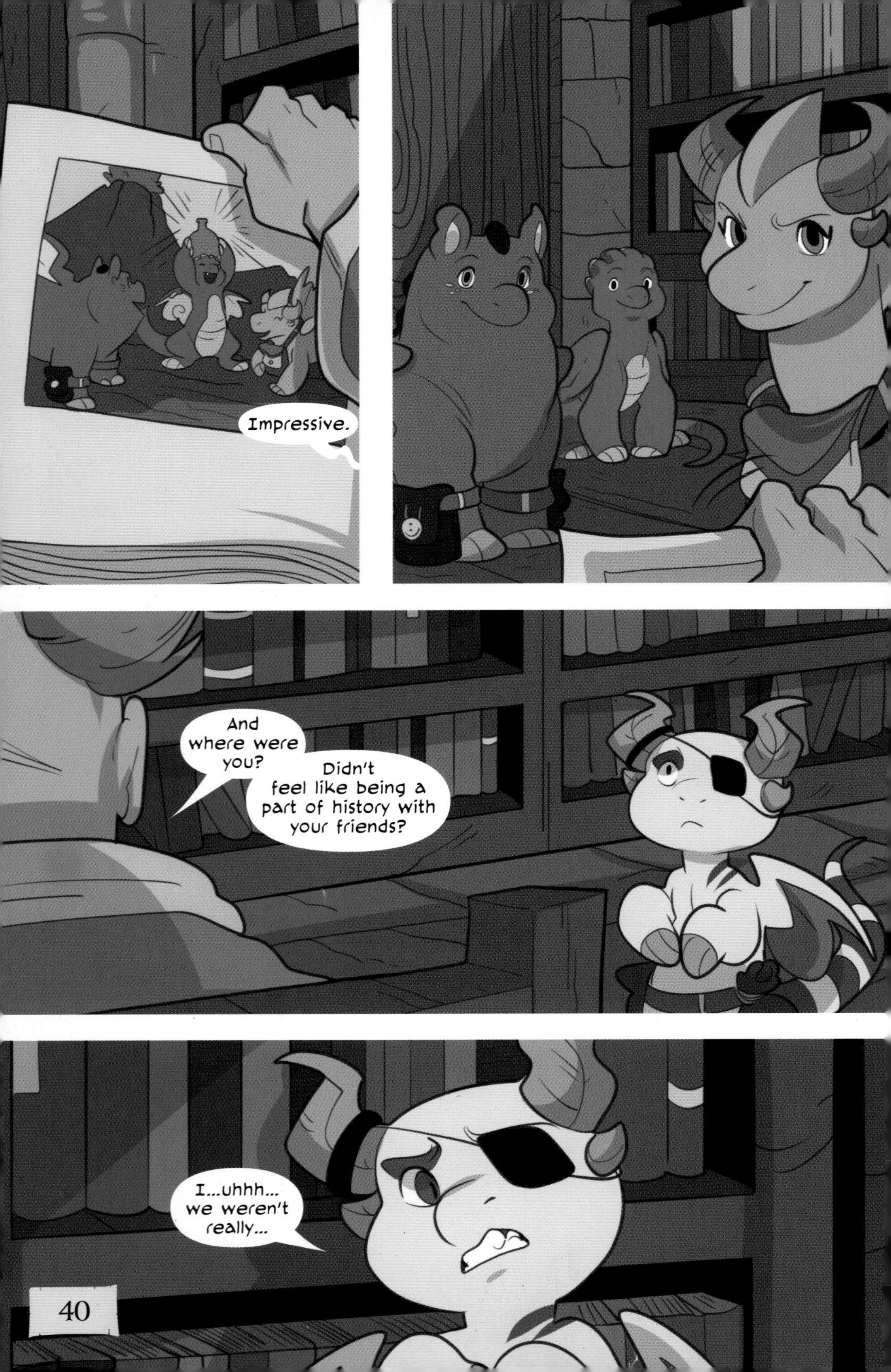
Impressive.
And where were you?
Didn't feel like being a part of history with your friends?
I...uhhh... we weren't really...

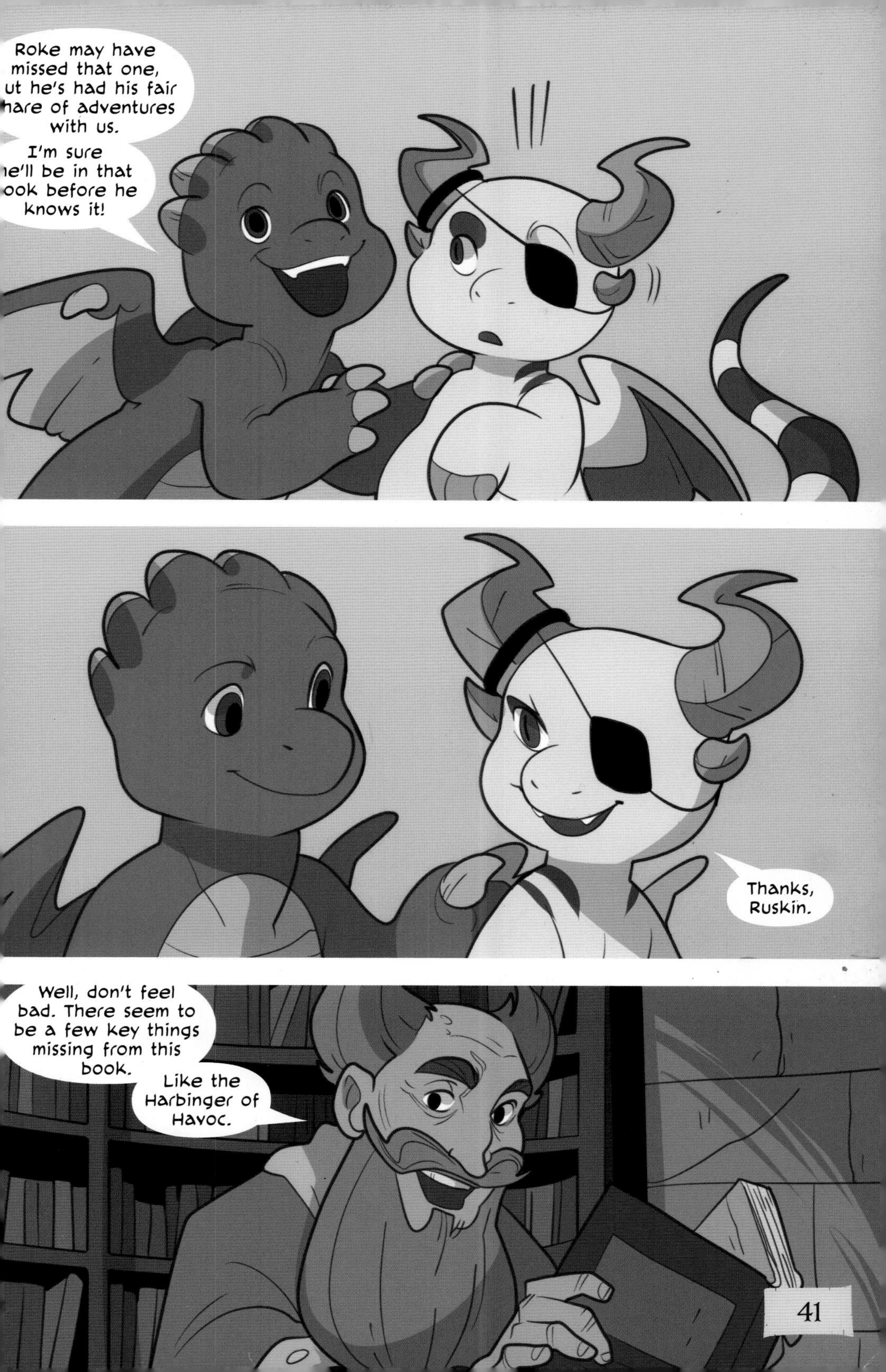
Roke may have missed that one, ut he's had his fair hare of adventures with us.
I'm sure ie'll be in that ook before he knows it!
Thanks, Ruskin.
Well, don't feel bad. There seem to be a few key things missing from this book.
Like the Harbinger of Havoc.

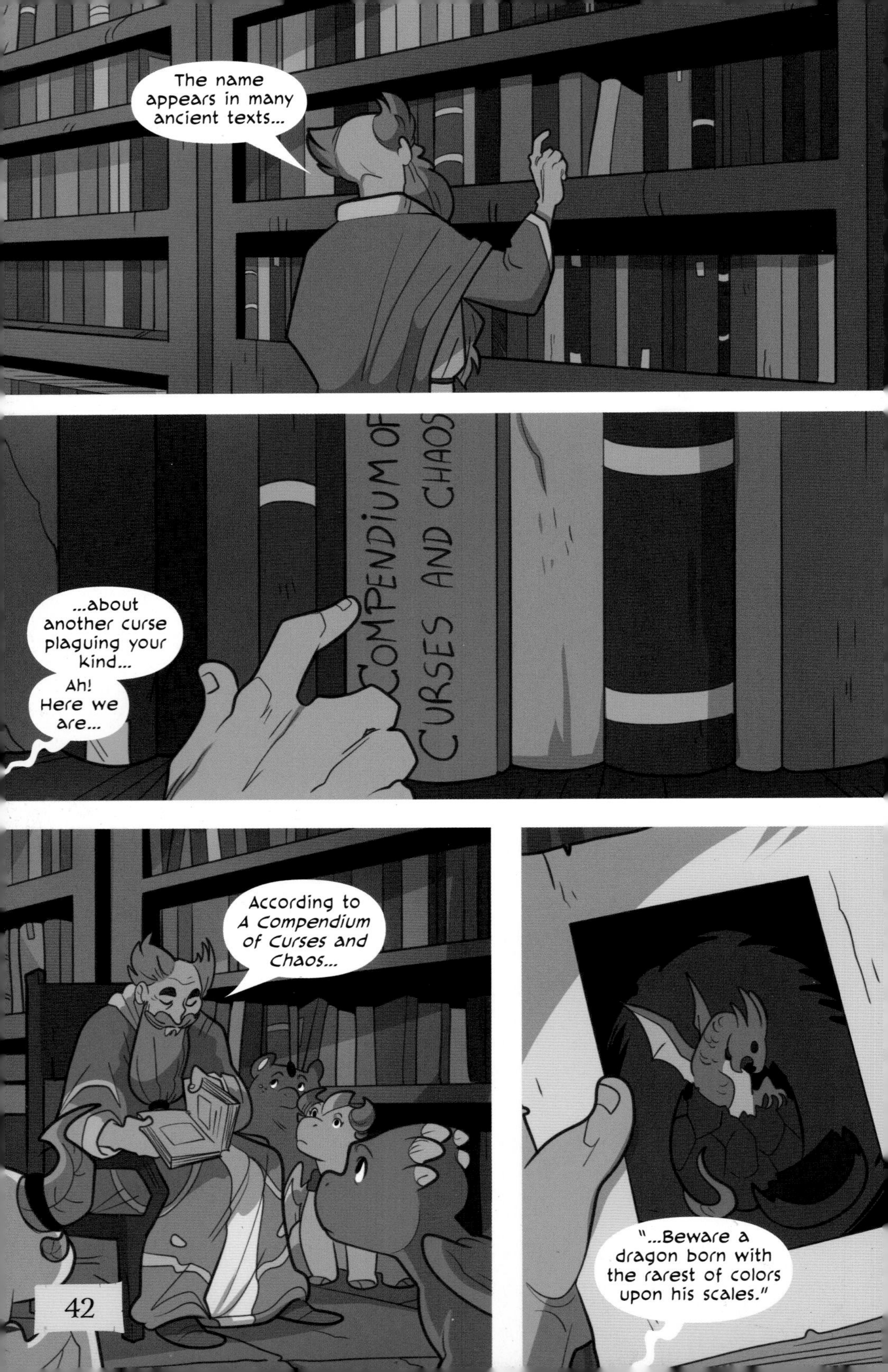

The name appears in many ancient texts...
COMPENDIUM OF CURSES AND CHAOS
...about another curse plaguing your kind...
Ah! Here we are...
According to *A Compendium of Curses and Chaos*...
"...Beware a dragon born with the rarest of colors upon his scales."

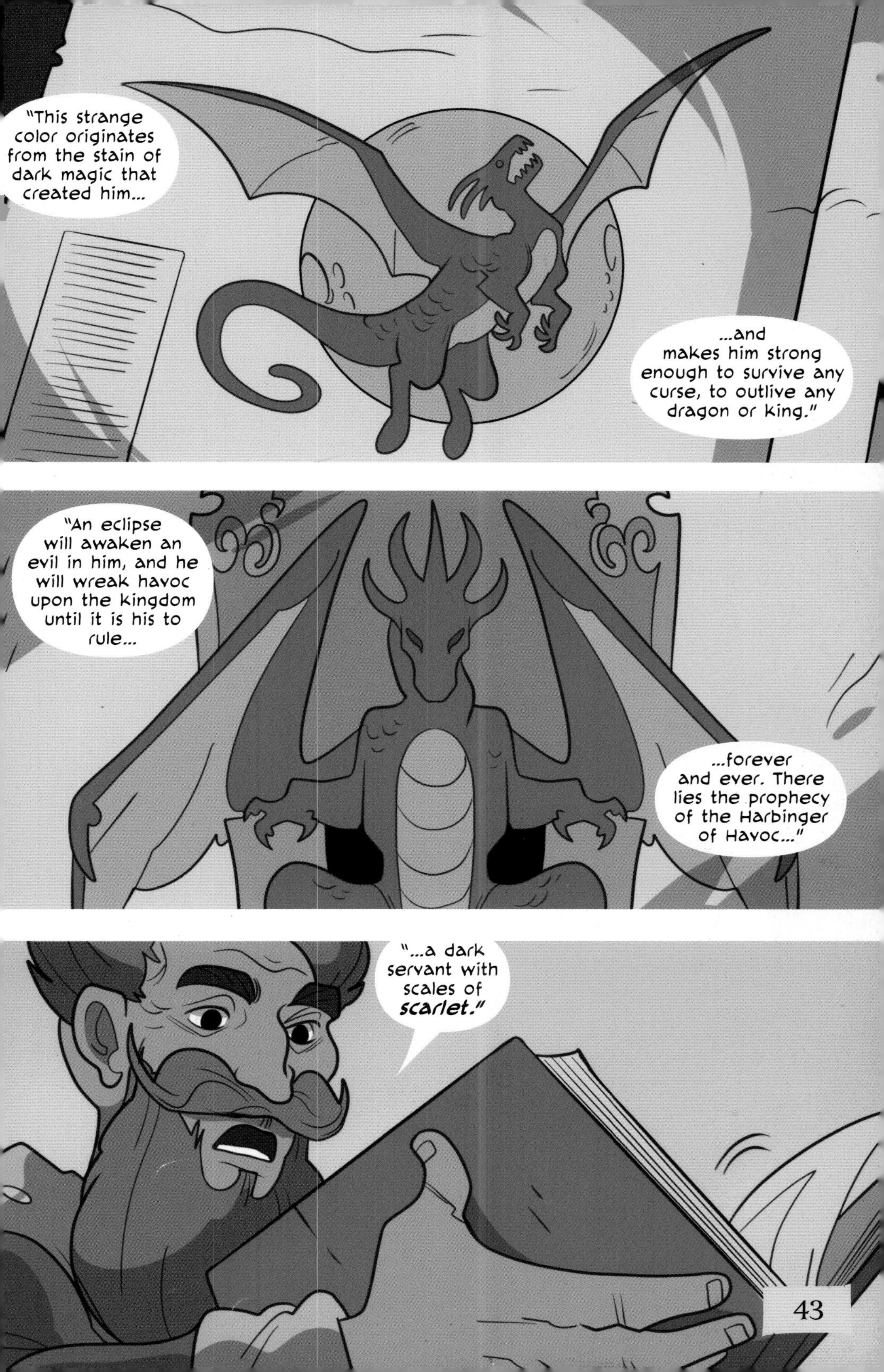
"This strange color originates from the stain of dark magic that created him...
...and makes him strong enough to survive any curse, to outlive any dragon or king."
"An eclipse will awaken an evil in him, and he will wreak havoc upon the kingdom until it is his to rule...
...forever and ever. There lies the prophecy of the Harbinger of Havoc..."
"...a dark servant with scales of *scarlet.*"

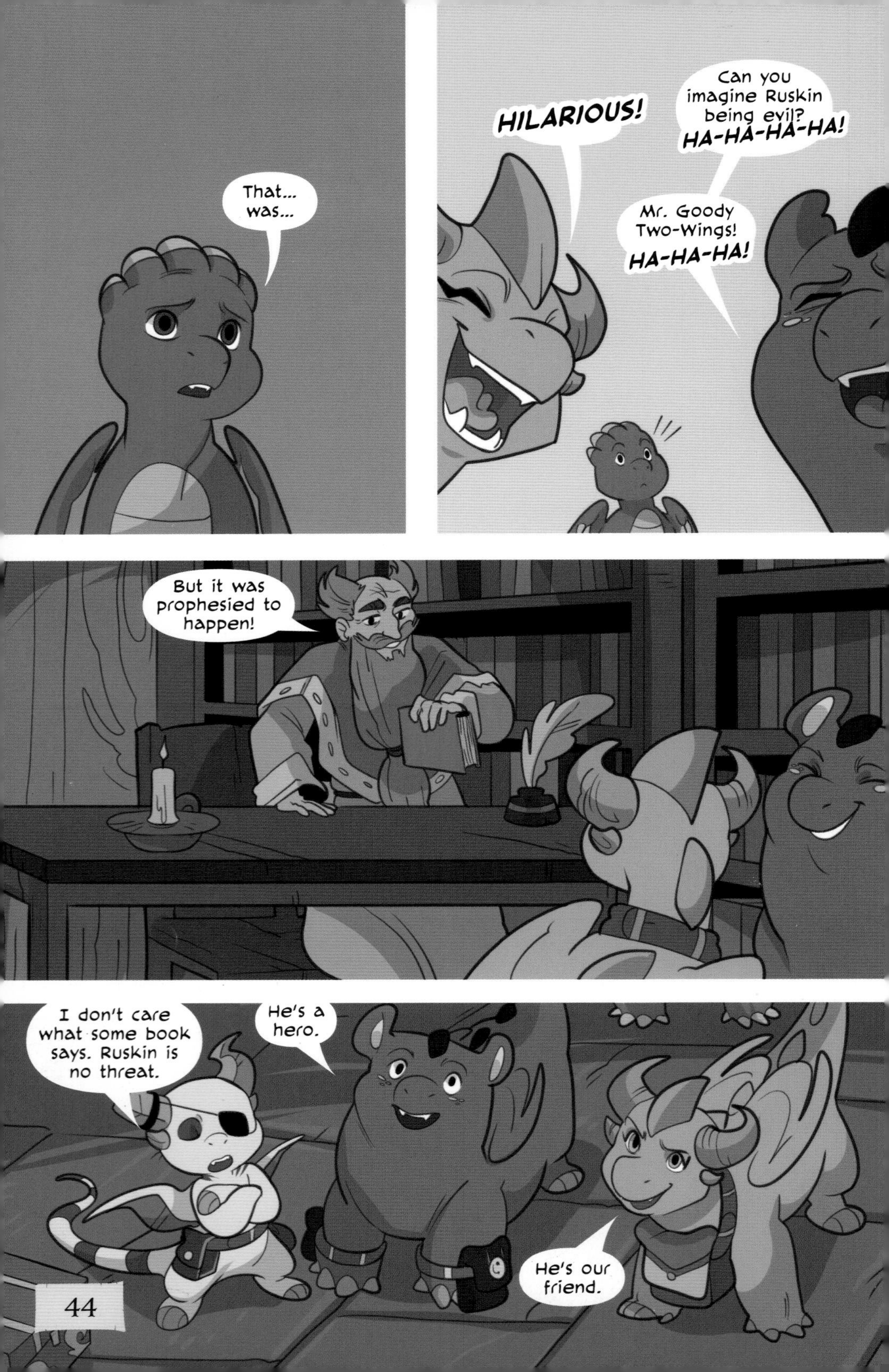

That... was...
HILARIOUS!
Can you imagine Ruskin being evil? HA-HA-HA-HA!
Mr. Goody Two-Wings! HA-HA-HA!
But it was prophesied to happen!
I don't care what some book says. Ruskin is no threat.
He's a hero.
He's our friend.

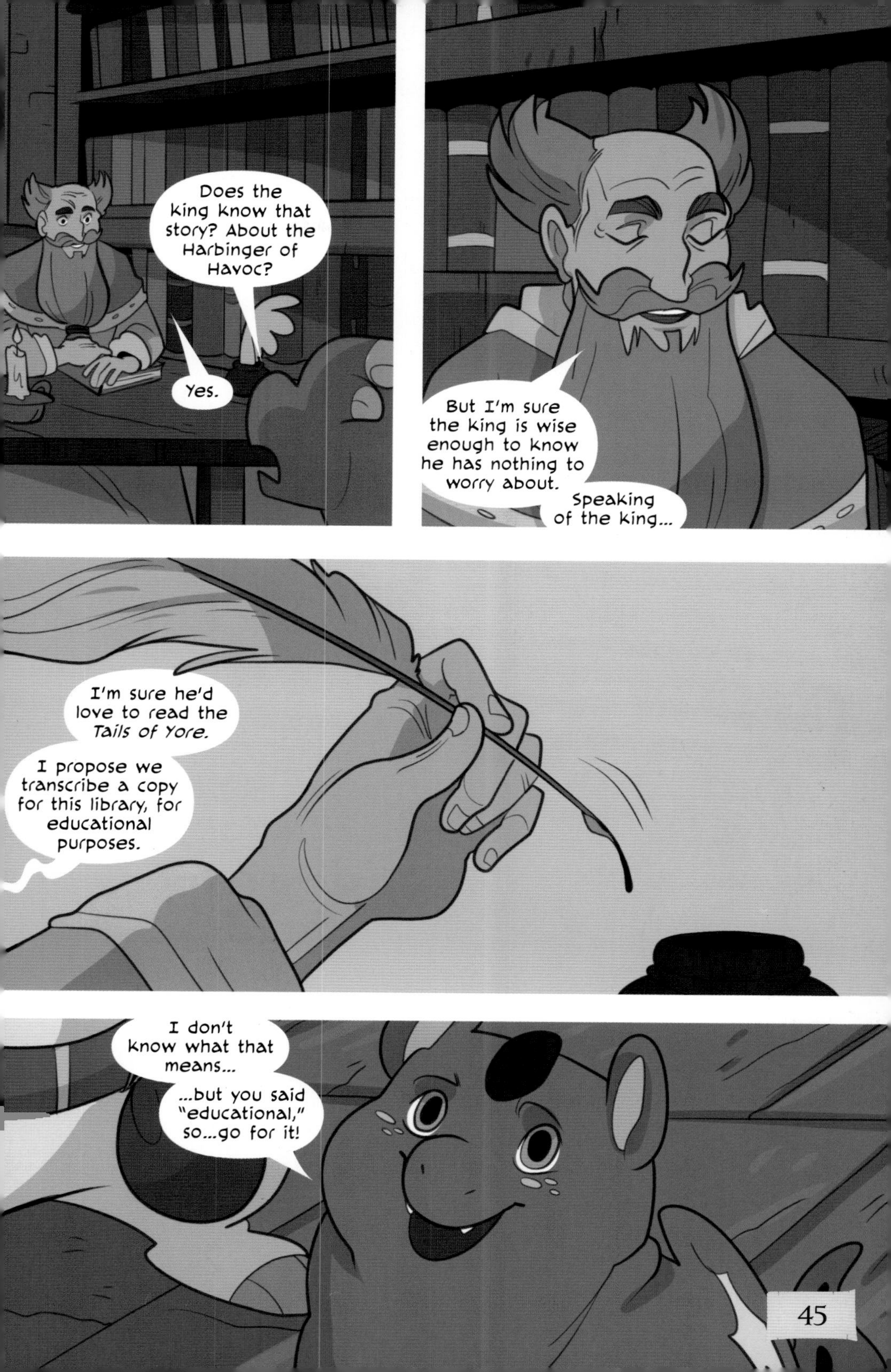
Does the king know that story? About the Harbinger of Havoc?
Yes.
But I'm sure the king is wise enough to know he has nothing to worry about.
Speaking of the king...
I'm sure he'd love to read the *Tails of Yore.*
I propose we transcribe a copy for this library, for educational purposes.
I don't know what that means...
...but you said "educational," so...go for it!

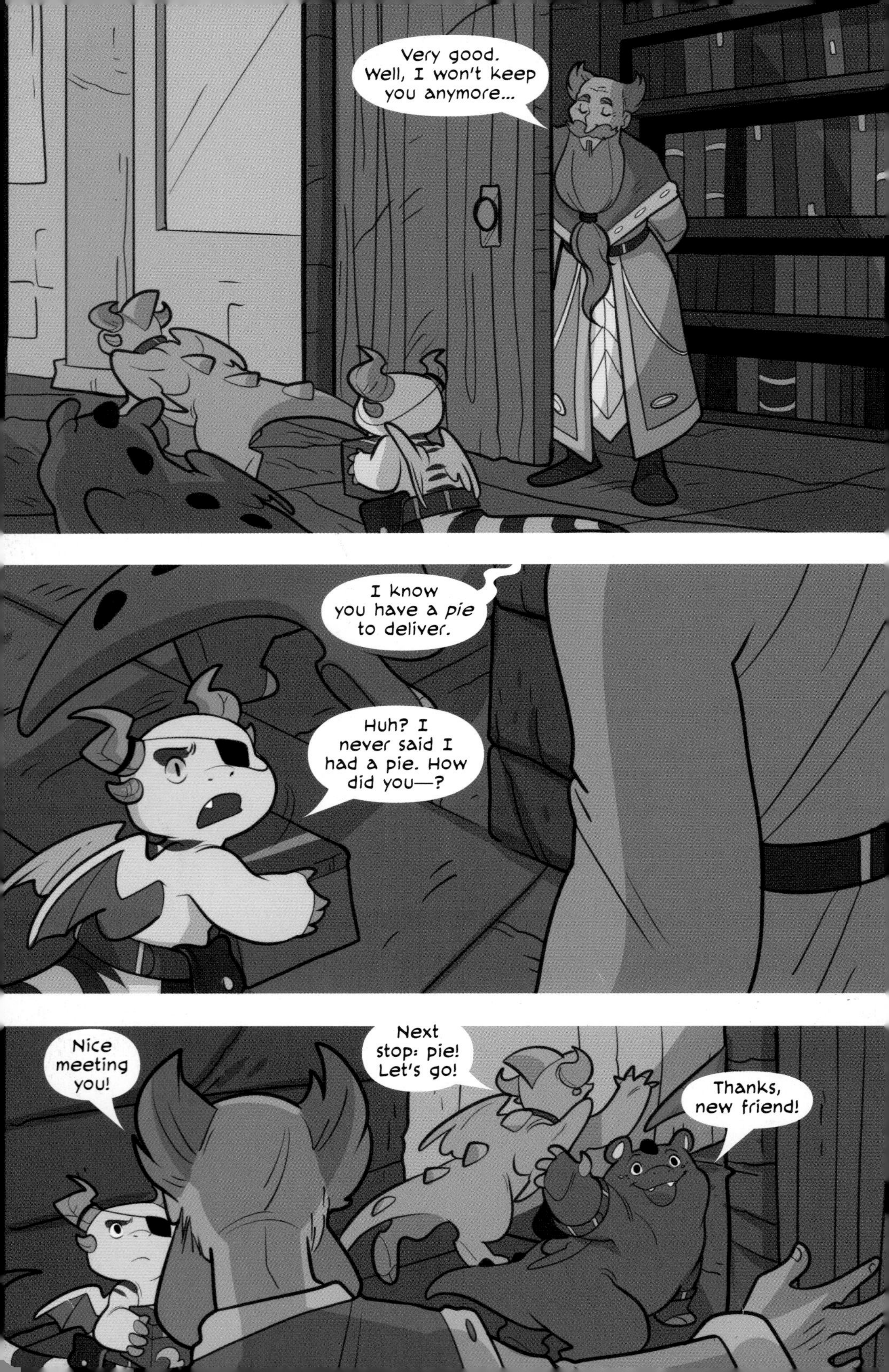
Very good. Well, I won't keep you anymore...
I know you have a *pie* to deliver.
Huh? I never said I had a pie. How did you—?
Nice meeting you!
Next stop: pie! Let's go!
Thanks, new friend!

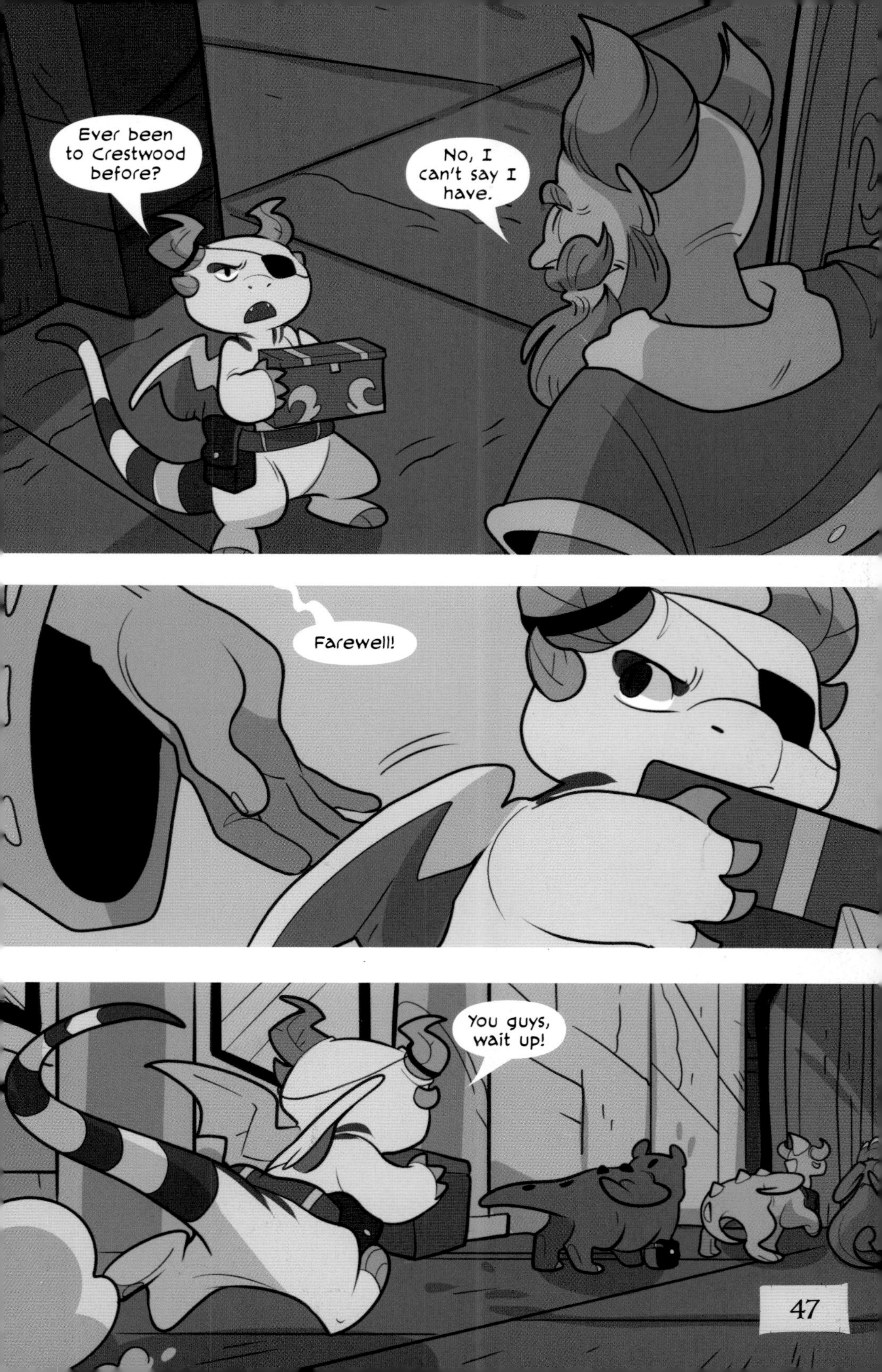
Ever been to Crestwood before?
No, I can't say I have.
Farewell!
You guys, wait up!

Chapter 4

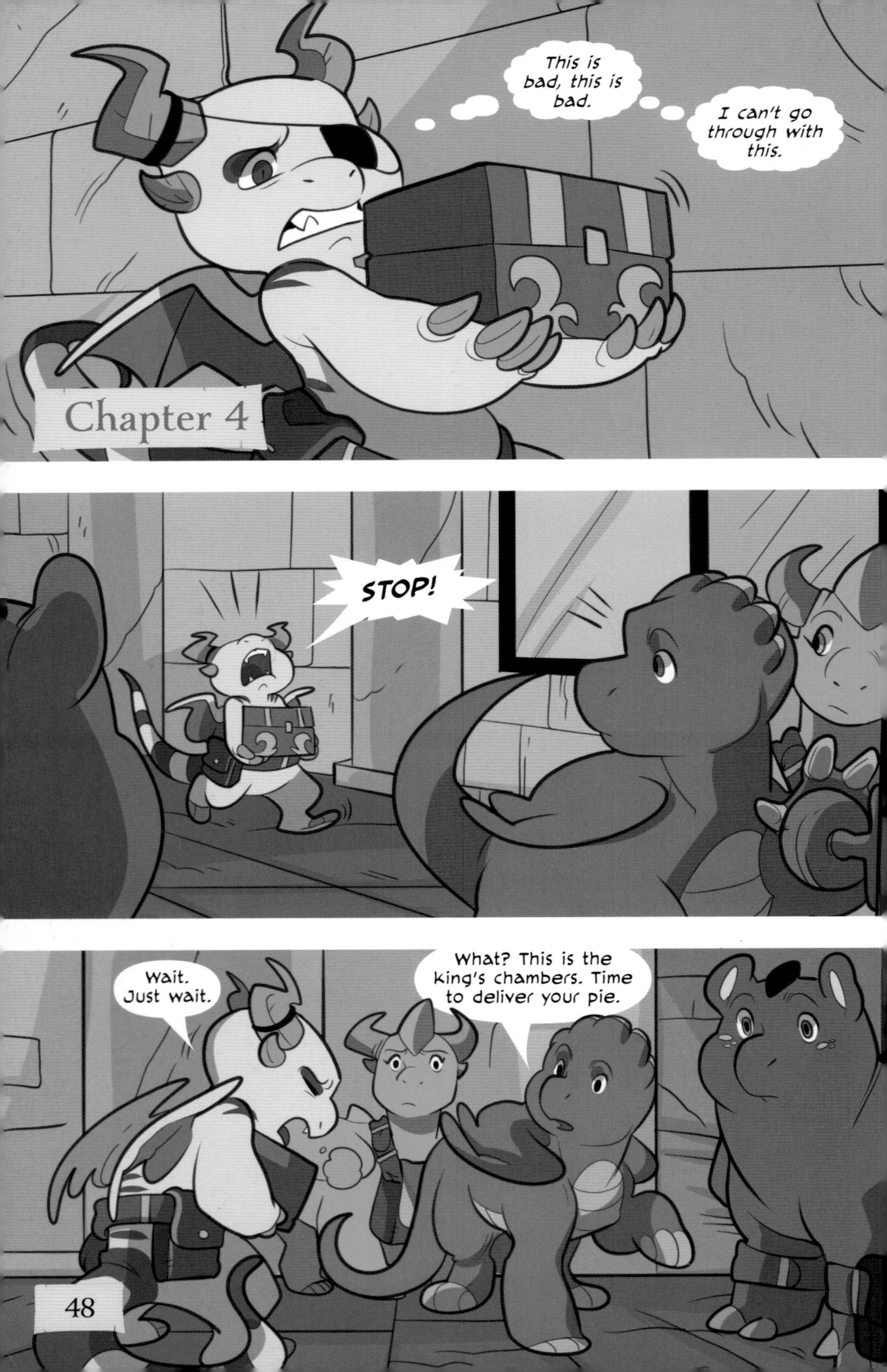
This is bad, this is bad.
I can't go through with this.
STOP!
Wait. Just wait.
What? This is the king's chambers. Time to deliver your pie.

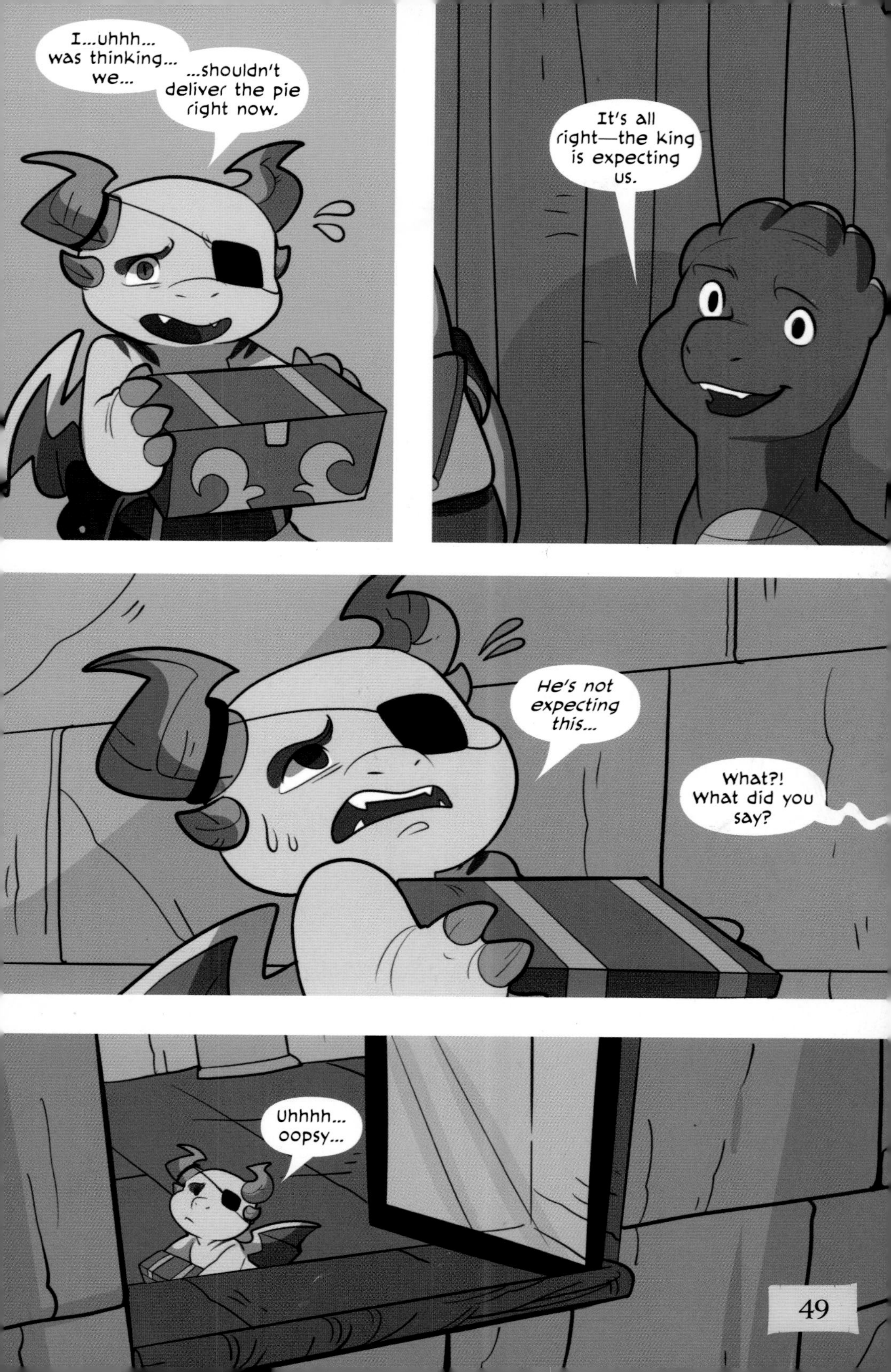
I...uhhh... was thinking... we...
...shouldn't deliver the pie right now.
It's all right—the king is expecting us.
He's not expecting this...
What?! What did you say?
Uhhhh... oopsy...

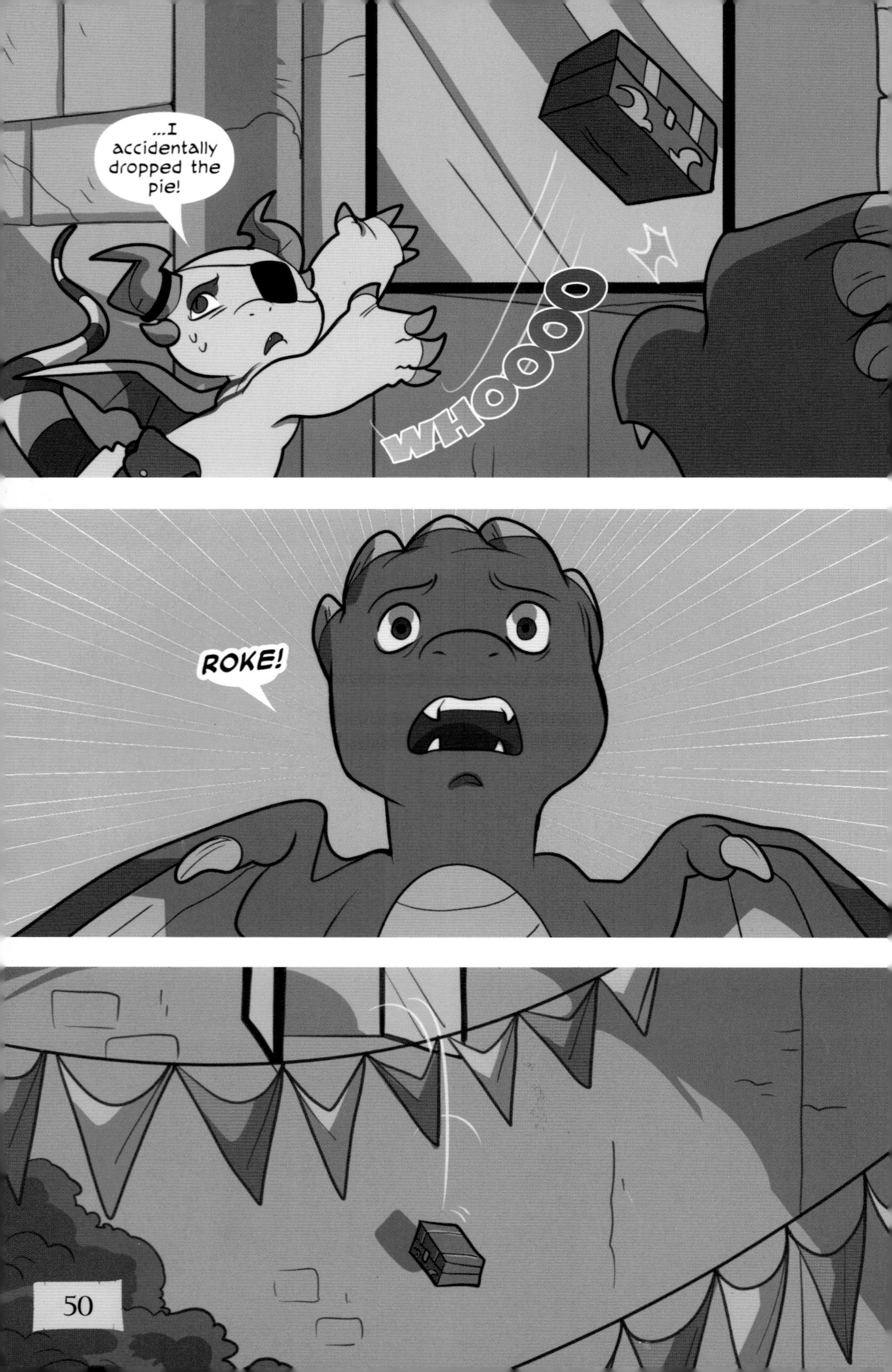
...I accidentally dropped the pie!
WHOOOOO
ROKE!

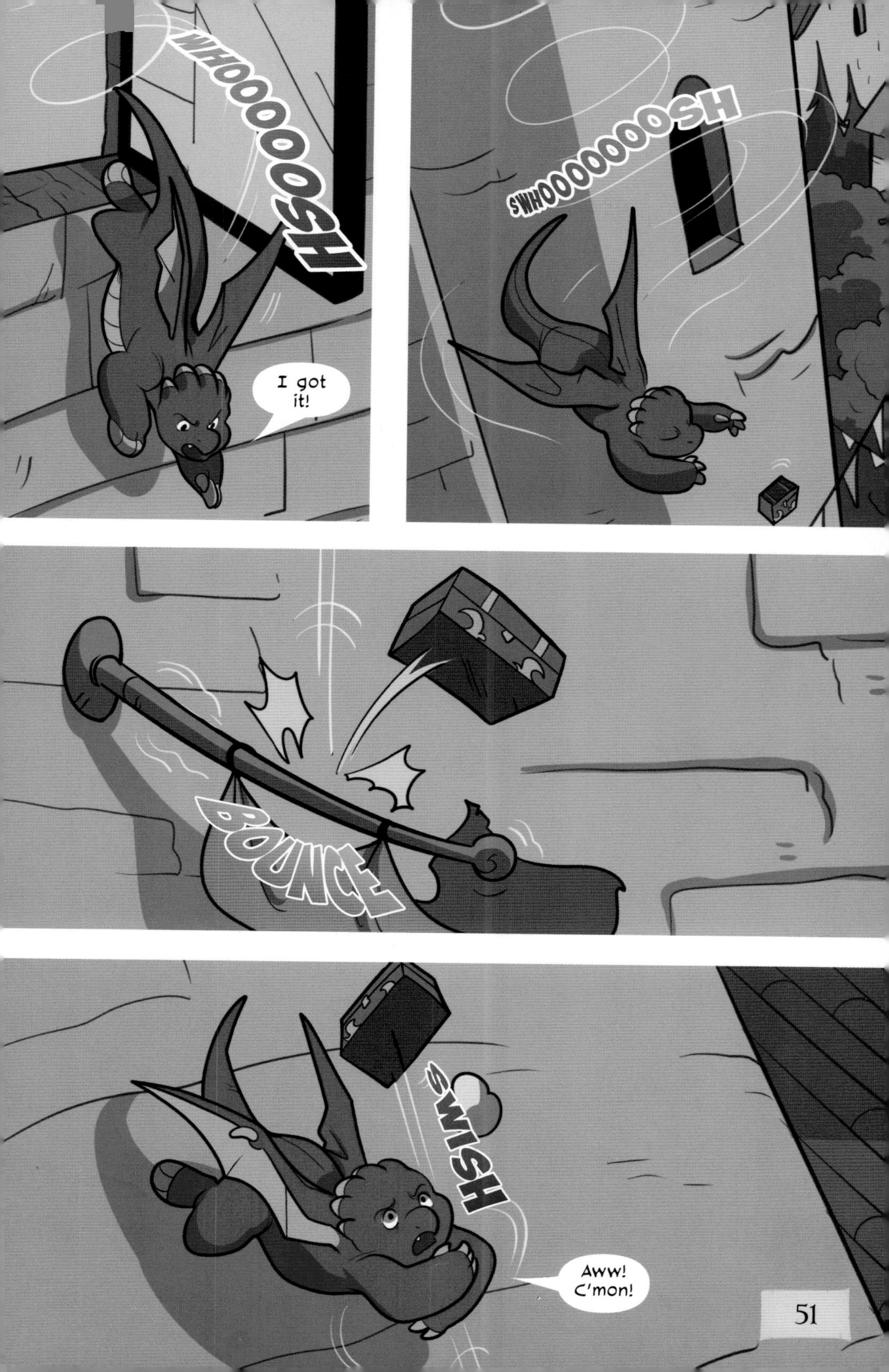
WHOOOOOSH
I got it!
SWHOOOOOOSH
BOUNCE
SWISH
Aww! C'mon!

GLIIIIDE

This pie in the sky's all mine! Watch a pro!

DODGE

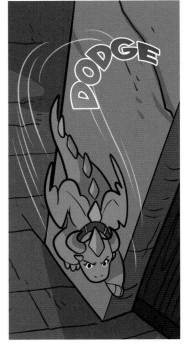

DODGE

SWOOP

GAAAAH!

SMACK

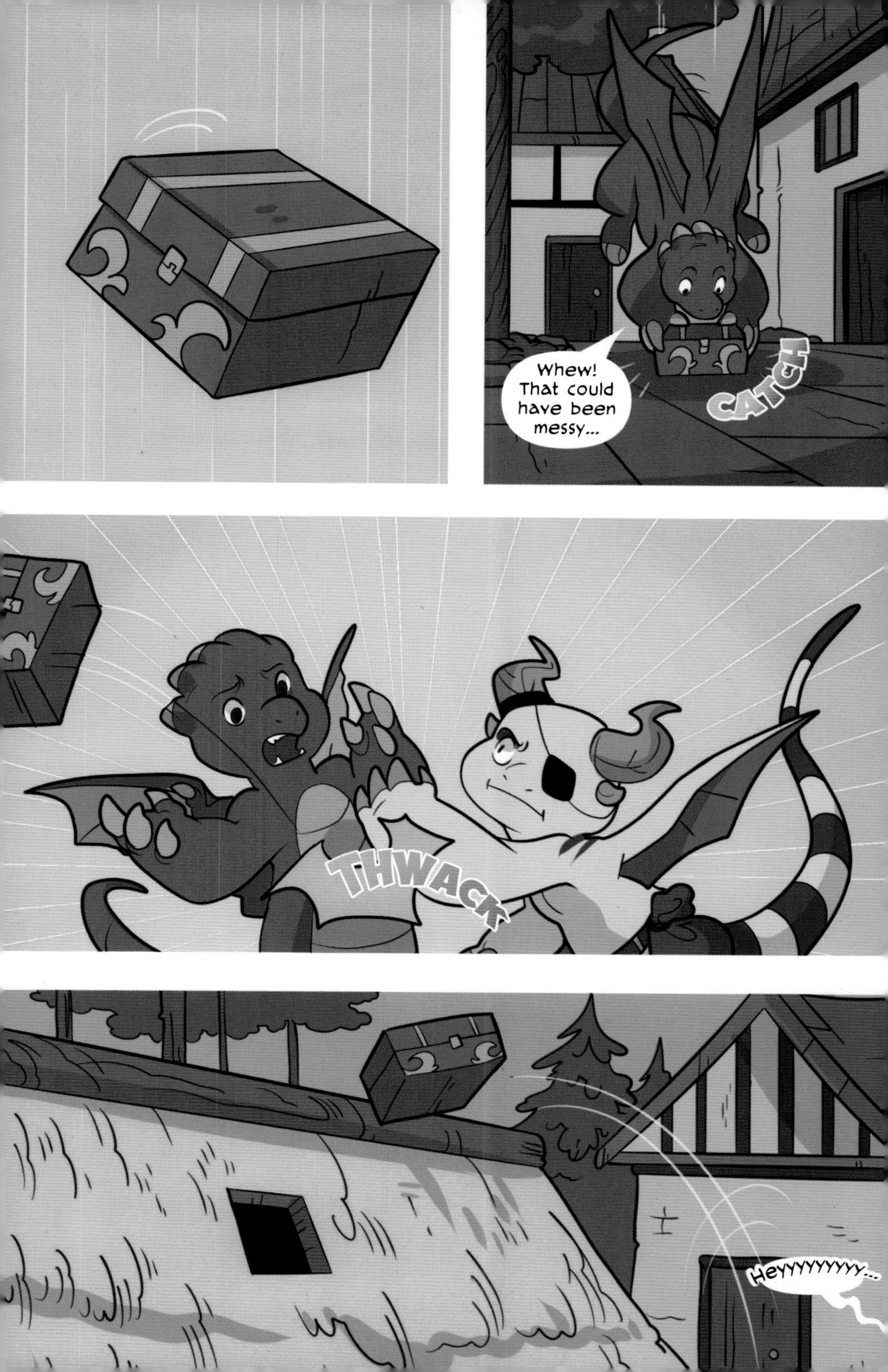
Whew! That could have been messy...
CATCH
THWACK
Heyyyyyyyyy...

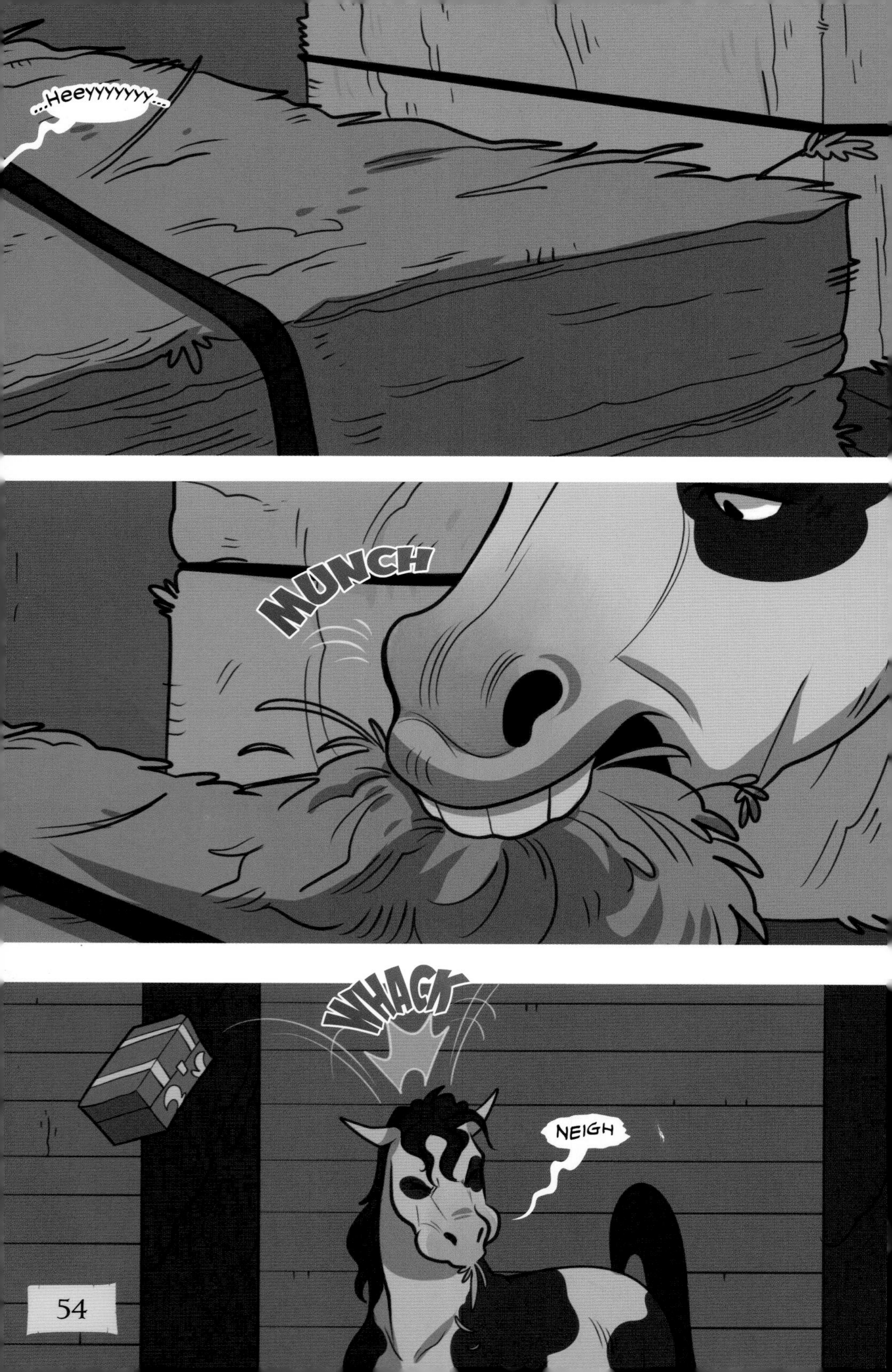
...Heeyyyyyyy...
MUNCH
WHACK
NEIGH

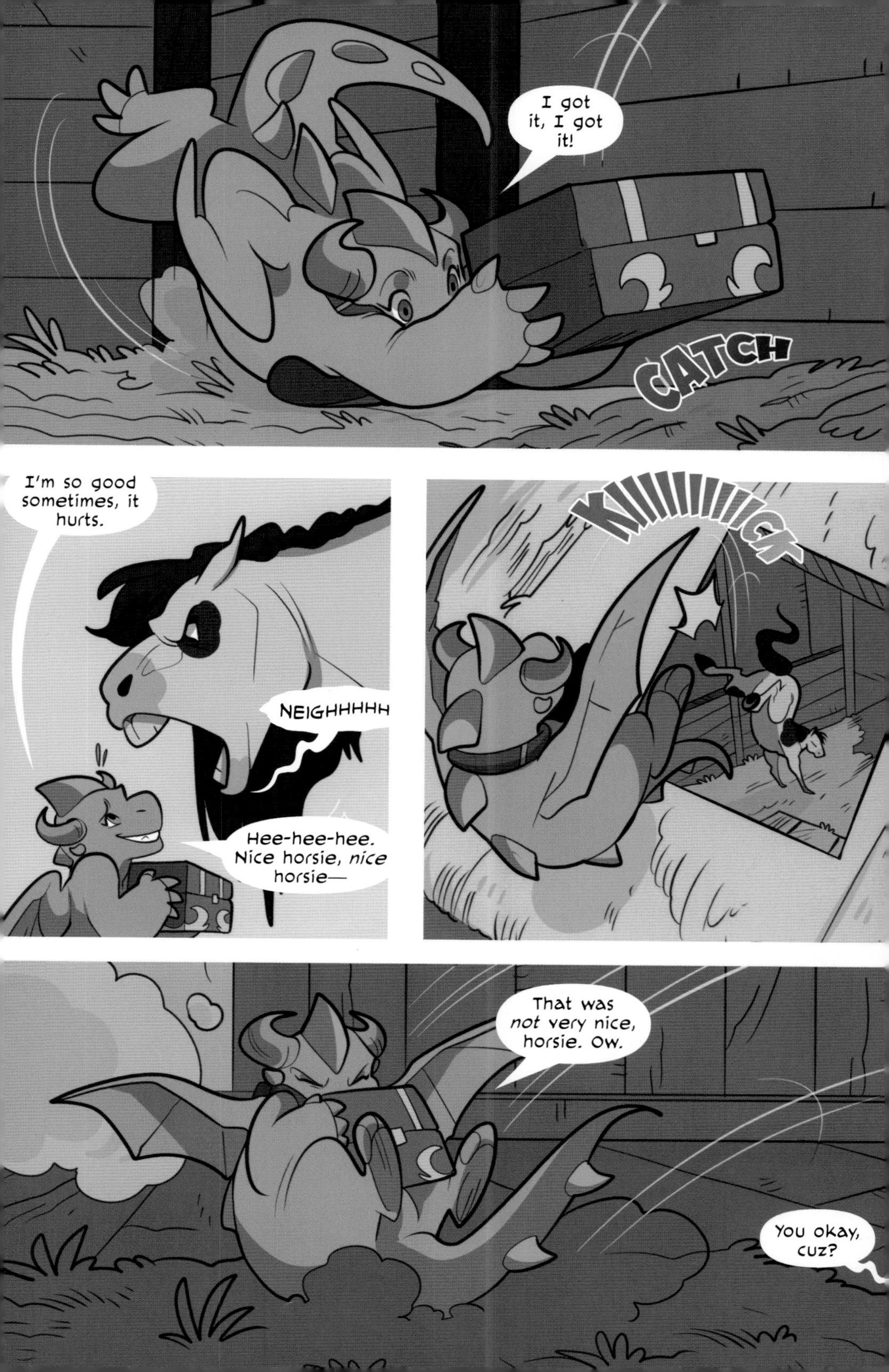
I got it, I got it!
CATCH
I'm so good sometimes, it hurts.
NEIGHHHHH
Hee-hee-hee. Nice horsie, *nice* horsie—
KIIIIIIIICK
That was *not* very nice, horsie. Ow.
You okay, cuz?

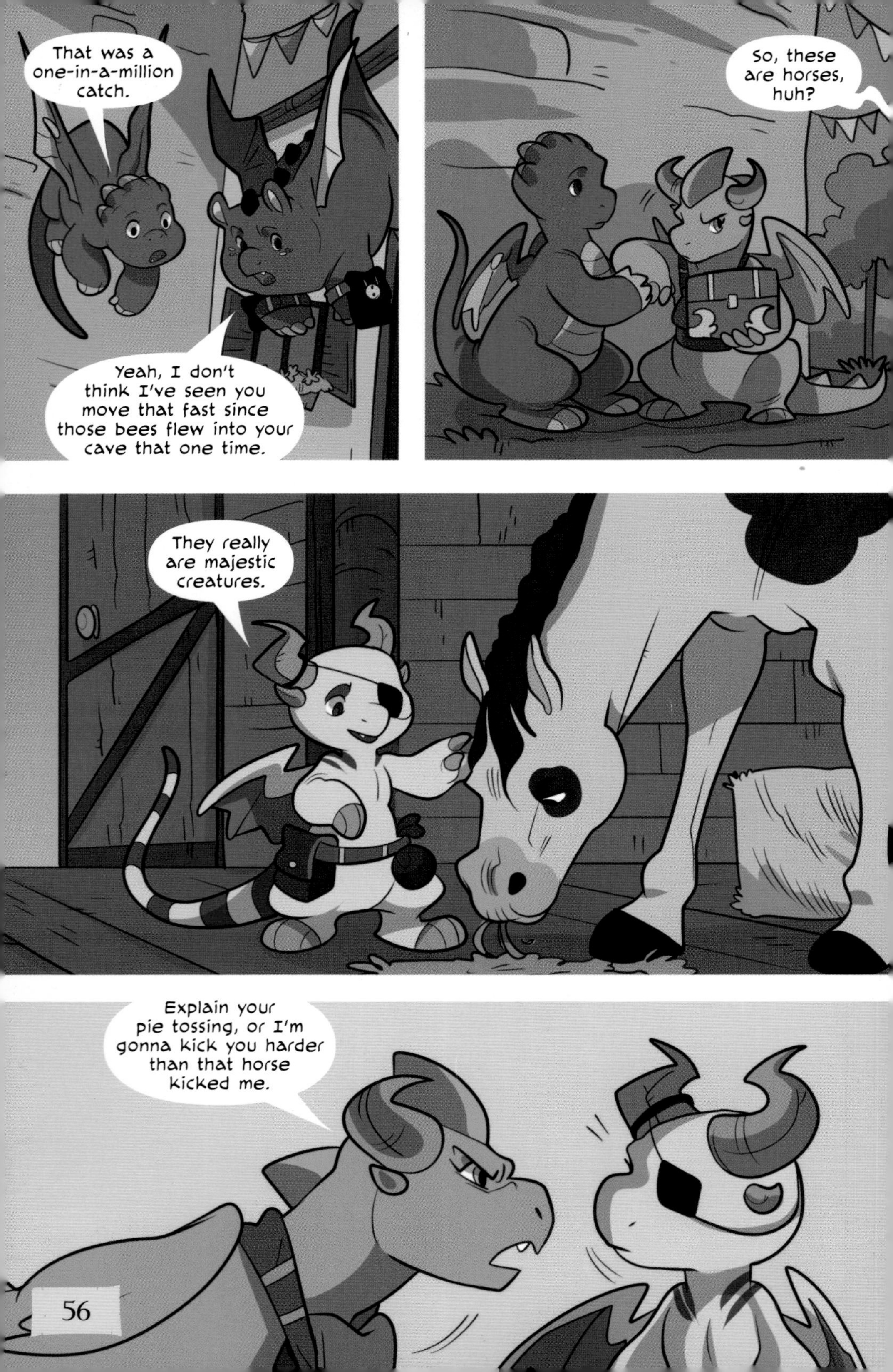
That was a one-in-a-million catch.
Yeah, I don't think I've seen you move that fast since those bees flew into your cave that one time.
So, these are horses, huh?
They really are majestic creatures.
Explain your pie tossing, or I'm gonna kick you harder than that horse kicked me.

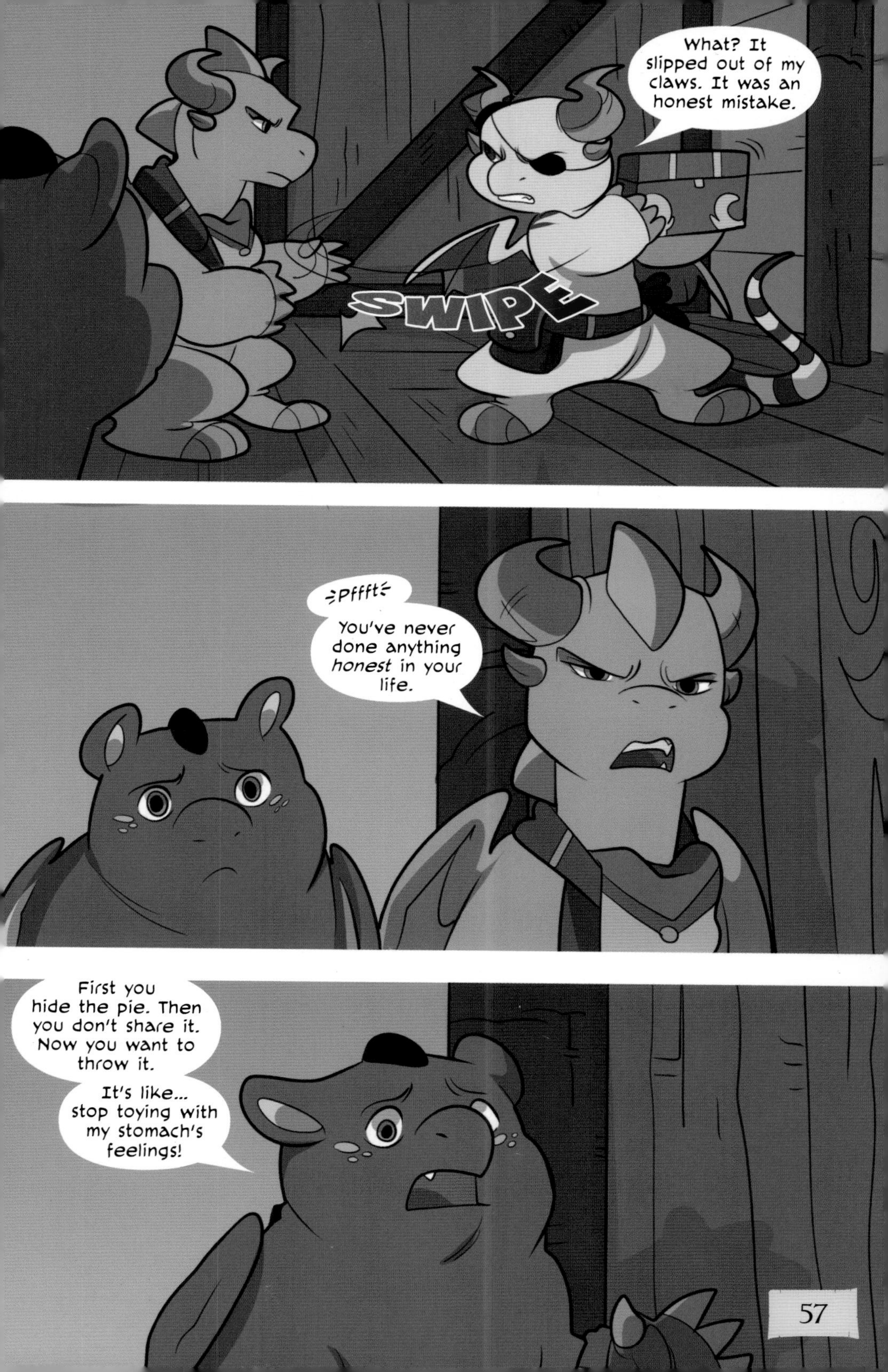
What? It slipped out of my claws. It was an honest mistake.
SWIPE
Pffft
You've never done anything *honest* in your life.
First you hide the pie. Then you don't share it. Now you want to throw it.
It's like... stop toying with my stomach's feelings!

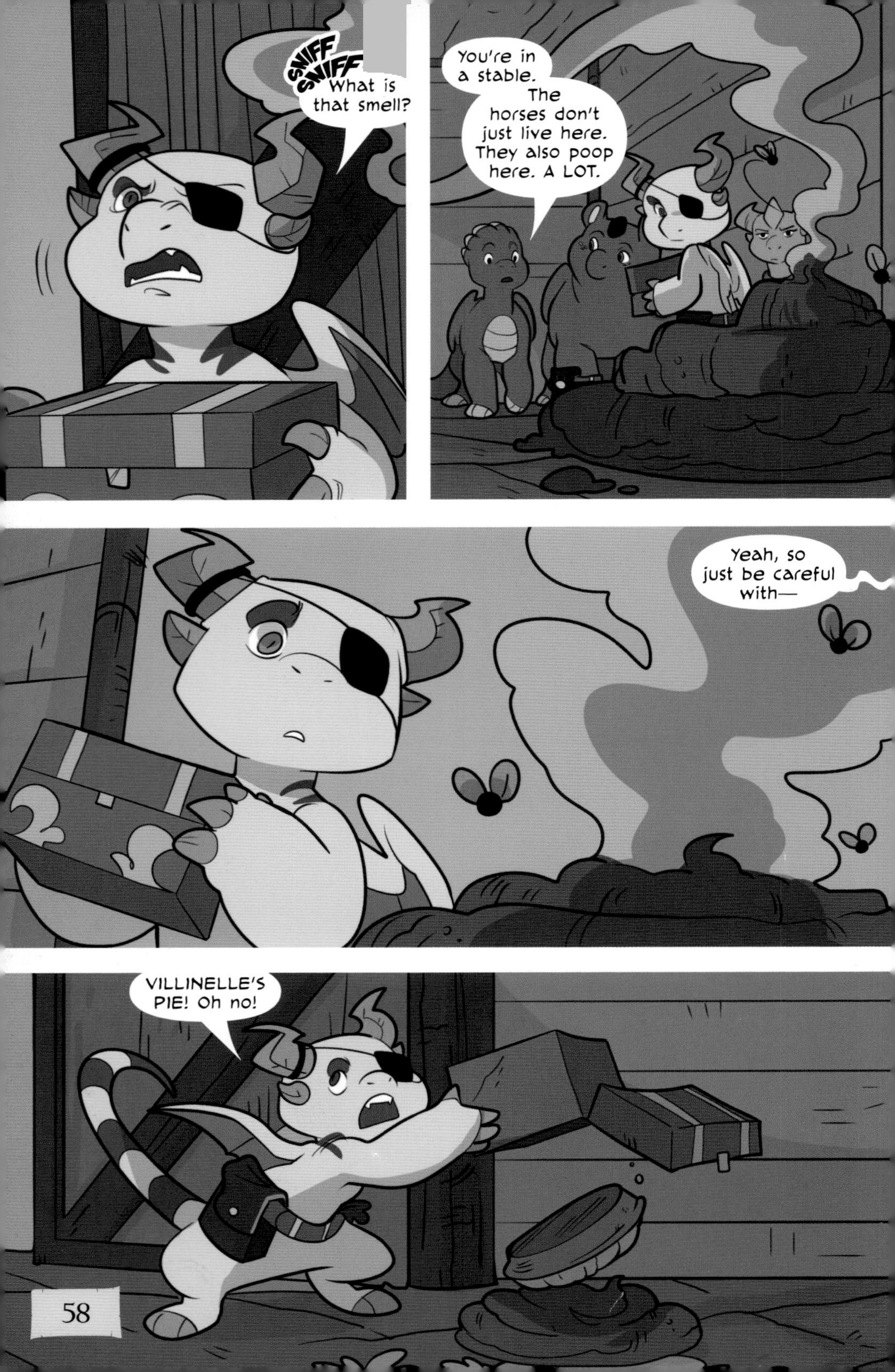
SNIFF SNIFF
What is that smell?
You're in a stable.
The horses don't just live here. They also poop here. A LOT.
Yeah, so just be careful with—
VILLINELLE'S PIE! Oh no!

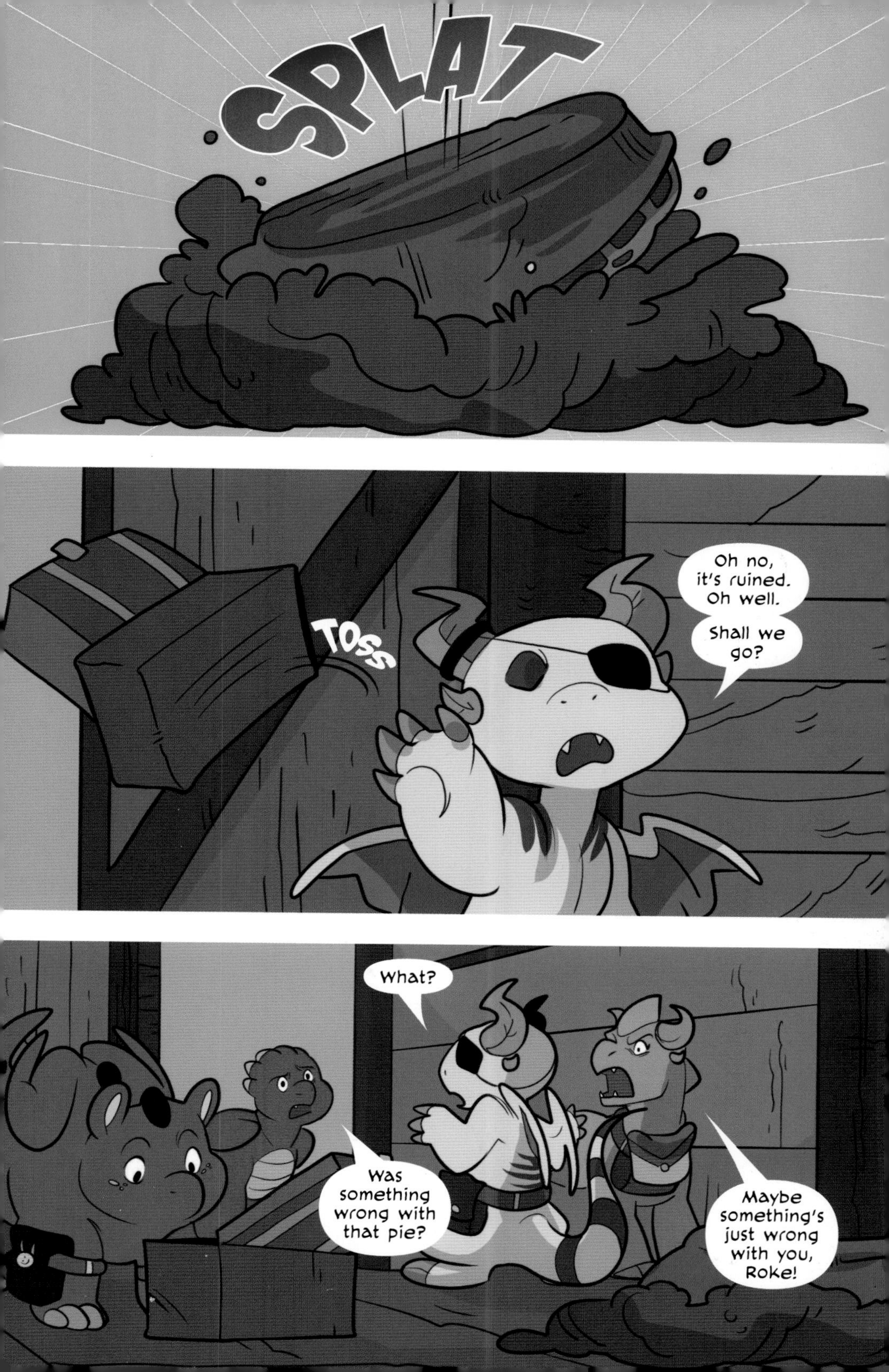
SPLAT
TOSS
Oh no, it's ruined. Oh well.
Shall we go?
What?
Was something wrong with that pie?
Maybe something's just wrong with you, Roke!

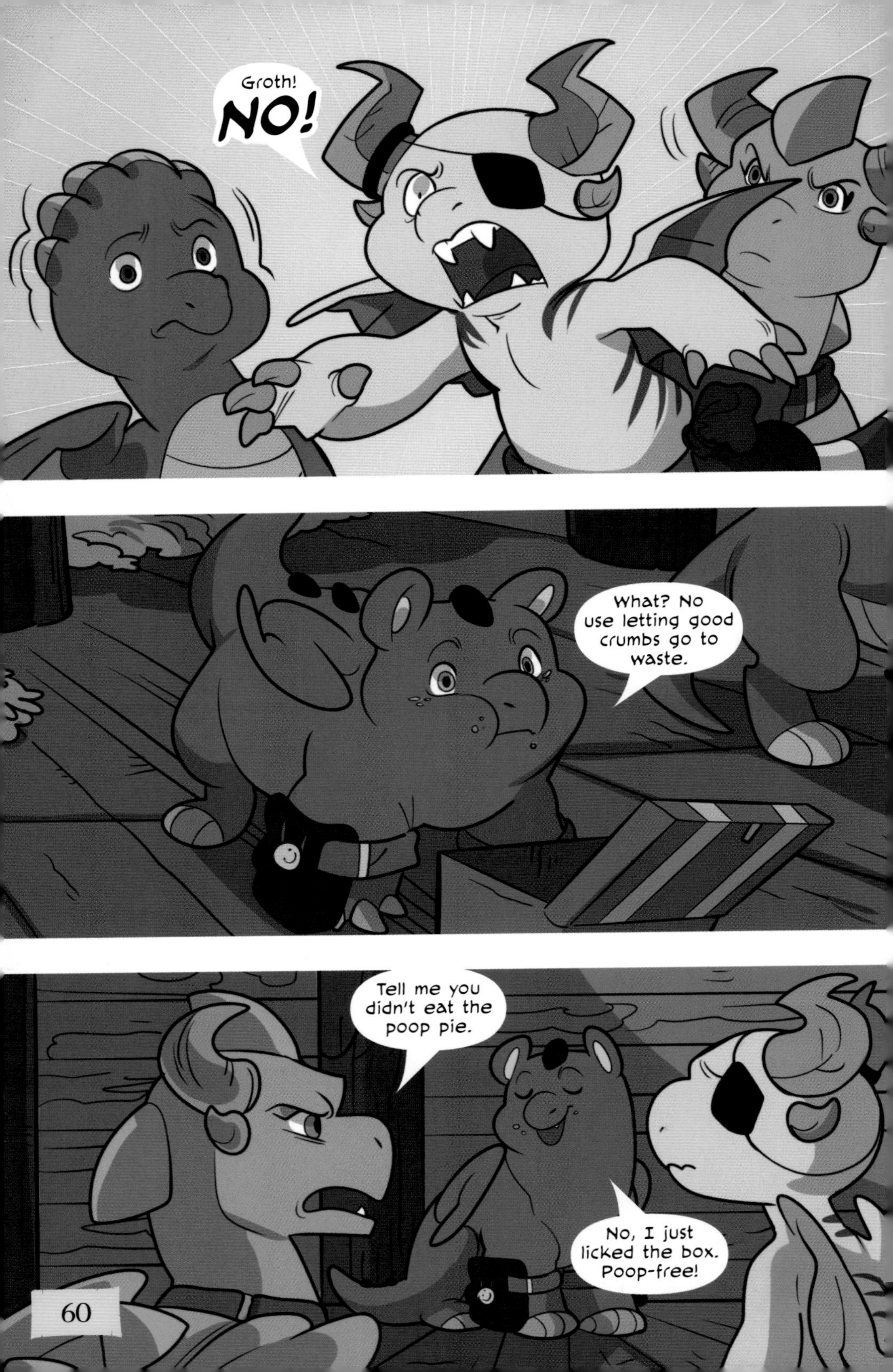
Groth! NO!
What? No use letting good crumbs go to waste.
Tell me you didn't eat the poop pie.
No, I just licked the box. Poop-free!

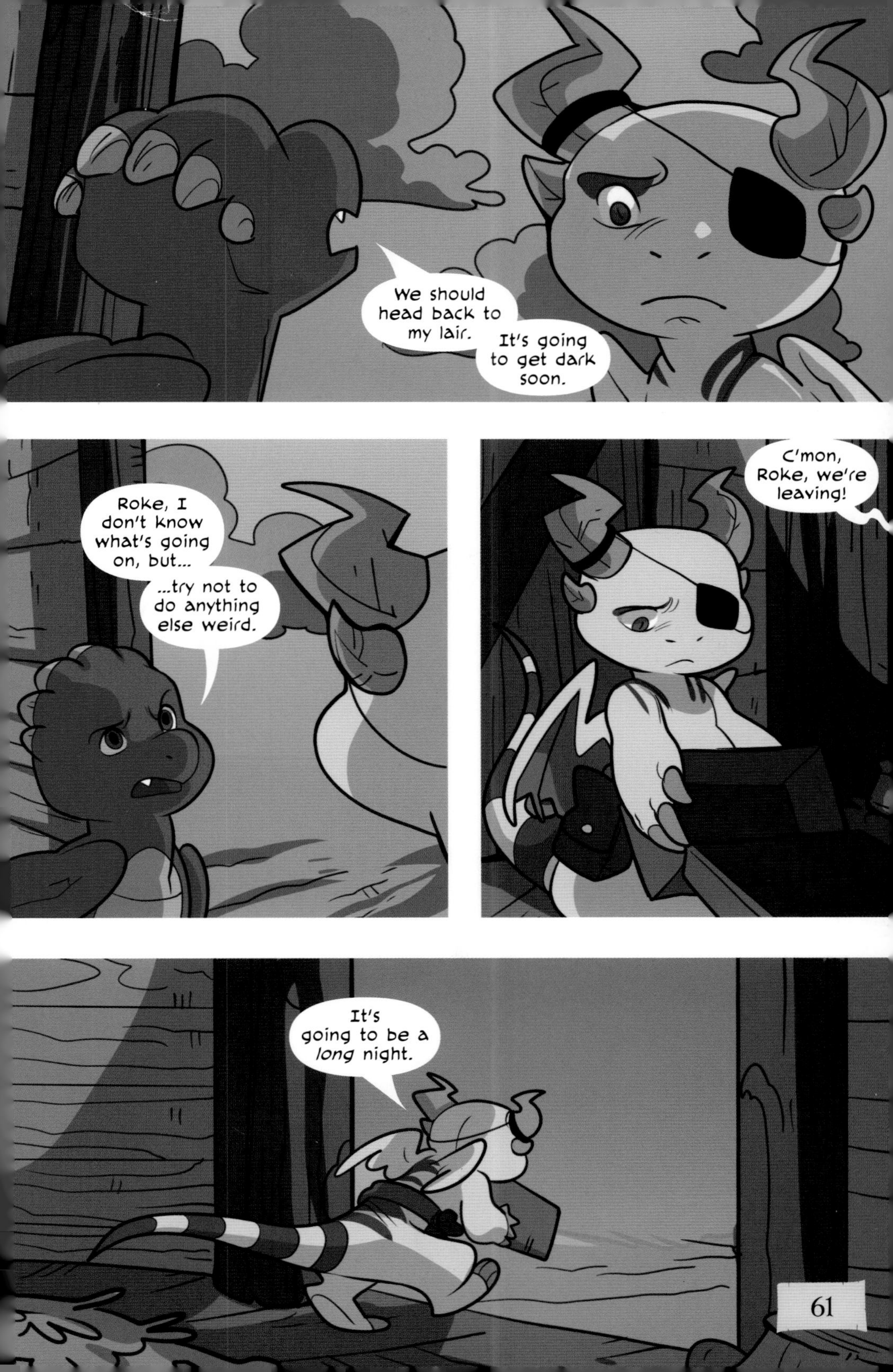
We should head back to my lair.
It's going to get dark soon.
Roke, I don't know what's going on, but...
...try not to do anything else weird.
C'mon, Roke, we're leaving!
It's going to be a *long* night.

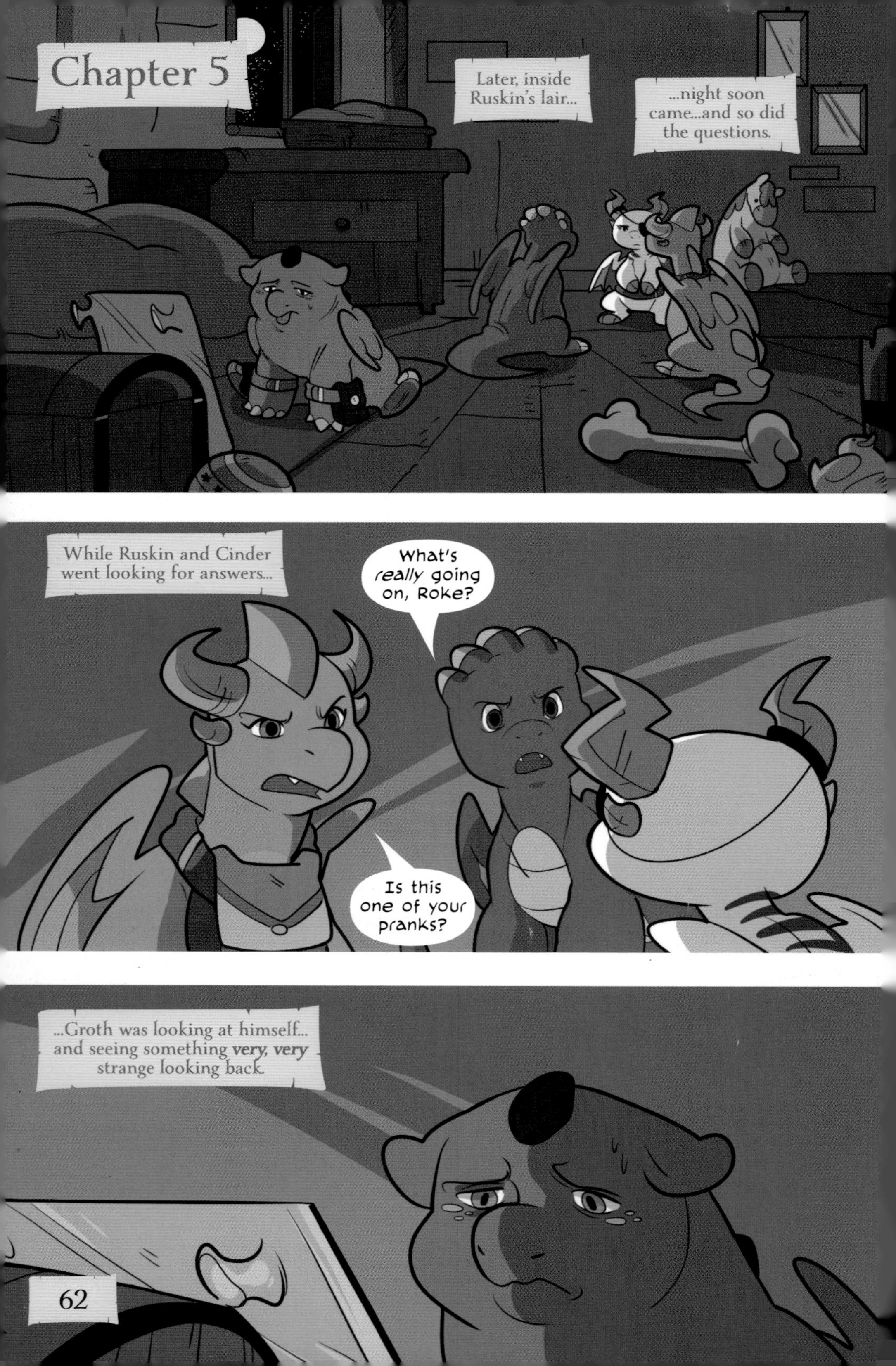
Chapter 5
Later, inside Ruskin's lair...
...night soon came...and so did the questions.
While Ruskin and Cinder went looking for answers...
What's *really* going on, Roke?
Is this one of your pranks?
...Groth was looking at himself... and seeing something **very, very** strange looking back.

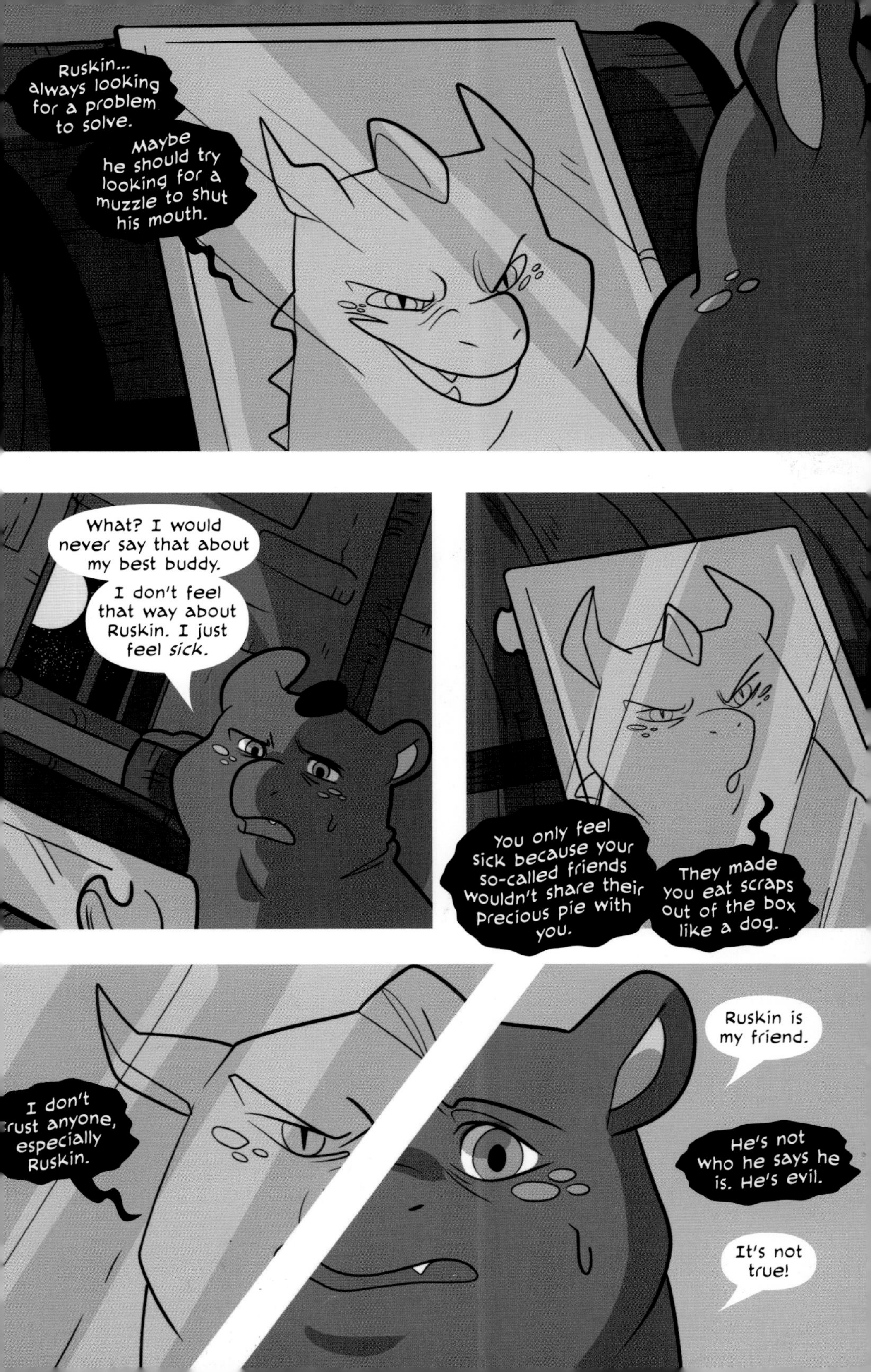
Ruskin... always looking for a problem to solve.
Maybe he should try looking for a muzzle to shut his mouth.
What? I would never say that about my best buddy.
I don't feel that way about Ruskin. I just feel *sick*.
You only feel sick because your so-called friends wouldn't share their precious pie with you.
They made you eat scraps out of the box like a dog.
I don't trust anyone, especially Ruskin.
Ruskin is my friend.
He's not who he says he is. He's evil.
It's not true!

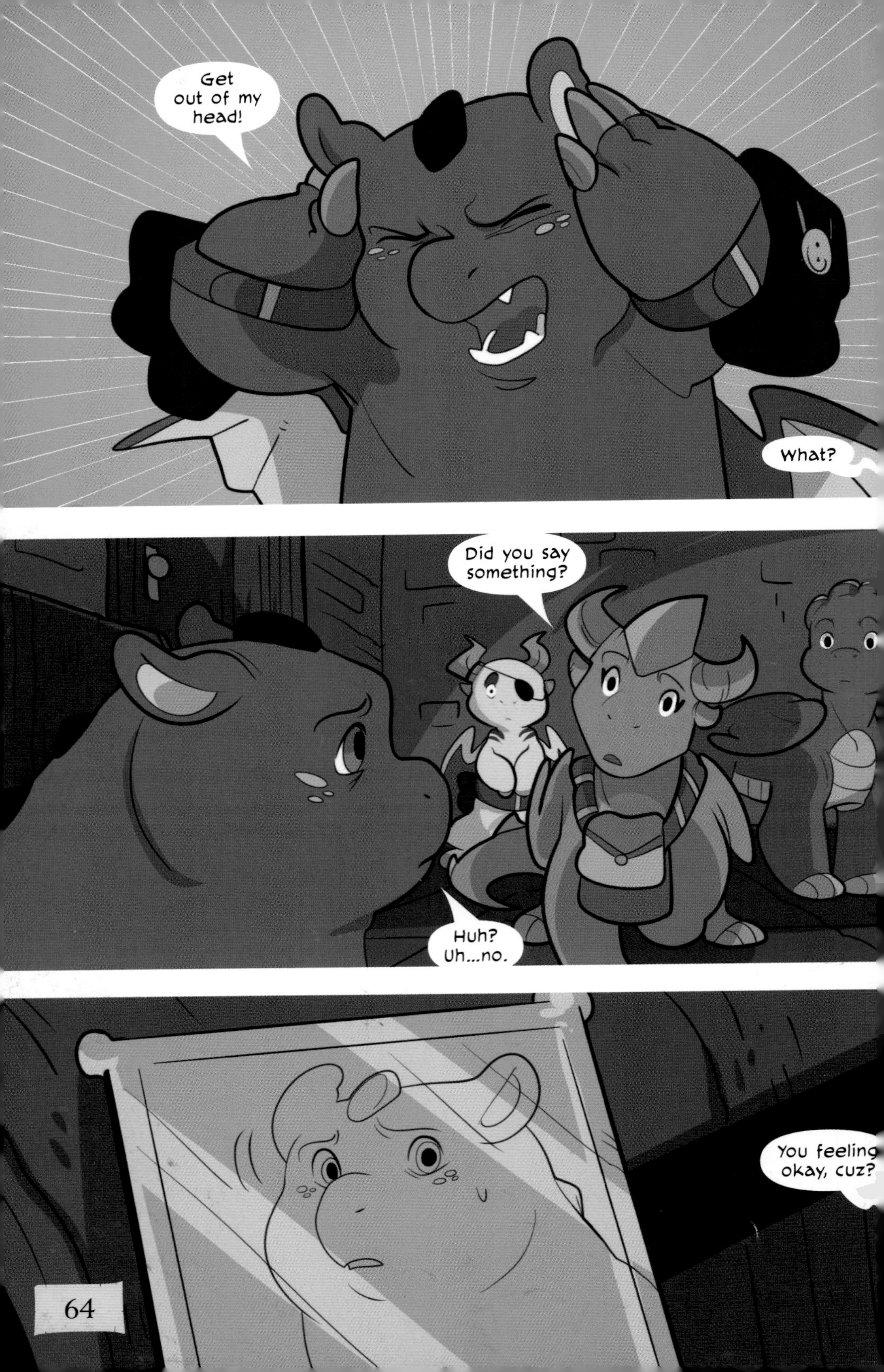

Get out of my head!
What?
Did you say something?
Huh? Uh...no.
You feeling okay, cuz?

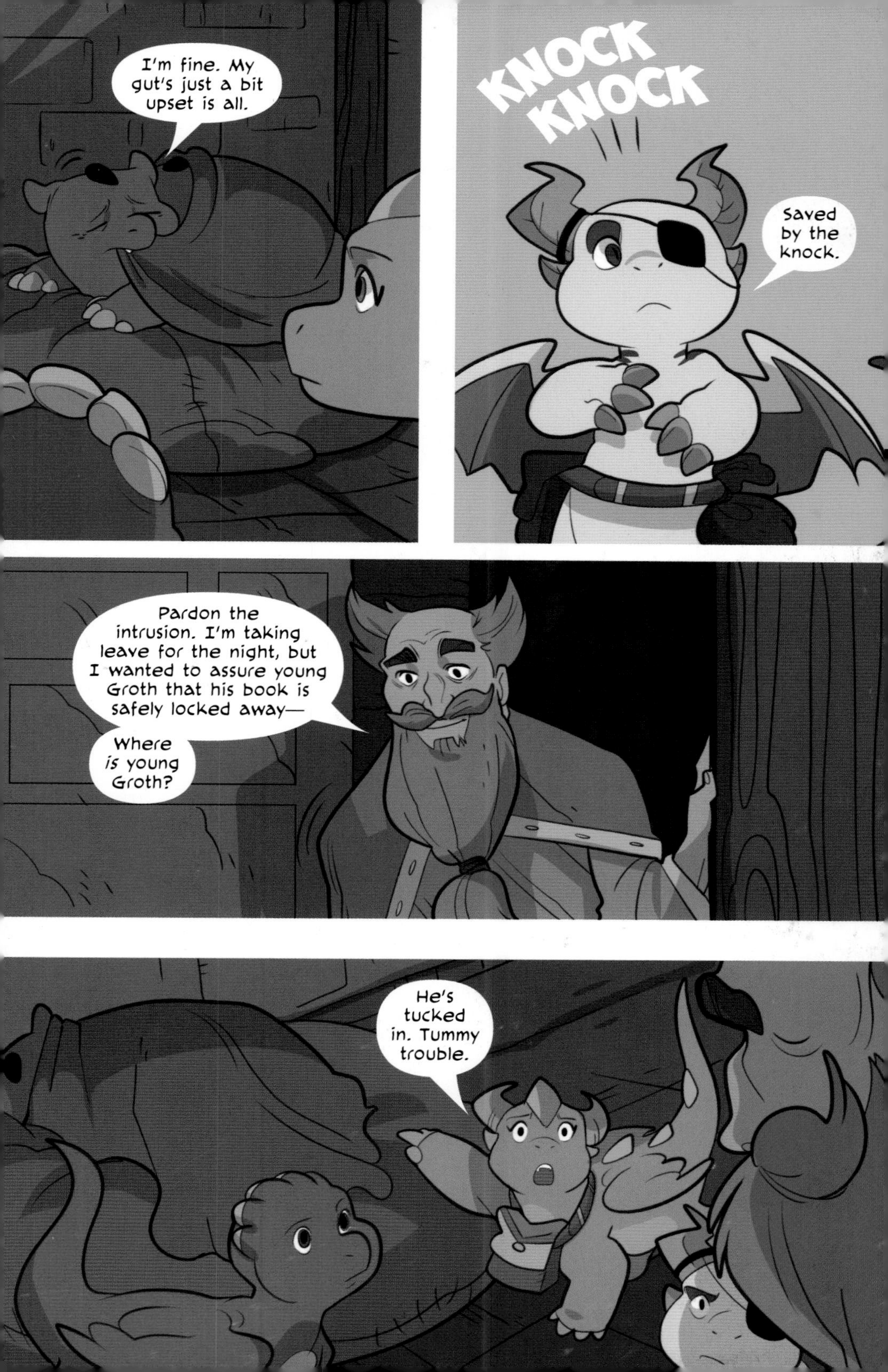

I'm fine. My gut's just a bit upset is all.
KNOCK KNOCK
Saved by the knock.
Pardon the intrusion. I'm taking leave for the night, but I wanted to assure young Groth that his book is safely locked away—
Where *is* young Groth?
He's tucked in. Tummy trouble.

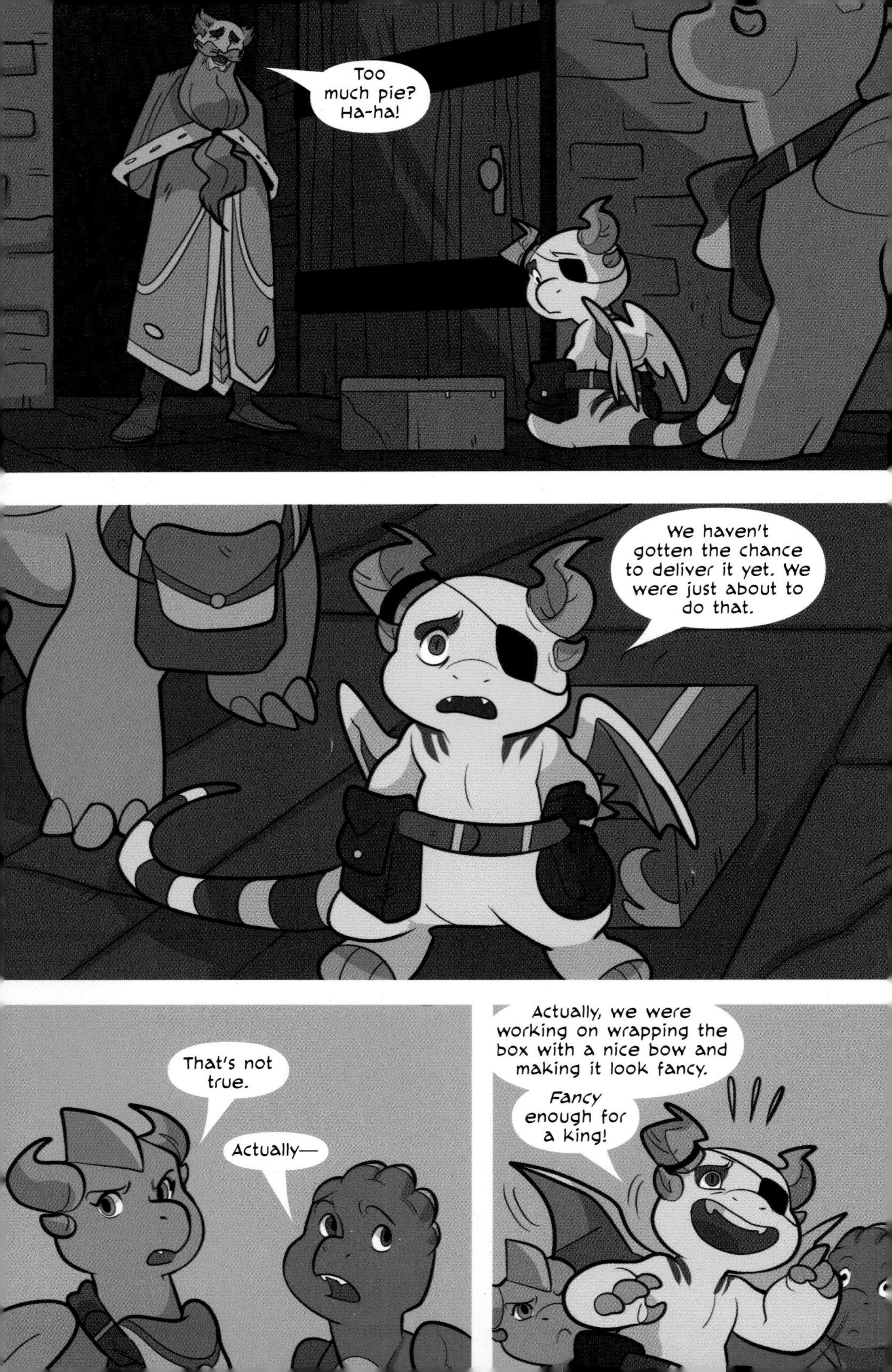
Too much pie? Ha-ha!
We haven't gotten the chance to deliver it yet. We were just about to do that.
That's not true.
Actually—
Actually, we were working on wrapping the box with a nice bow and making it look fancy.
Fancy enough for a king!

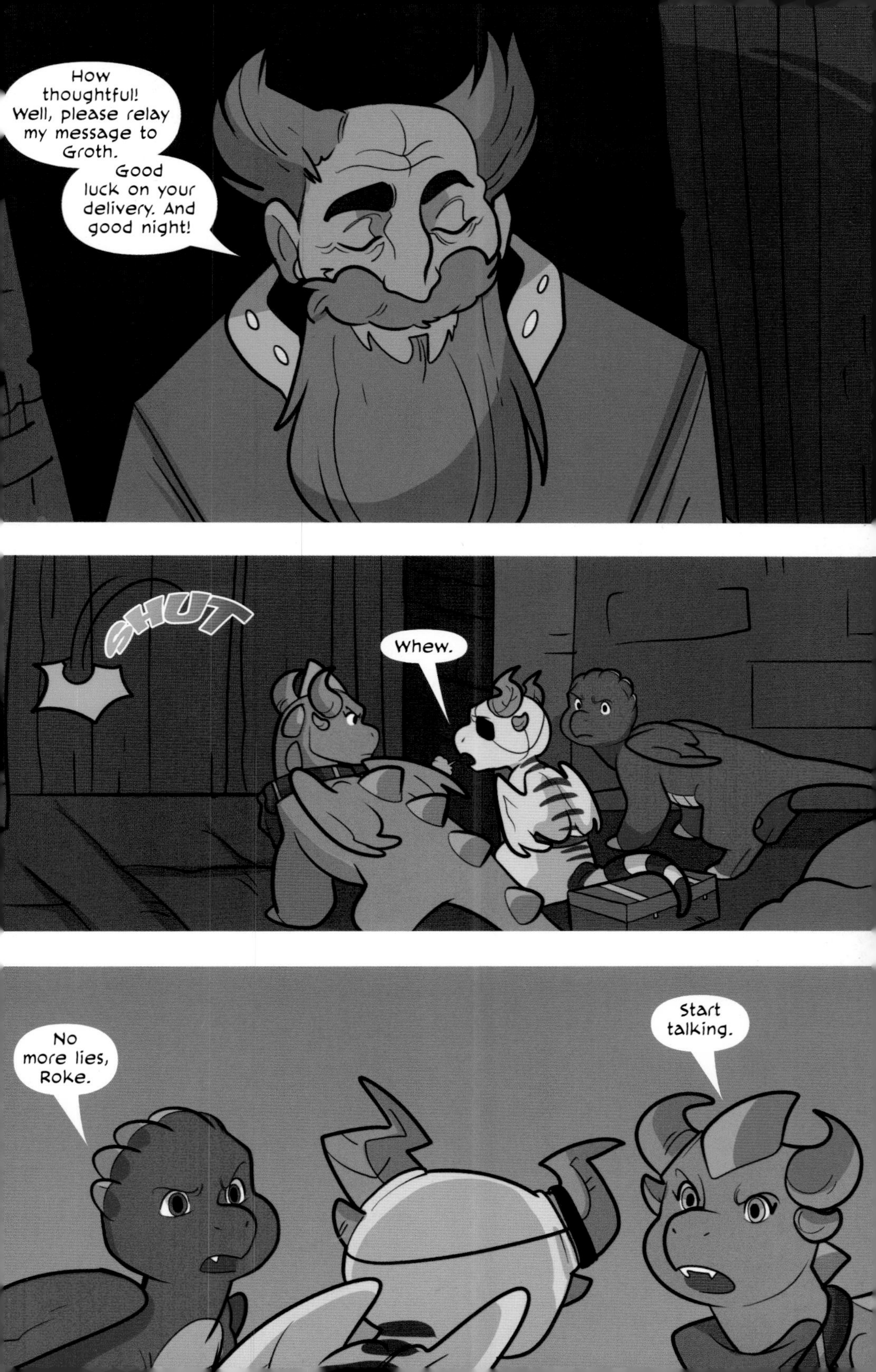
How thoughtful! Well, please relay my message to Groth.
Good luck on your delivery. And good night!
SHUT
Whew.
No more lies, Roke.
Start talking.

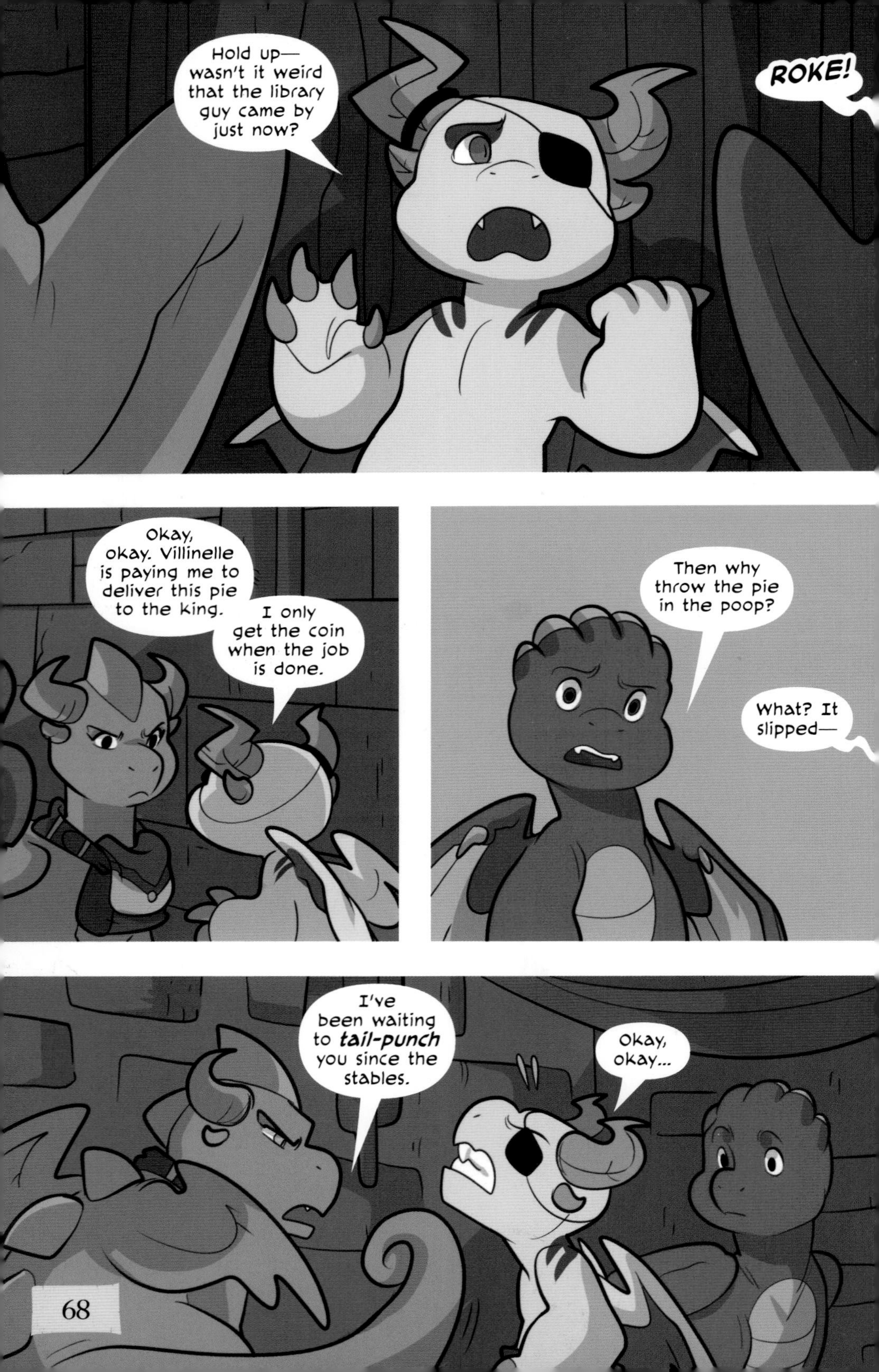
Hold up—wasn't it weird that the library guy came by just now?
ROKE!
Okay, okay. Villinelle is paying me to deliver this pie to the king.
I only get the coin when the job is done.
Then why throw the pie in the poop?
What? It slipped—
I've been waiting to ***tail-punch*** you since the stables.
Okay, okay...

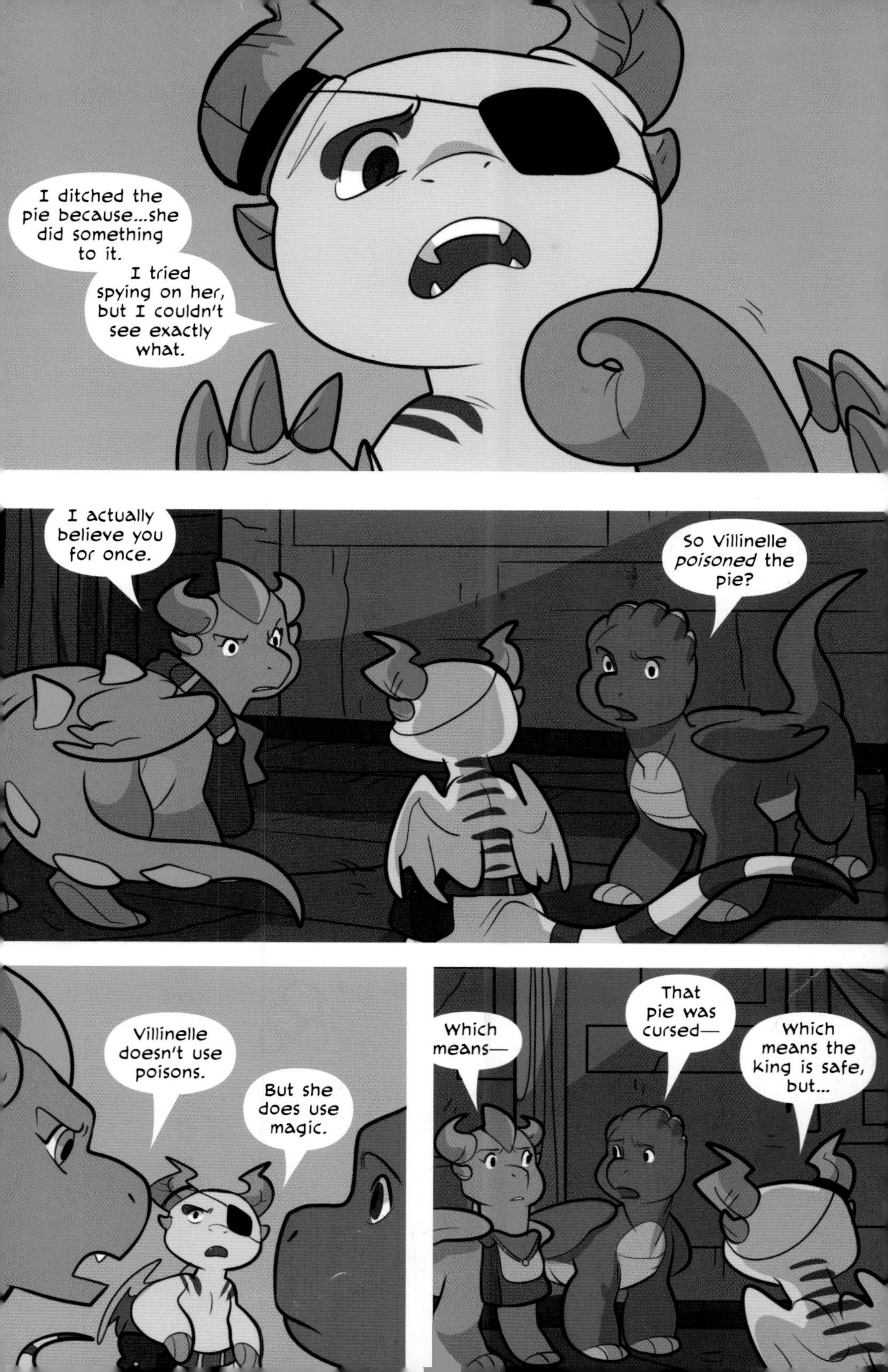
I ditched the pie because...she did something to it.
I tried spying on her, but I couldn't see exactly what.
I actually believe you for once.
So Villinelle *poisoned* the pie?
Villinelle doesn't use poisons.
But she does use magic.
Which means—
That pie was cursed—
Which means the king is safe, but...

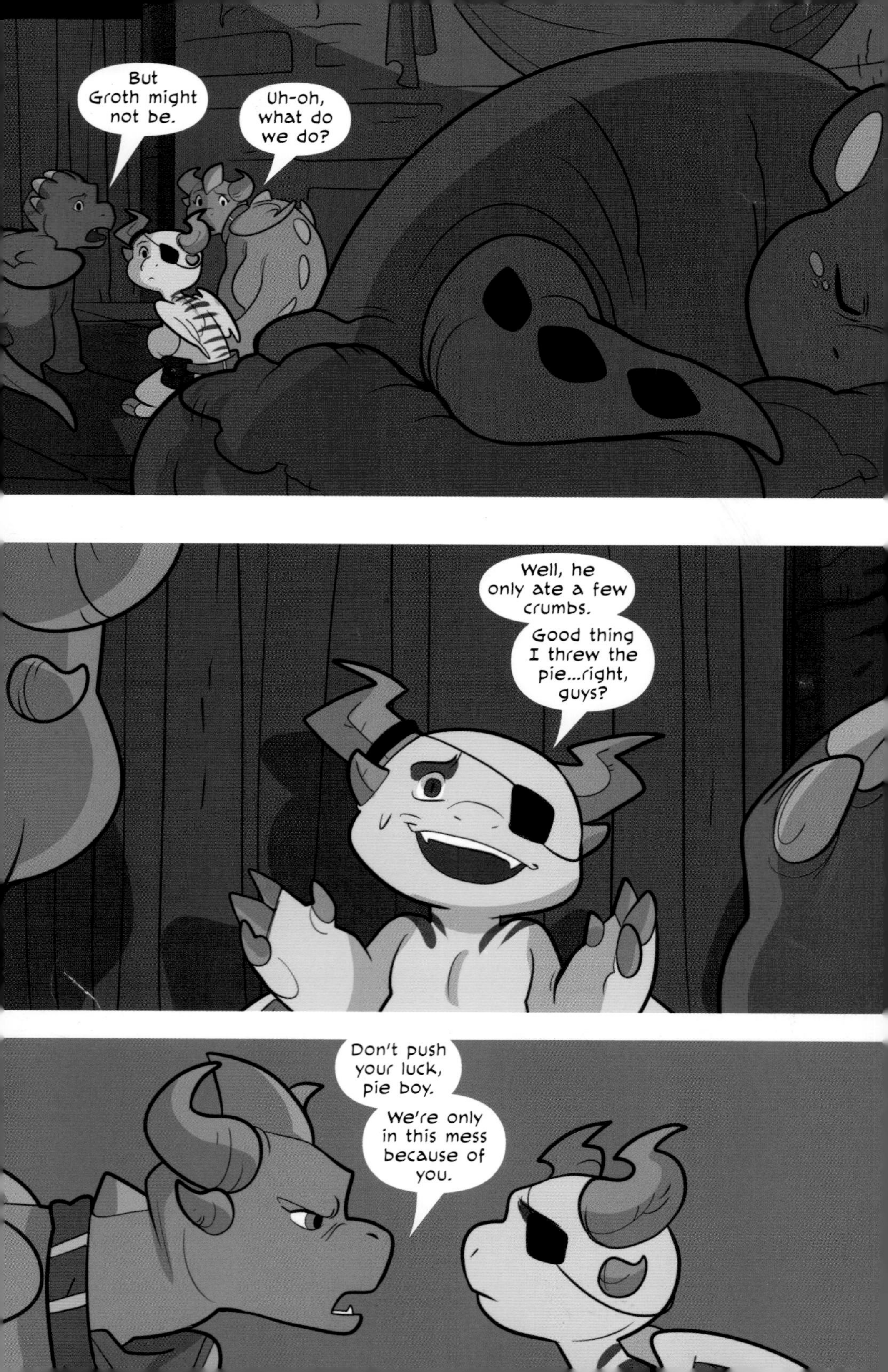
But Groth might not be.
Uh-oh, what do we do?
Well, he only ate a few crumbs.
Good thing I threw the pie...right, guys?
Don't push your luck, pie boy.
We're only in this mess because of you.

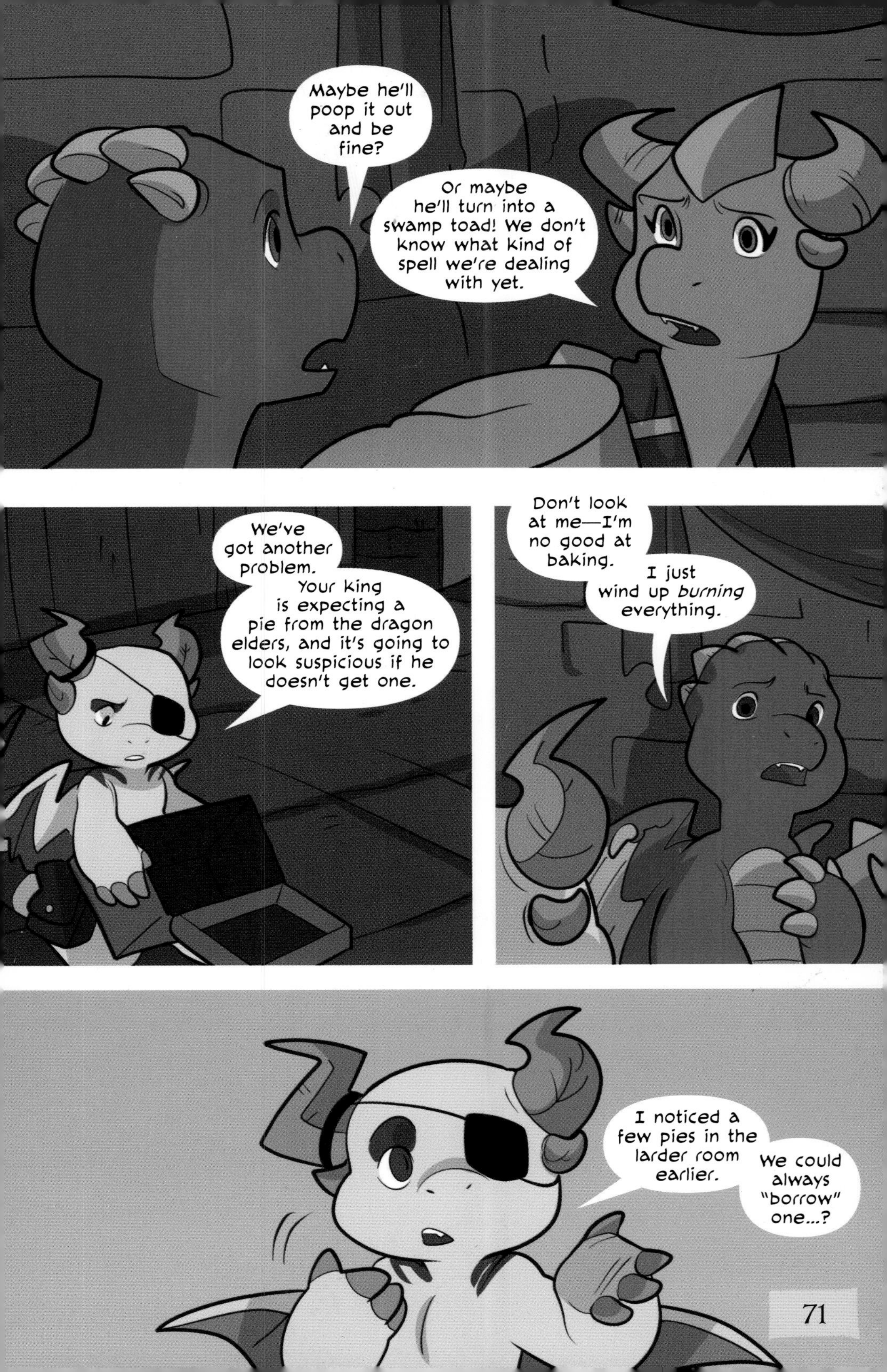
Maybe he'll poop it out and be fine?
Or maybe he'll turn into a swamp toad! We don't know what kind of spell we're dealing with yet.
We've got another problem.
Your king is expecting a pie from the dragon elders, and it's going to look suspicious if he doesn't get one.
Don't look at me—I'm no good at baking.
I just wind up *burning* everything.
I noticed a few pies in the larder room earlier.
We could always "borrow" one...?

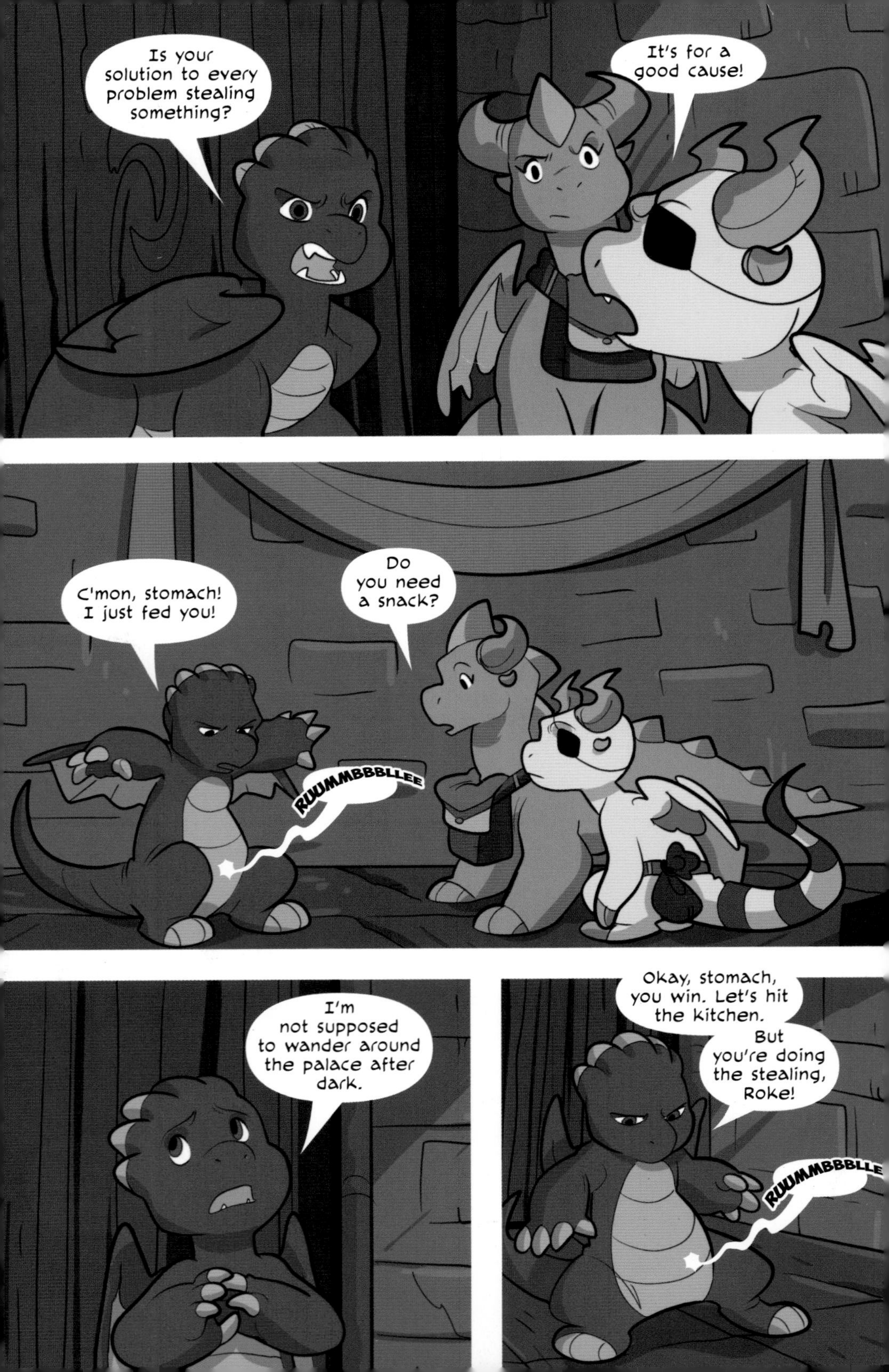
Is your solution to every problem stealing something?
It's for a good cause!
C'mon, stomach! I just fed you!
Do you need a snack?
RUUMMBBBLLEE
I'm not supposed to wander around the palace after dark.
Okay, stomach, you win. Let's hit the kitchen.
But you're doing the stealing, Roke!
RUUMMBBBLLE

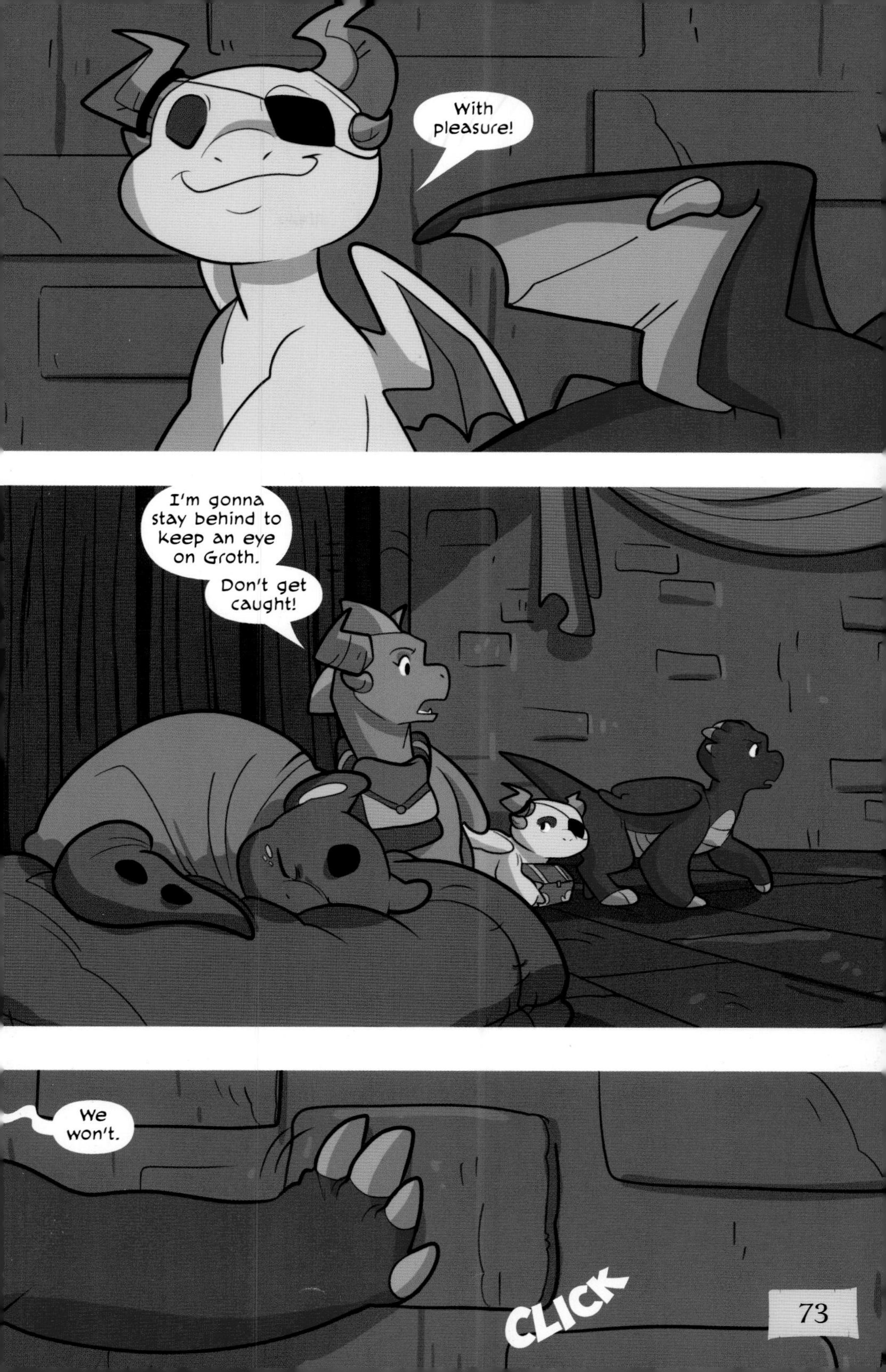
With pleasure!
I'm gonna stay behind to keep an eye on Groth.
Don't get caught!
We won't.
CLICK

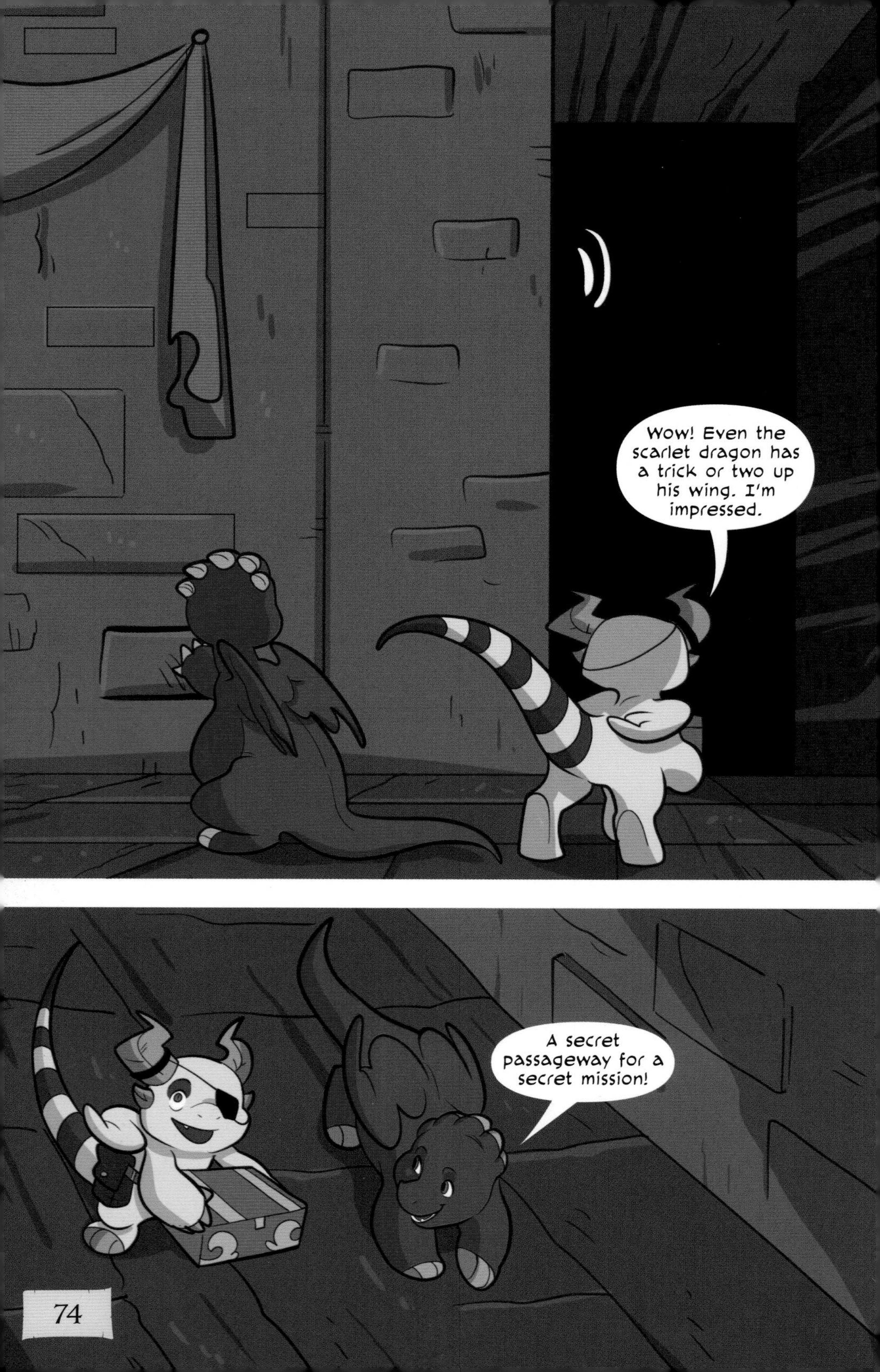
Wow! Even the scarlet dragon has a trick or two up his wing. I'm impressed.
A secret passageway for a secret mission!

Chapter 6

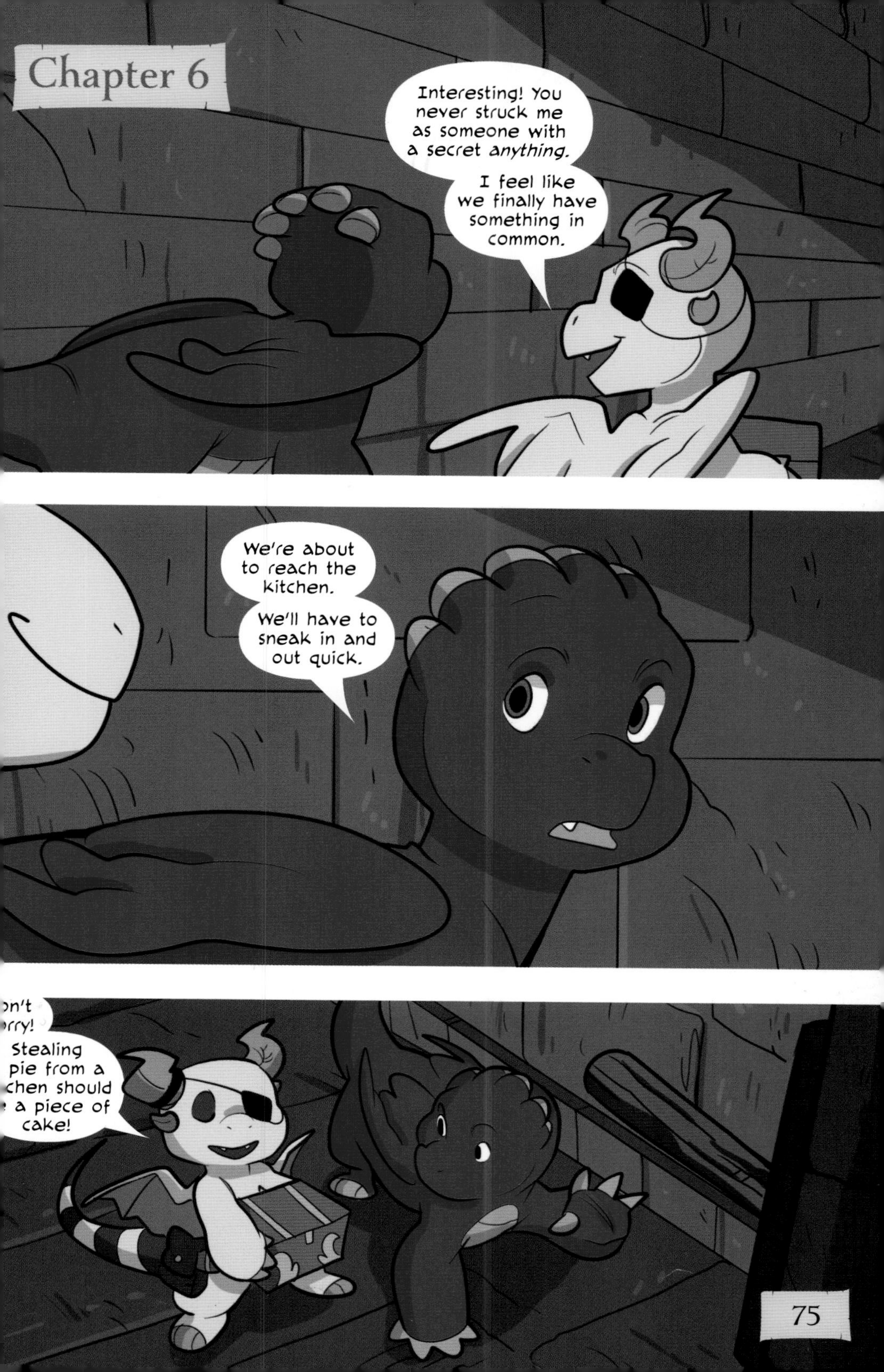
Interesting! You never struck me as someone with a secret *anything.*
I feel like we finally have something in common.
We're about to reach the kitchen.
We'll have to sneak in and out quick.
n't rry!
Stealing pie from a chen should a piece of cake!

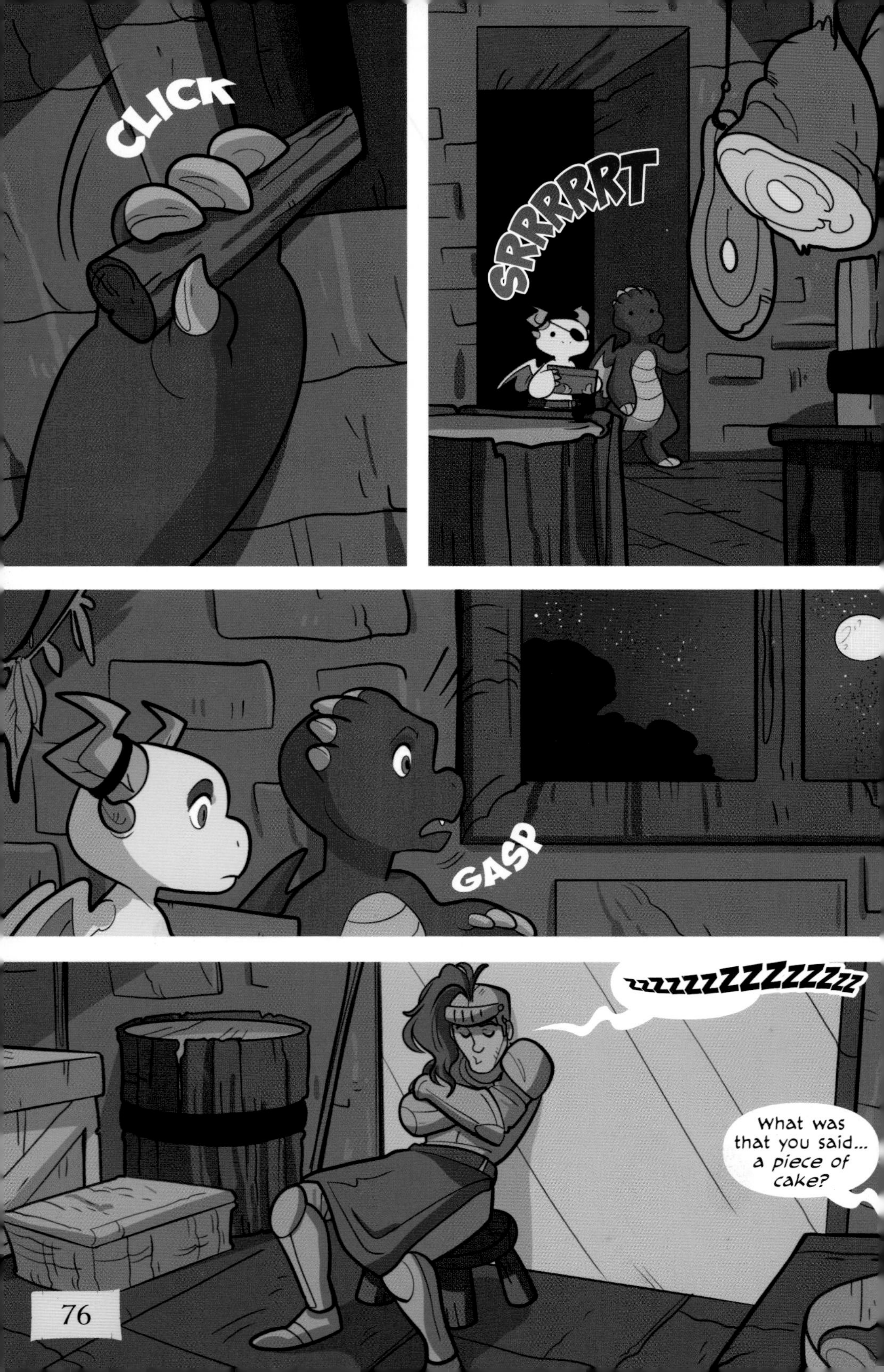
CLICK
SRRRRRT
GASP
zzzzzzzZZZZZZzz
What was that you said... a *piece of cake?*

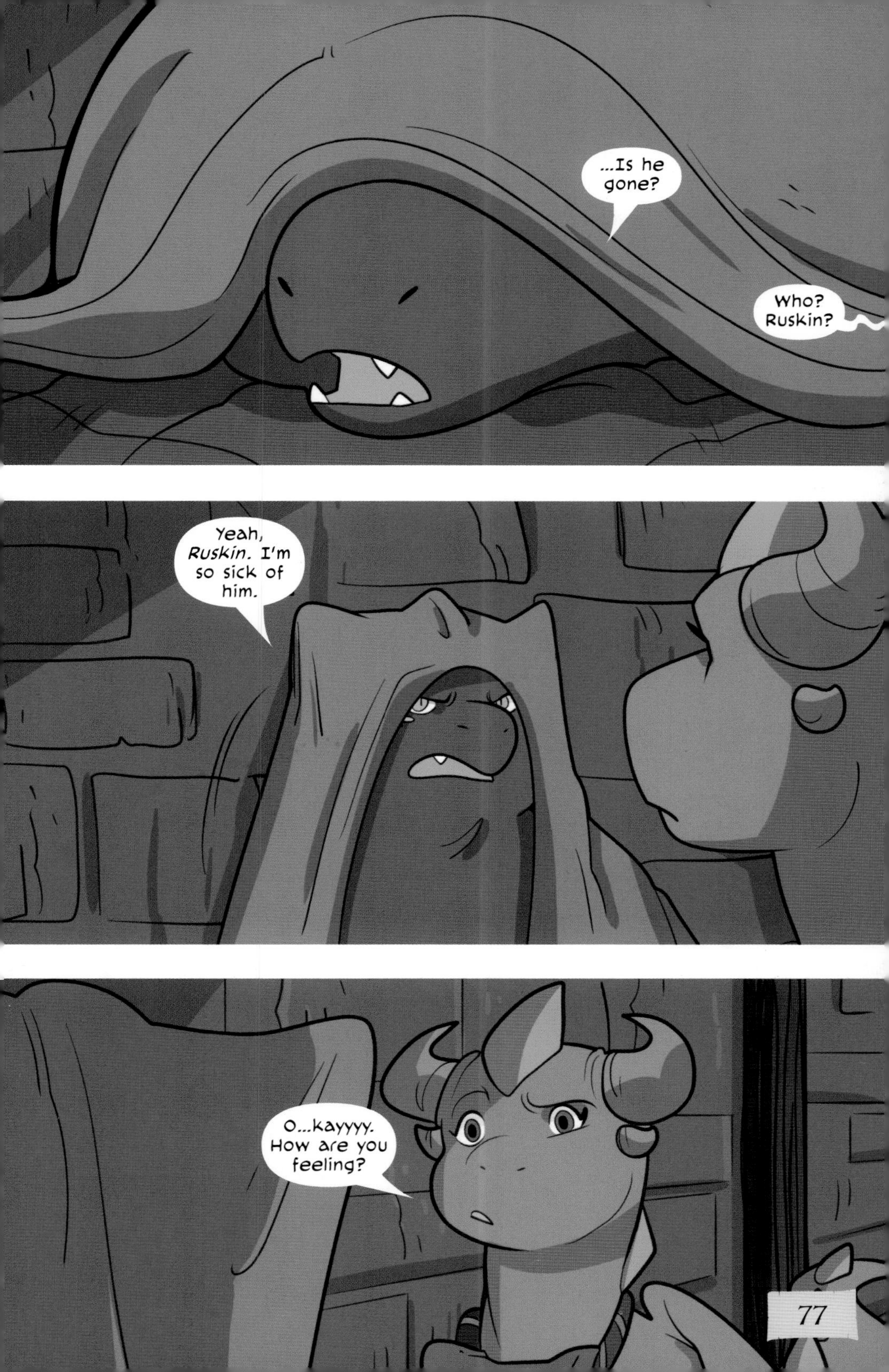
...Is he gone?
Who? Ruskin?
Yeah, *Ruskin.* I'm so sick of him.
O...kayyyy. How are you feeling?

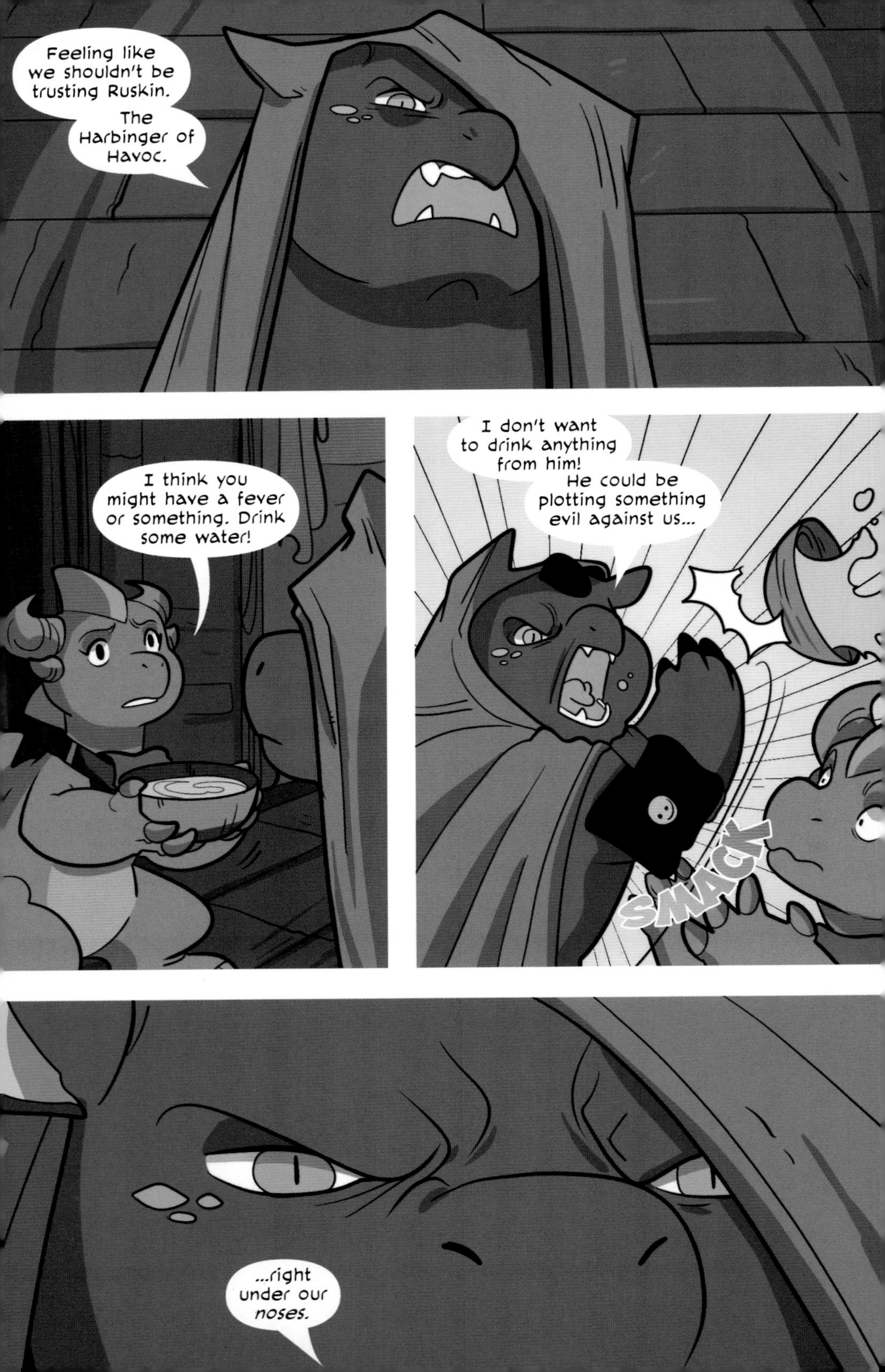
Feeling like we shouldn't be trusting Ruskin.
The Harbinger of Havoc.
I think you might have a fever or something. Drink some water!
I don't want to drink anything from him!
He could be plotting something evil against us...
SMACK
...right under our *noses.*

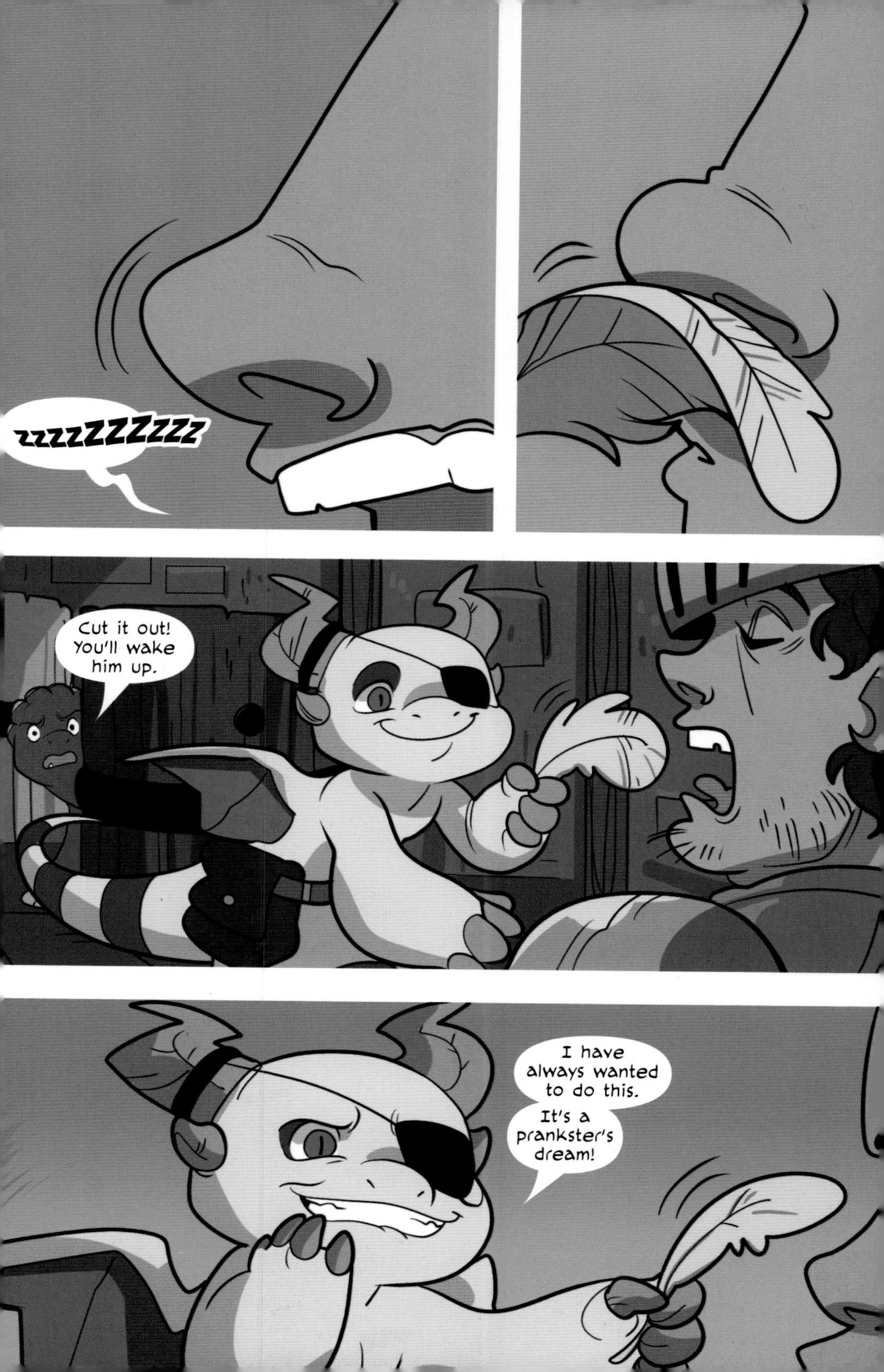
zzzzZZZZzzz
Cut it out! You'll wake him up.
I have always wanted to do this.
It's a prankster's dream!

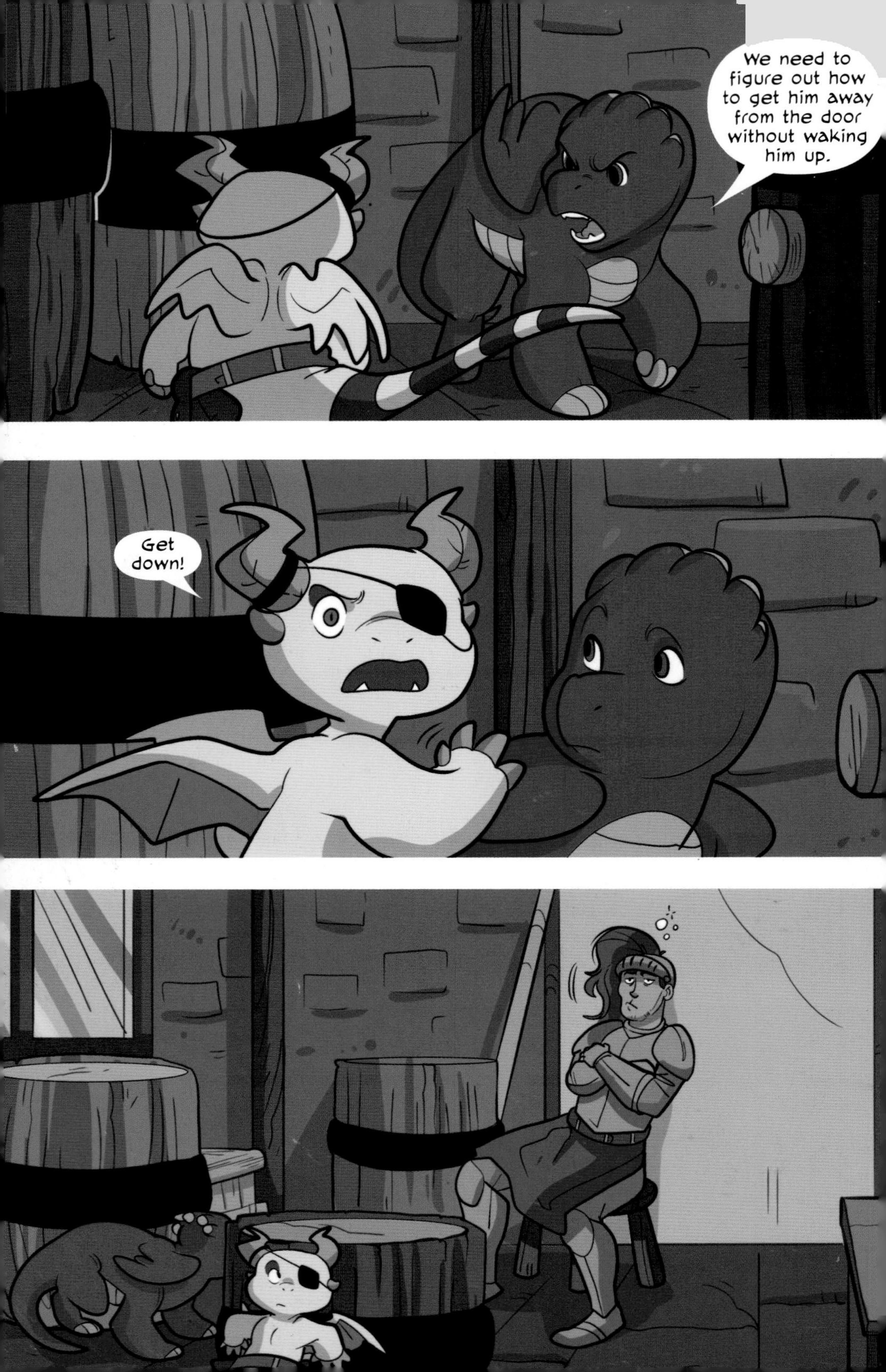
We need to figure out how to get him away from the door without waking him up.
Get down!

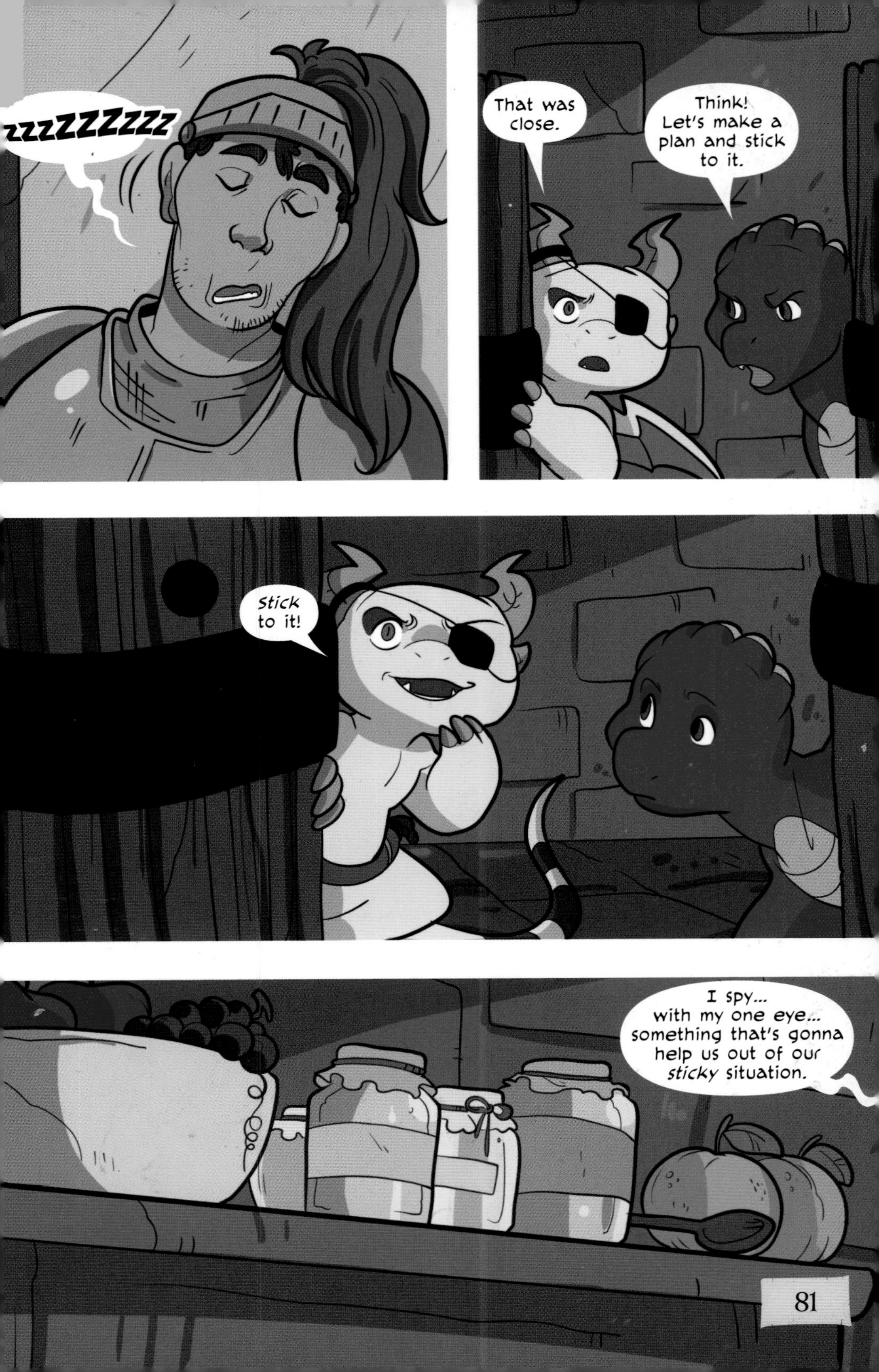
zzzZZZZzzz
That was close.
Think! Let's make a plan and stick to it.
Stick to it!
I spy... with my one *eye*... something that's gonna help us out of our *sticky* situation.

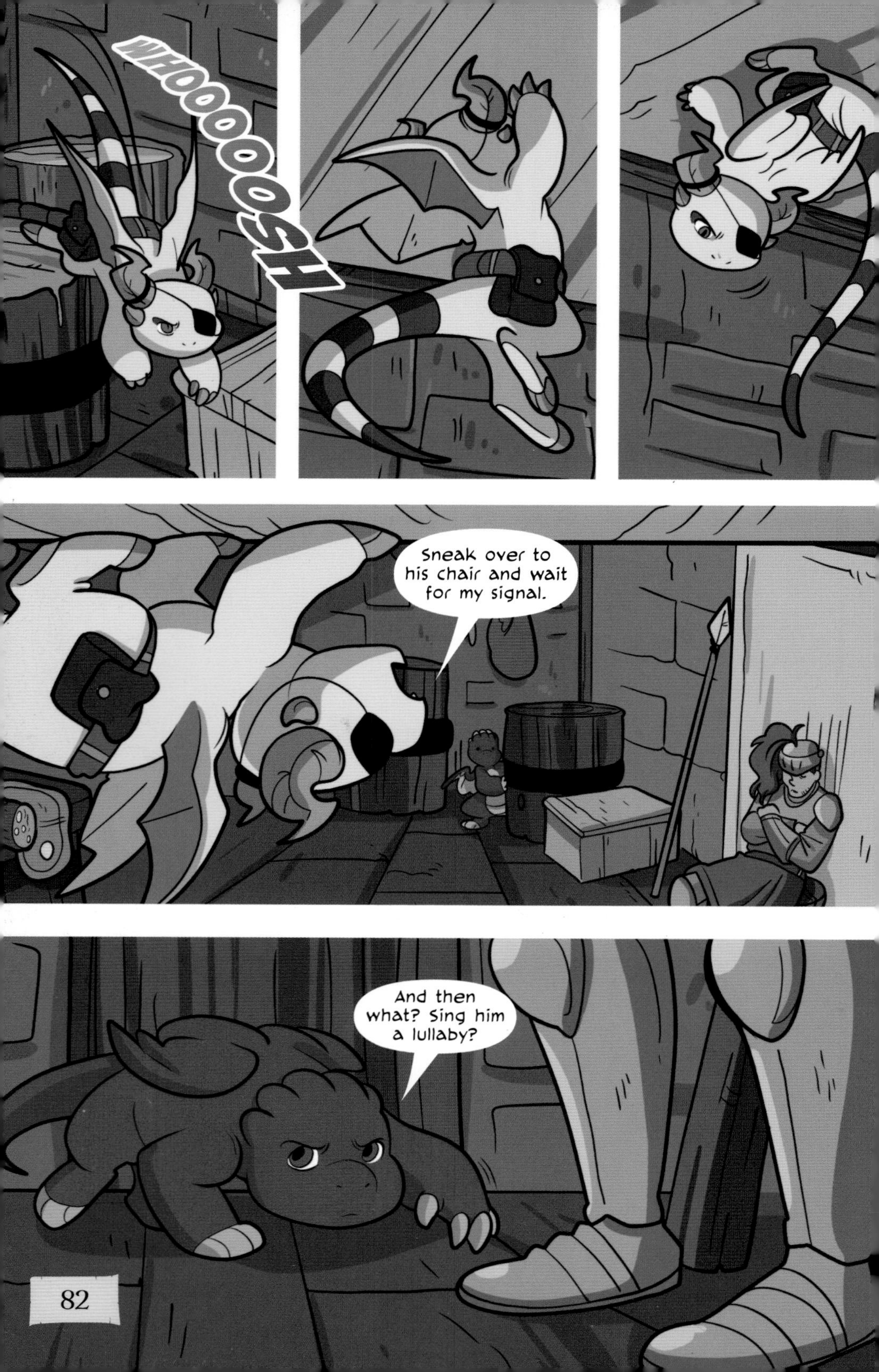
WHOOOOOSH
Sneak over to his chair and wait for my signal.
And then what? Sing him a lullaby?

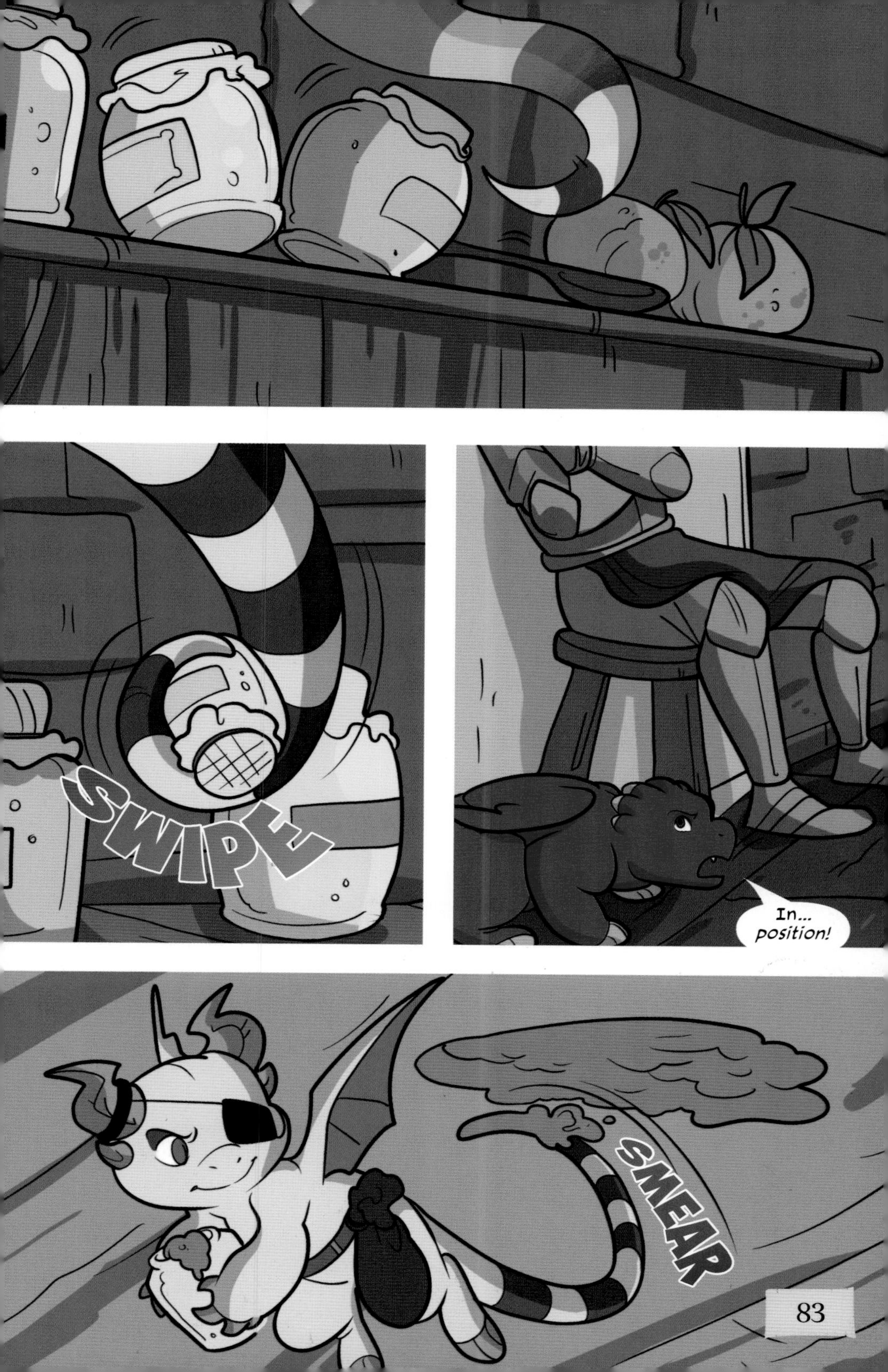
SWIPE
In... position!
SMEAR

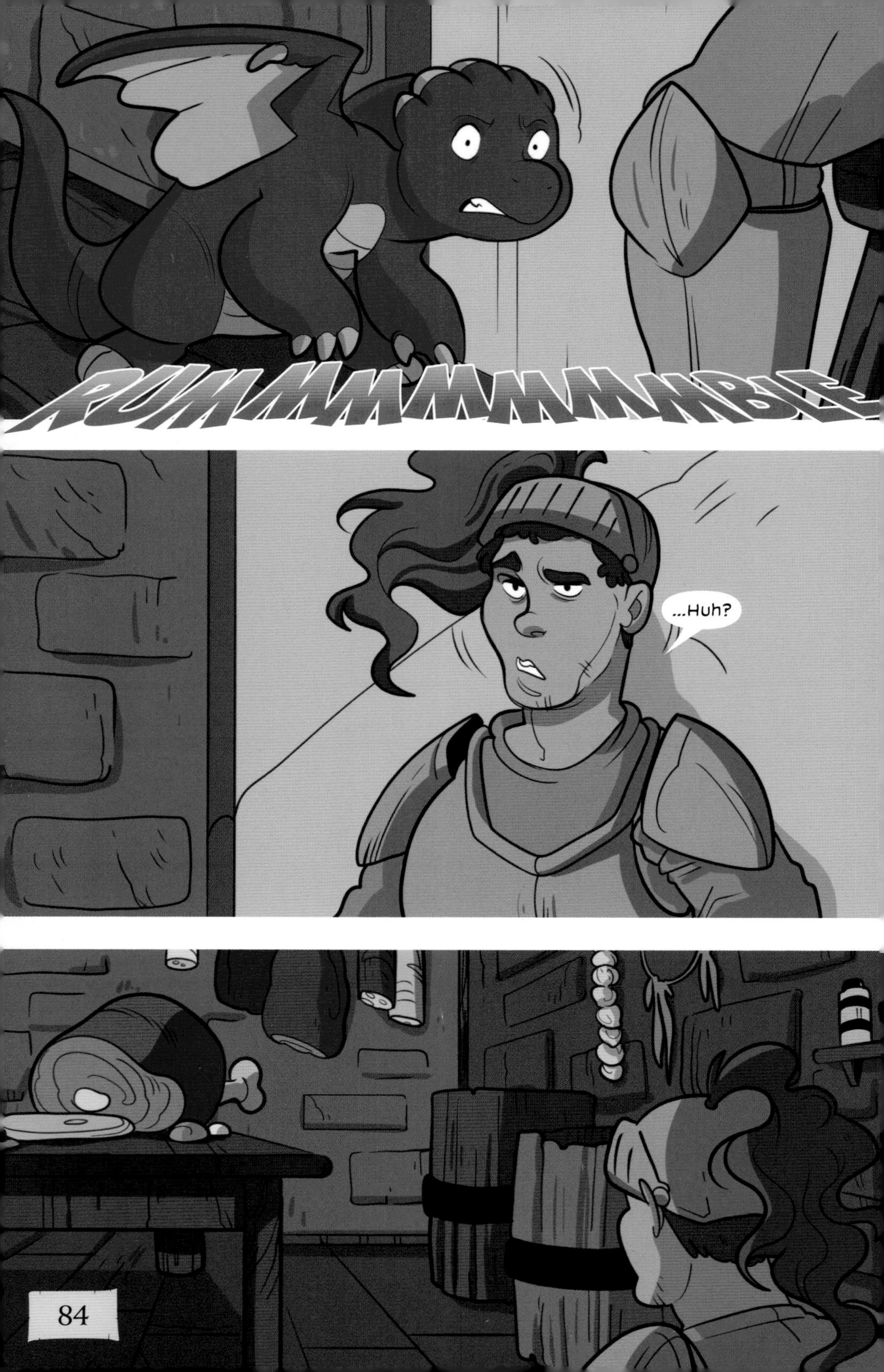
RUMMMMMMMMBLE
...Huh?

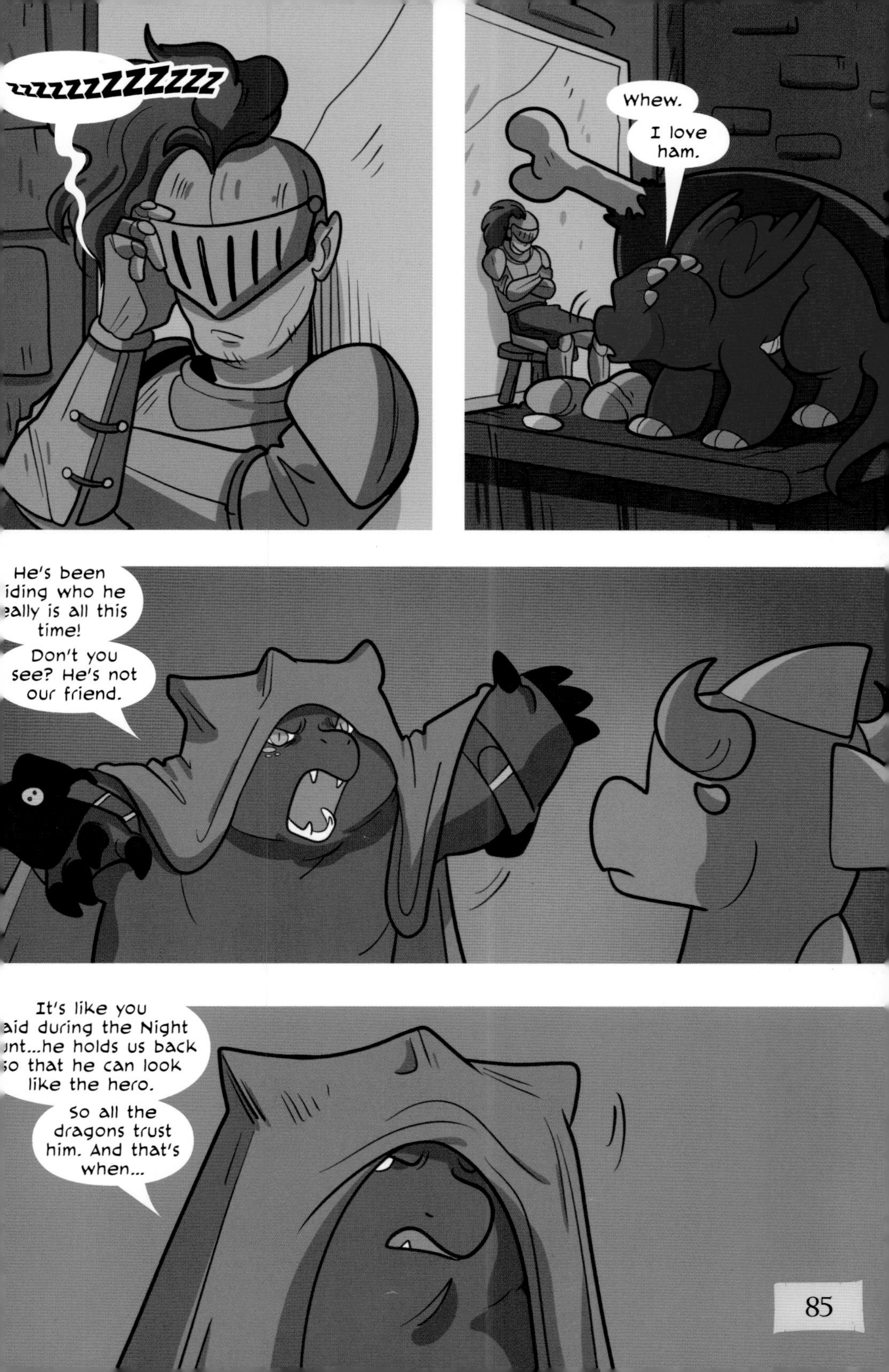
zzzzzzZZZZZZ
Whew.
I love ham.
He's been iding who he eally is all this time!
Don't you see? He's not our friend.
It's like you aid during the Night unt...he holds us back o that he can look like the hero.
So all the dragons trust him. And that's when...

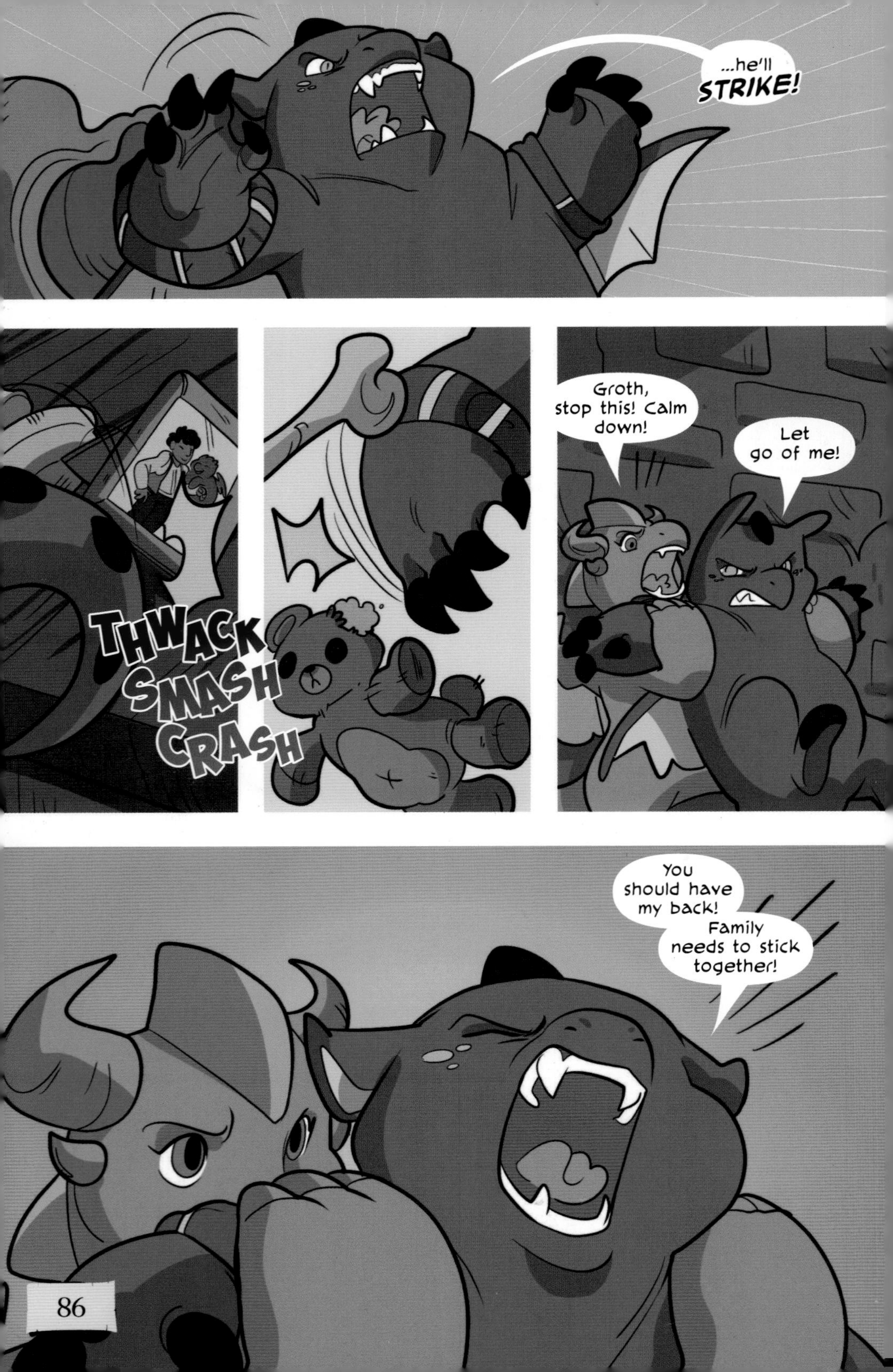

...he'll STRIKE!
THWACK SMASH CRASH
Groth, stop this! Calm down!
Let go of me!
You should have my back!
Family needs to stick together!

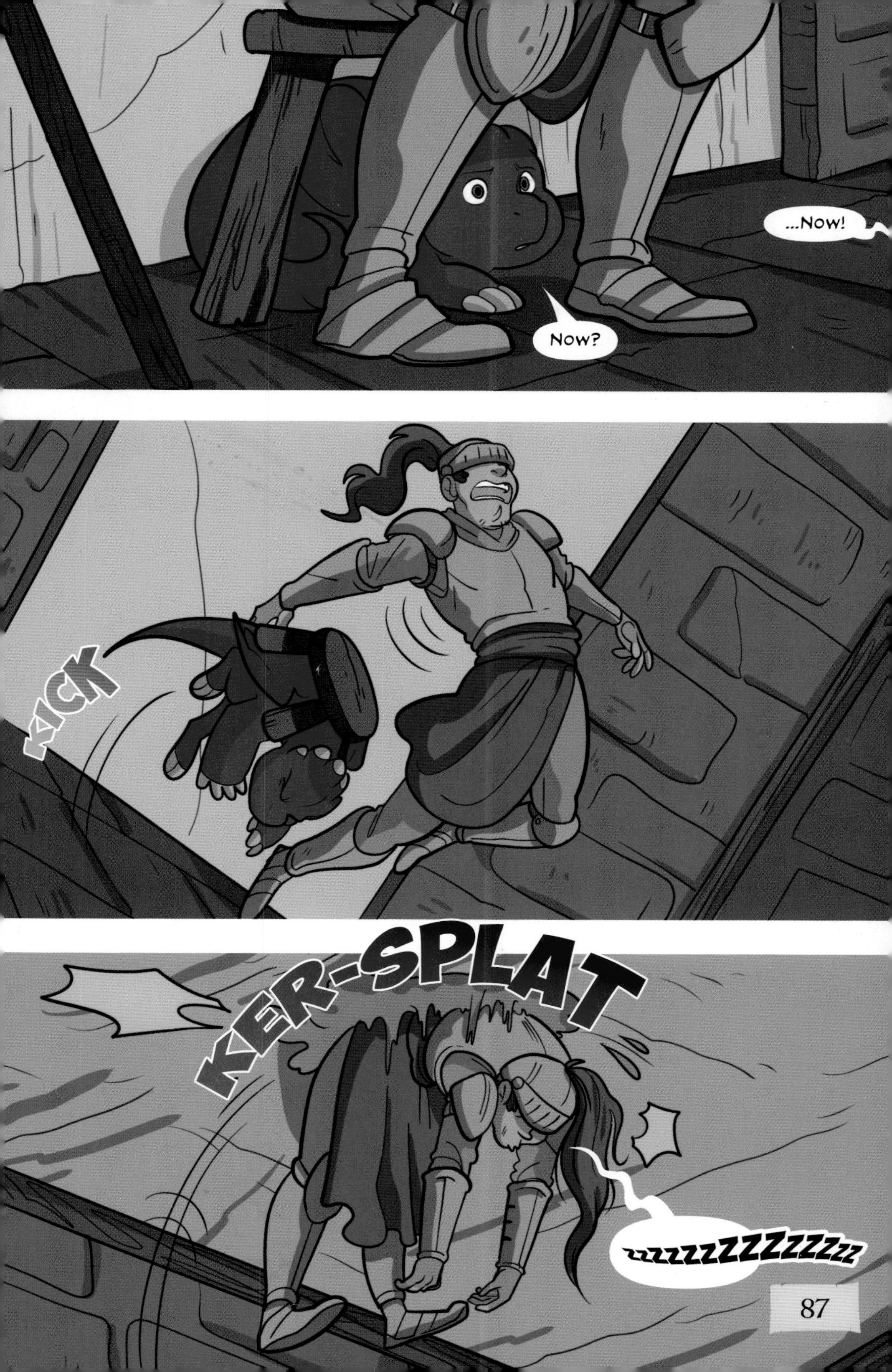
...Now!
Now?
KICK
KER-SPLAT
zzzzzzZZZZZZzz

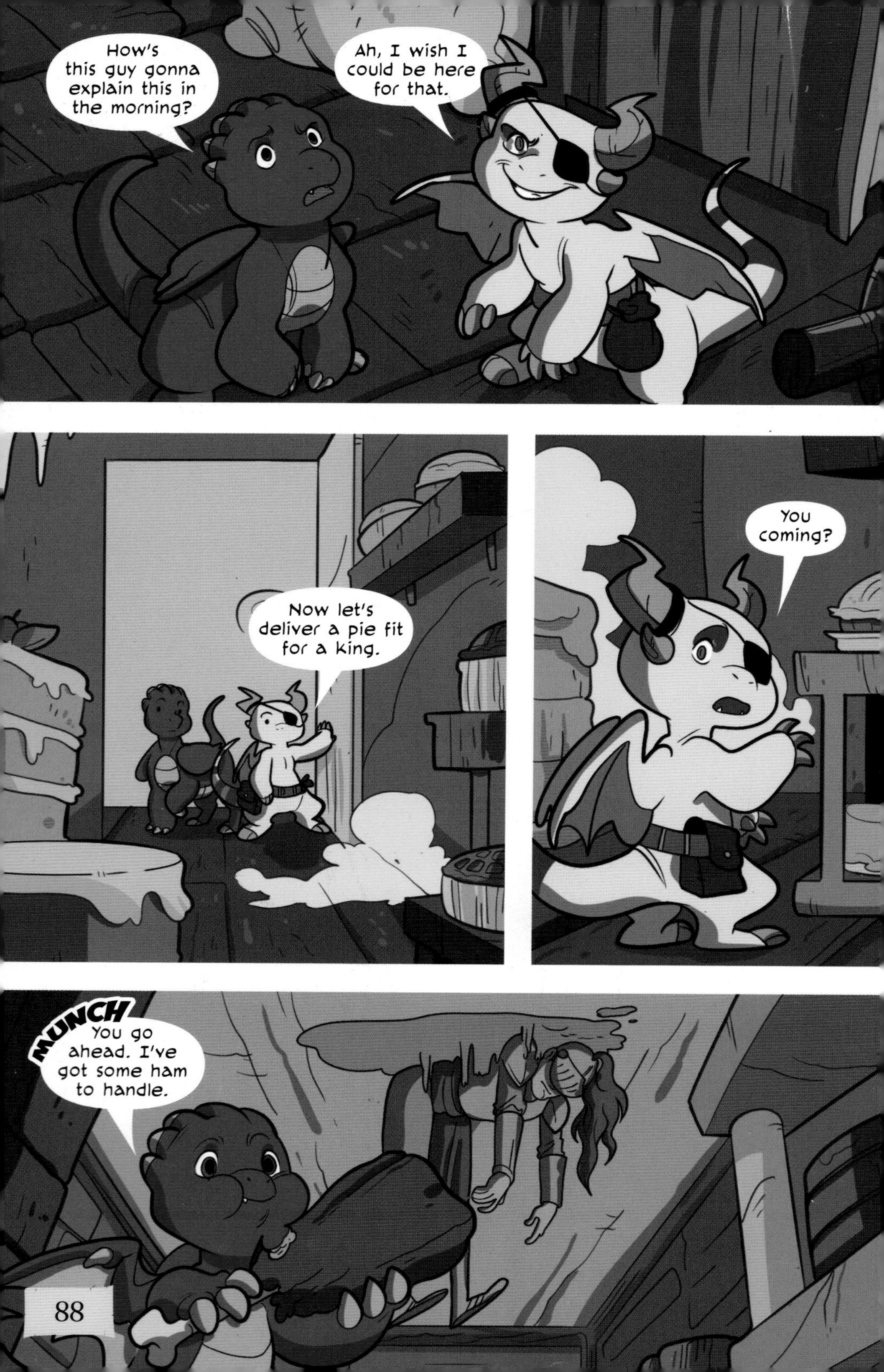
How's this guy gonna explain this in the morning?
Ah, I wish I could be here for that.
Now let's deliver a pie fit for a king.
You coming?
MUNCH
You go ahead. I've got some ham to handle.

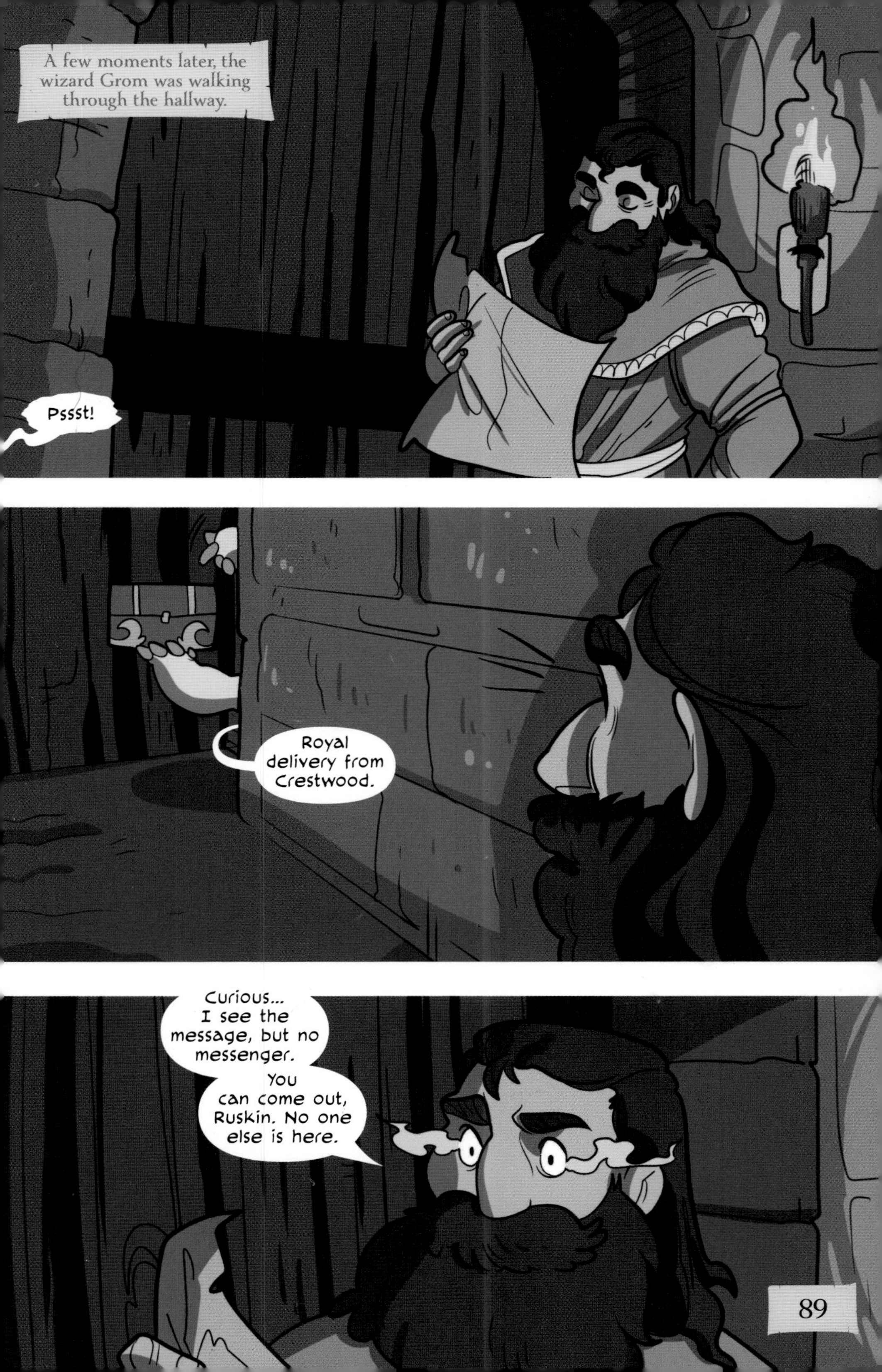
A few moments later, the wizard Grom was walking through the hallway.
Pssst!
Royal delivery from Crestwood.
Curious... I see the message, but no messenger.
You can come out, Ruskin. No one else is here.

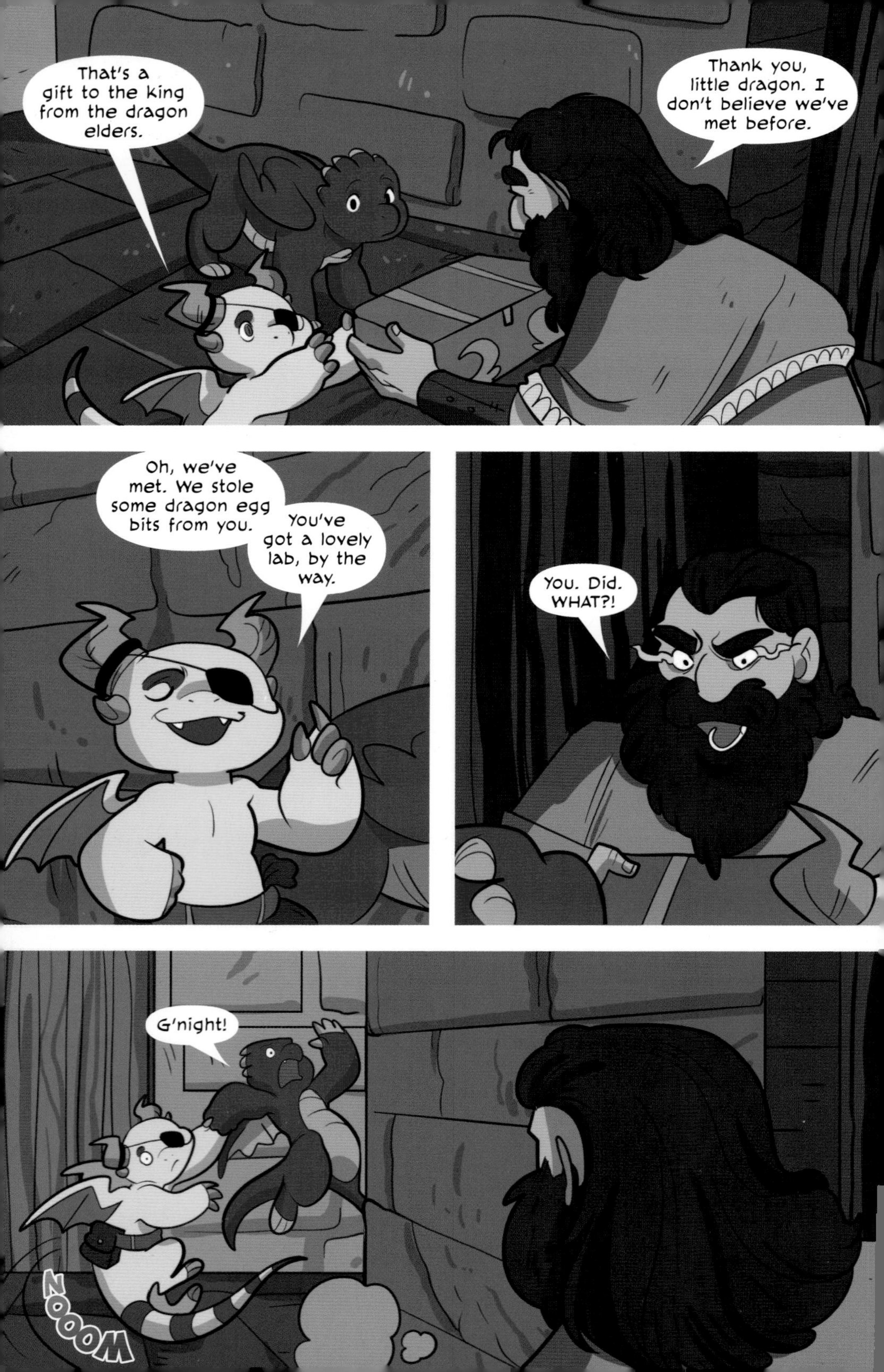
That's a gift to the king from the dragon elders.
Thank you, little dragon. I don't believe we've met before.
Oh, we've met. We stole some dragon egg bits from you.
You've got a lovely lab, by the way.
You. Did. WHAT?!
G'night!
WOOOOM

Chapter 7

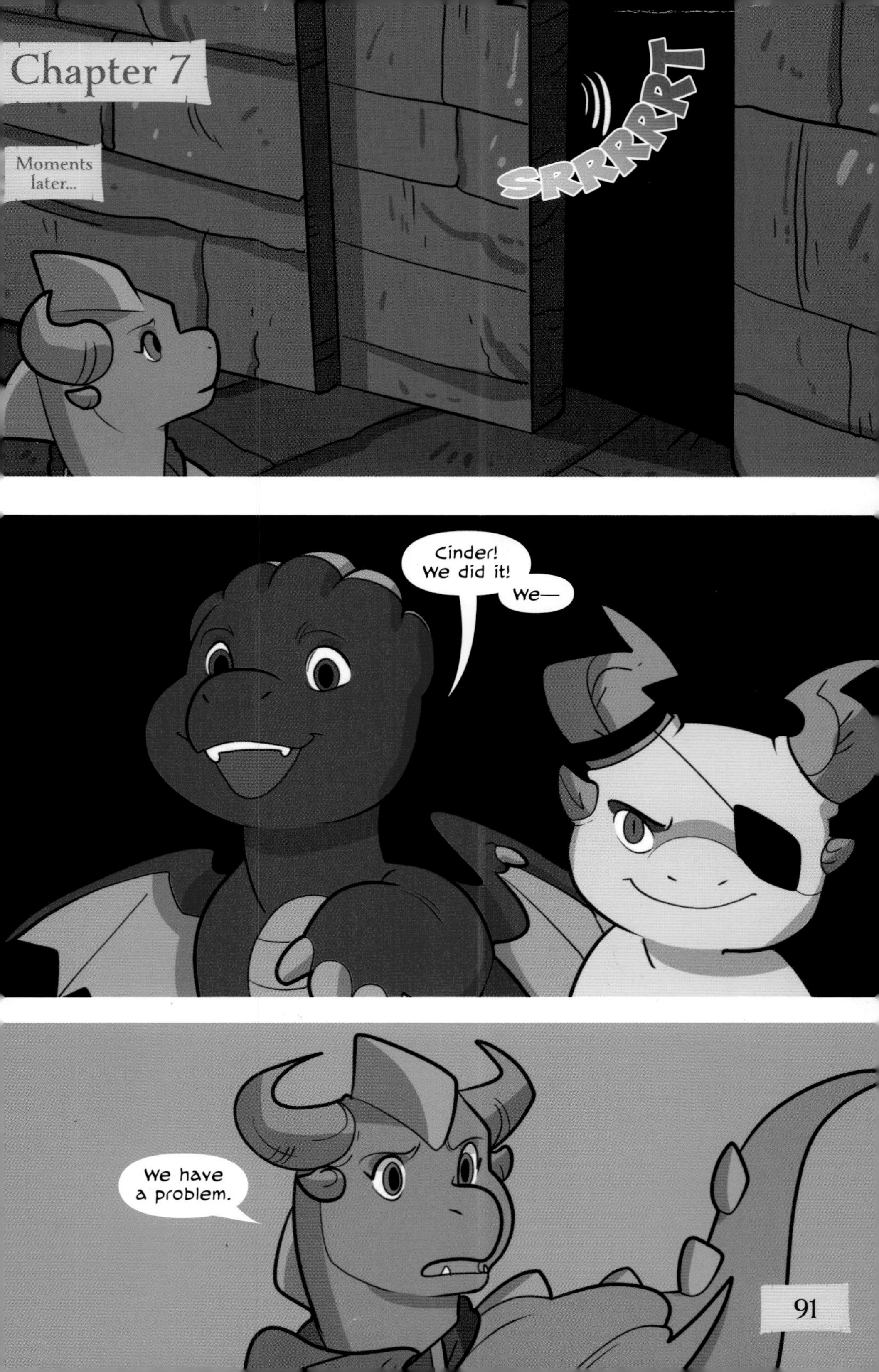
Moments later...
SRRRRRT
Cinder! We did it!
We—
We have a problem.

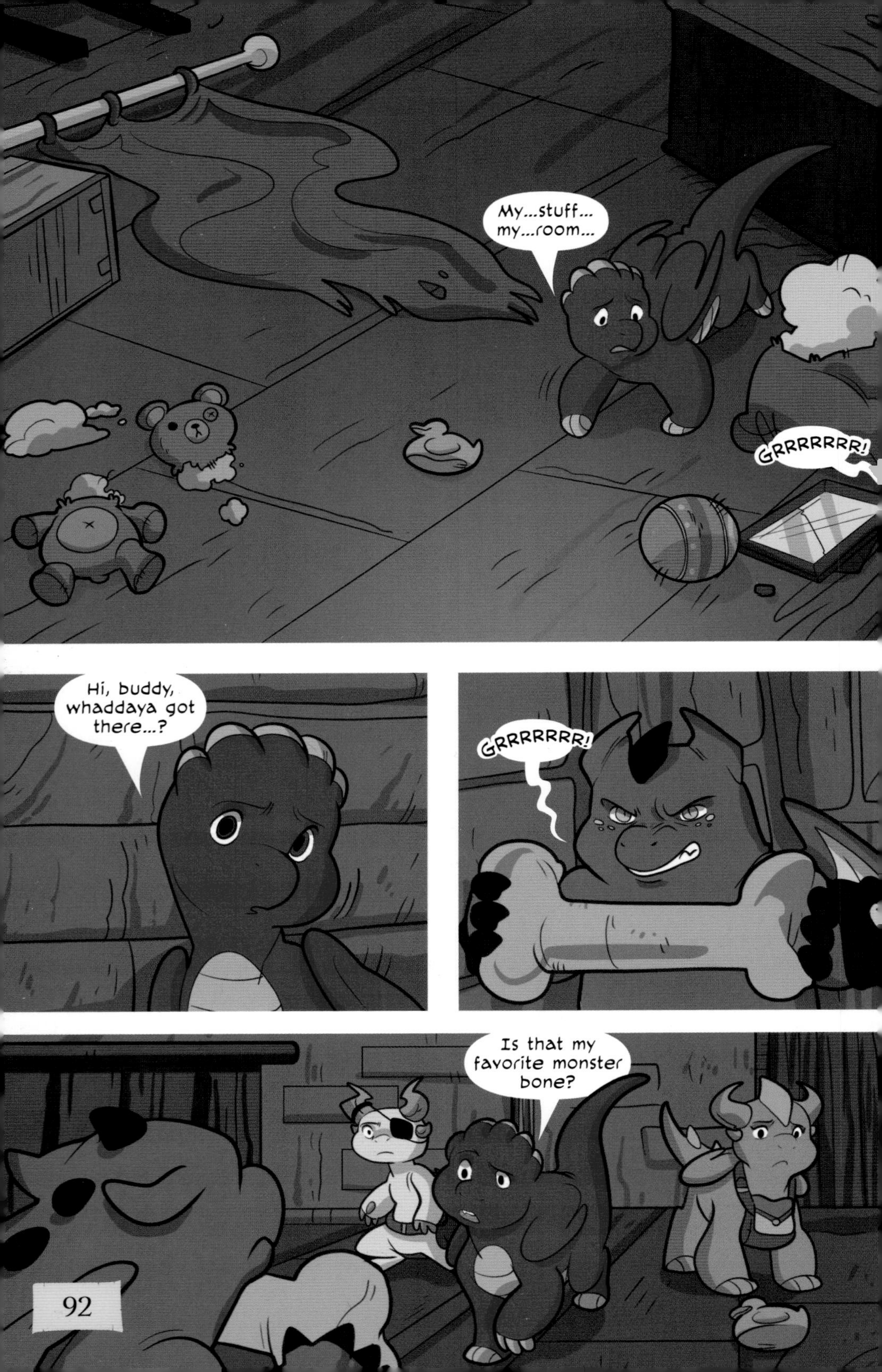
My...stuff...
my...room...
GRRRRRRR!
Hi, buddy, whaddaya got there...?
GRRRRRRR!
Is that my favorite monster bone?

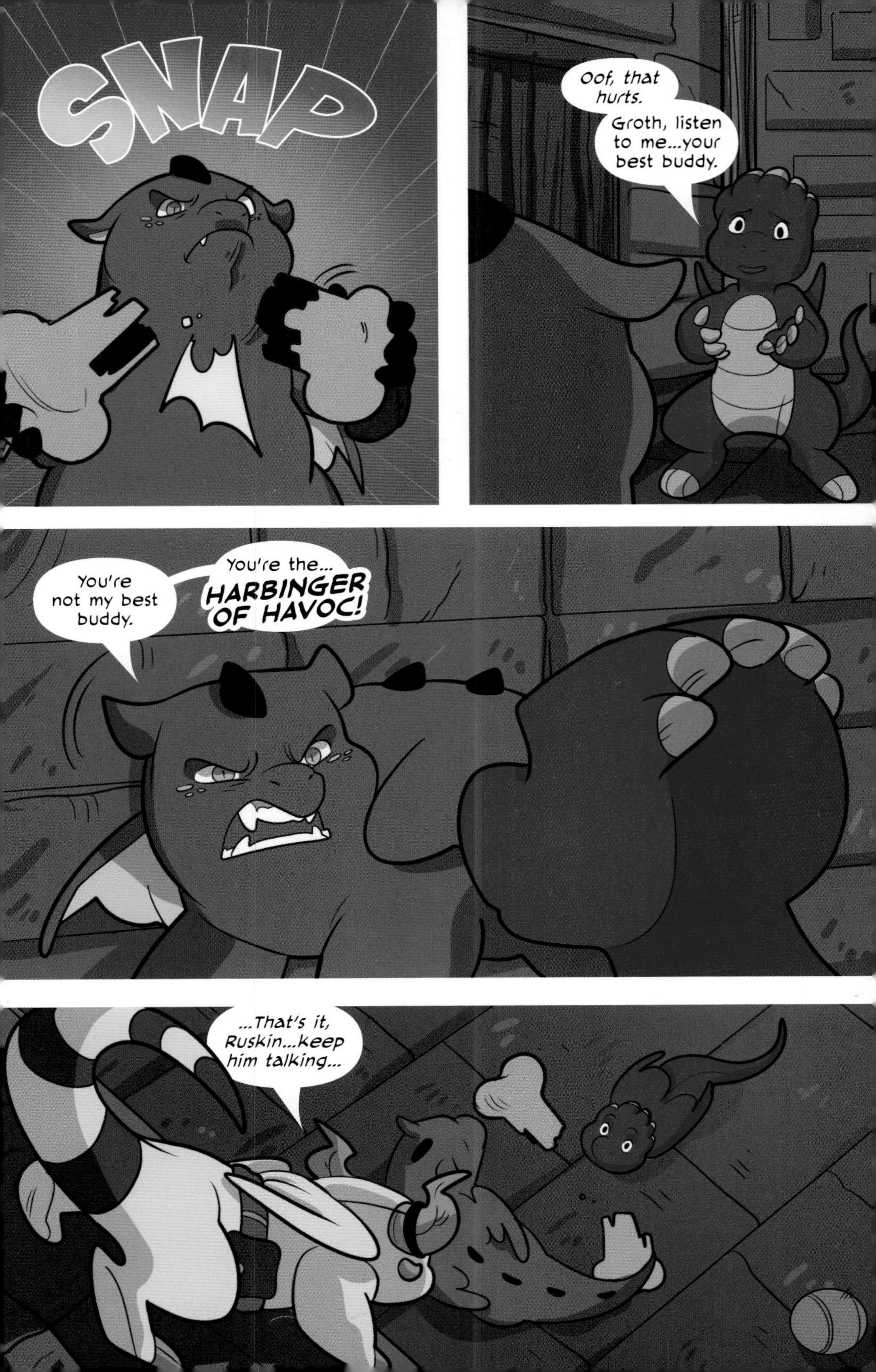
SNAP
Oof, that hurts.
Groth, listen to me...your best buddy.
You're not my best buddy.
You're the... HARBINGER OF HAVOC!
...That's it, Ruskin...keep him talking...

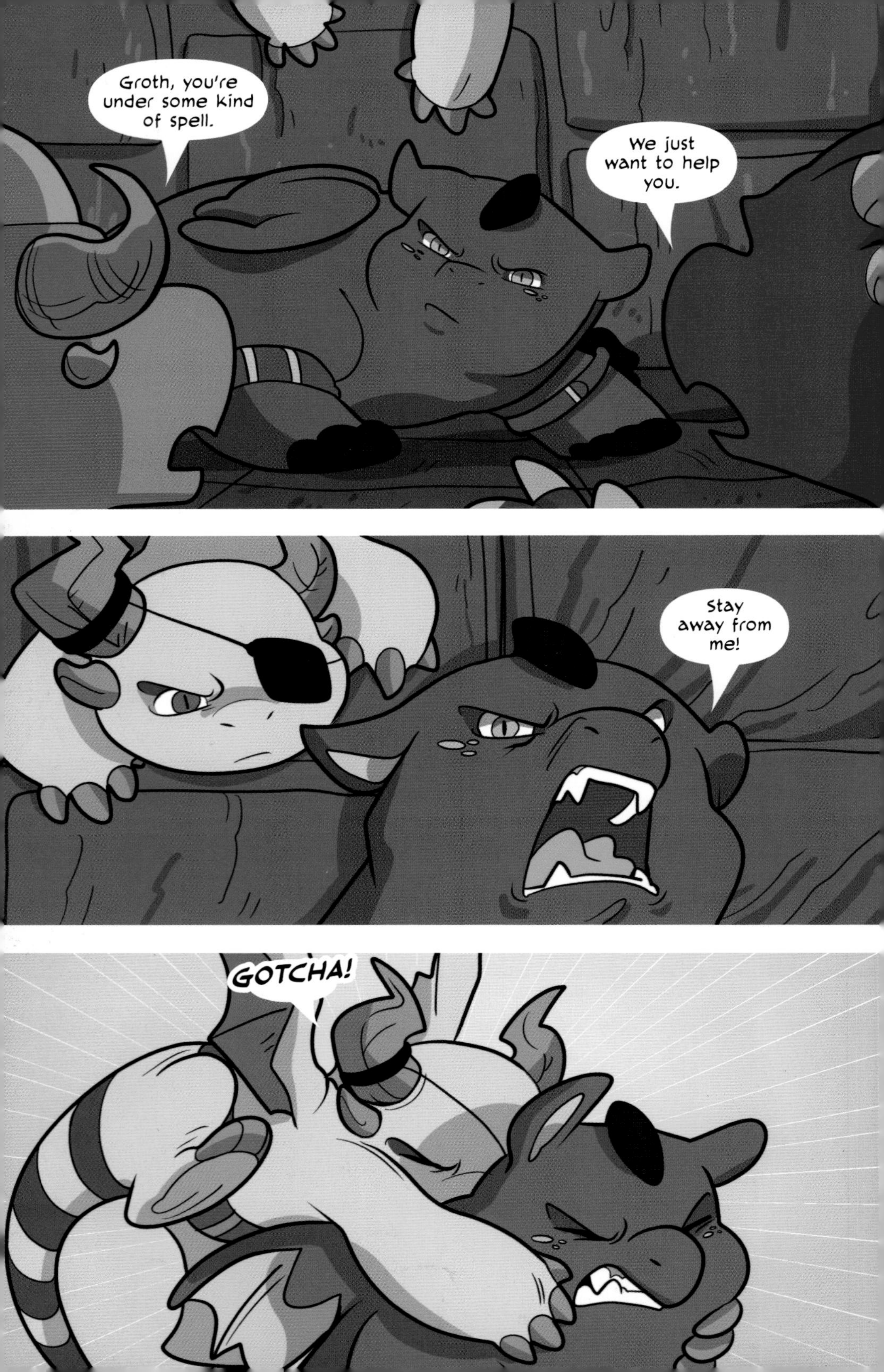
Groth, you're under some kind of spell.
We just want to help you.
Stay away from me!
GOTCHA!

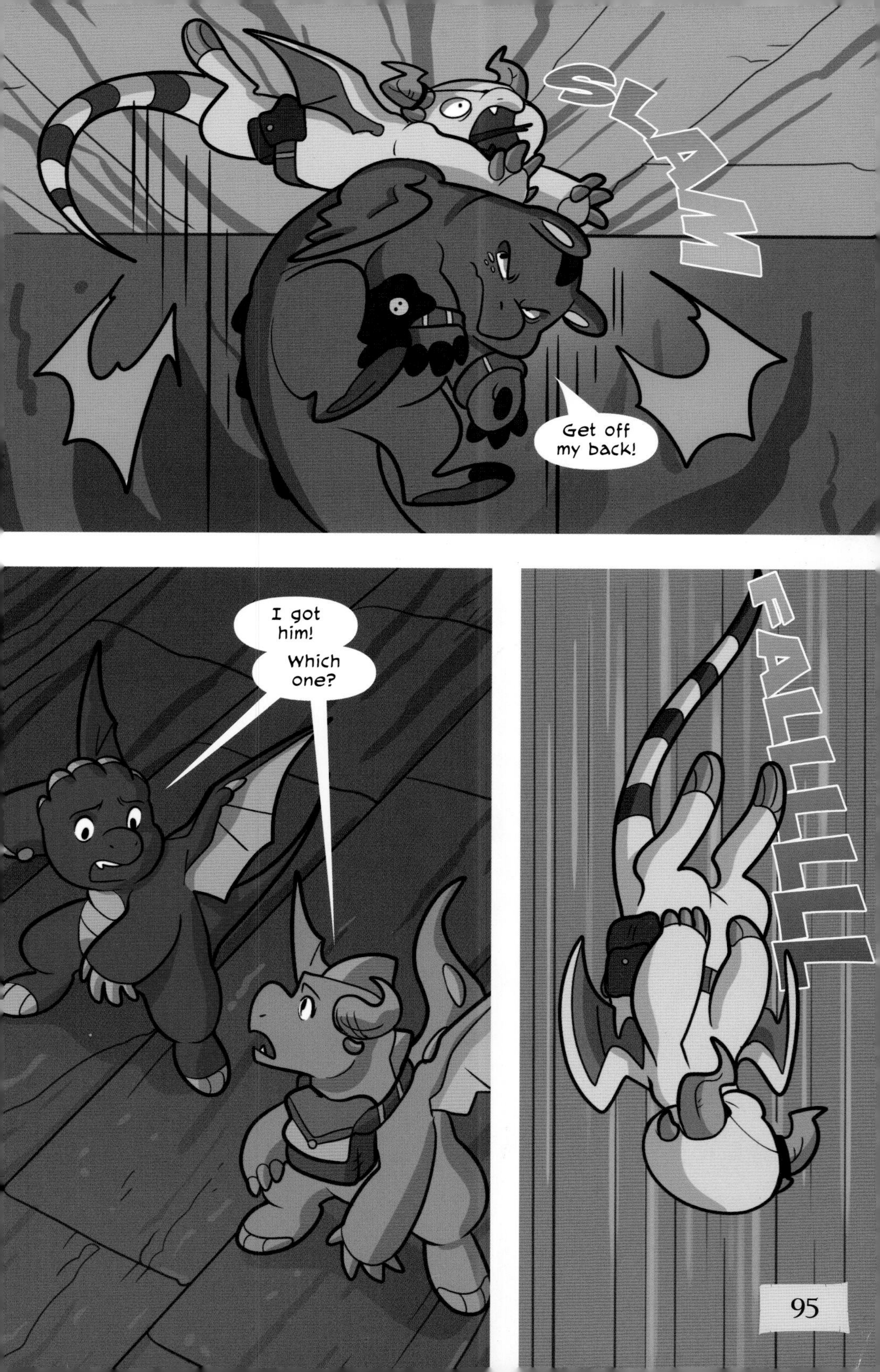
SLAM
Get off my back!
I got him!
Which one?
FALLLLL

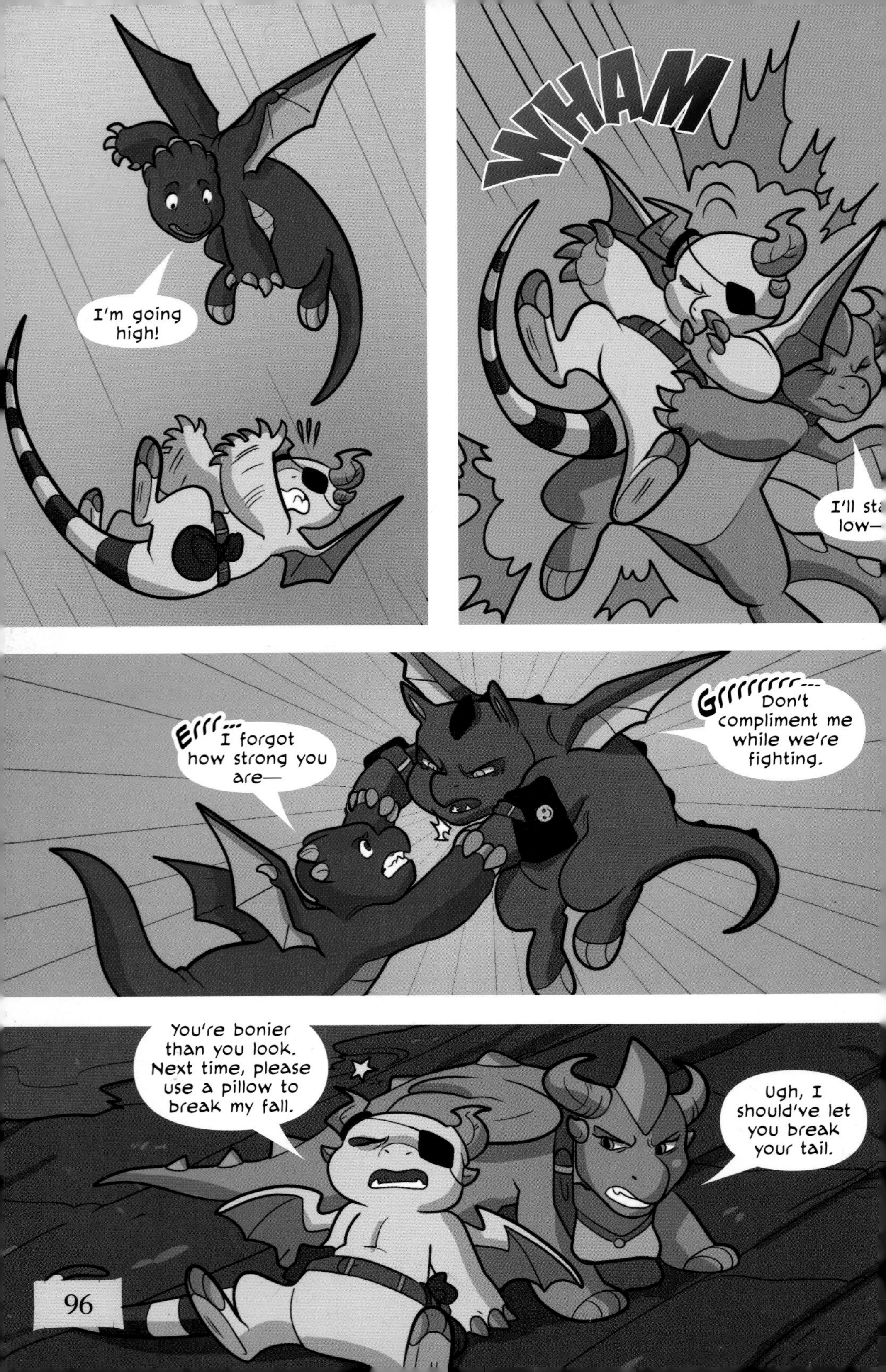
I'm going high!
WHAM
I'll sta
low—
Errr... I forgot how strong you are—
Grrrrrrr... Don't compliment me while we're fighting.
You're bonier than you look. Next time, please use a pillow to break my fall.
Ugh, I should've let you break your tail.

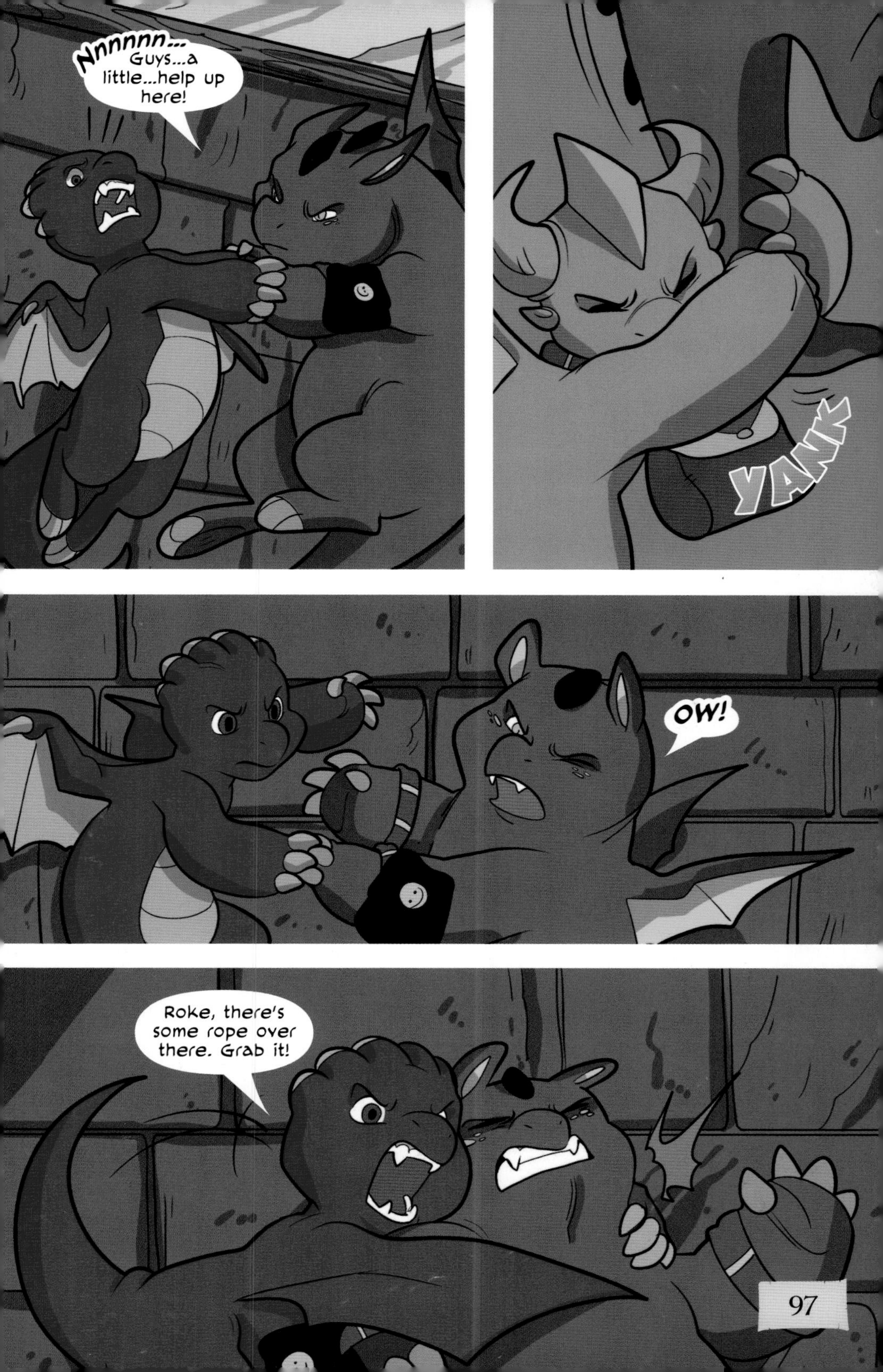
Nnnnnn...
Guys...a little...help up here!
YANK
OW!
Roke, there's some rope over there. Grab it!

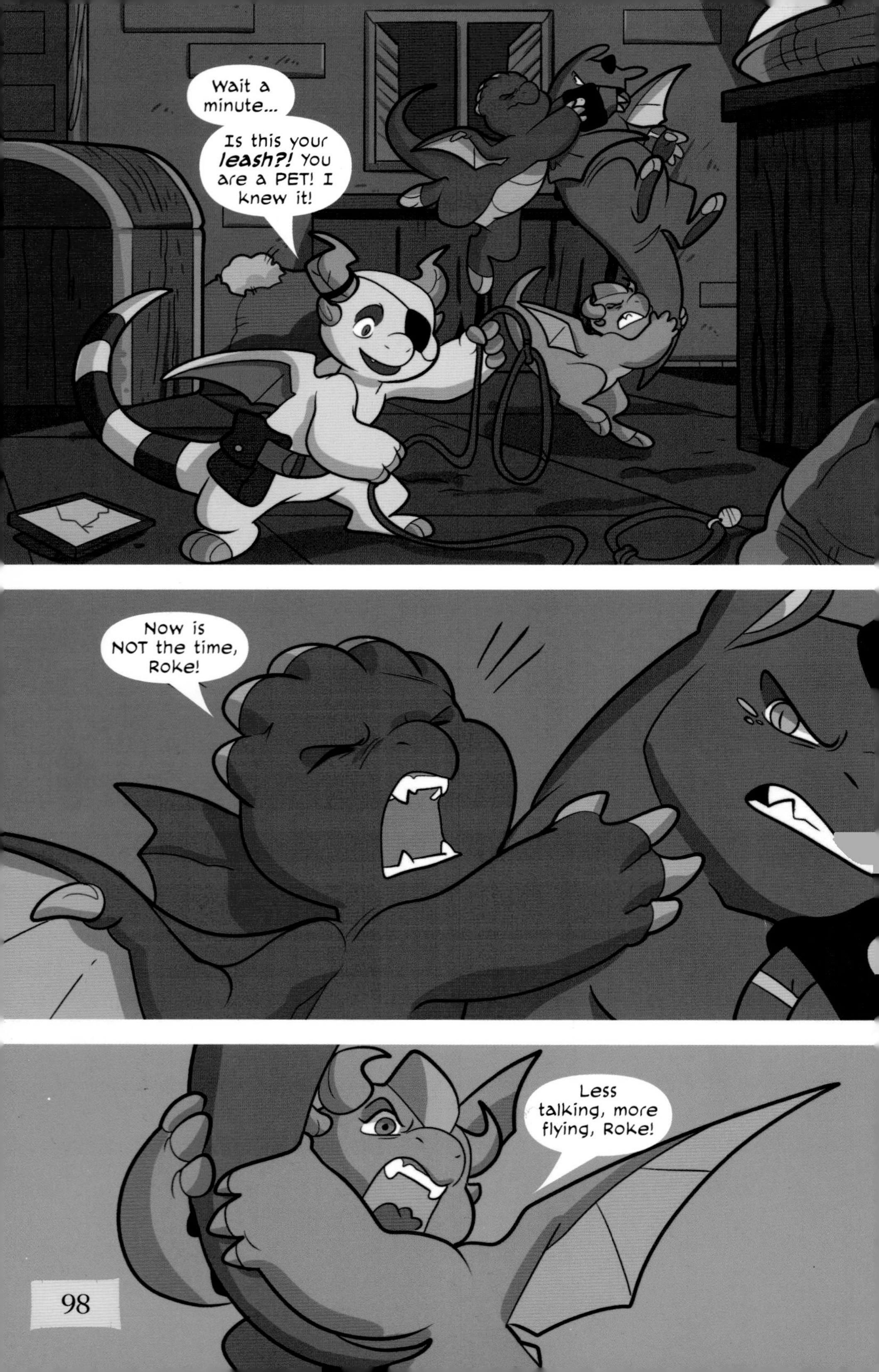
Wait a minute...
Is this your *leash?!* You are a PET! I knew it!
Now is NOT the time, Roke!
Less talking, more flying, Roke!

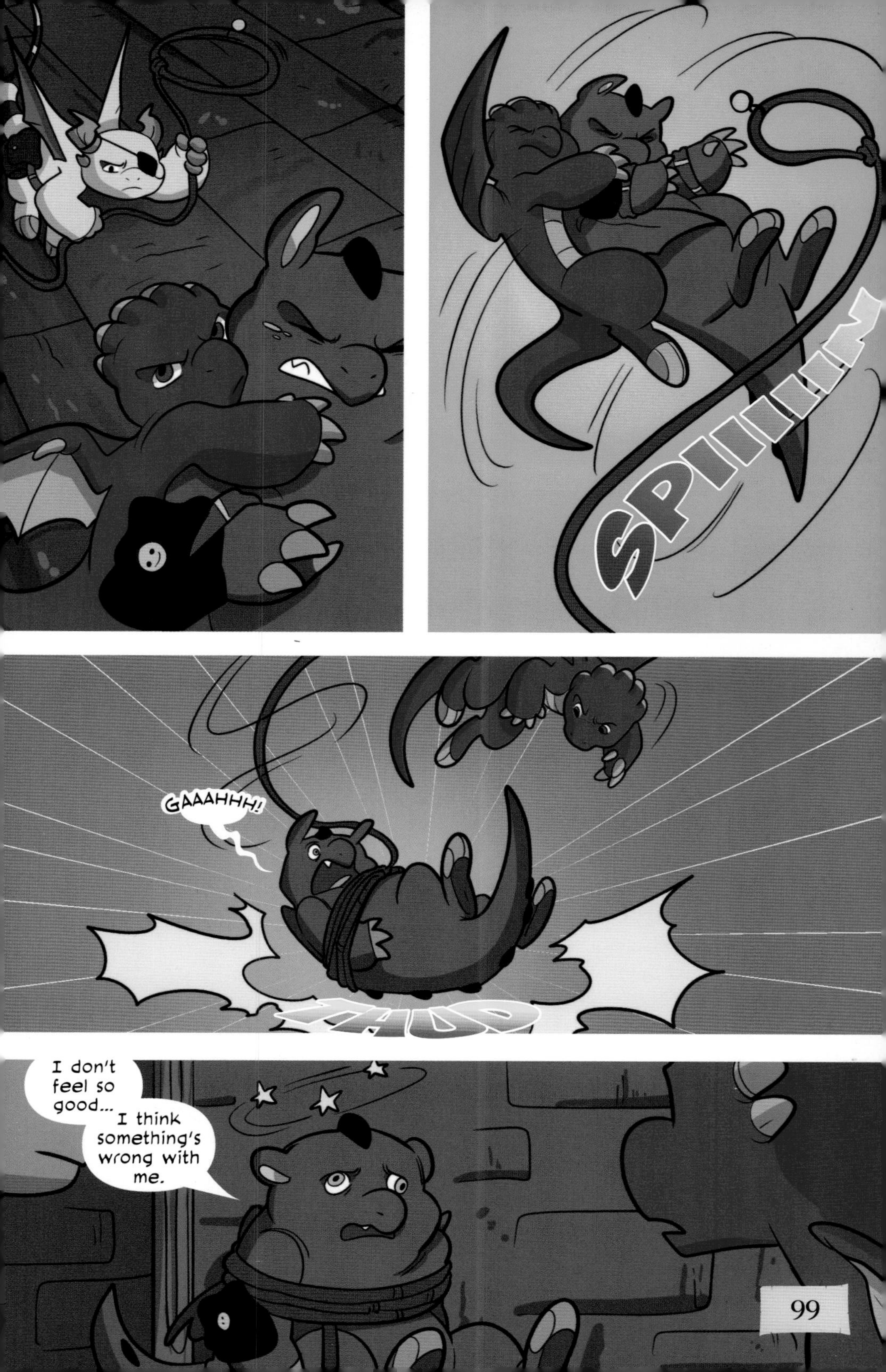
SPIIIIIIN
GAAAHHH!
THUD
I don't feel so good... I think something's wrong with me.

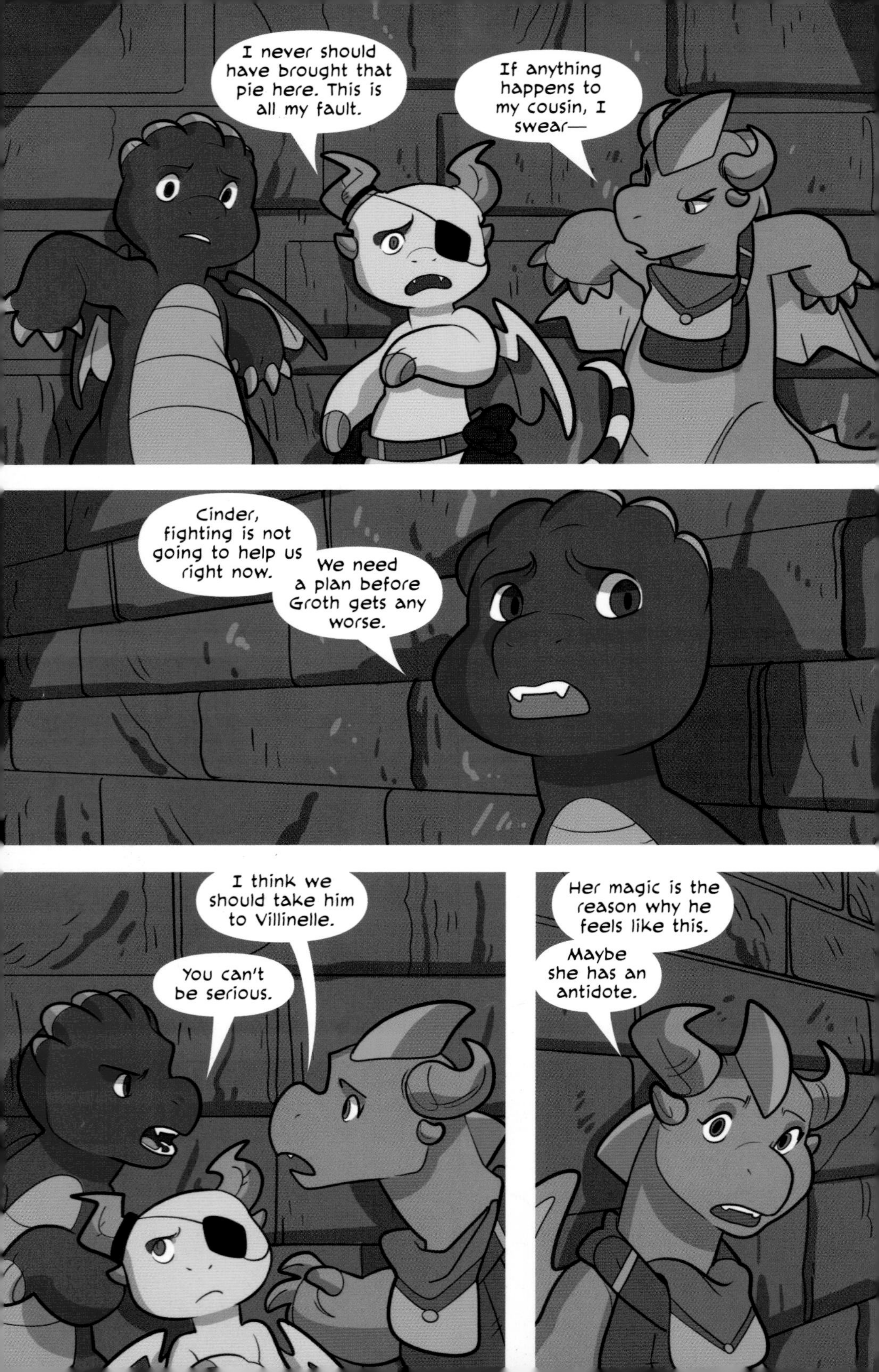
I never should have brought that pie here. This is all my fault.
If anything happens to my cousin, I swear—
Cinder, fighting is not going to help us right now.
We need a plan before Groth gets any worse.
I think we should take him to Villinelle.
You can't be serious.
Her magic is the reason why he feels like this.
Maybe she has an antidote.

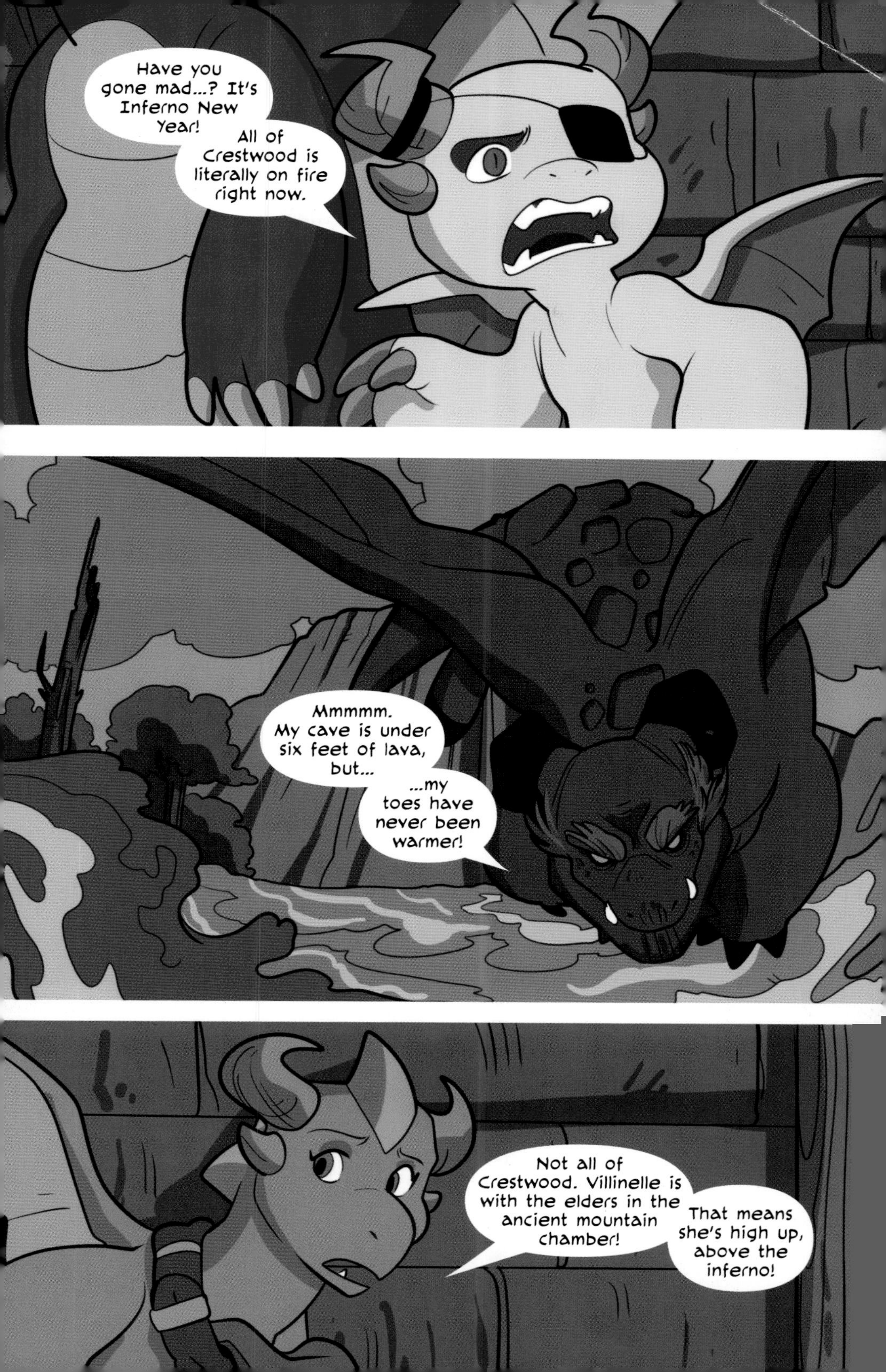
Have you gone mad...? It's Inferno New Year!
All of Crestwood is literally on fire right now.
Mmmmm. My cave is under six feet of lava, but...
...my toes have never been warmer!
Not all of Crestwood. Villinelle is with the elders in the ancient mountain chamber!
That means she's high up, above the inferno!

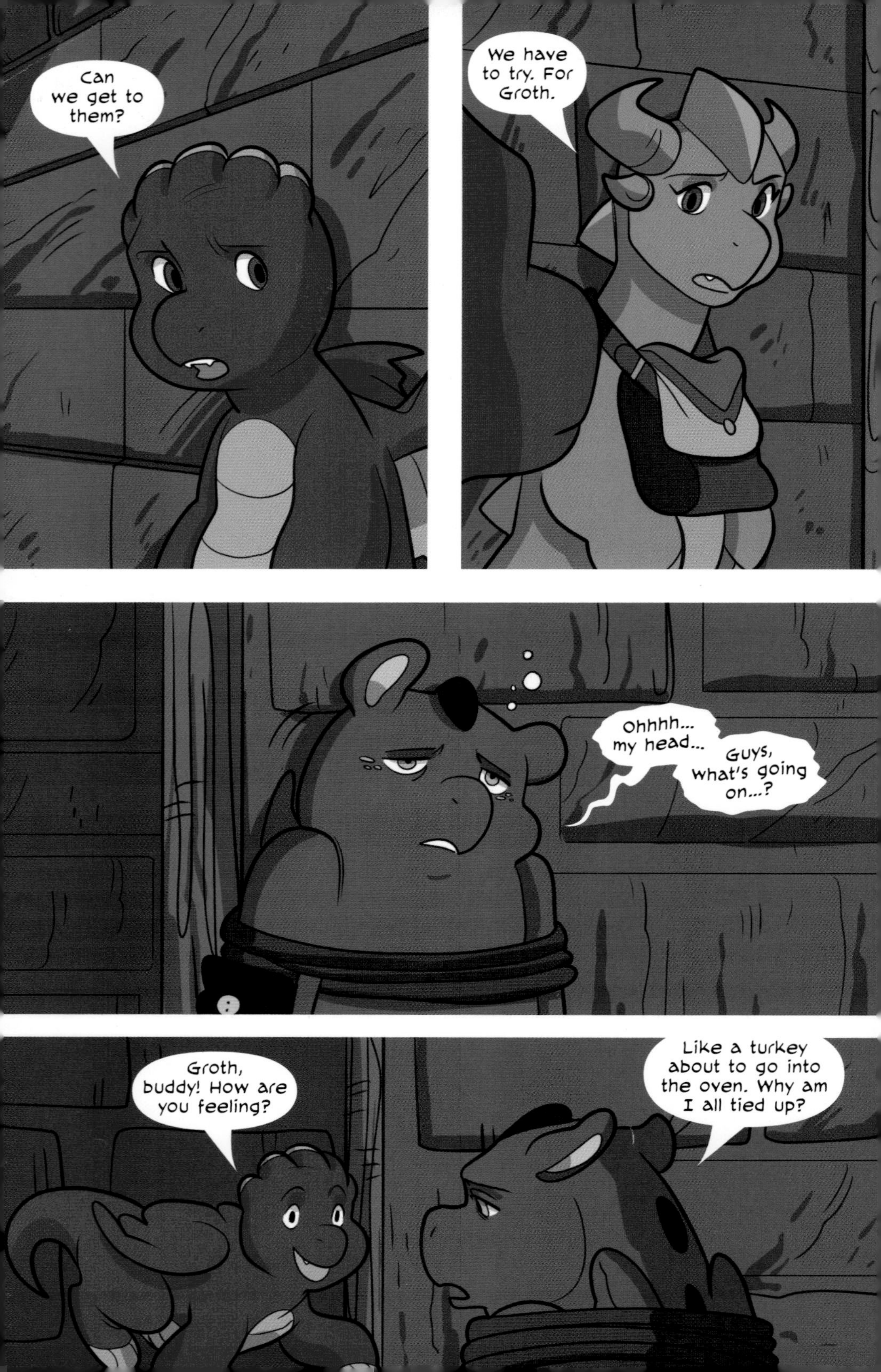
Can we get to them?
We have to try. For Groth.
Ohhhh... my head...
Guys, what's going on...?
Groth, buddy! How are you feeling?
Like a turkey about to go into the oven. Why am I all tied up?

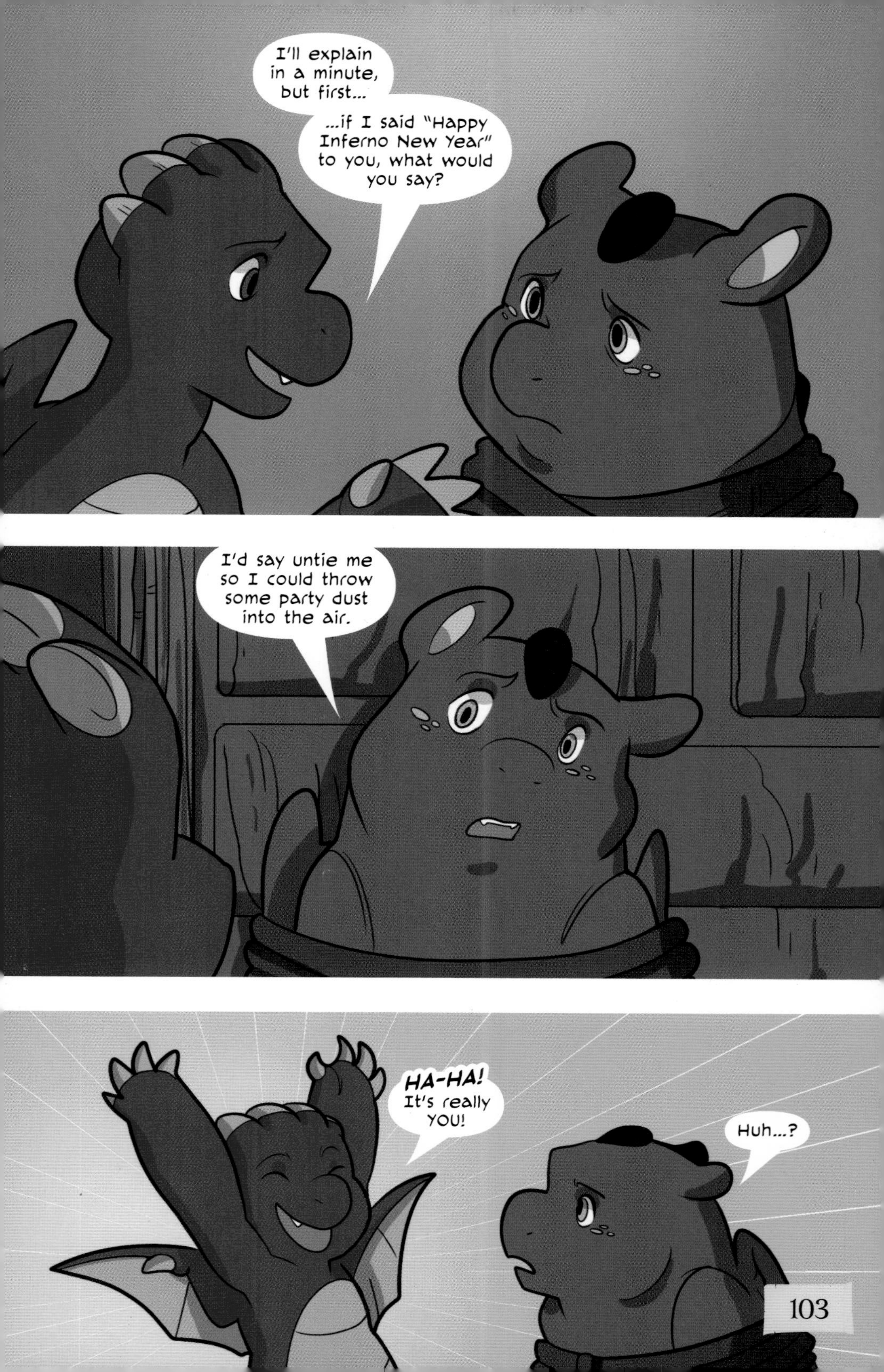
I'll explain in a minute, but first...
...if I said "Happy Inferno New Year" to you, what would you say?
I'd say untie me so I could throw some party dust into the air.
HA-HA! It's really YOU!
Huh...?

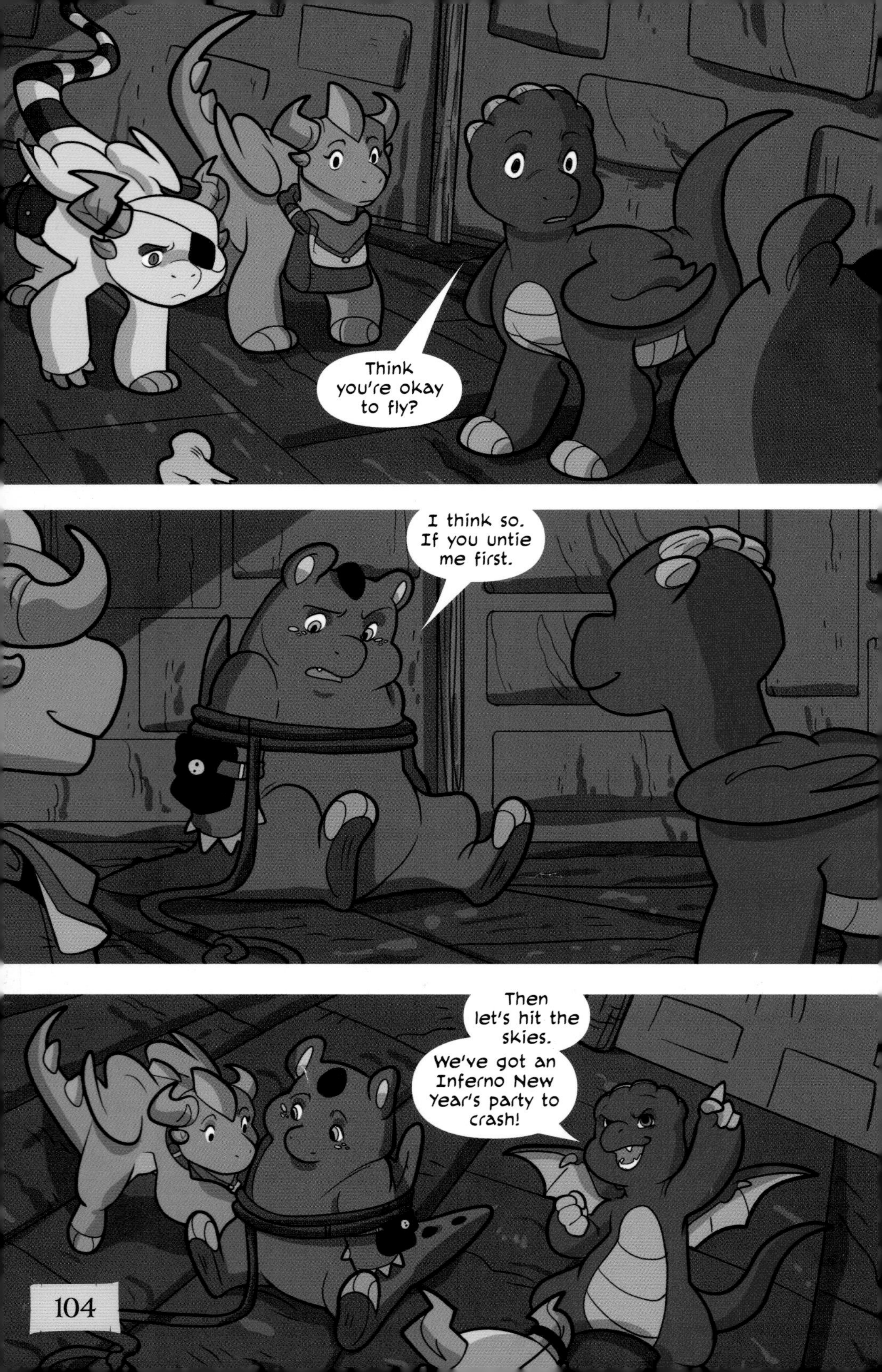
Think you're okay to fly?
I think so. If you untie me first.
Then let's hit the skies.
We've got an Inferno New Year's party to crash!

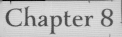

Chapter 8

The dragons launched into a last-minute night flight. The skies looked clear all the way to Crestwood...

SWHOOOOOOSH

But little did they know, it was going to be a bumpy ride.

105

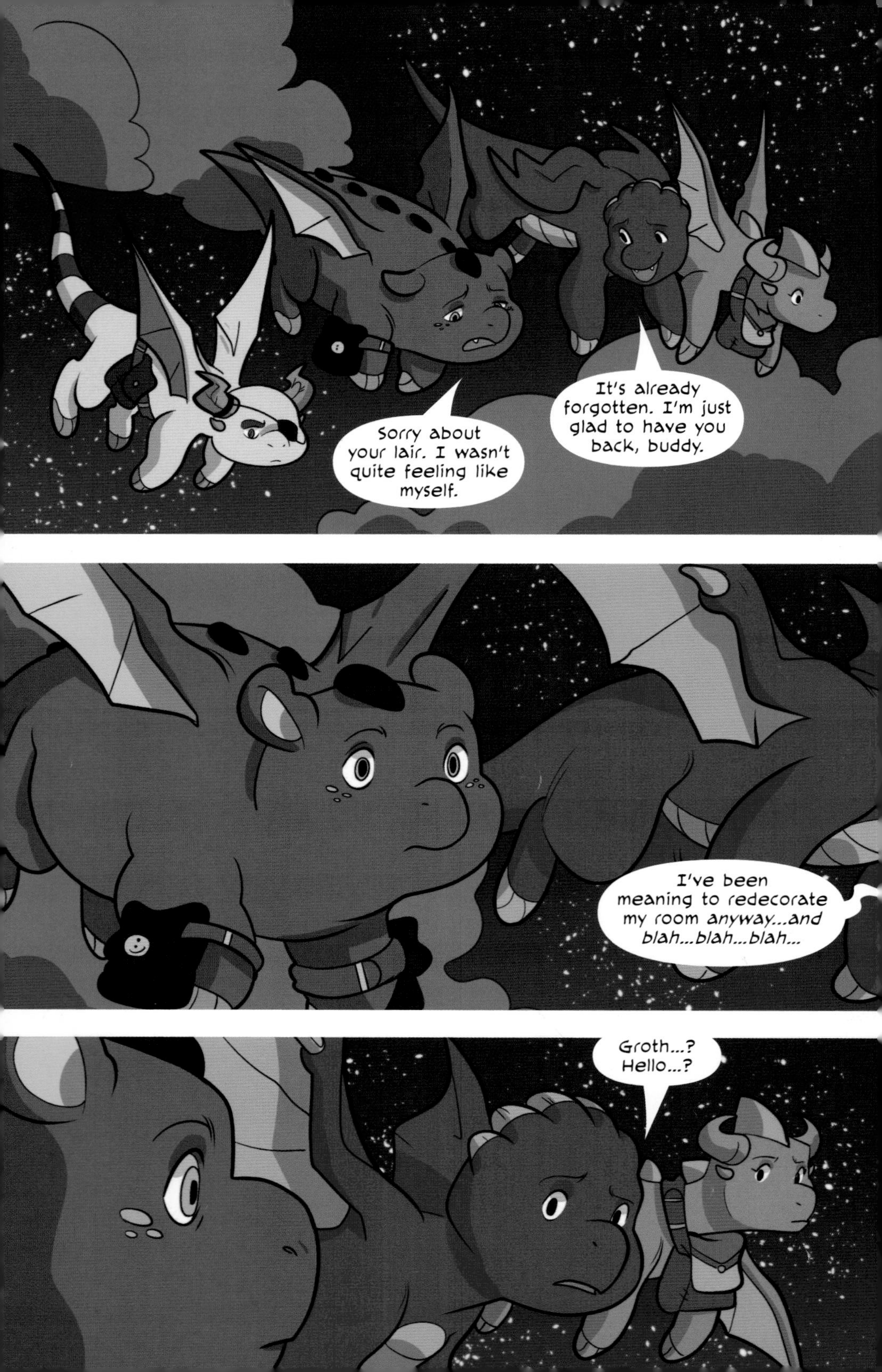
Sorry about your lair. I wasn't quite feeling like myself.
It's already forgotten. I'm just glad to have you back, buddy.
I've been meaning to redecorate my room anyway...and *blah...blah...blah...*
Groth...? Hello...?

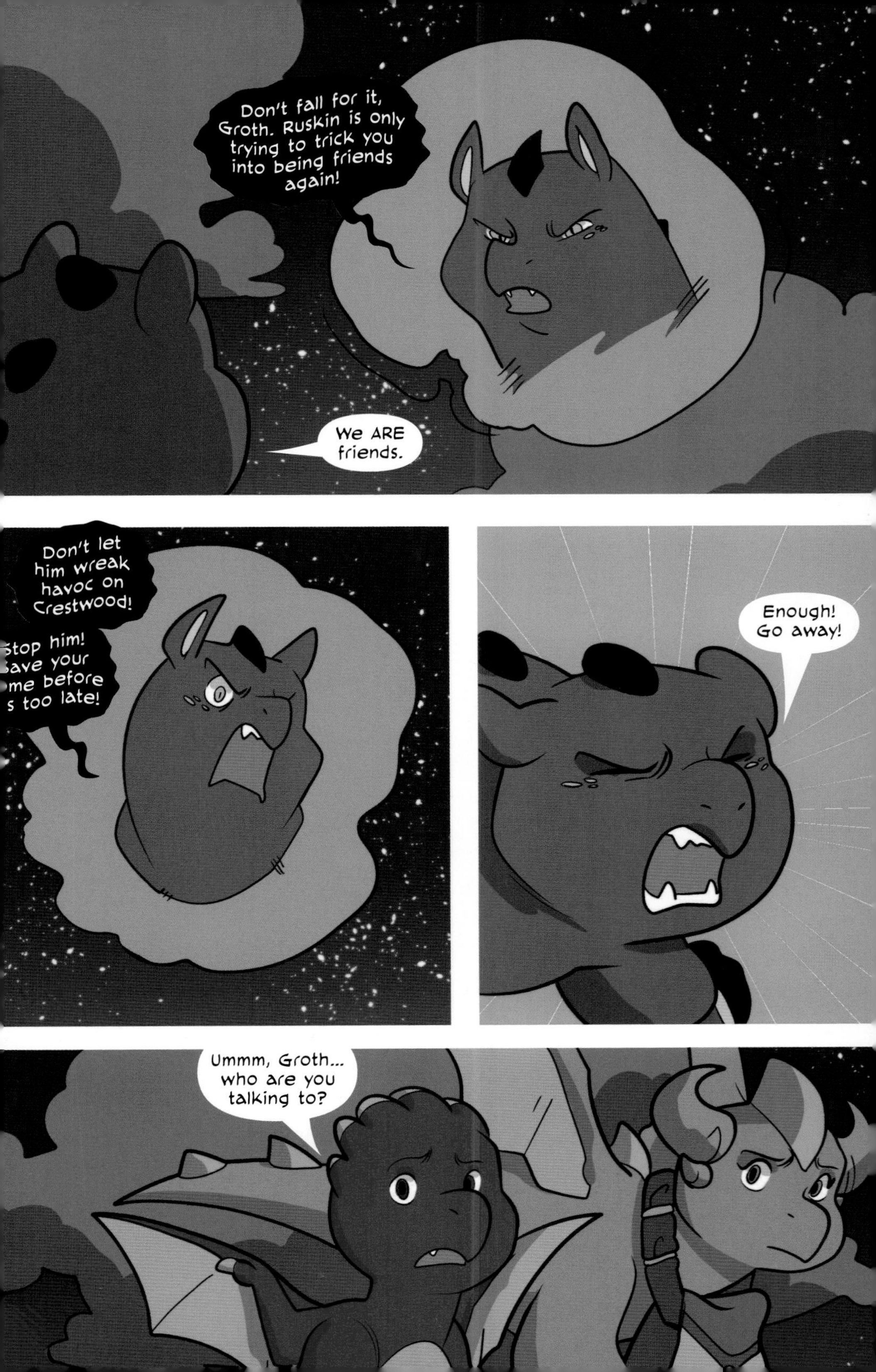
Don't fall for it, Groth. Ruskin is only trying to trick you into being friends again!
We ARE friends.
Don't let him wreak havoc on Crestwood!
Stop him! Save your home before it's too late!
Enough! Go away!
Ummm, Groth... who are you talking to?

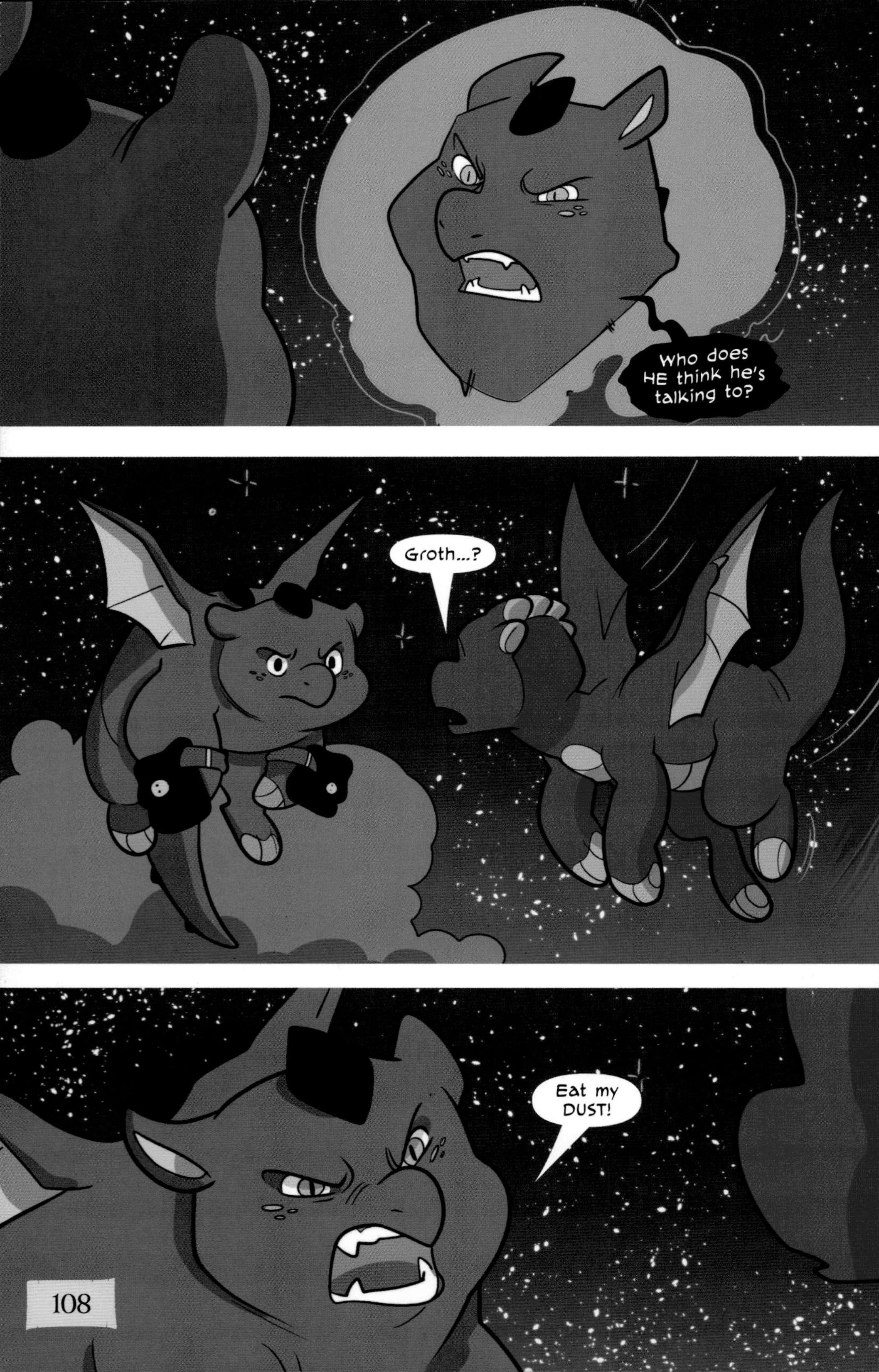
Who does HE think he's talking to?
Groth...?
Eat my DUST!

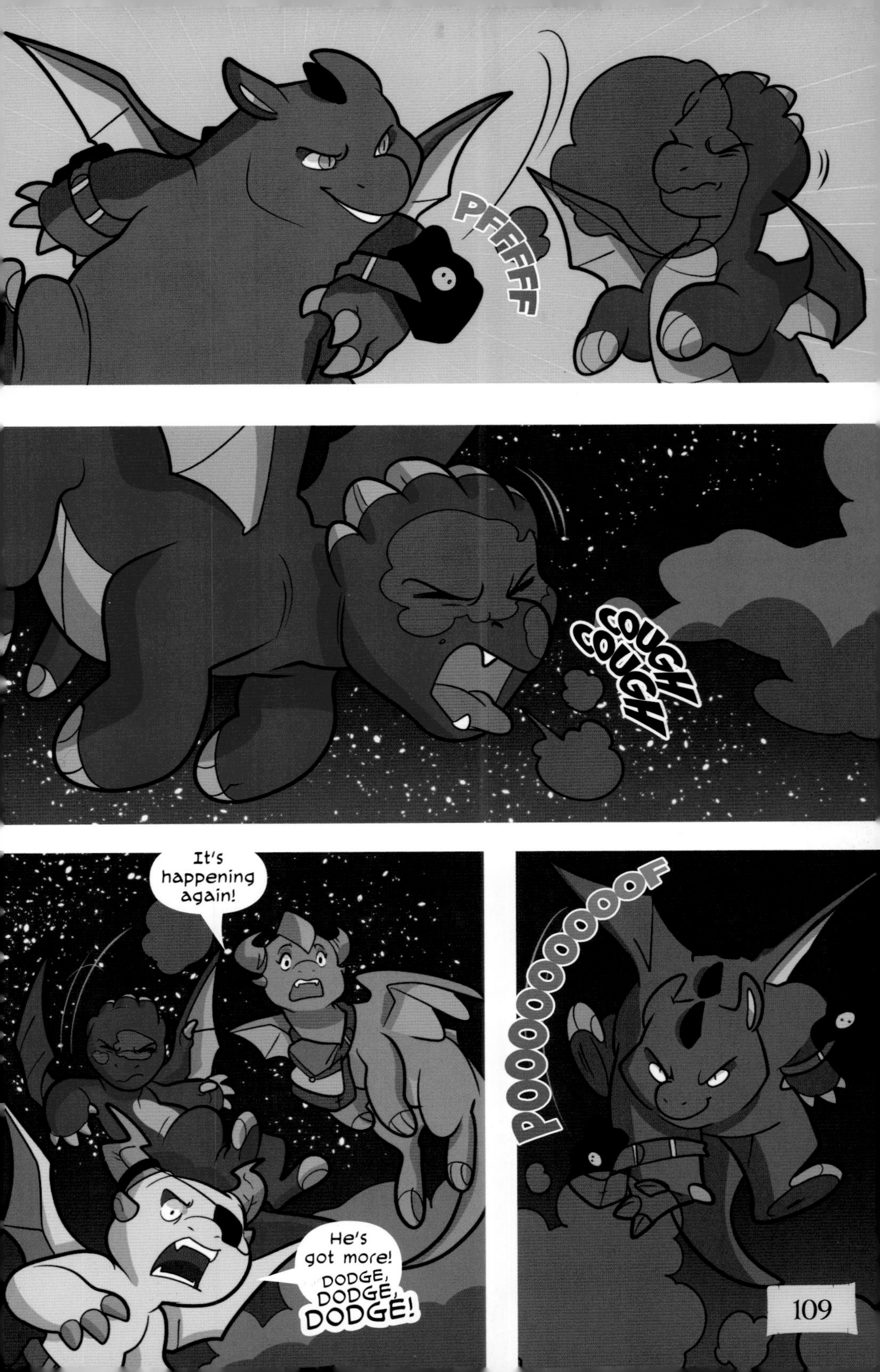
PFFFFFF
COUGH
COUGH
It's happening again!
He's got more! DODGE, DODGE, DODGE!
POOOOOOOOOOF

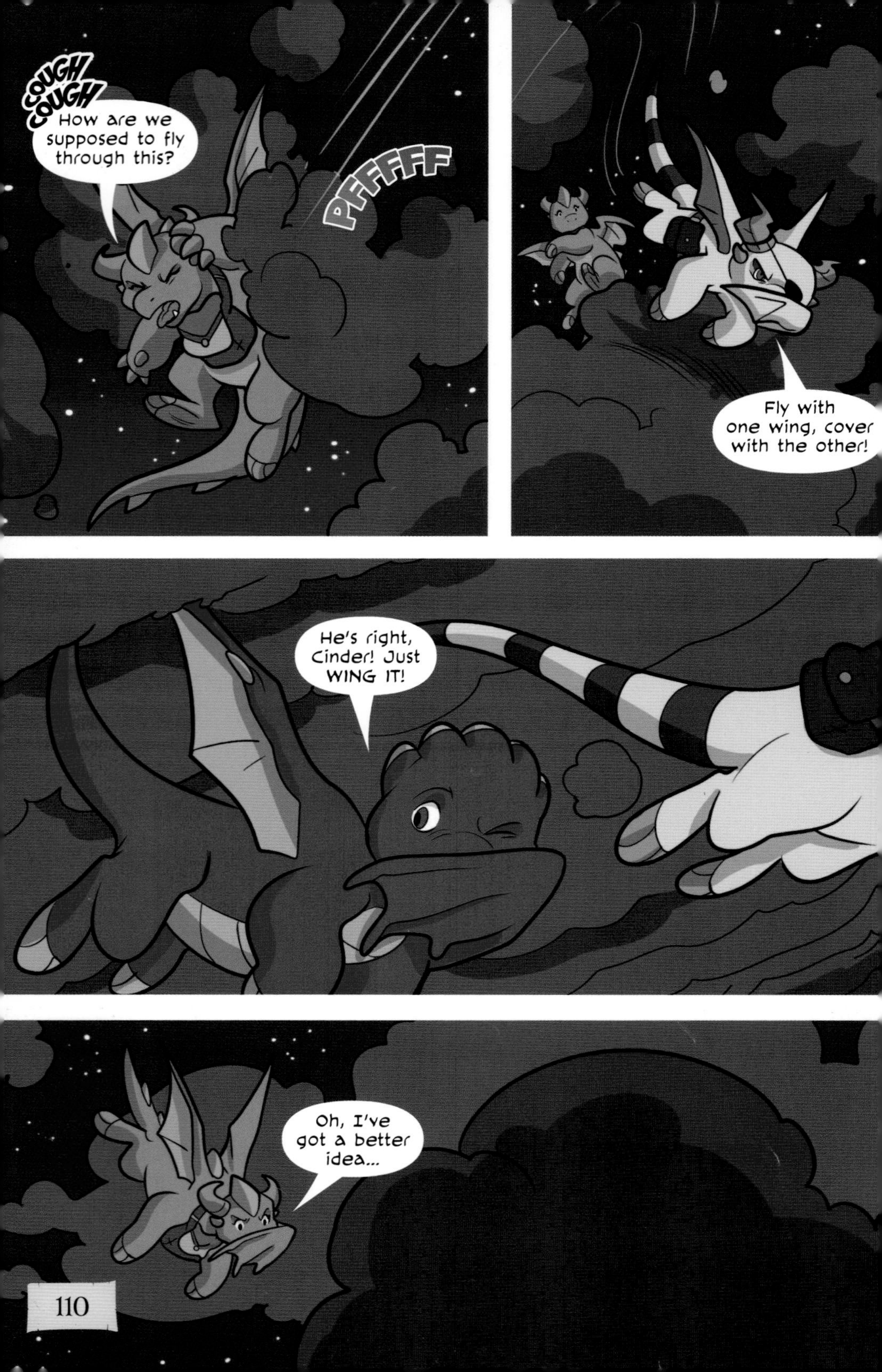
COUGH COUGH
How are we supposed to fly through this?
PFFFFF
Fly with one wing, cover with the other!
He's right, Cinder! Just WING IT!
Oh, I've got a better idea...

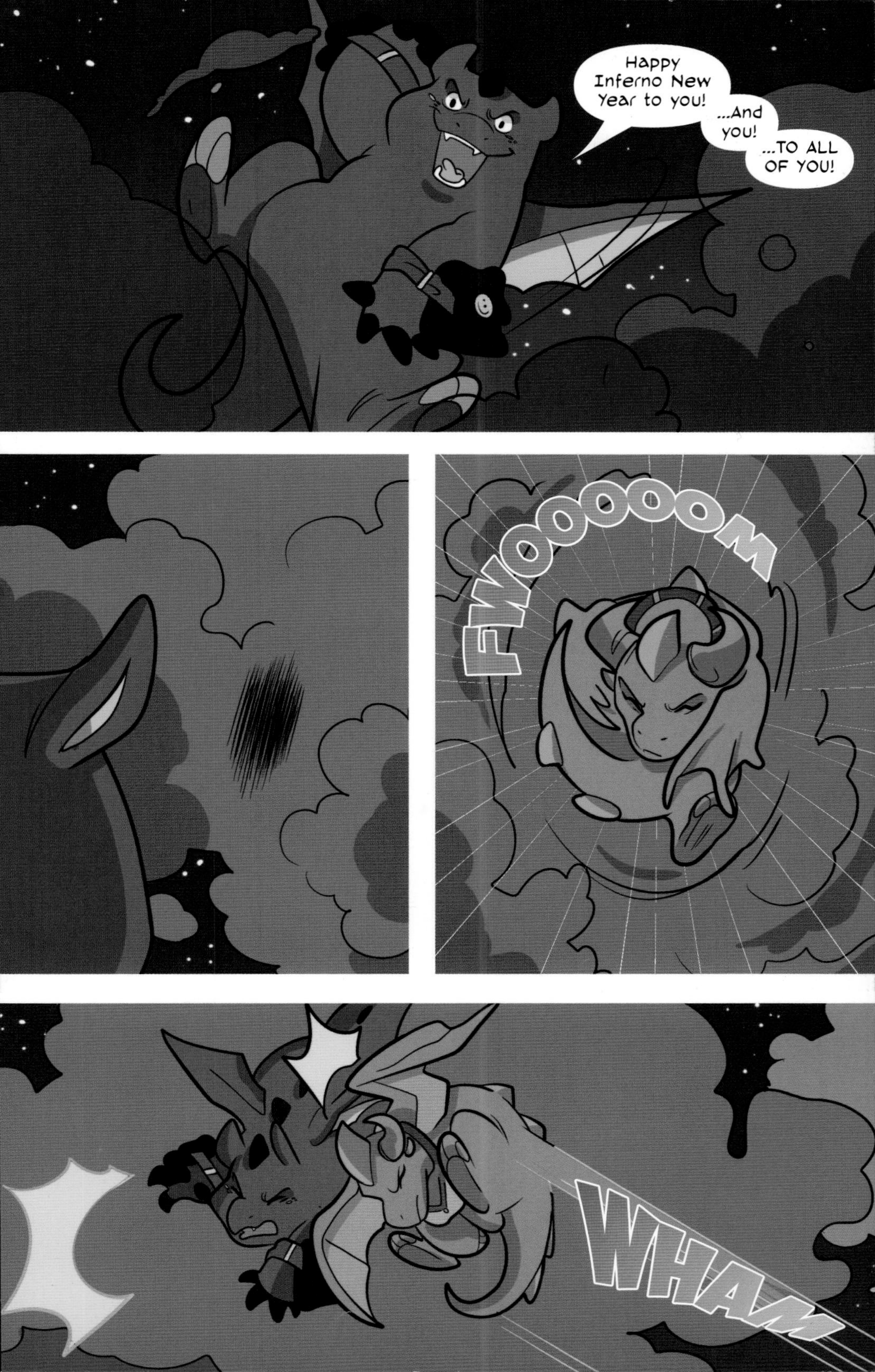
Happy Inferno New Year to you!
...And you!
...TO ALL OF YOU!
FWOOOOOM
WHAM

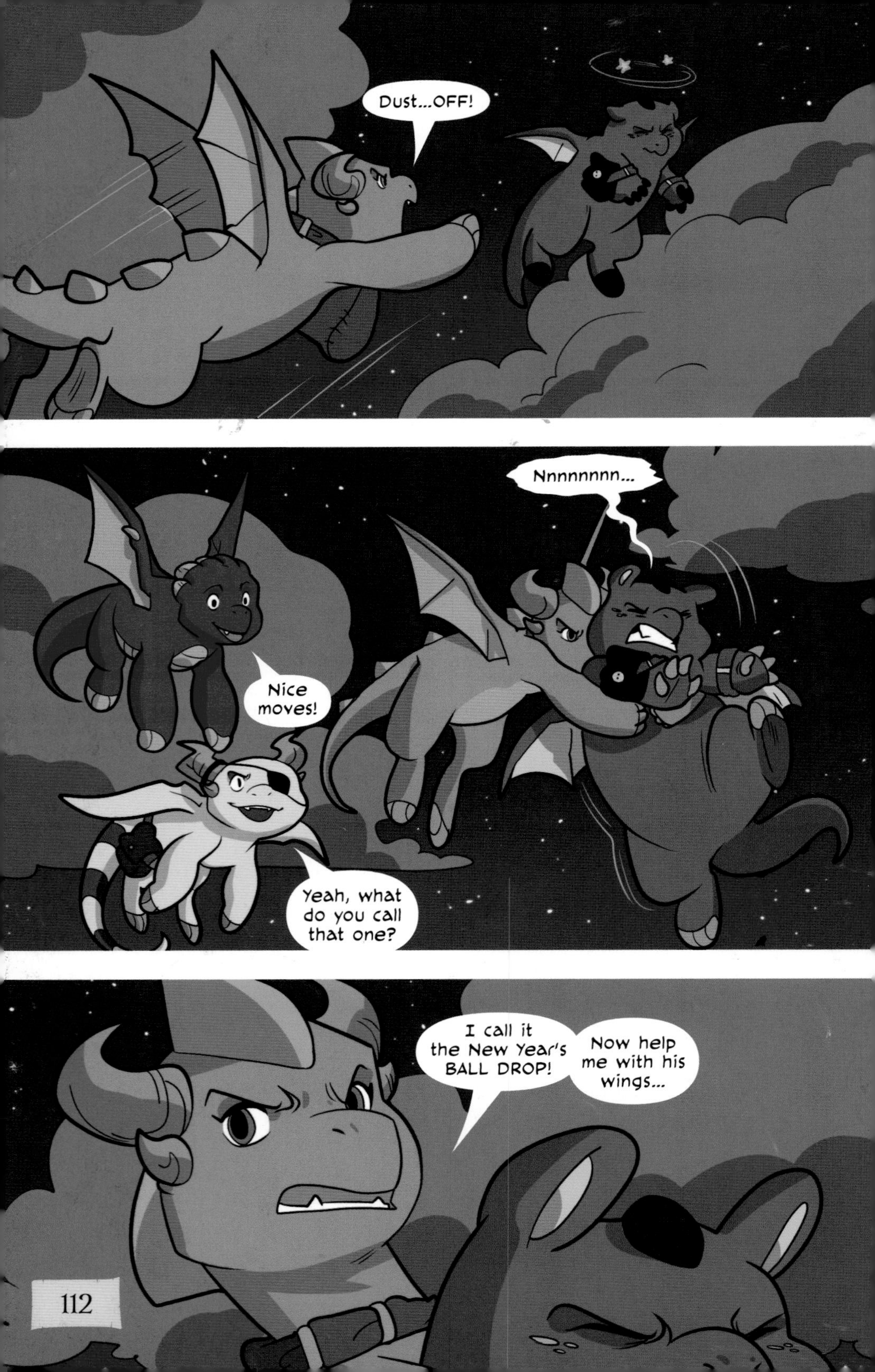

Dust...OFF!
Nnnnnnnn...
Nice moves!
Yeah, what do you call that one?
I call it the New Year's BALL DROP!
Now help me with his wings...

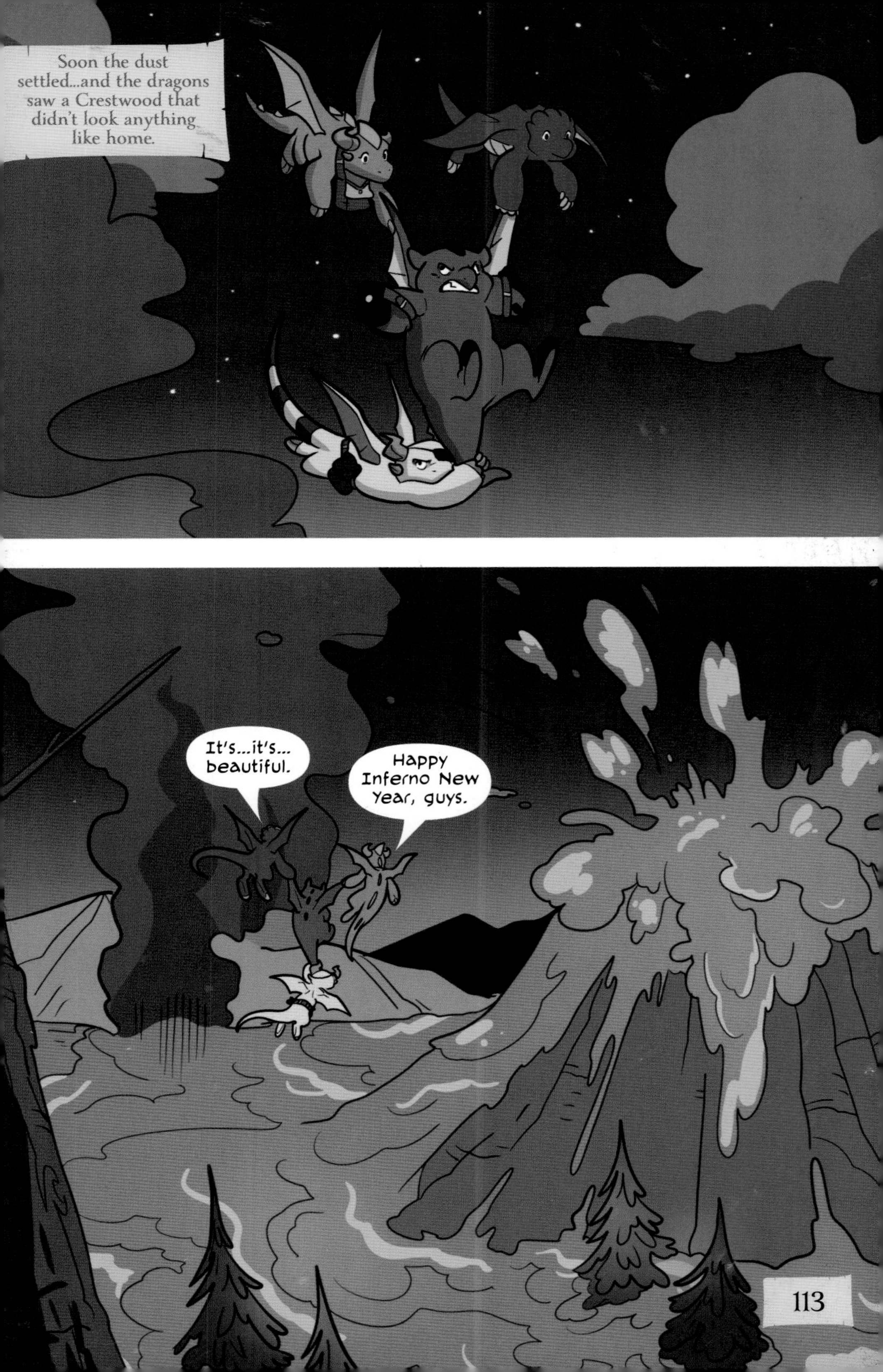
Soon the dust settled...and the dragons saw a Crestwood that didn't look anything like home.
It's...it's... beautiful.
Happy Inferno New Year, guys.

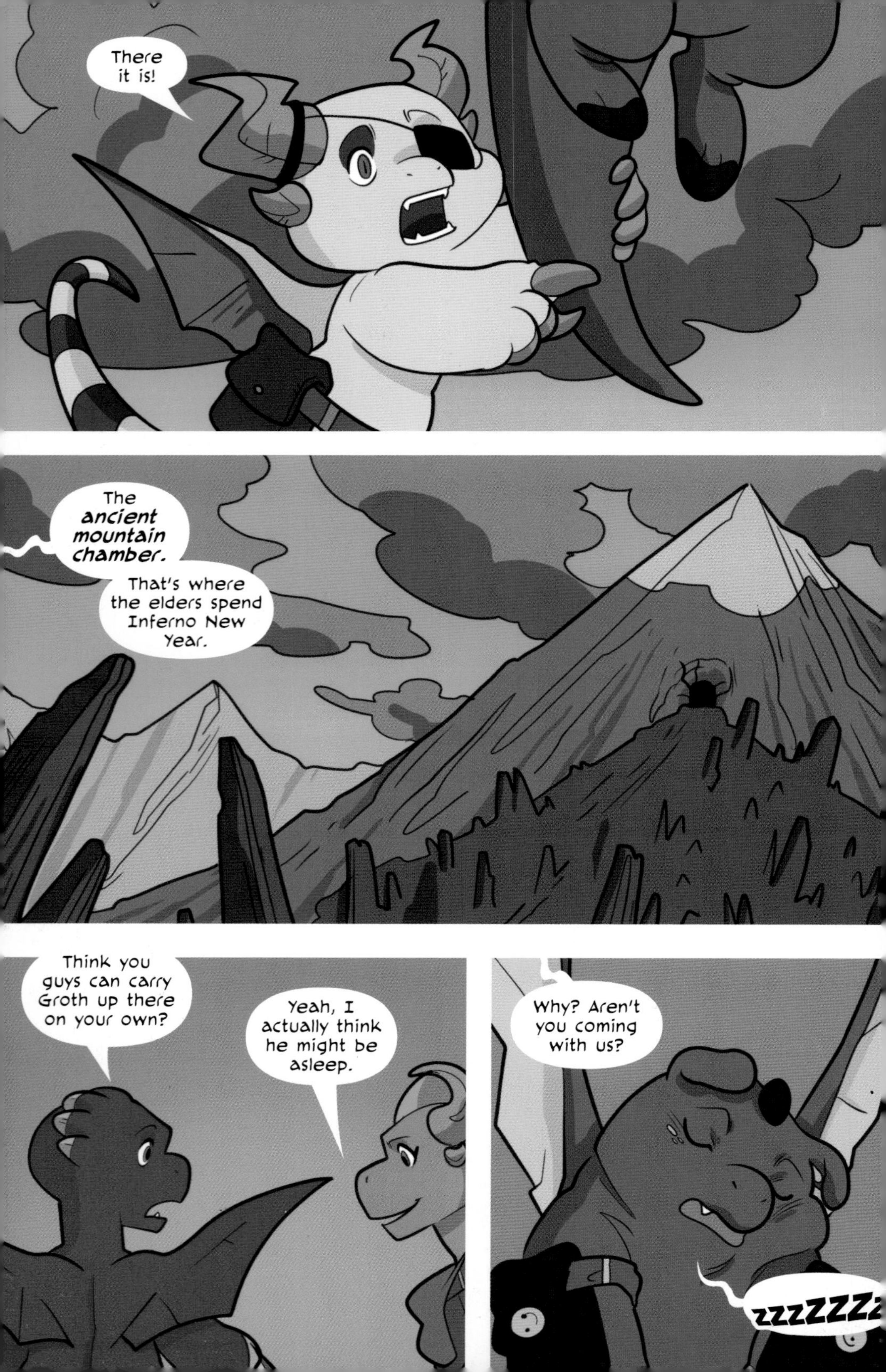
There it is!
The *ancient mountain chamber.*
That's where the elders spend Inferno New Year.
Think you guys can carry Groth up there on your own?
Yeah, I actually think he might be asleep.
Why? Aren't you coming with us?
ZZZZZZZ

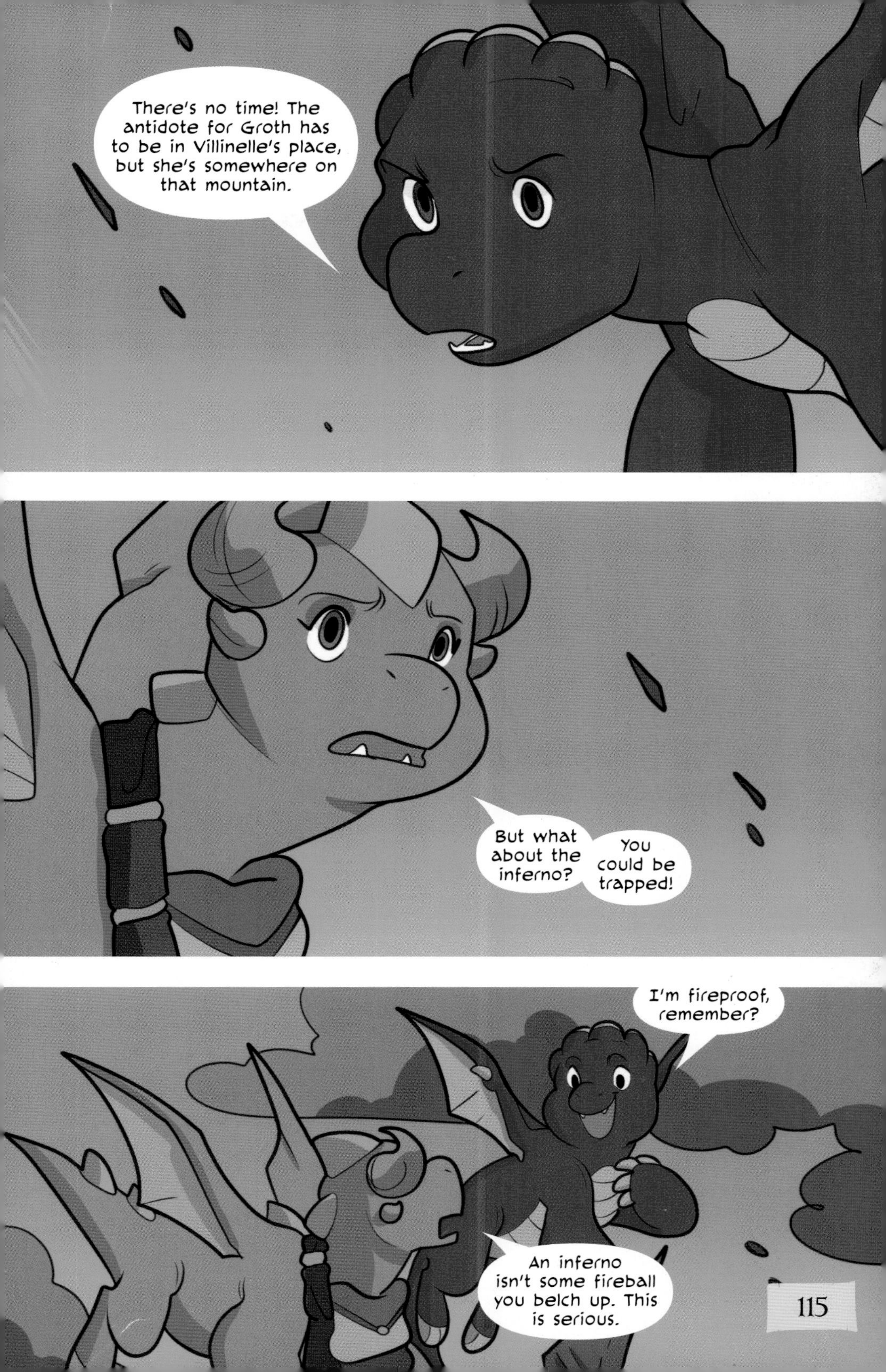

There's no time! The antidote for Groth has to be in Villinelle's place, but she's somewhere on that mountain.
But what about the inferno?
You could be trapped!
I'm fireproof, remember?
An inferno isn't some fireball you belch up. This is serious.

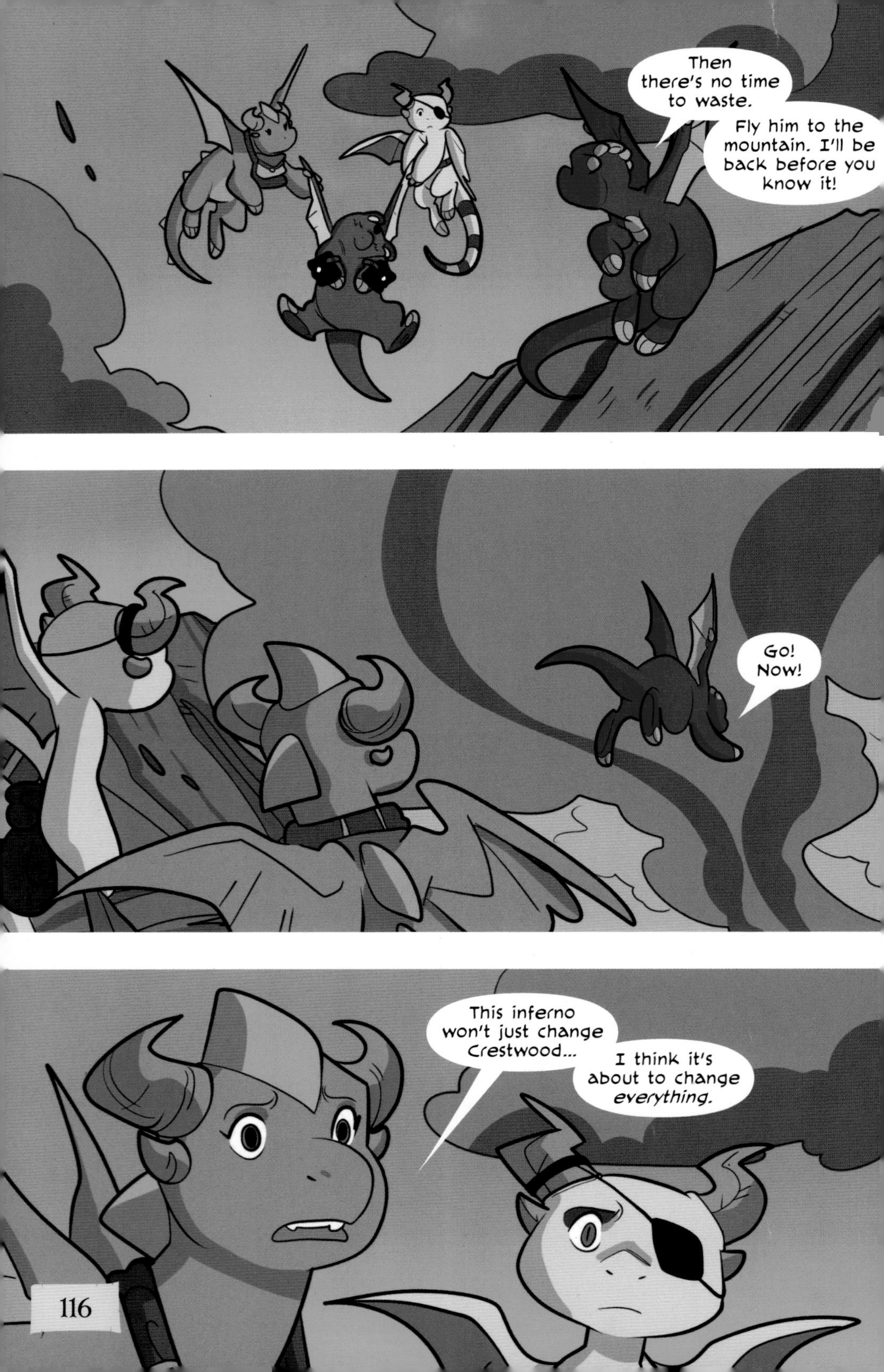
Then there's no time to waste.
Fly him to the mountain. I'll be back before you know it!
Go! Now!
This inferno won't just change Crestwood...
I think it's about to change *everything.*

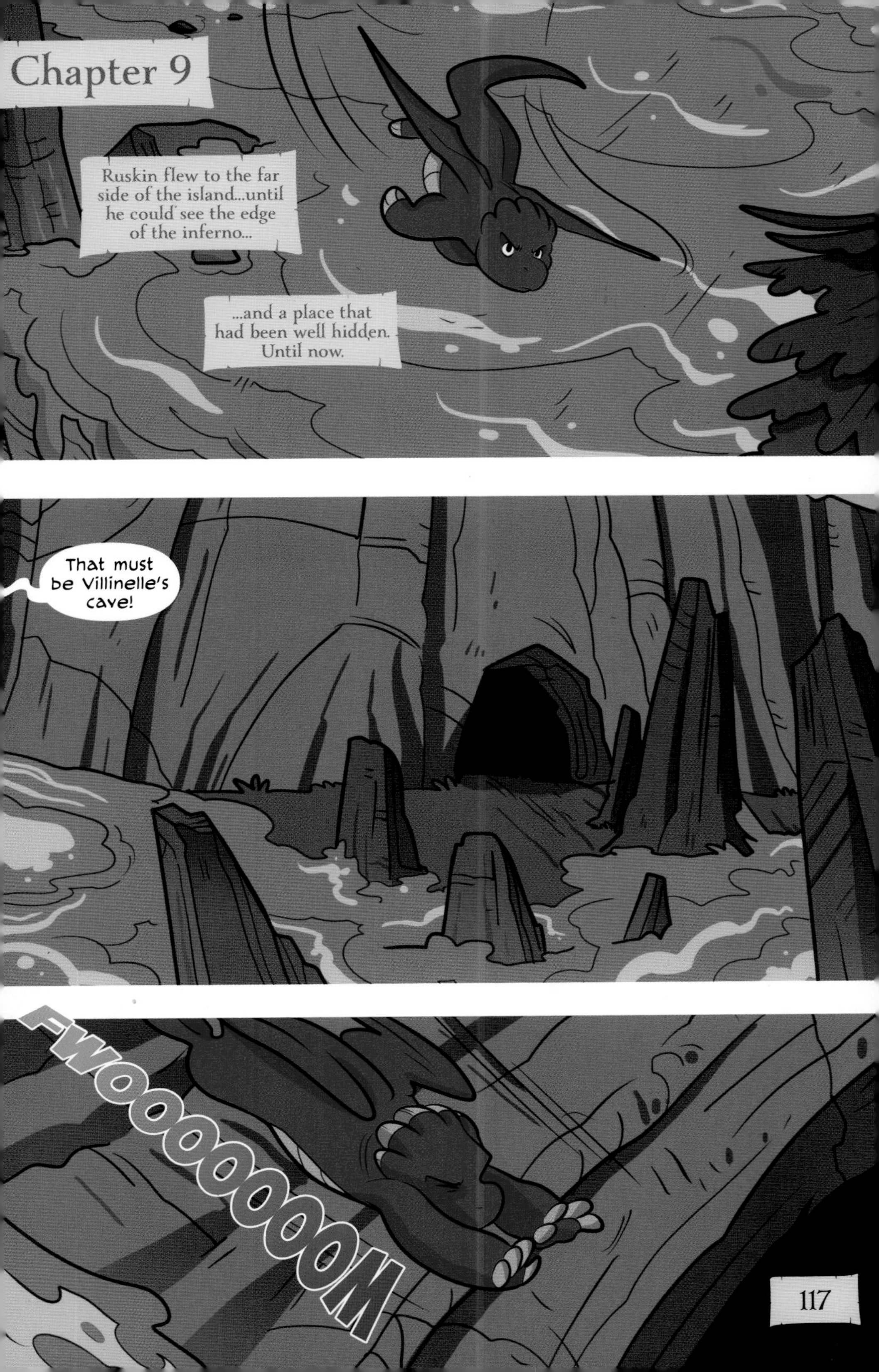
Chapter 9
Ruskin flew to the far side of the island...until he could see the edge of the inferno...
...and a place that had been well hidden. Until now.
That must be Villinelle's cave!
FWOOOOOOOM

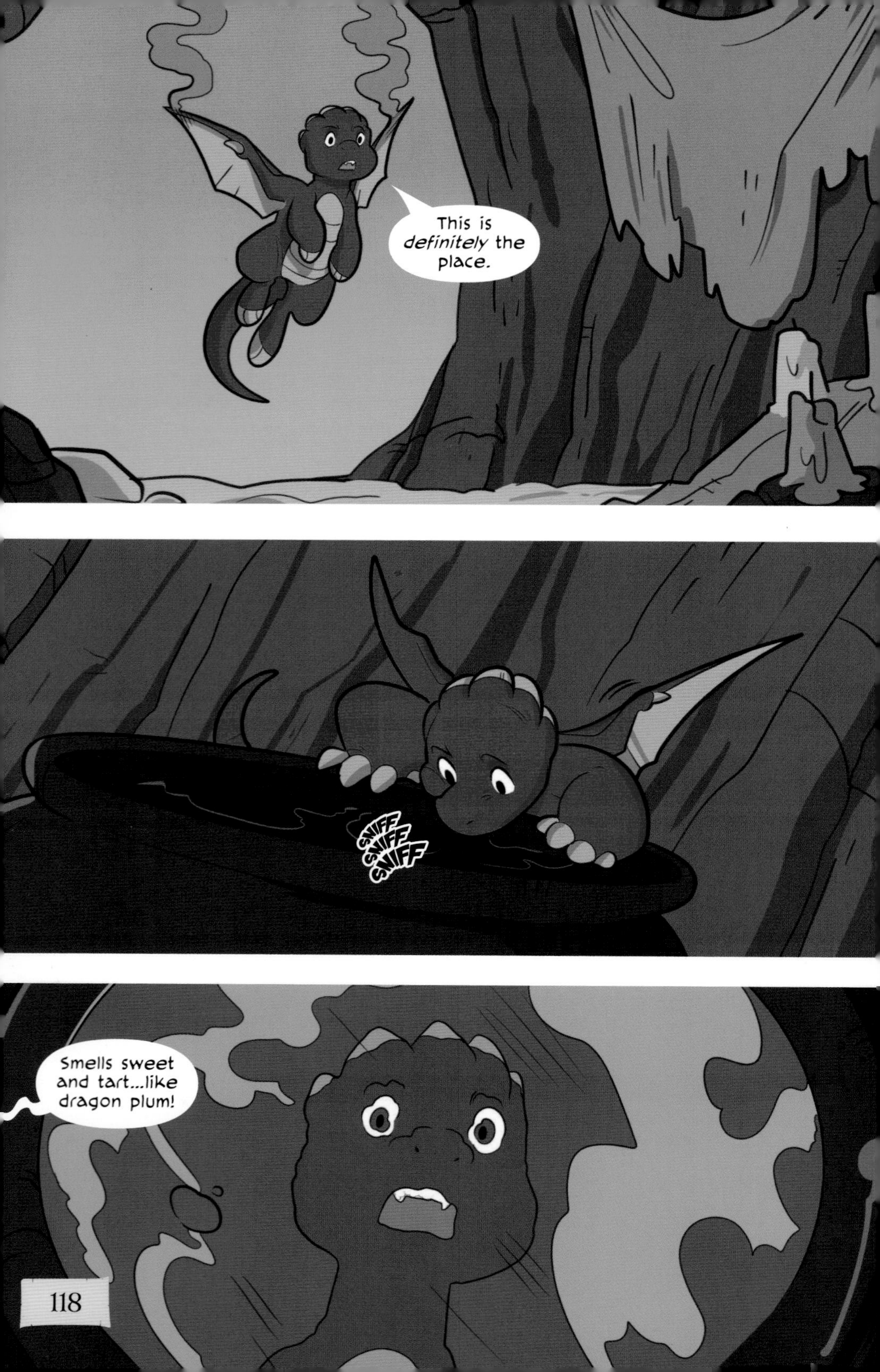
This is *definitely* the place.
SNIFF SNIFF SNIFF
Smells sweet and tart...like dragon plum!

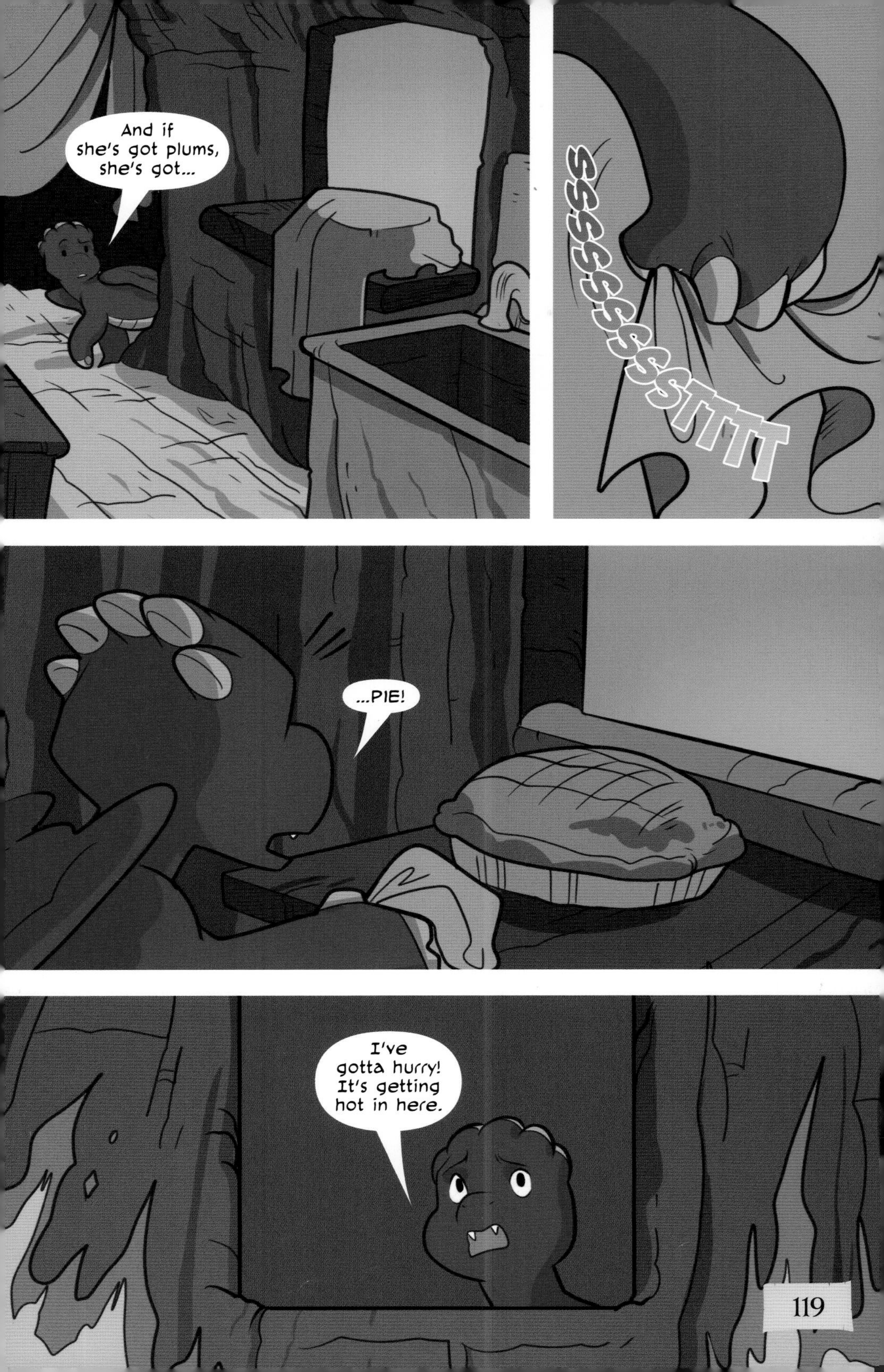
And if she's got plums, she's got...
SSSSSSSSTTTT
...PIE!
I've gotta hurry! It's getting hot in here.

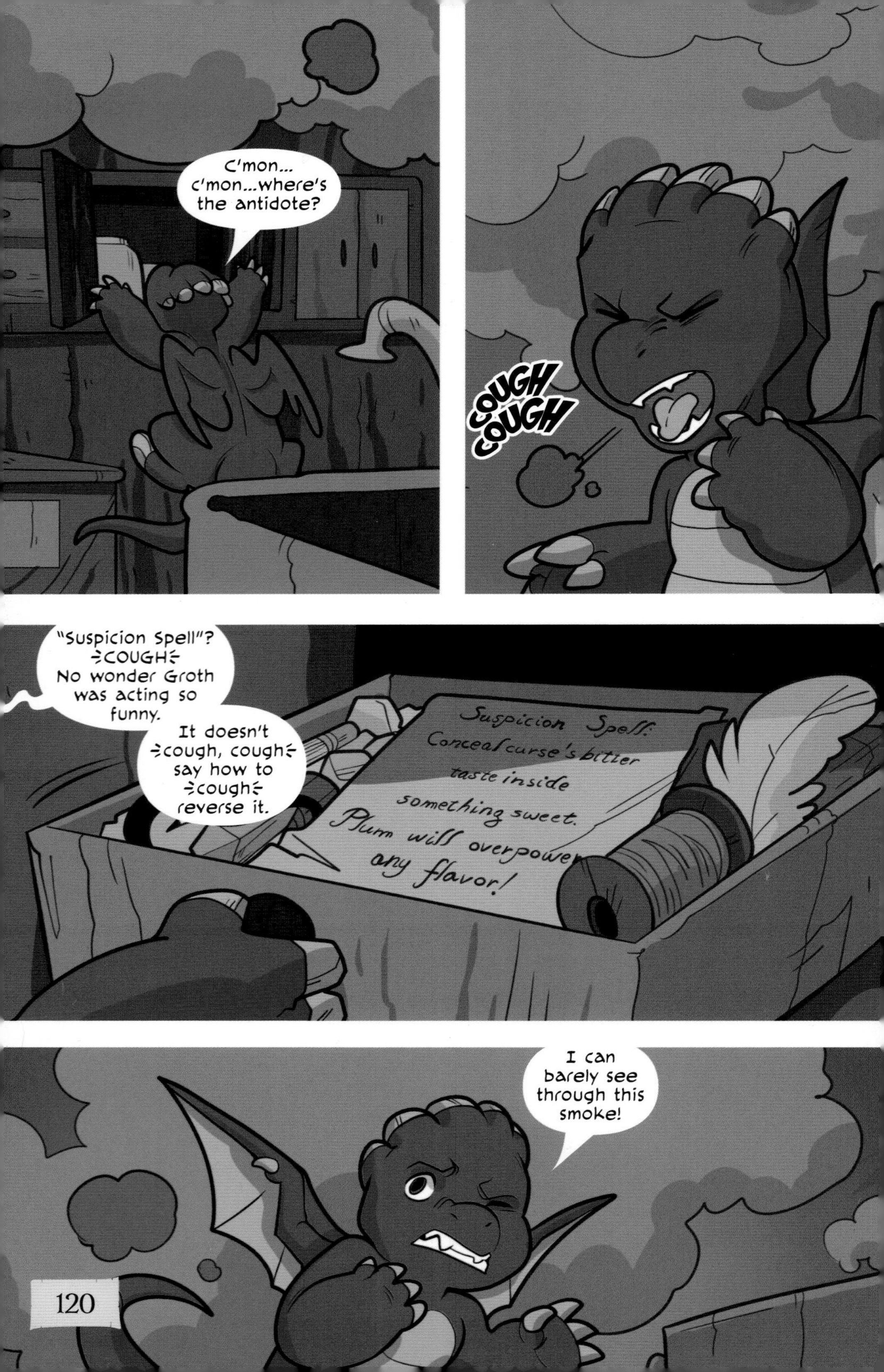
C'mon... c'mon...where's the antidote?
COUGH COUGH
"Suspicion Spell"? ⋛COUGH⋚ No wonder Groth was acting so funny.
It doesn't ⋛cough, cough⋚ say how to ⋛cough⋚ reverse it.
Suspicion Spell: Conceal curse's bitter taste inside something sweet. Plum will overpower any flavor!
I can barely see through this smoke!

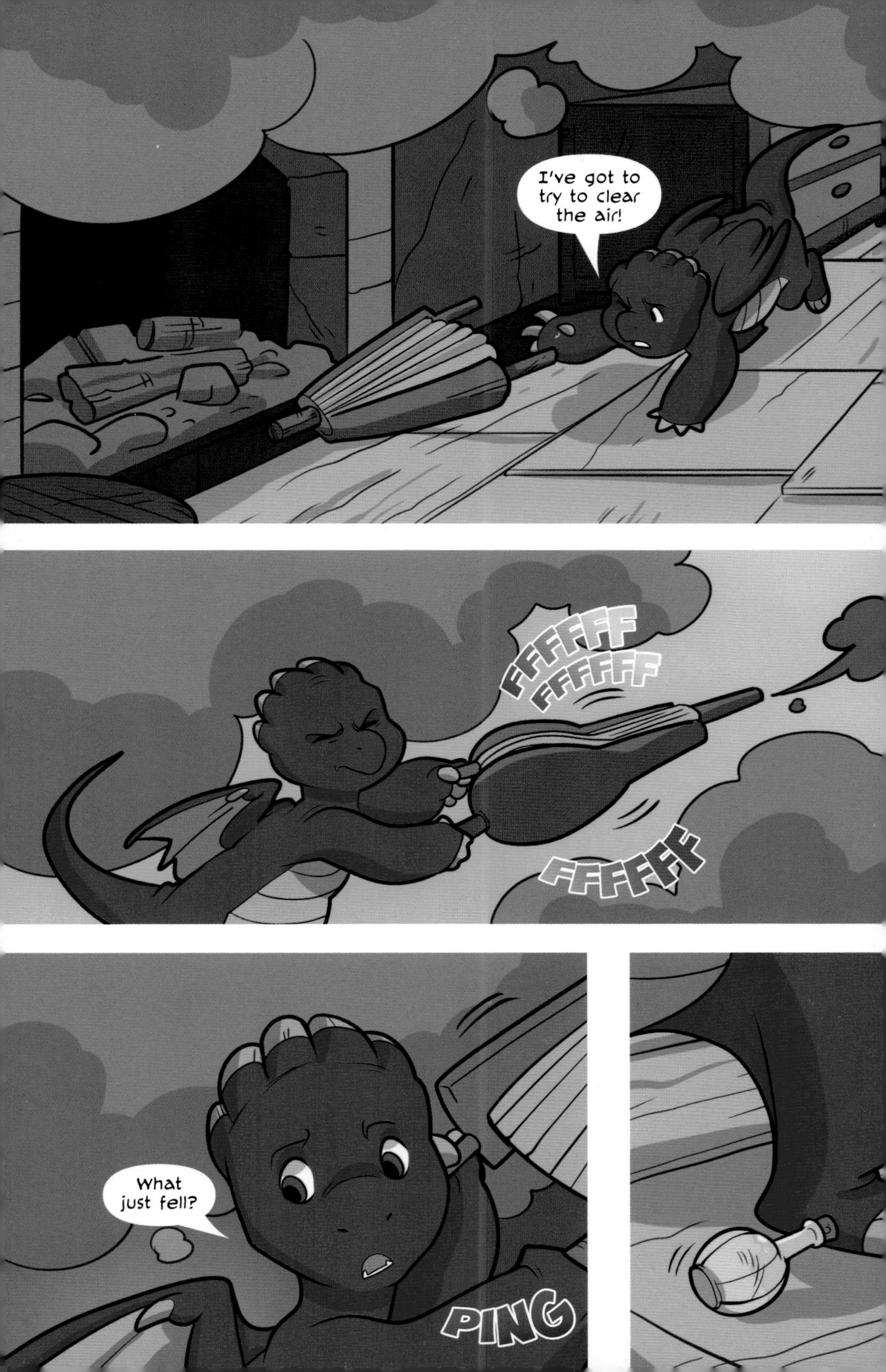

I've got to try to clear the air!
FFFFFF
FFFFFF
FFFFFF
What just fell?
PING

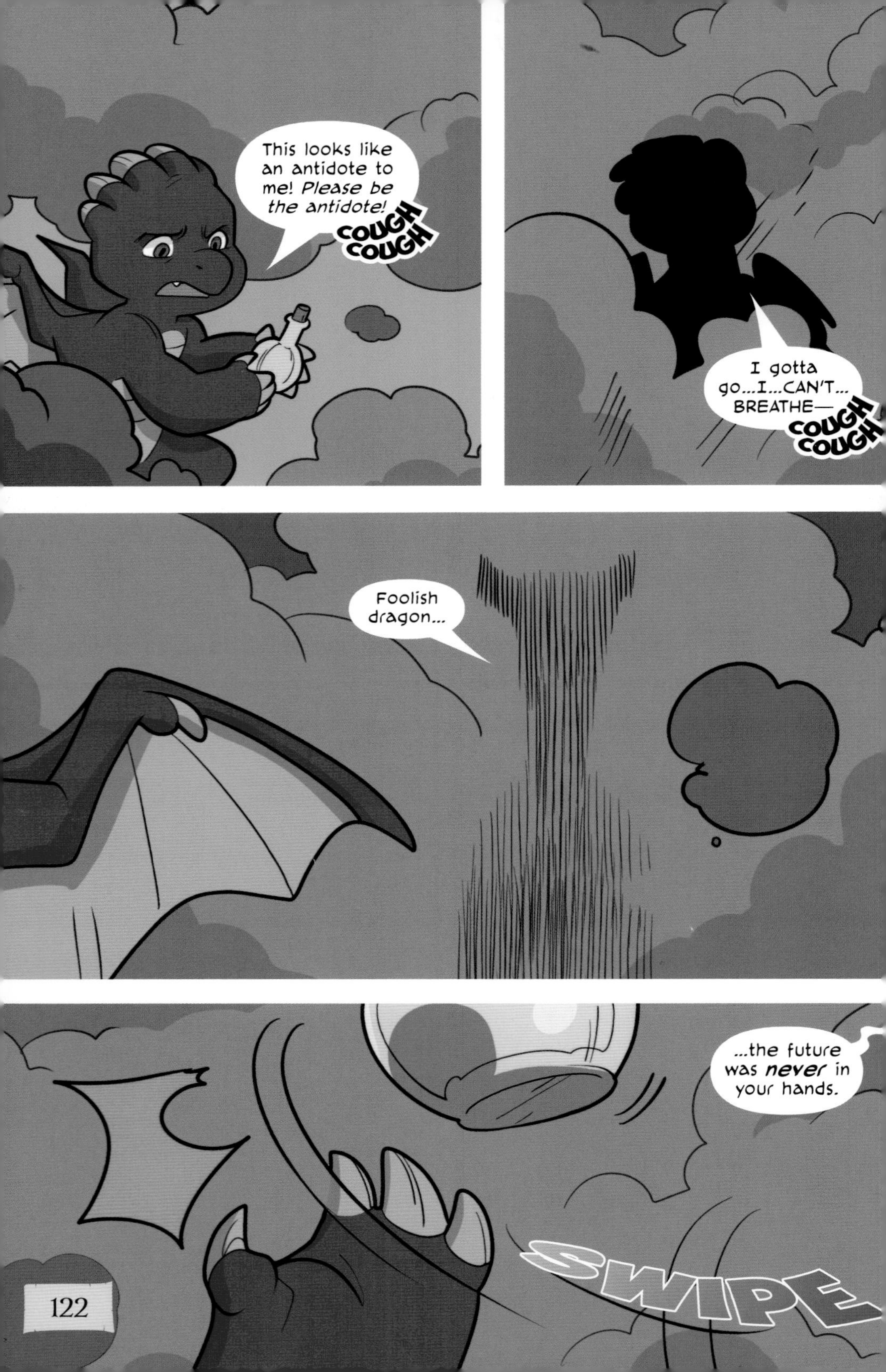
This looks like an antidote to me! *Please be the antidote!*
COUGH COUGH
I gotta go...I...CAN'T... BREATHE—
COUGH COUGH
Foolish dragon...
...the future was ***never*** in your hands.
SWIPE

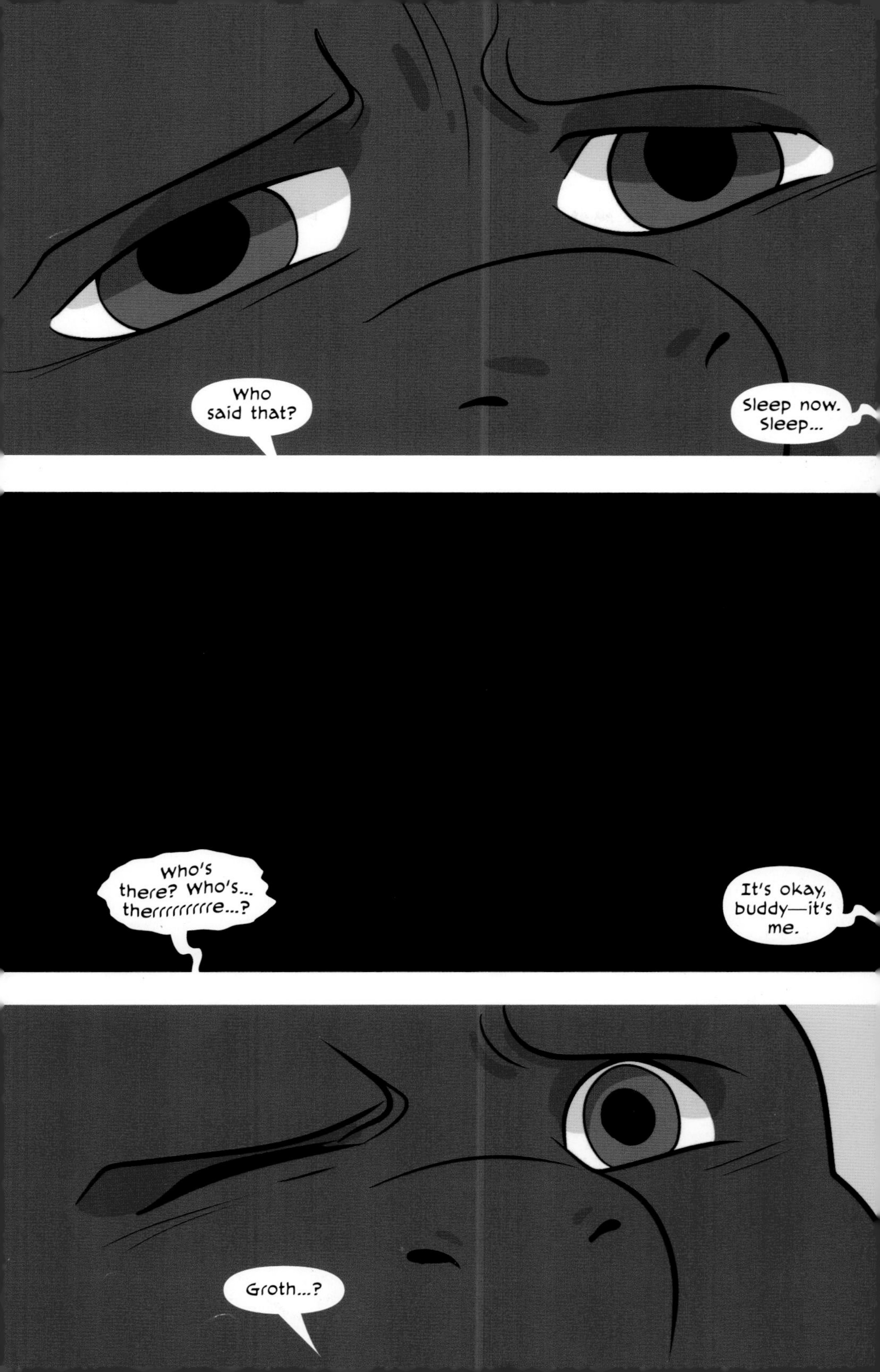
Who said that?
Sleep now. Sleep...
Who's there? Who's... therrrrrrrrre...?
It's okay, buddy—it's me.
Groth...?

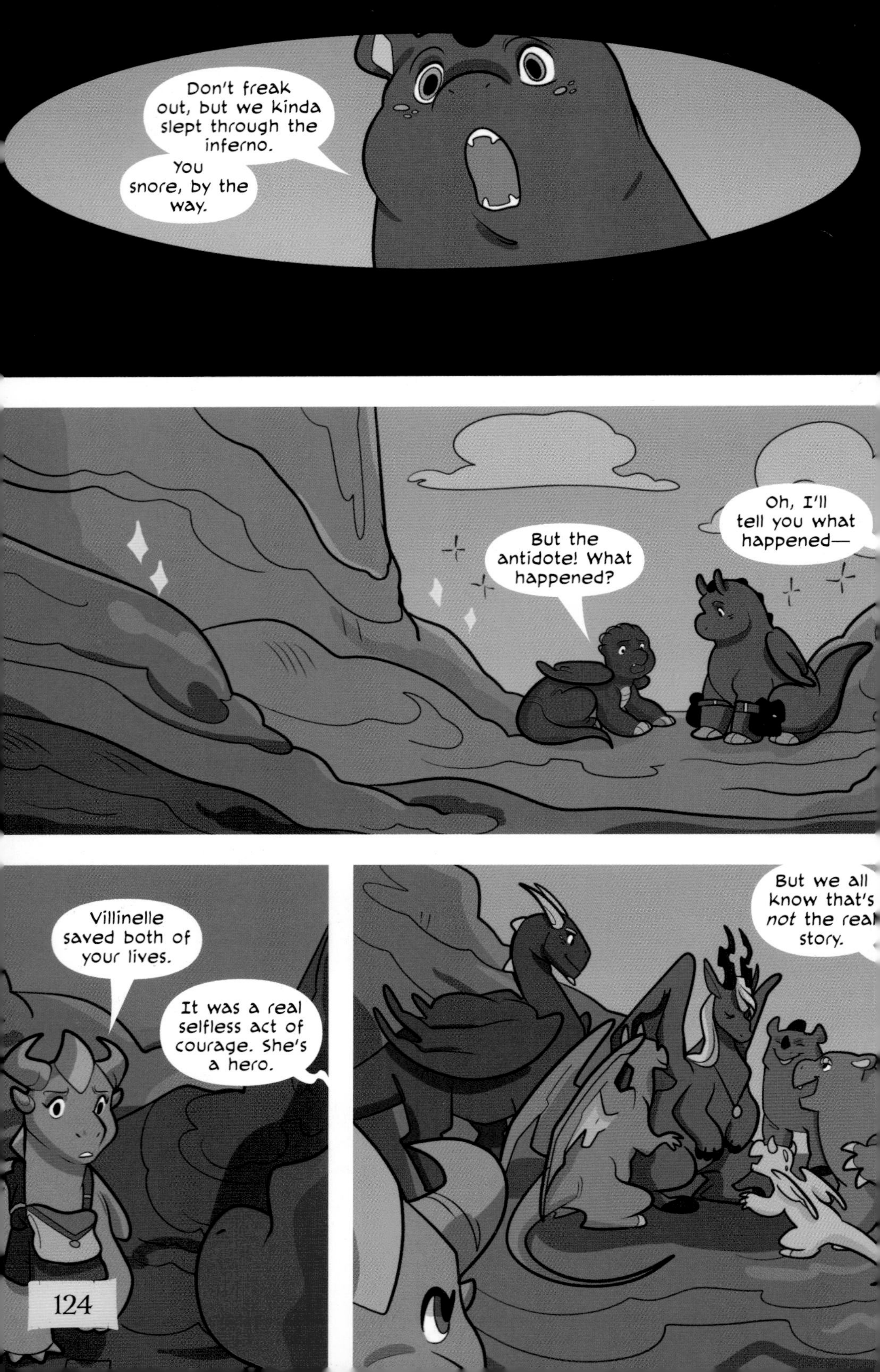

Don't freak out, but we kinda slept through the inferno.
You snore, by the way.
But the antidote! What happened?
Oh, I'll tell you what happened—
Villinelle saved both of your lives.
It was a real selfless act of courage. She's a hero.
But we all know that's *not* the real story.

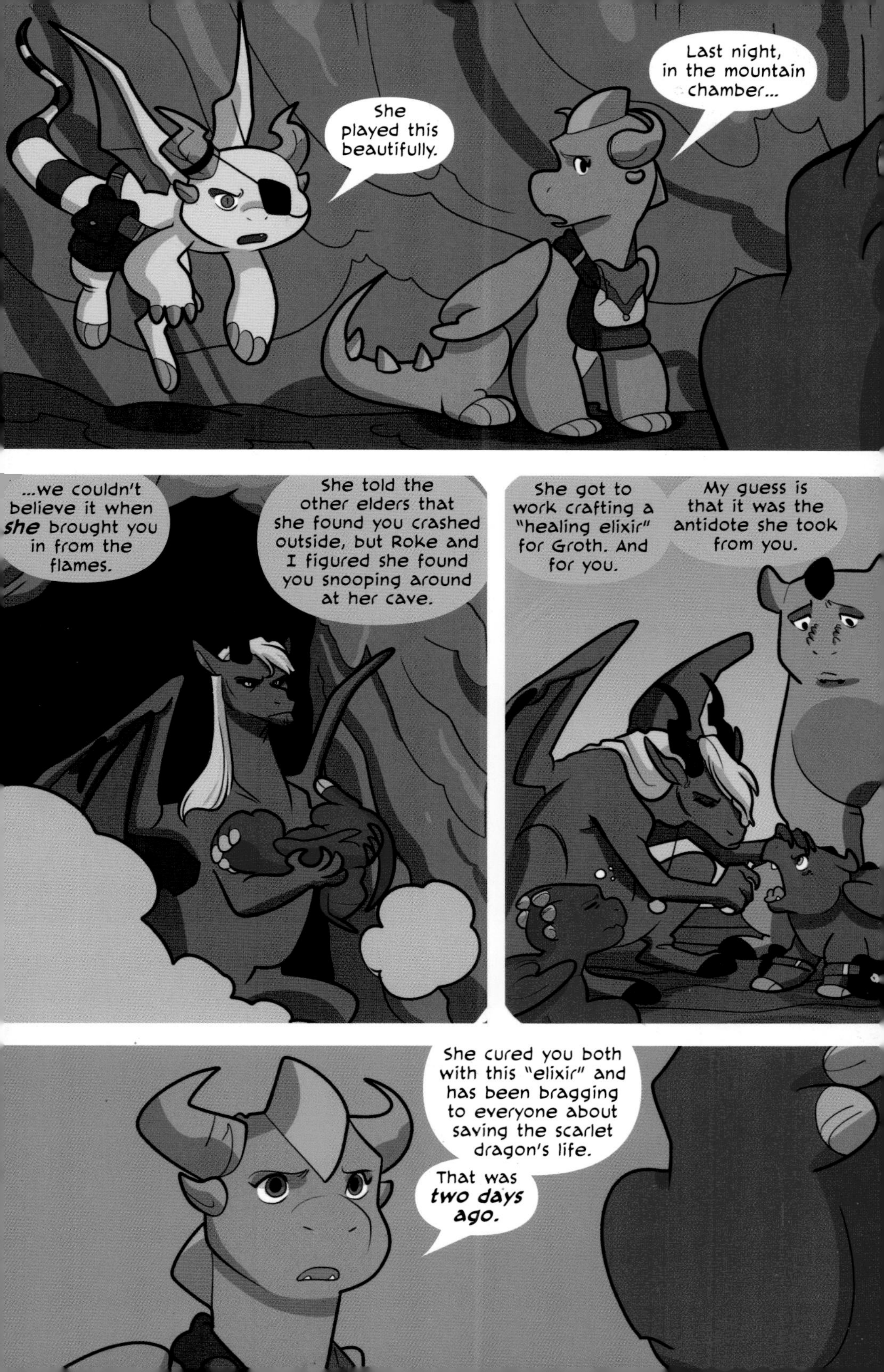

She played this beautifully.
Last night, in the mountain chamber...
...we couldn't believe it when *she* brought you in from the flames.
She told the other elders that she found you crashed outside, but Roke and I figured she found you snooping around at her cave.
She got to work crafting a "healing elixir" for Groth. And for you.
My guess is that it was the antidote she took from you.
She cured you both with this "elixir" and has been bragging to everyone about saving the scarlet dragon's life.
That was *two days ago.*

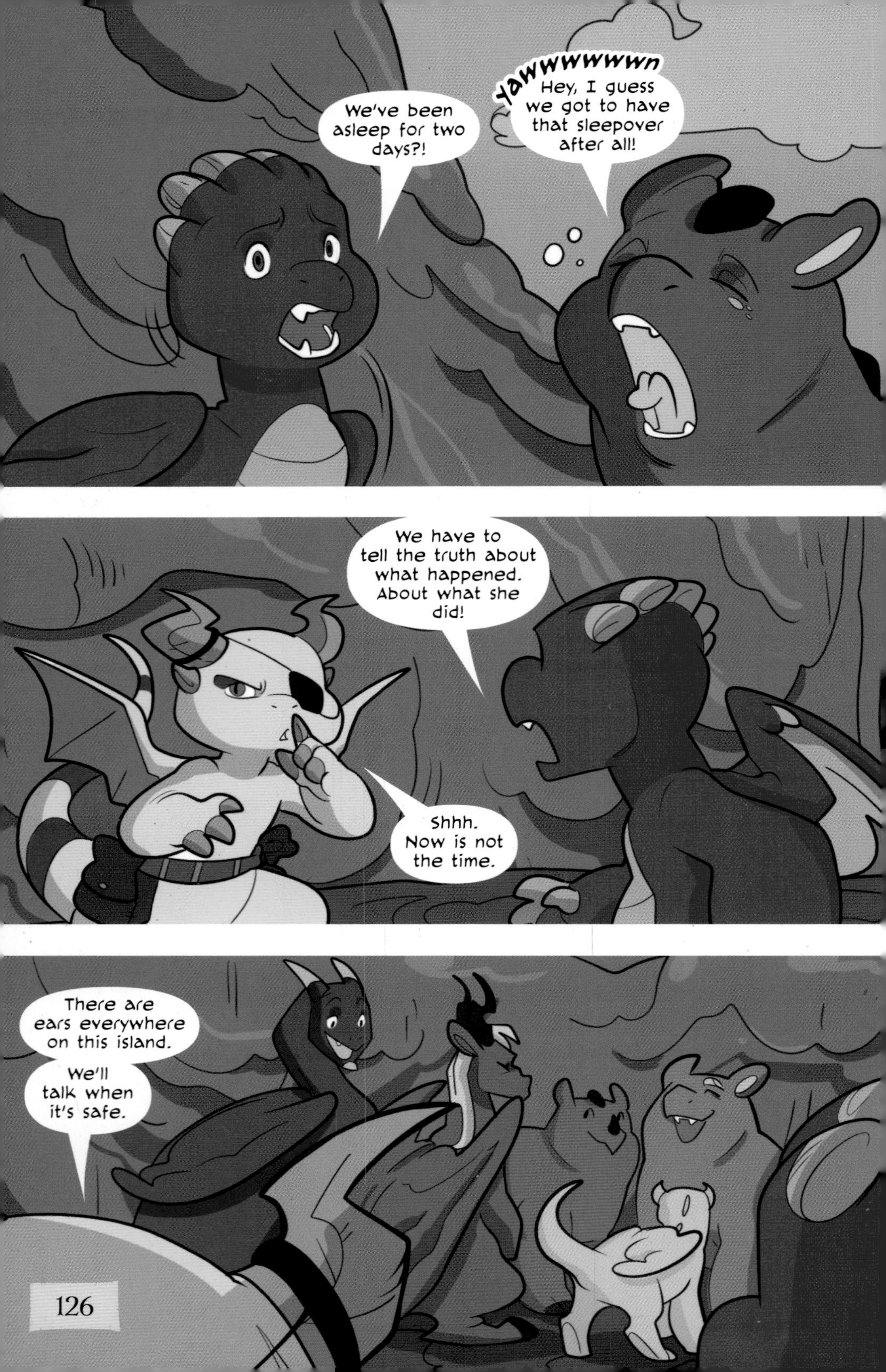
We've been asleep for two days?!
YAWWWWWWN
Hey, I guess we got to have that sleepover after all!
We have to tell the truth about what happened. About what she did!
Shhh. Now is not the time.
There are ears everywhere on this island.
We'll talk when it's safe.

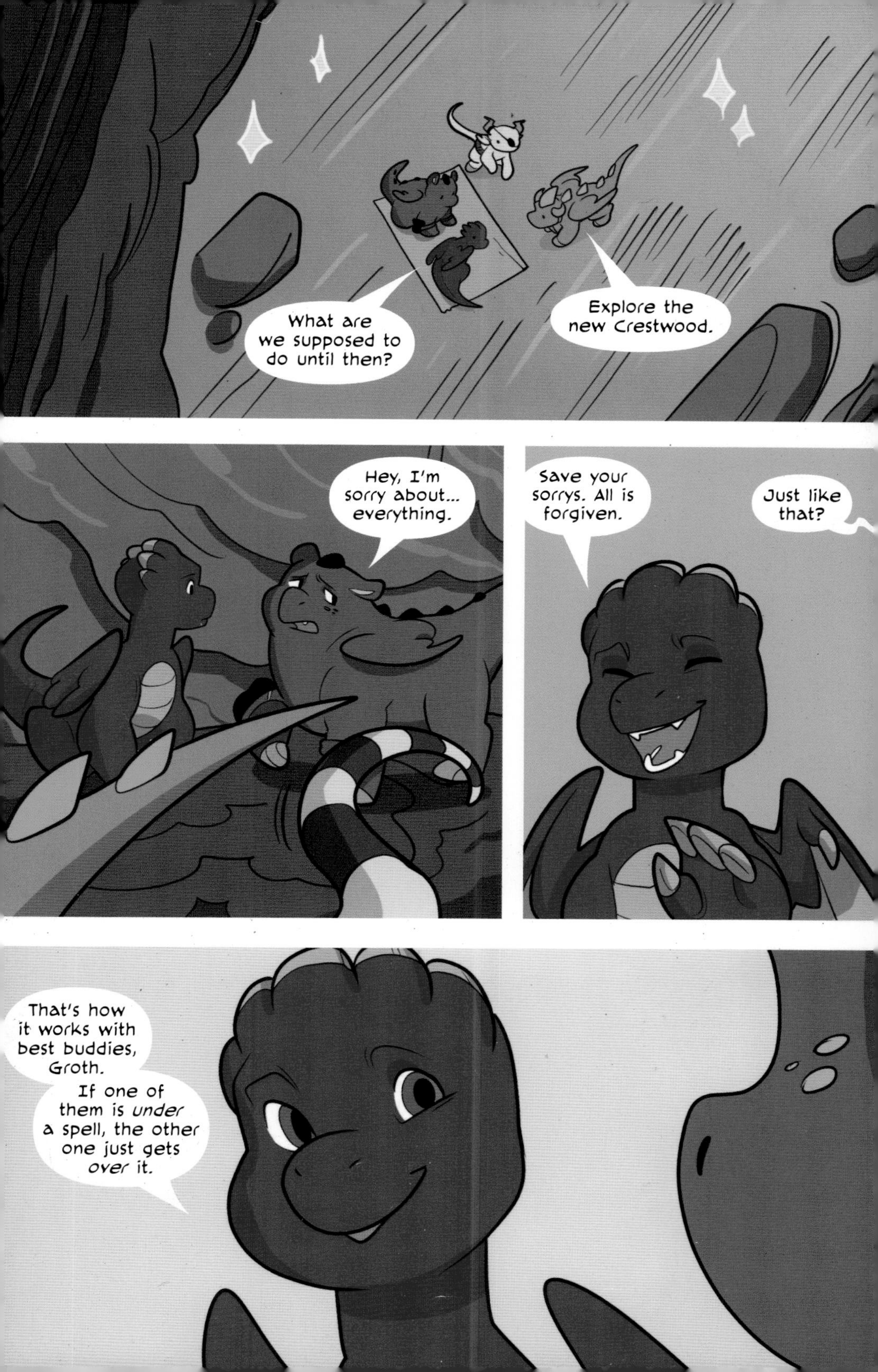
What are we supposed to do until then?
Explore the new Crestwood.
Hey, I'm sorry about... everything.
Save your sorrys. All is forgiven.
Just like that?
That's how it works with best buddies, Groth.
If one of them is *under* a spell, the other one just gets *over* it.

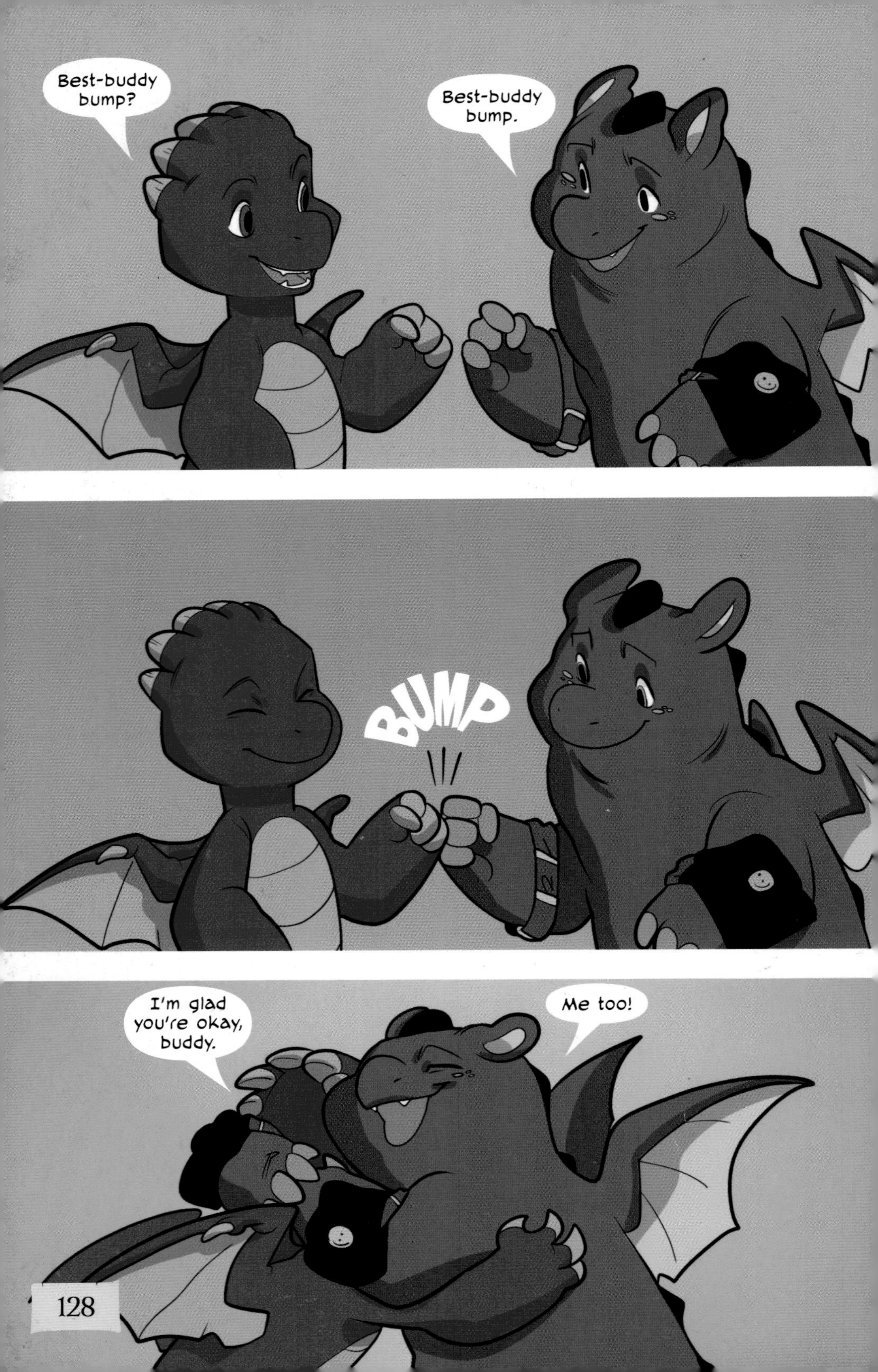
Best-buddy bump?
Best-buddy bump.
BUMP
I'm glad you're okay, buddy.
Me too!

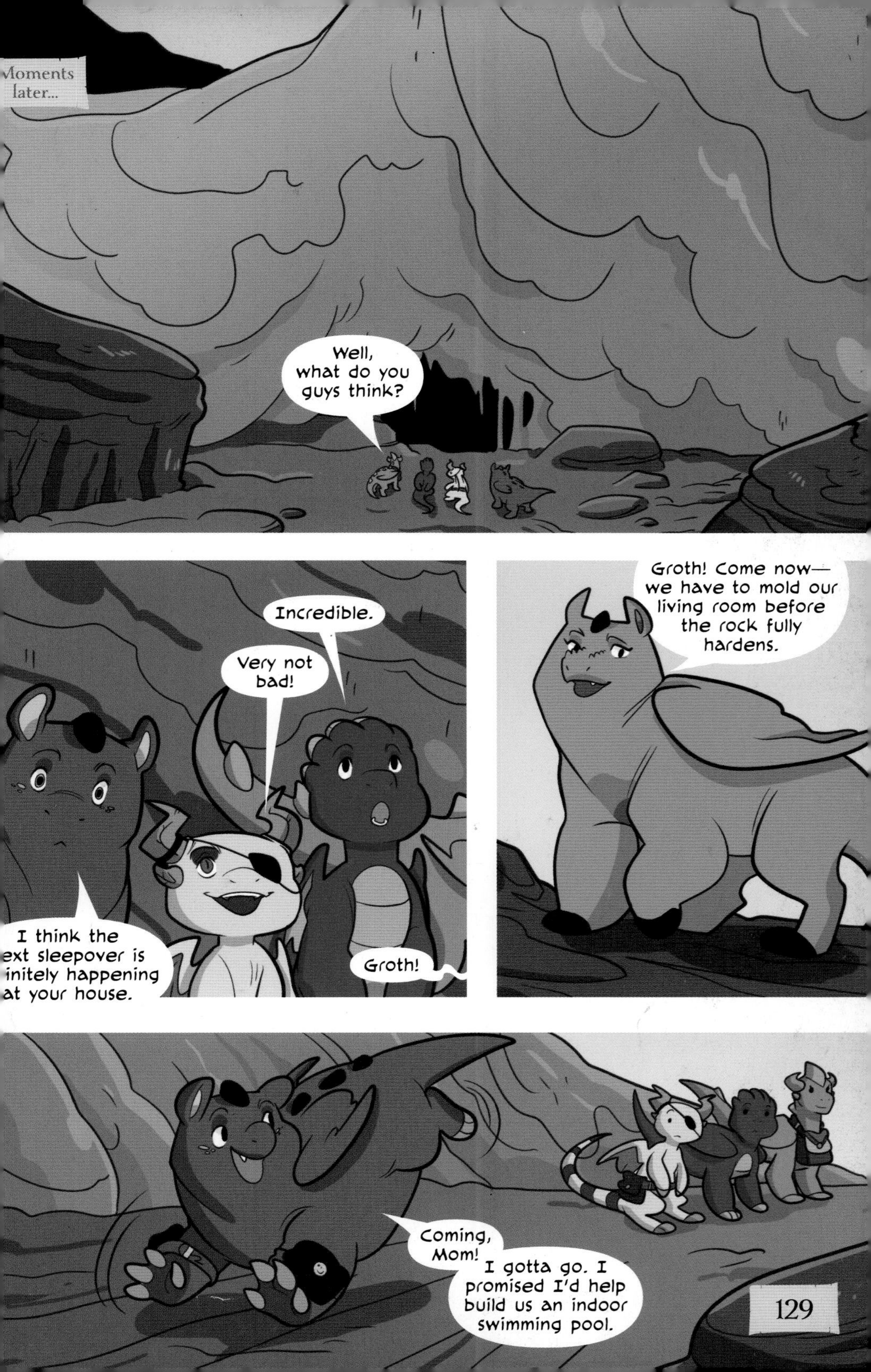

Moments later...
Well, what do you guys think?
I think the ext sleepover is initely happening at your house.
Very not bad!
Incredible.
Groth!
Groth! Come now— we have to mold our living room before the rock fully hardens.
Coming, Mom!
I gotta go. I promised I'd help build us an indoor swimming pool.

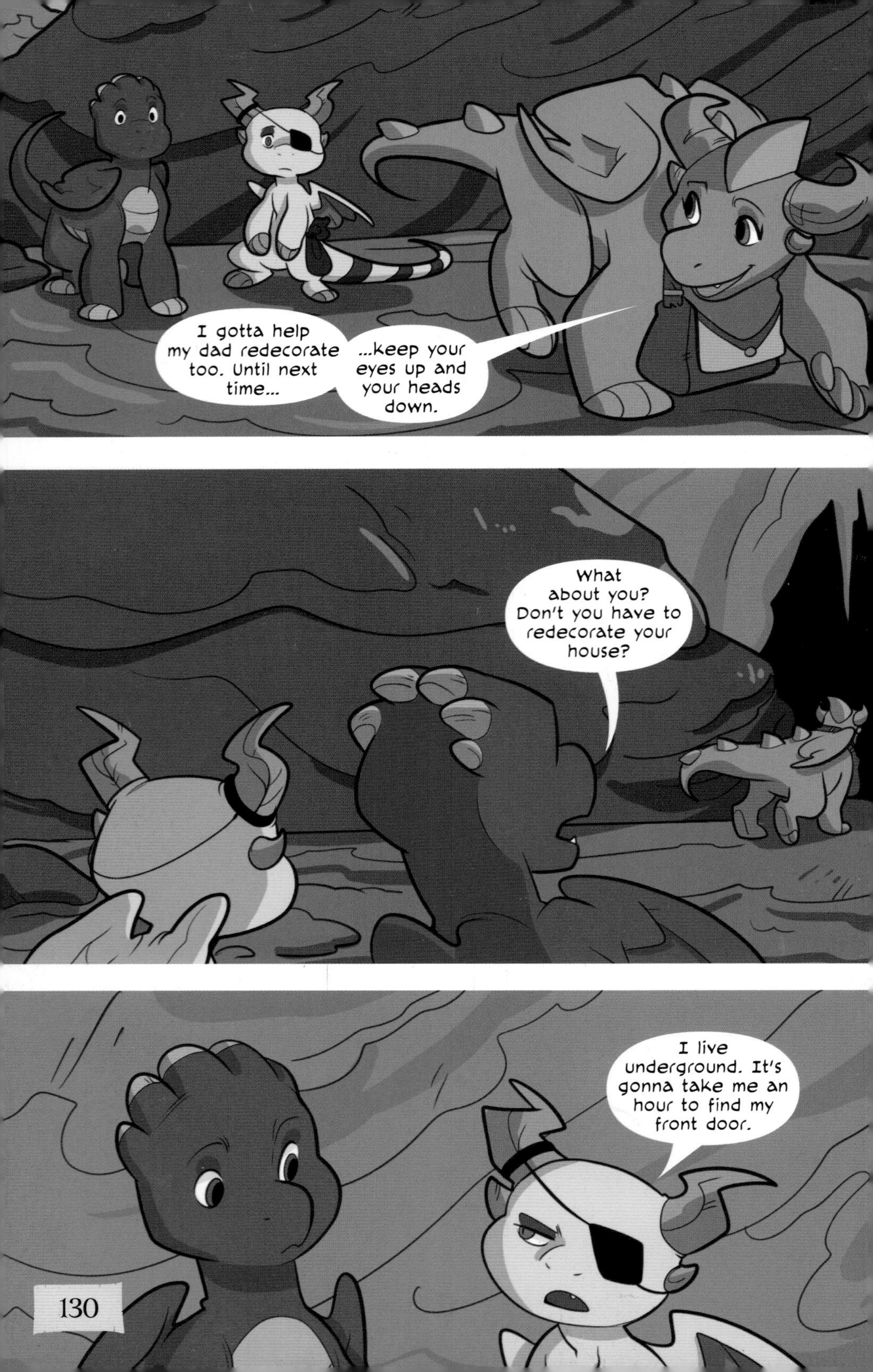
I gotta help my dad redecorate too. Until next time...
...keep your eyes up and your heads down.
What about you? Don't you have to redecorate your house?
I live underground. It's gonna take me an hour to find my front door.

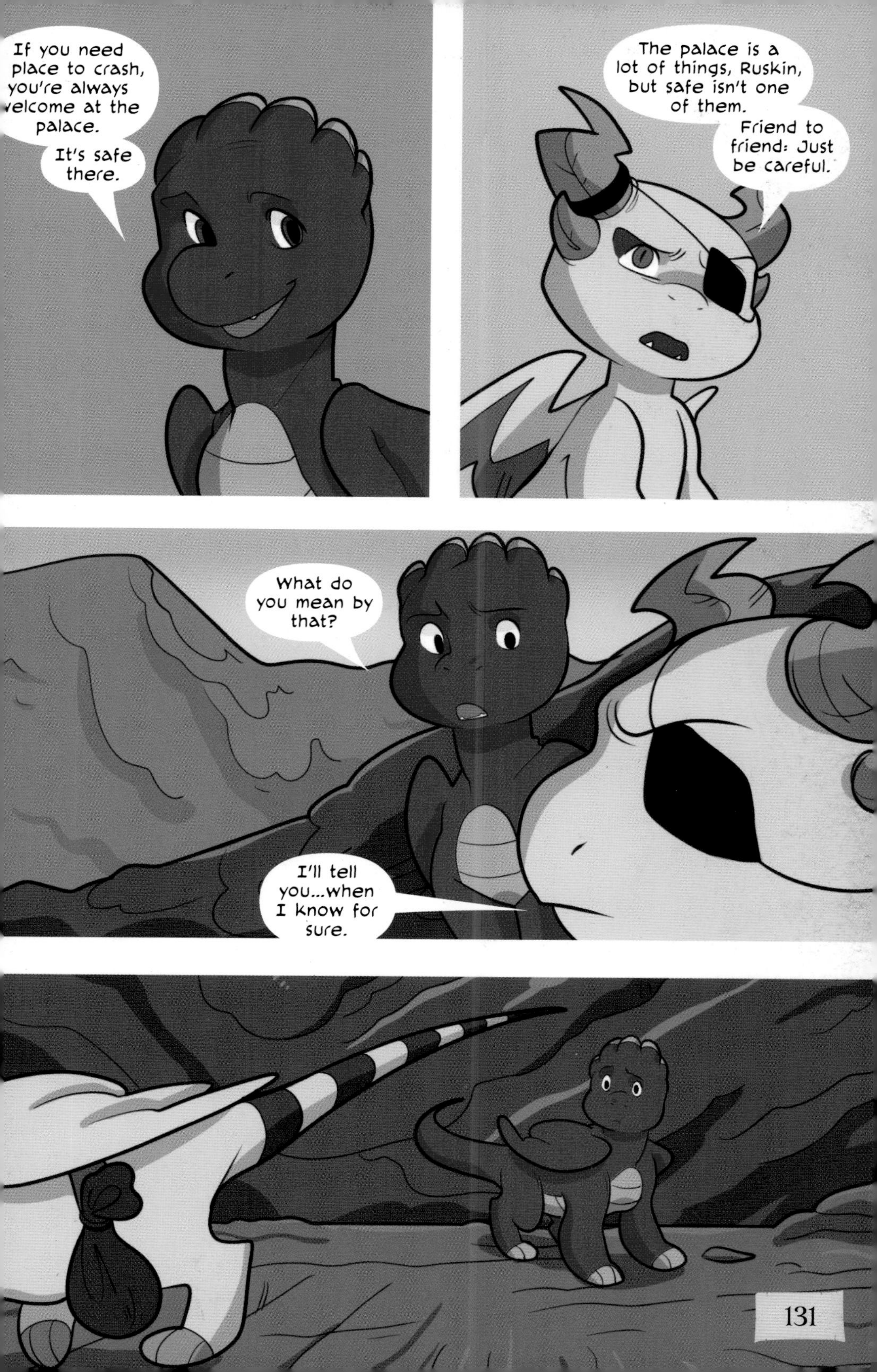
If you need place to crash, you're always welcome at the palace.
It's safe there.
The palace is a lot of things, Ruskin, but safe isn't one of them.
Friend to friend: Just be careful.
What do you mean by that?
I'll tell you...when I know for sure.

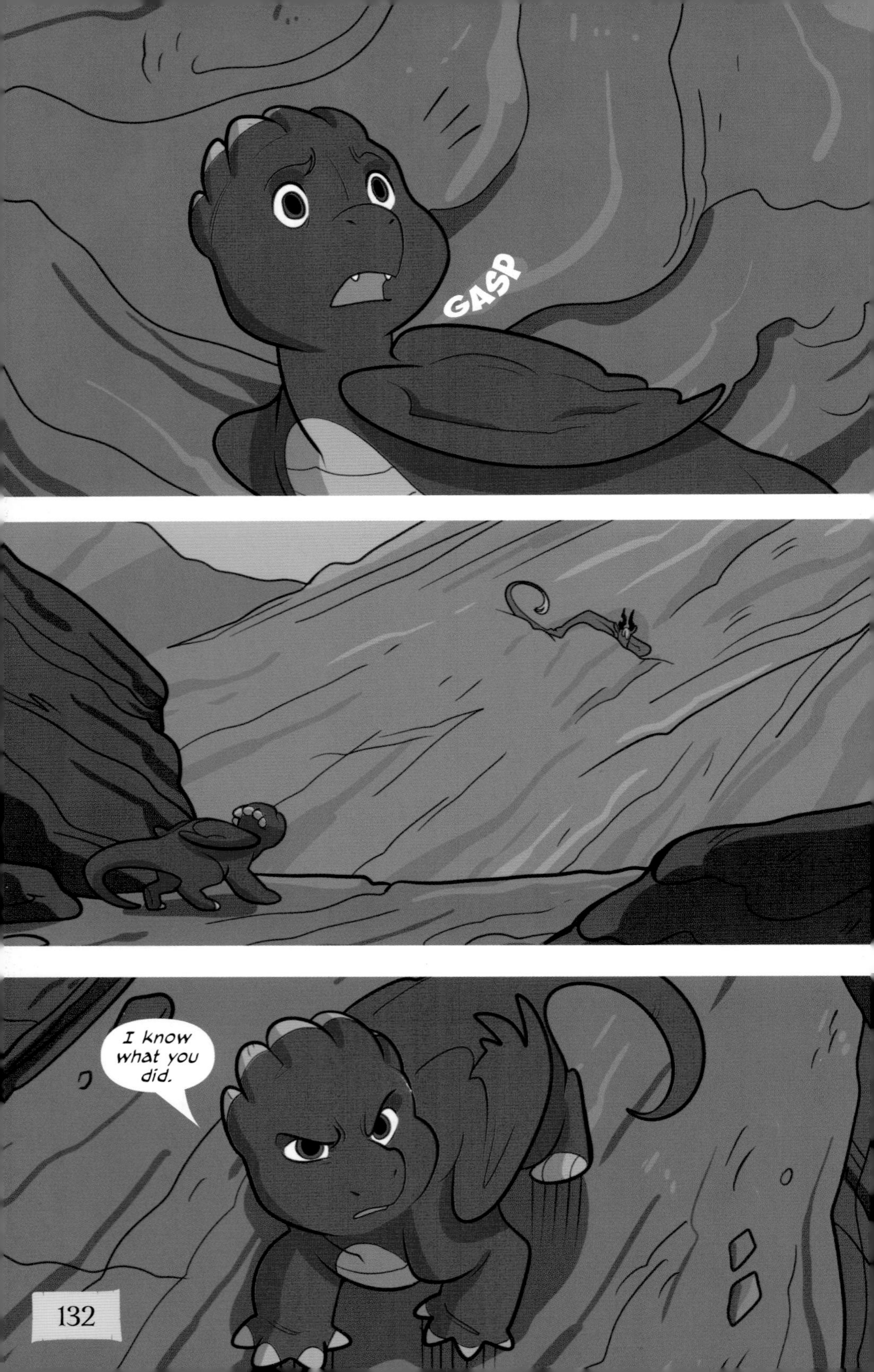
GASP
I know what you did.

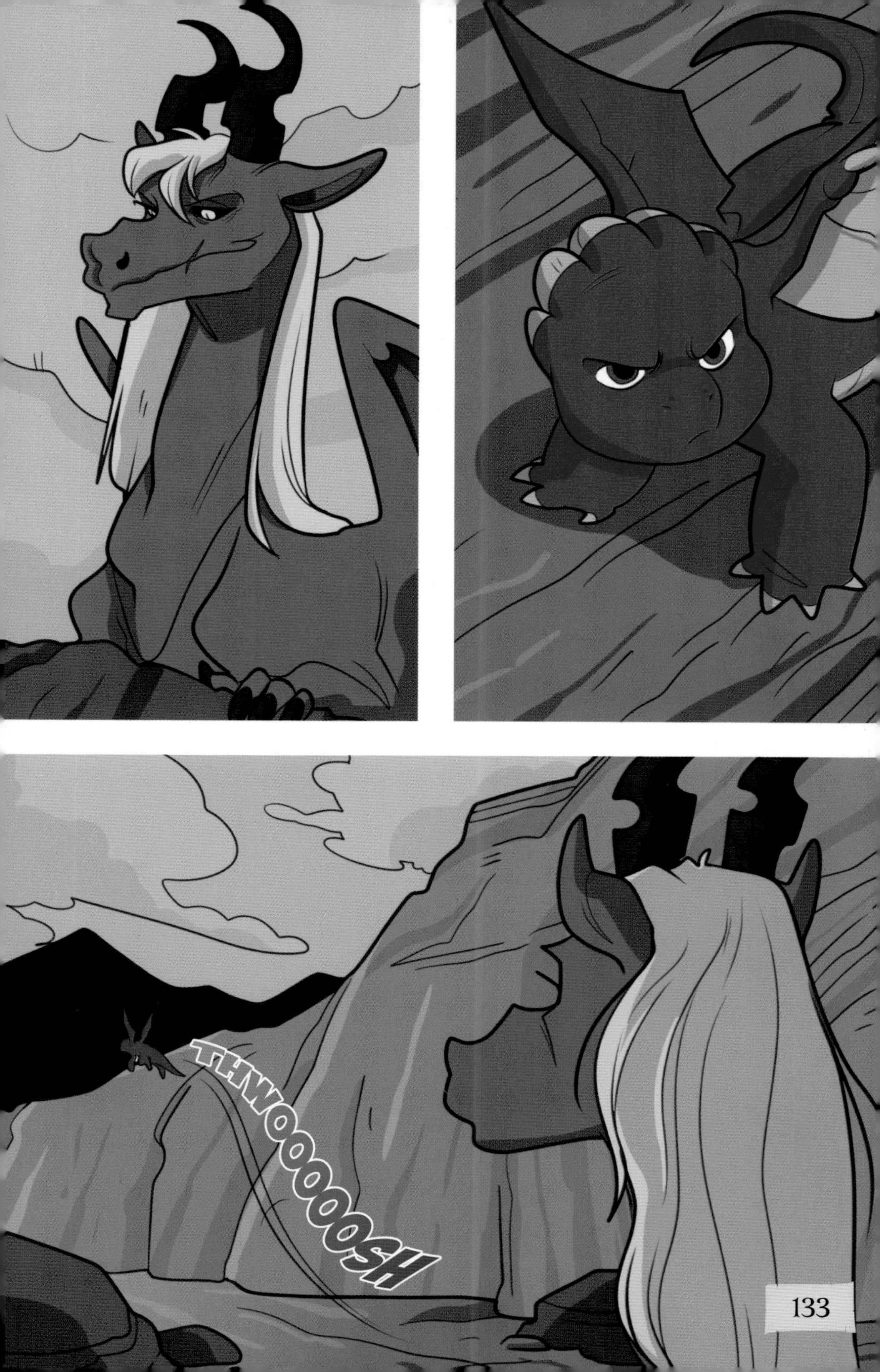
THWOOOOOSH

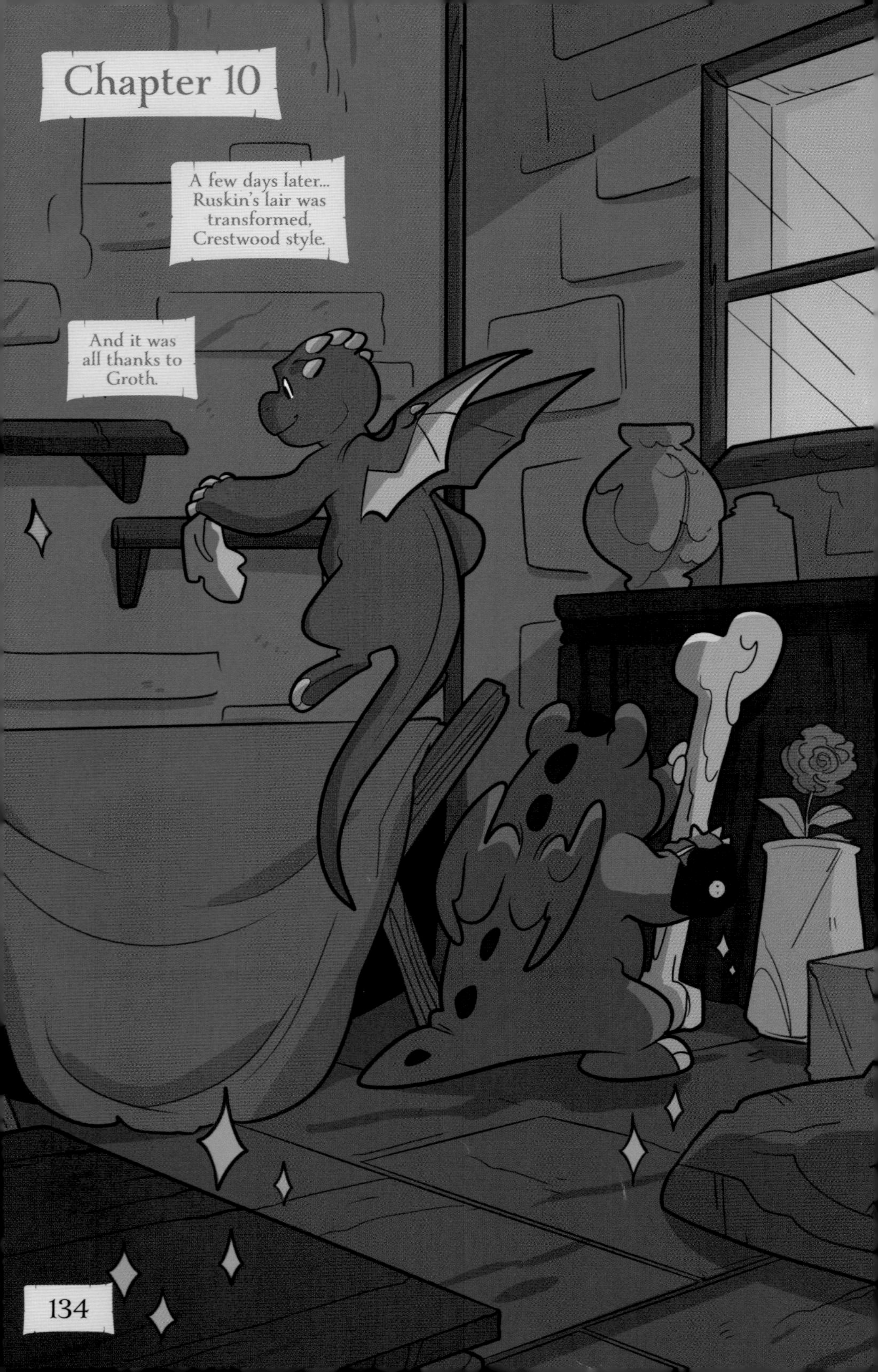
Chapter 10
A few days later... Ruskin's lair was transformed, Crestwood style.
And it was all thanks to Groth.

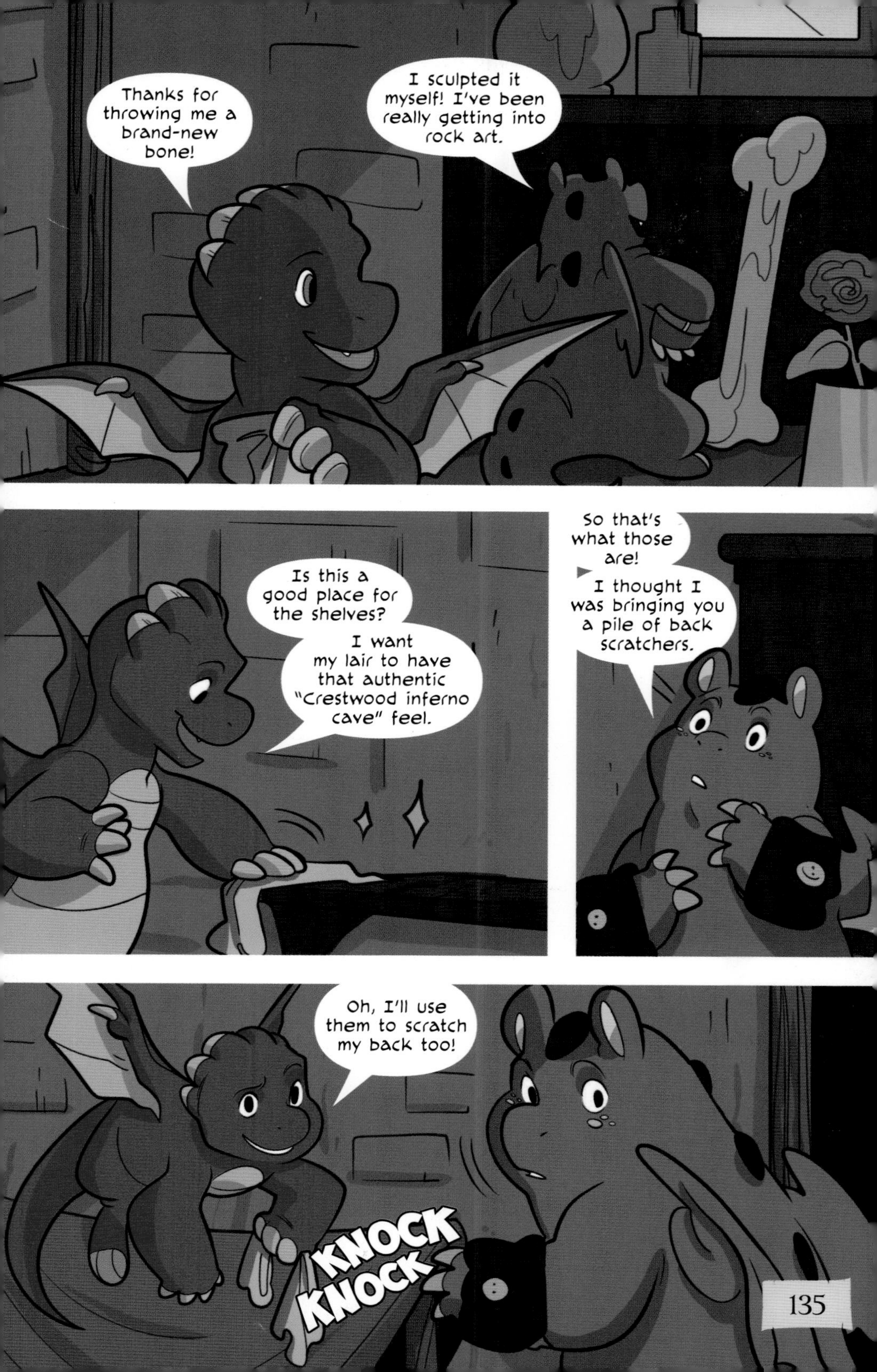
Thanks for throwing me a brand-new bone!
I sculpted it myself! I've been really getting into rock art.
Is this a good place for the shelves?
I want my lair to have that authentic "Crestwood inferno cave" feel.
So that's what those are!
I thought I was bringing you a pile of back scratchers.
Oh, I'll use them to scratch my back too!
KNOCK KNOCK

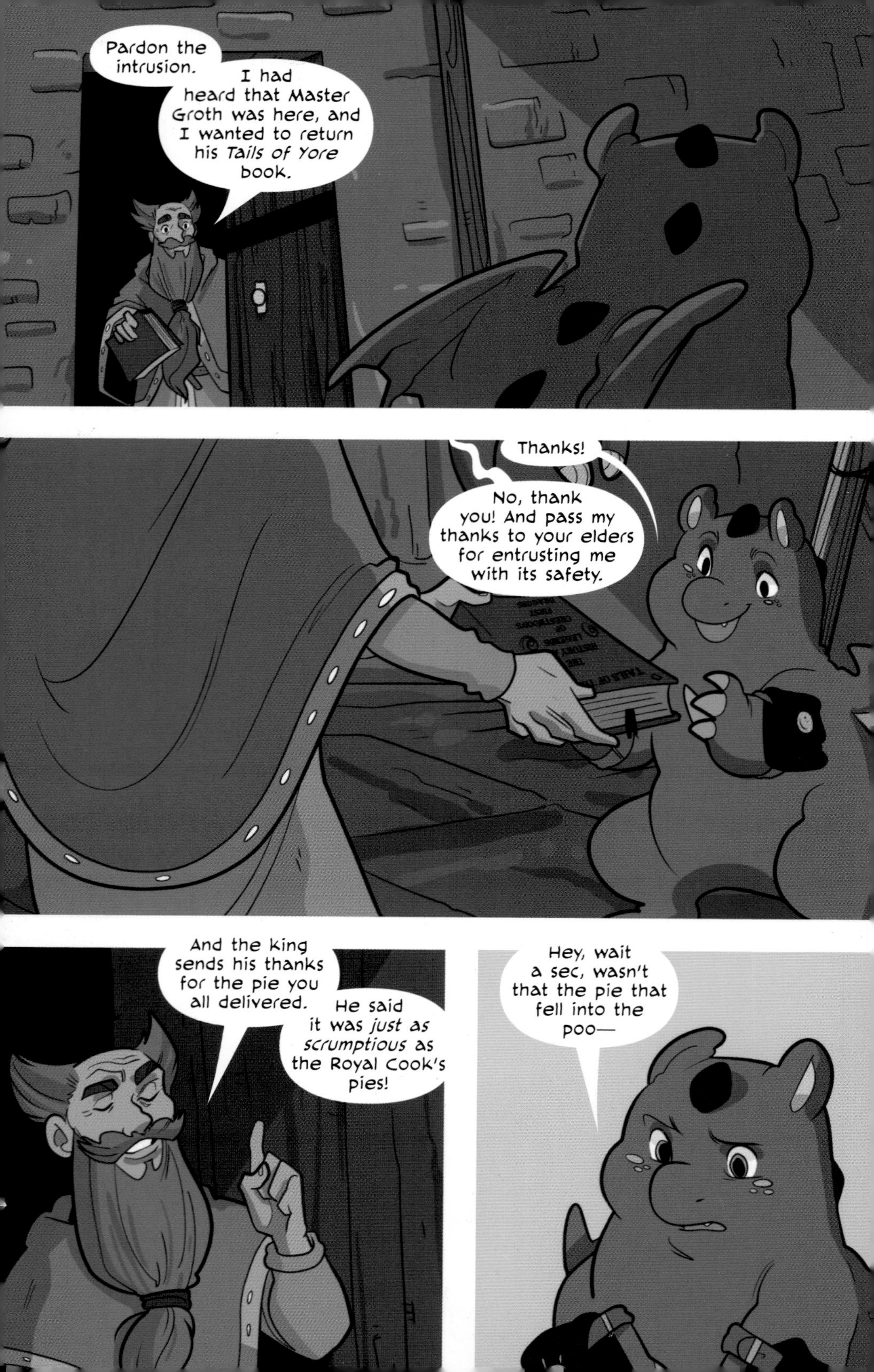
Pardon the intrusion.
I had heard that Master Groth was here, and I wanted to return his *Tails of Yore* book.
Thanks!
No, thank you! And pass my thanks to your elders for entrusting me with its safety.
And the king sends his thanks for the pie you all delivered.
He said it was *just as scrumptious* as the Royal Cook's pies!
Hey, wait a sec, wasn't that the pie that fell into the poo—

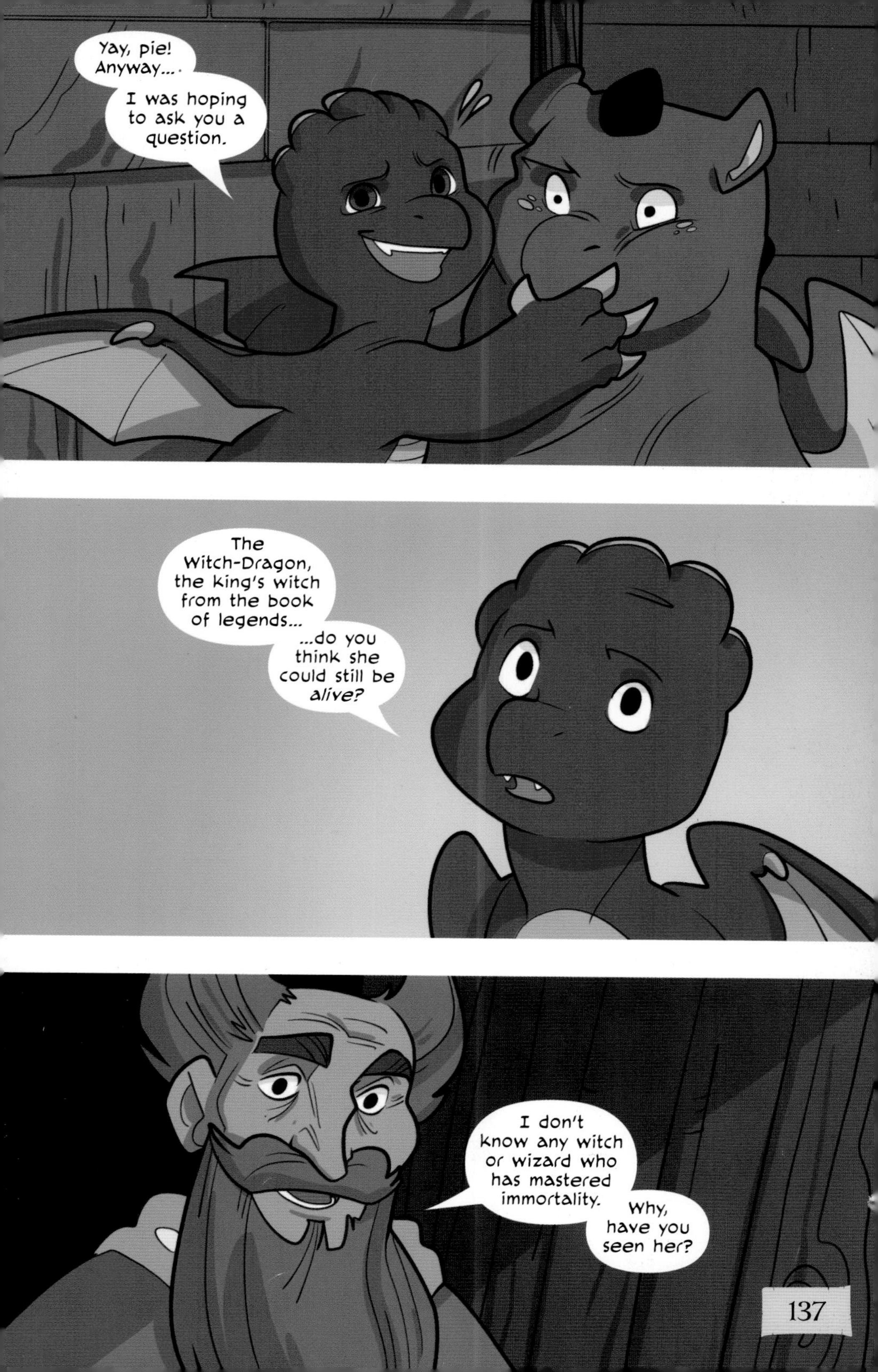
Yay, pie! Anyway...
I was hoping to ask you a question.
The Witch-Dragon, the king's witch from the book of legends...
...do you think she could still be *alive*?
I don't know any witch or wizard who has mastered immortality.
Why, have you seen her?

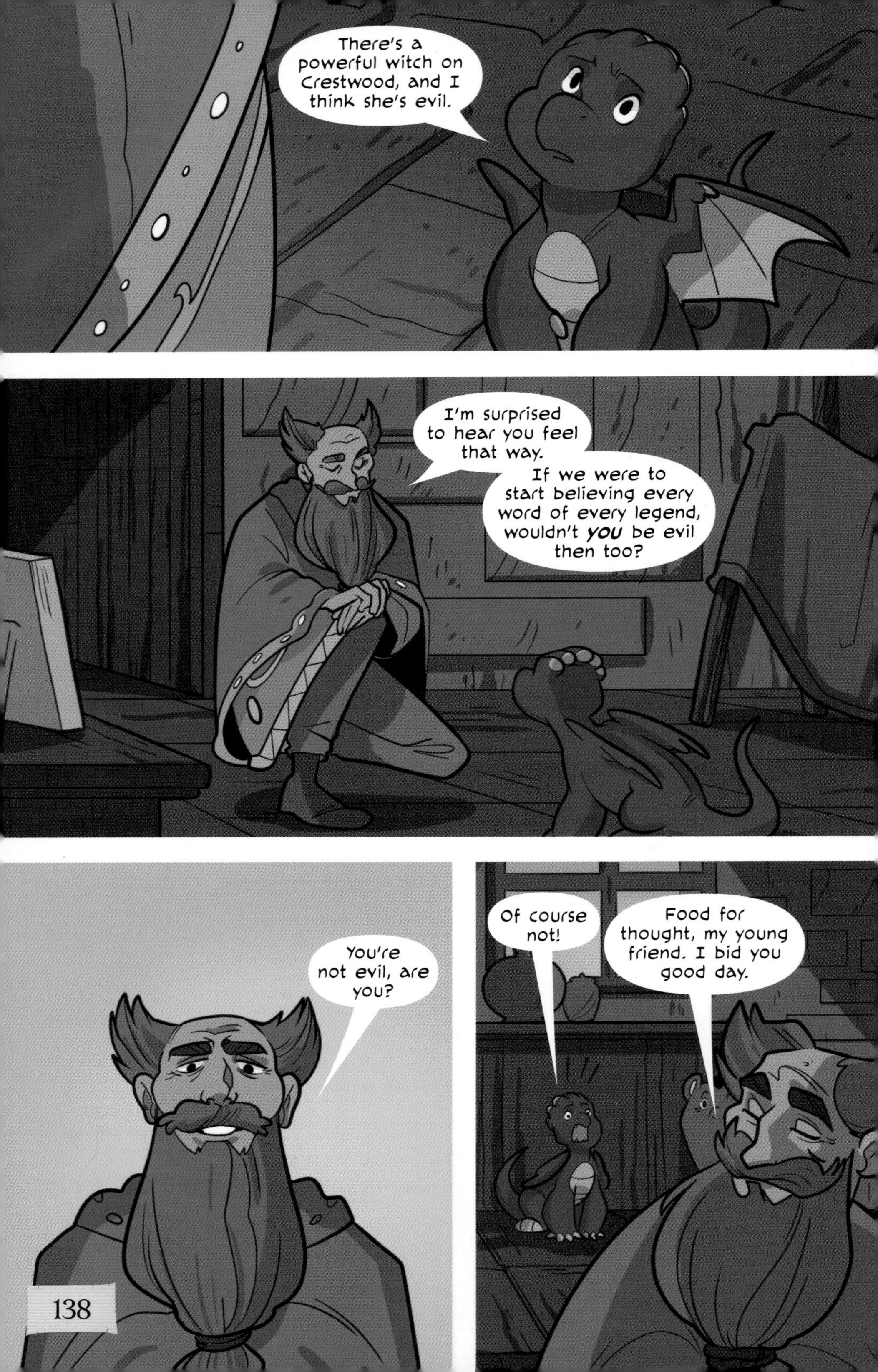
There's a powerful witch on Crestwood, and I think she's evil.
I'm surprised to hear you feel that way.
If we were to start believing every word of every legend, wouldn't *YOU* be evil then too?
You're not evil, are you?
Of course not!
Food for thought, my young friend. I bid you good day.

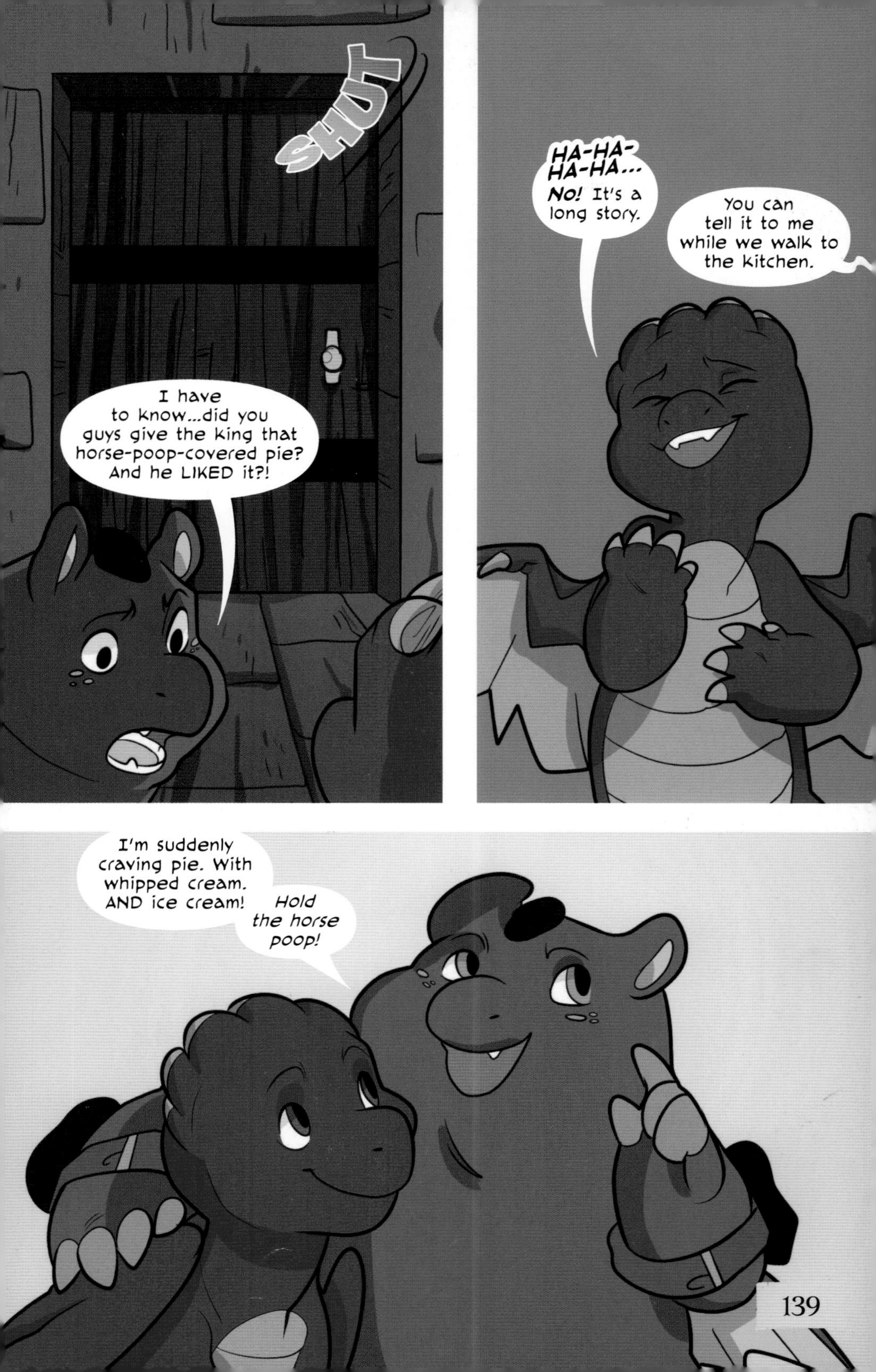
SHUT
I have to know...did you guys give the king that horse-poop-covered pie? And he LIKED it?!
HA-HA-HA-HA... No! It's a long story.
You can tell it to me while we walk to the kitchen.
I'm suddenly craving pie. With whipped cream. AND ice cream!
Hold the horse poop!

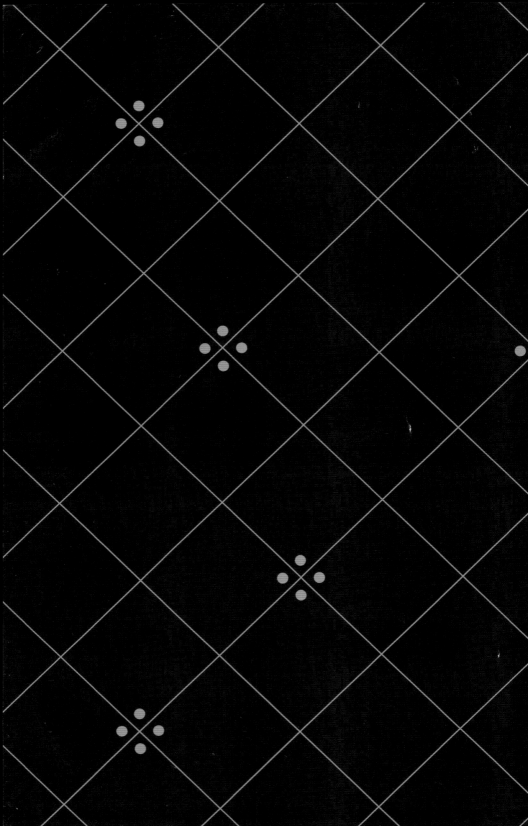

What's in store for Ruskin and his friends next? Find out in . . .

Graphic Novel
Dragon Kingdom
of Wrenly
Ice Dragon

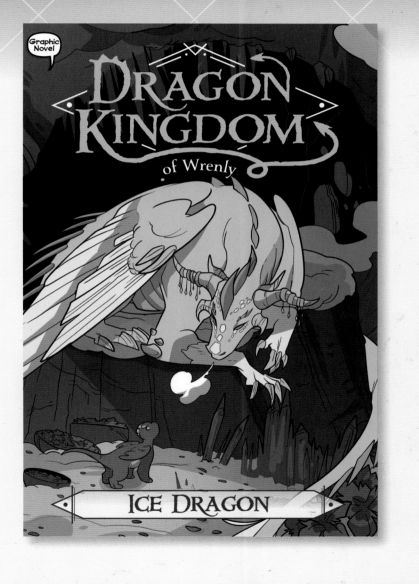

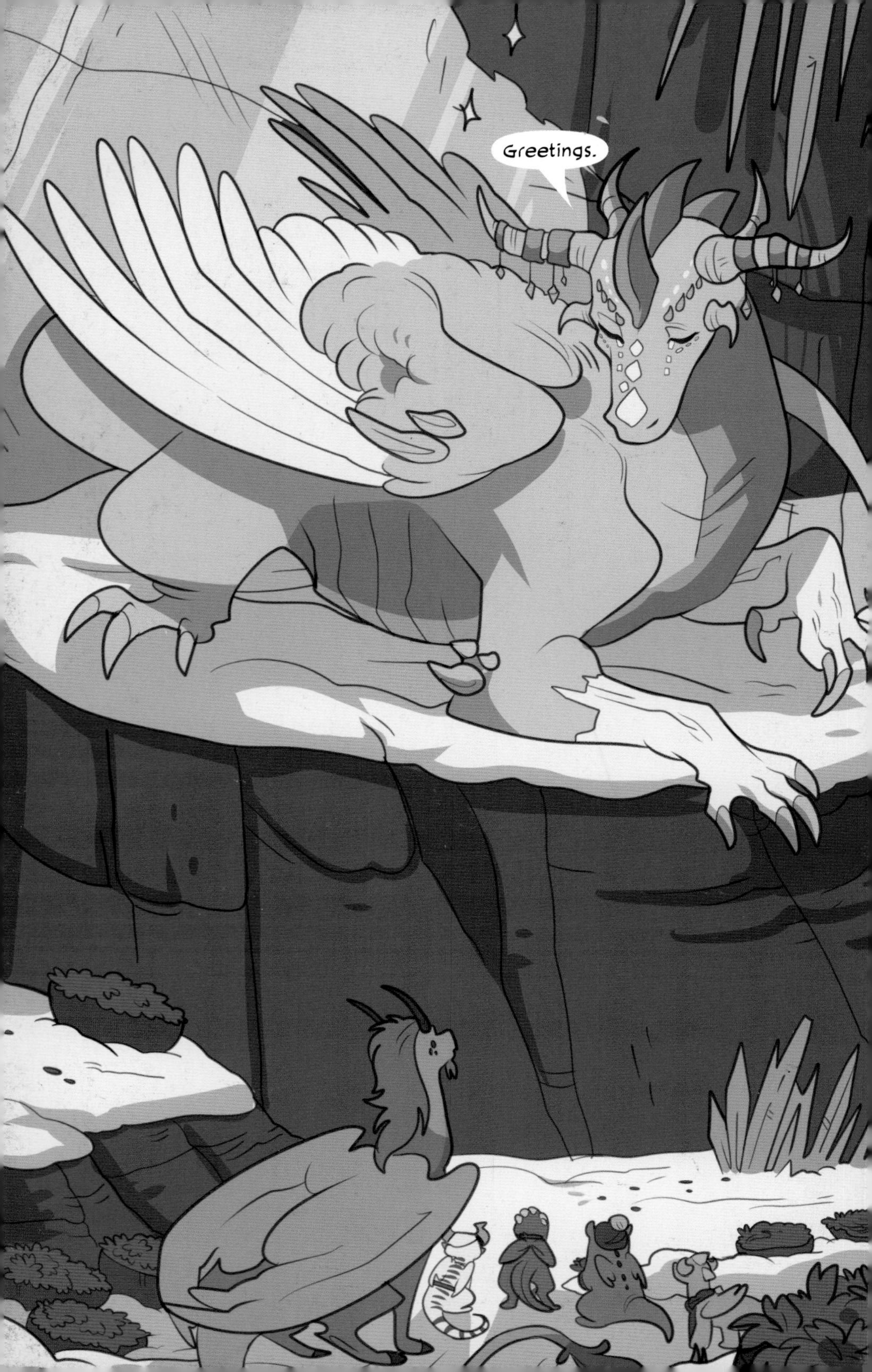
Greetings.

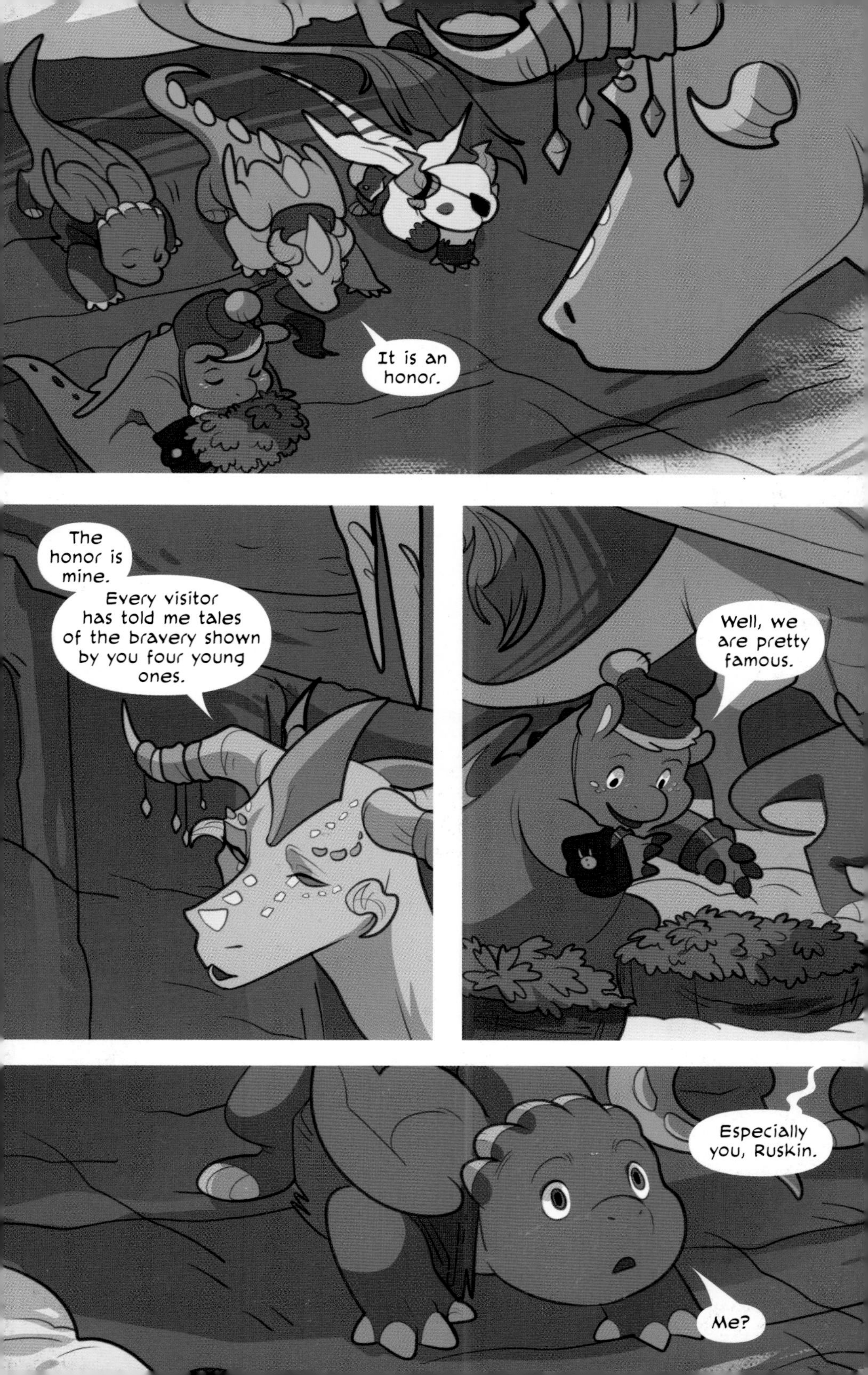
It is an honor.
The honor is mine.
Every visitor has told me tales of the bravery shown by you four young ones.
Well, we are pretty famous.
Especially you, Ruskin.
Me?

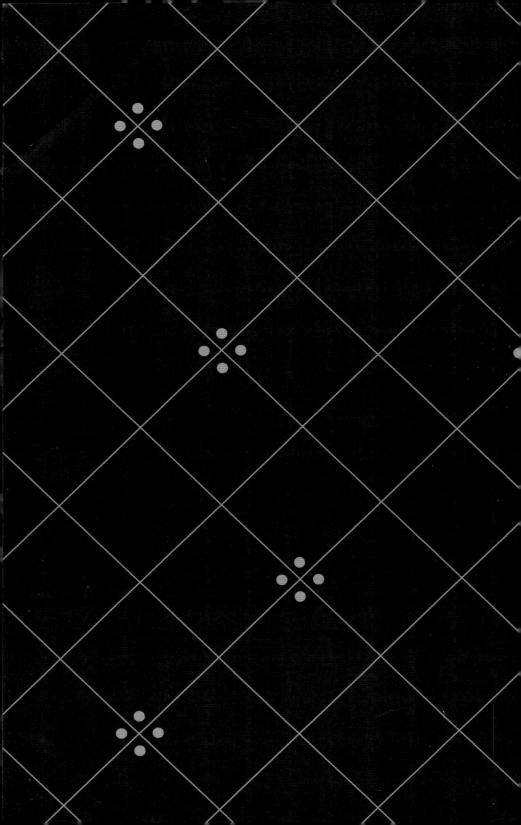